Also by Arthur Rosenfeld...

Novels
Diamond Eye
A Cure for Gravity
Dark Tracks
Dark Money
Harpoons
Trigger Man

Nonfiction
The Truth About Chronic Pain
Exotic Pets

Forthcoming Novels
The Crocodile and the Crane

ARTHUR ROSENFELD

YMAA Publication Center
Boston, Mass. USA

ARTHUR ROSENFELD

YMAA Publication Center, Inc.
Main Office
4354 Washington Street
Boston, Massachusetts, 02131
1-800-669-8892 • www.ymaa.com • ymaa@aol.com

Editor: Leslie Takao
Cover Design: Vanessa Luchtan

ISBN-13: 978-1-59439-082-1
ISBN-10: 1-59439-082-7

10   9   8   7   6   5   4   3   2   1

Publisher's Cataloging in Publication

Rosenfeld, Arthur.

The cutting season / Arthur Rosenfeld. -- 1st ed. -- Boston, Mass. :
YMAA Publication Center, 2007.

p. ; cm.

ISBN-13: 978-1-59439-082-1
ISBN-10: 1-59439-082-7

1. Martial arts--Fiction. 2. Reincarnation--Fiction. 3. Martial arts
fiction, Chinese. I. Title.

PS3568.O812 C88 2007   2007922384
813/.54--dc22   0706

Printed in Canada.

For Master Max Gaofei Yan. I must have done something truly wonderful in a past life to deserve such a gifted teacher and generous friend in this one.

Acknowledgments

In writing this book, I became hugely grateful for the number of friends I have and their eagerness to help me. That might just be the finest thing a man can say about his life.

My meager science background was never up to the task of getting all the medical details in this book right. Any technical mistakes are mine and mine alone, and all accuracies are thanks to the illustrious Dr. Lloyd Zucker, my great friend the loyal and insightful Dr. Ronald Weisberg, and my long-time friend and student, the swashbuckling Dr. E. Scott Leaderman.

Howard Korn and Daniel O'Malley contributed greatly to my under-standing of blades, while my friend Dellana, whose work is always with me, taught me what I needed to know of bladesmithing. Of course, my personal armorer Sam Curry gets a bow too, for making me weapons far better than I deserve.

Thanks to Leslie Takao for her terrific editing, to Pam Barr for her careful read, and to my friends Dr. Manuel Garcia, and Britin Haller for their great sense of character and story. Thanks to my pal Detective Jim Dees for helping me get my bomb and procedural points right, and to Steven Beer for his keen legal assistance. Special thanks, to my publisher, David Ripianzi, for his vision, commitment, and enthusiasm.

Last, but far from least, thanks to Janelle and Tasman for putting up with the countless hours it took to make this book what it is.

1

The young boy's soul emerged from his body, hesitated as if getting its bearings, made a circuit of the operating theater, and flitted upward toward the radiance of the halogen lamp like a wispy white pigeon homing in on the sun. I have often wondered about that ineffable thing I know to be present in the living and absent in the dead, but the shock of seeing the ethereal transit so clearly cost me the grip on my scalpel. The blade slipped inside the turgid surgical stage, and a tiny cut was born. Blood from a vertebral artery shot me in the goggles, a thin, angry stream hissing fast to the glass before I could even duck. Vicky Sanchez, one of the hospital's best surgical nurses, used her clamp bravely, I sutured in fast motion, but the monitors screamed and the boy came crashing down and neither the paddles nor my desperate blows to his heart could bring him back.

"No more," Vicky said at last.

I put my finger on the boy's carotid artery, hoping desperately but finding no pulse.

"Let go now," she said gently.

I stood there, breathing hard, feeling hollow and desperate and angry. He was only eleven; Rafik, the little Russian boy. Despite how much I relish their grateful looks when I go and pat them on the cheek in recovery, this very risk and unpredictability—this flying in the face of all that is medically rational and right—is what makes working on kids so tough.

I tried to sort out the order of events. The white wings flapped off before my slip-up, I was sure of that. I couldn't help wondering if that meant that the soul was prescient, knew what was about to happen, and simply took wing in the face of death. The encumbrances of medical practice—insurance regulations, legal considerations, and institutional politics—are usually unfair, but I wouldn't be able to blame anyone for believing the boy died after I cut him, and not before.

I bent close to the blonde peach fuzz at the base of his neck. His head and face were swollen and distorted by the most furious array of dents and cuts and holes I had ever seen on a patient, yet for all that he managed to look almost angelic. "I'm sorry," I whispered, knowing hearing is the last sense to go.

I closed the skin flap and made my way out of the theater. In the changing room, I tore off my mask and splashed my face with cold water, letting it run down my chest. I collapsed onto the bench by the lockers and relived the operation sequence, growing less sure of it by the moment. Maybe the white wings I saw were merely a mote in my eye. Maybe my brain was scrambling the order in which things had unfolded because I couldn't handle it any other way.

Roan Cole, the anesthesiologist, came in. One out of five conversations with Roan give me a sense of déjà vu; honestly, if I didn't know better, I'd say we'd known each other in a previous life. The last time we worked together, it was on a woman with a mass in her head. The procedure started as a look-see; turned into cancer removal. The tumor was the size of a pomegranate, and I needed to take out a chunk of her brain along with it. It was hard to know if I got it all. Keeping his eye on the numbers the way sleep jockeys do, Roan said she'd be a drooler if she ever woke up, a carrot stick if she didn't. Roan's a good man, but his sensitivity scores are low enough to get him into trouble, especially when alcohol is present. Usually I pocket my opinions, but that time I got angry with him. Even though the proof of it keeps rolling in, I'm the only member of the team that believes people hear things while they are asleep on the table.

"Rough one," he said.

"You got that right."

"It wasn't just that artery, Zee. He was in pieces. A busted leg and one arm too, ribs looking like a butcher shop, damage around the middle. We were just the first in the rotation. Jeff Ketchmer was waiting for you to finish, and Franks was right behind him."

Ketchmer is an abdominal surgeon. I've seen him fashion recognizable organs out of red mud. Pete Franks worked for one of the sports teams, mostly on knees, sometimes on shoulders and elbows and wrists. I had read enough of the boy's file before going to work to know that speed was of the essence, but the way things worked, surgical patients were most often reduced to fields of flesh and organs eerily disconnected from the rest of the body.

"Well, you can call those guys off," I said.

I went back out to the body. I pulled off the drapes and towels, revealing systematic destruction painted in sickening greens, yellows, and blues.

"The parents said he fell off his bicycle," Roan said, appearing at my elbow.

"I'd say somebody beat the shit out of him."

"Agreed. Paralysis and respiratory failure were just waiting to happen. The autopsy will confirm that."

"Still, it may have been my bleeder that put him over the edge," I said.

Most surgeons would never make such an admission, not even to their intimates, not even in the freshness of the moment. Tort law has glued our lips, crippled our hands, too. Still, when it comes right down to it, I'm the kind of man who would rather take responsibility than duck it.

Roan shook his head. "He was shocky coming in. You didn't kill him; someone else did. I'll put that in writing."

"Listen, I need to collect my thoughts. If you run into the parents out there, will you stall them for me?"

He nodded as I stripped down for the shower. Doctors who don't put their hands inside people can afford to pack it on, but surgeons tend to be fit. No doubt this is because of our intimate relationship with fat, with the oozing yellow of it, the way it bogs procedures down, doubles, even triples our work. Surgeons exercise because we don't like fat on ourselves any more than we like it on patients; I exercise more than most.

"You're looking leaner," Roan remarked.

"I've added a morning workout."

Soaping up, I began to rationalize my mistake, to convince myself that Rafik's death really wasn't my fault. Surgery is a nuts-and-bolts affair; you can't live with doubts in your fingers, you have to work the angles and command the odds. The boy had died before I made him bleed, and if he hadn't, his injuries would have cost him any kind of normal life anyway. Perhaps it had been a vision rather than an apparition, a miniature weather front whose associated vortices and winds spawned gossamer threads. Already the white of it was growing less distinct, less concrete. Memory will do that; will toy with you until uncertainty creeps in to replace the crisp edges of an image, an odor or a sound. Give it enough lead and memory will render even the most palpable truth as insubstantial as a sigh.

When I came out of the stall, Wu Tie Mei was waiting. My teacher wore the green silk outfit she'd died in, but her eyes showed no holes. As always, she smelled of fresh almonds. I wiped my eyes, took a breath, and opened them again. She was still there. I felt my heart pound and my mouth go dry. I steadied myself against the locker with one hand and reached out to her. She shimmered more brightly as my hand grew close and I found no substance.

"Is it really you?" I asked.

She smiled. "There are so very many ideas of me."

"You've been dead ten years," I said.

"And you dream of me less and less often."

"Perhaps I'm dreaming now. I work so much and sleep so little I can't trust myself sometimes."

"That's why I'm here. To help you trust yourself more. To help you remember who you are."

"I know who I am."

"You only think you do."

"This is because of the Russian boy, isn't it? I didn't kill him."

"I know."

"It's a tragedy—probably it's a crime—but I didn't do it."

"Of course not," Wu Tie Mei soothed.

I withdrew my hand and used it to tighten my towel. "I know what's going on. I'm having a stress reaction. That's what this is. I'm having a little breakdown. Goddamnit if I could get some decent sleep I'd be stronger than this."

"You're about to get stronger," said my old teacher. "It's not going to be easy, but big change is coming."

She faded after that, and no amount of rubbing my eyes would bring her back. I pinched myself; I wondered why she had come to this cold

4

and antiseptic place to mark the death of a child she did not know. I worried that she might come back suddenly, perhaps even when I was talking to the boy's parents. The thought scared me. I could not with any confidence hold both past and present in my hands at once. I waited as long as I dared, but felt no sea change within me. At last, I dressed and went out to meet the Petrossovs.

They were waiting on blue plastic chairs, leaning slightly toward the television, which ran a daytime soap with the sound turned off. On a different day they might have radiated wealth and power, but all I saw was exhaustion. The mother was a small, wiry blonde vibrating with intensity, and three degrees off beautiful. Fleshy, big, and white, the father had a broad Slavic face and a high forehead. His little ears cupped forward and his jaw receded, lending him the appearance of someone who had been vertically compressed nearly to the popping point. Only his fine suit saved him from hoggishness, along with a thin, elegant, wristwatch.

"How is he?" he asked, managing a certain charm. "How is my son?"

The chart said his name was Vlexei. She was Natalya. Because my own father had come over from Lvov, I knew how to pronounce their names, hers with the accent on the middle syllable, his with the accent on the last. I considered addressing them in Russian, but decided it would introduce an element of inappropriate intimacy.

"I'm Dr. Xenon Pearl," I said. "I operated on Rafik's neck."

"Will he be all right?" Natalya's accent was so heavy I got the question from her look more than her lips.

"His injuries were severe," I said. "There was a great deal of damage."

She began a small, hungry rocking. "What are you saying?"

"We worked it right to the end, but I'm afraid we lost him. I'm so very sorry."

She gave me a strange look, then slid to the floor without a sound. Her husband made no effort to help her.

"You could have struggled," he said. "You could have fought."

"Believe me, we tried."

I waited for the usual spasms of grief to seize him, waited for the inevitable quiver of the chin, the tiny twitches of the skin under the eyes that children set off when they die before their parents do. Instead, the rocking turned to rage as Petrossov dropped his charm like a hot coal,

gathered my scrubs at the collar, and lifted me clear off the ground. He had big, ropy farmer's forearms; adapted to city life, to American life, but after his own fashion.

"You don't know what trying is," he said.

My training kicked in at once, and I sensed the direction he was moving, the slightest, subtlest turn of his fingers. I knew how to follow those movements, and how to use them devastatingly against him, but I left his grip alone. The pain helped clear my head of doubt and confusion, and anger rushed in to fill the void. "Would you like to tell me what really happened to your son?" I asked, looking calmly into his eyes.

Petrossov put his face so close to mine I could smell the knots in his stomach on his breath.

"Forget my son," he said. "And hope we forget you."

2

It might have been the energetic imprint of the Russian's fingers on my arm that sent me off to see the swordsmith after lunch, but more likely it was my teacher's reference to change. I don't like change, even when a person long dead suggests it. I may not get much sleep—indeed I have my issues with Morpheus even when my surgical schedule allows me some shuteye—but I always sit with my back to the wall, and if some kind of transition was nigh, I felt the itch for a weapon.

I left the hospital for the waning sun along an asphalt river that was once grass and filled with alligators and frogs. I ride a bright yellow Triumph Thruxton, the most powerful of the famous marque's retro offerings. I love the rhythmic thumping of its twin cylinders, and the forward urge they provide. My colleagues tell me I'm a fool to live on a motorcycle in Florida. They cite the statistics, point out the blue-hairs driving west in the eastbound lane, cluck at the coked-up kids weaving from lane to lane, generally rehash what I of all people know so damn well about head injury. They're right, I know they're right, but the blast of the wind on my flesh satisfies some visceral yearning my martial training doesn't. Besides, riding adds nuance to my relationship with gravity, and if gravity is not on your side, you cannot possibly win a fight.

I made it to the Fort Lauderdale bedroom community of Plantation, and rang the doorbell at the address I was after. A woman in her late twenties answered the door. She wore work boots and overalls but even so I could see she was lovely; built like a swimmer, tall and lean with big shoulders, thin hips, light brown hair cropped short enough to barely challenge a cap.

"Yes?" she said, using her foot for a doorstop.

"I'm looking for Thaddeus Jones," I said.

"My father died two years ago. What can I do for you?"

I rocked the full-face helmet off my head and wiped the sweat off my forehead.

"I'm sorry for your loss," I said. "I heard his work was fine."

"And you are?"

"Xenon Pearl. Speak it with a z, spell it with an x."

She took me in, up and down. "I'm Jordan," she said. "Xenon's a noble gas, isn't it? Inert, rare, glows when electricity goes through it, doesn't want to react with other compounds?"

"I don't meet a lot of people who know that."

"How did you get a gas for a name?"

"My dad made an investment in a technology stock back before half those companies were scams. The outfit made xenon light bulbs. Shares went through the roof the day I was born; dad took it for a sign."

"I can't tell yet if you're rare, but you don't seem to be inert. Now, how can I help you, Xenon Pearl?"

"I have an interest in swords."

She took her foot away from the door, but aside from that, nothing changed."

"Are you a collector?"

"I wouldn't say so."

The foot came back, and on top of that, Jordan's eyes grew narrow.

"Your father's card has been in my wallet for a long time. I hadn't realized it was years. Are any of his blades still available?"

"They are not. But I've taken over his forging and have a few of my own for sale."

"People claim the living are more important than the dead," I said. "I'm not so sure that's true. Life and death are two sides of the same coin. Each is what makes the other important."

"What are you talking about?" she hugged herself impatiently.

"Family traditions are very valuable. I'd be happy to look at your work if you're willing to show it."

A drizzle started. She appraised me long enough for my head and shoulders to get pretty wet. "I don't usually let strangers in," she said. "But I have a piece of sword steel heating and I've got to get back to it. You can come in and watch me forge, if you like."

The house was *un salon des fleurs*, it was as simple as that—one big greenhouse with skylights, an arboretum filled with tropical plants: bromeliads, ferns, philodendrons, and small palms and cycads by the windows. It was remarkable, even for Florida, and I said so. She reached out to touch a large purple orchid. "This is a species specimen," she said. "Breeders are all about crosses, but I like my plants the way nature intended."

"So you're a purist."

"A naturist, maybe, although I'm not keen on labels."

We went through a door and into what had once been the garage. I have been in a couple of other shops. Usually they are as charred and masculine as a side of beef, dirty too, with flat dusty tables, bruised benches, pin-up calendars on the wall. Jordan's place was immaculate.

"I do my finish work here," she said, her finger dragging across the rows of little drawers. "It's where I store the handle materials, sheath leather, too. I like semiprecious stones like chrysoprase and citrine, also oosic, fossilized mastodon ivory and stag."

"Oosic?"

"Fossilized walrus penis."

"Bet it feels great in the hand."

She shot me a look, but I beat it back with a grin and followed her out to a little shed in the yard. The heat from the forge was so ferocious I had to wait in the doorway.

"See the lemon-yellow of the caowool?" Jordan asked, pointing to the material lining the glowing oven. "That means the temperature is right."

She slipped on a pair of gloves, donned welder's glasses, and pulled a glowing billet the size of a thick pack of cigarettes out of the fire by the handle. She put it between the dies and hit it with a power hammer. The muscles in her forearms bulged. Sparks like stars lit up the shed, and a moment later lightning came under the door, and then a thunderclap shook us.

"What type of metal is that?" I asked.

"My proprietary Damascus. I like a combination of water-hardened high-carbon tool steel and low-carbon oilrig scrap. Gives me a beautiful contrast and the flexibility and edge-holding so important to the Asian masters."

A burning ember of white-hot slag flew into the cuff of her welding glove. She barely even winced.

"Probably should take care of that," I said, smelling her flesh burn.

"Later," she replied, watching the glowing metal. "I have to work with it before it cools. There's only a short window before molecular changes take place."

I dodged the debris flying from the forge, not wanting an ember to land on me. I dug a piece of chocolate out of my pocket. It was a bit the worse for wear from the heat and the ride, but still serviceable.

"Maybe this will take your mind off the pain," I said. I went to put it in her mouth. She hesitated and then let me. I saw her tongue and her even white teeth.

"Goodness." She rolled deep gray eyes.

"It certainly is. Made by a boutique company in the Midwest from Hawaiian fruit: 70 percent cacao, very little sugar; the dark, pure stuff. Chocolate has medicinal properties modern medicine is only just beginning to fathom."

"Swords and chocolate," she mused.

"I hope that makes you think I have both depth and complexity."

"You're pretty smooth," she said. "I'm not sure that's good."

She took a chop saw to the billet then, and sparks flew as if in some intimate cosmic collision. She cut it, folded it, and heated it again. I watched her go through this twice more, and when she had the layering she wanted, we retired to the living room. I sat down on the couch while she broke a piece off an aloe plant and put the fresh ooze on her burn.

"What do you like?" she asked me.

"I like you, if that's what you're asking."

She blushed. It was charming, tough as she looked in those overalls. "I meant in a sword."

"What's your specialty?"

"Japanese styles, like my father."

"May I see?"

She went out for a minute and came back with three magnificent samurai swords. The hamon, or temper line, was clean on each katana, and the traditional stingray handles well done.

"These are beautiful," I said.

"I've loved swords since I was a child."

We stood in awe of the specific gravity of the blades, their beauty, their familiar shape. Finally, reluctantly, I broke the spell. "I wish I had your talent. Could you create a sword for me in a Chinese design?"

She looked at me in surprise. For most collectors, the katana is the thing, but then most collectors don't have my particular history.

"Chinese? Really?"

"I know about Japanese purity of line," I said. "I know how the master smiths of yore prepared for forging with forty days of meditation and ablution. But Japanese blade designs were constrained, the result, I think, of the kind of short horizon that comes from living on an island. The Chinese had a bigger universe. There are so many distractions in that vast land of theirs that nobody spent forty days preparing to forge. On the other hand, the Chinese smiths were sensitive in what they picked up about nature and creative in the way they put the lessons they learned to steel."

"I've never heard it put quite that way," she said.

I smiled. "I think about the subject a great deal. The sword I'm after needs to be a straight sword, double-edged, flexible, with a voice through the air."

"How flexible?"

"I need it to be able to bend ninety degrees and then snap back to true."

She frowned. "It's very, very difficult to make a blade like that. The grind lines alone…."

"I understand," I said, standing up. "It's got to be a hell of a sword."

"I'm not saying I can't do it."

The more closely I looked at her work, the more certain I was that she could. She had a wonderful eye, a great sense of balance, and the ability to create lively steel out of inanimate materials; a conjury really, magical and rare.

"So you might give it a stab?"

"You won't feel like punning when you get the bill."

"That's all right."

"It is? What are you, last of the Internet millionaires?"

"A surgeon."

"Really? What, boobs and noses?"

"Brains and spines," I said.

She crossed her beautiful legs, uncrossed them, and crossed them again.

"A neurosurgeon?"

"That's right."

She looked at me as if in a new light. I get that a lot, riding a motorbike and dressing as casually as I do.

"Even so, there are people ahead of you," she said at last.

"I did feed you chocolate. Maybe that's worth a bump to the head of the line."

She gave me a smile as natural as a greyhound let out to run after being cooped up in the house for too long. "I'll think about it," she said.

3

That night I rode south on the interstate through a gap in the rain. I crossed Biscayne Bay on the causeway to North Miami Beach, where my father, Asher, lives in a senior residence. The place is a frenzy of mad motion and energy, so busy even death has to wait in line for a room. At any hour, but especially late, the canasta tables are crowded, bridge players in demand, chess queens are on the prowl, and old cocks are, too. I've seen lower libidos on the Riviera and met smaller egos on Wall Street.

Dad was on the patio when I pulled up, deep in a novel, reading by the light of a Tiki torch, his feet on a table made from an old Cadillac grill.

"A man and his Caddy," I said.

He glanced up at my helmet. "Less dangerous than a bike," he said.

"Don't complain. I got here on time."

He glanced at his watch. "Barely."

"Mom knows we're thinking of her whenever we do it, and it's still an hour to midnight."

He got up and we hugged. "Can't argue about the time, but you know I hate riding on the back of that thing."

"So we'll eat here."

"The cardboard food is killing me. I haven't shit for a week."

"Eat more fruit and stop hanging out with old people. Why don't we go somewhere fun?"

"Because I'm scared of that bike."

This is a sham. Actually, he loves to ride. He doesn't think I know that he used to ride an orange BMW R90S when I was young and he was younger. It was a famous bike, because it represented the last gasp of European racing dominance before the Japanese completely took over the field. The bike, rare and expensive even in its day, came only in orange, and a less-desirable smoke color. I found one just like it in the paper in very rough shape, paid too much for it, and put it in the garage. Someday soon I plan to restore it to its former, burbling glory.

"I'll go slow," I said. "And I'll buy dinner, too. Make it worth your while. What do you say?"

"If you're buying, how come we're still standing here?" he grinned. He dog-eared his Irving Stone novel, glanced around like a spy, saw nobody was watching, and tucked it under a cushion. I gave him my helmet. He made a show of wiping it out with his shirttail before sliding it on.

I drove him over to Calle Ocho, the heart of the Cuban section of town, and parked in front of Versailles, a crammed-together restaurant filled with high-volume Spanish and smelling of garlic chicken and yucca fries. We got comfortable and I ordered a half-pitcher of sangria. I poured most of it in his glass when it arrived, saving just a splash for myself on account of my strict rule on biking and boozing.

"Happy Birthday, Mom," I raised my glass. "We miss you."

He clinked with me. "If you really want to show her you love her, sell the motorcycle. She wouldn't like that you're a thug."

"I'm not a thug, Dad. I'm a doctor."

"A doctor and a thug, with all that kicking and punching."

The comment was a revelation. Throughout my childhood, Wu Tie Mei had secretly shared martial information of great power and importance, and demanded utter discretion from me.

"What are you talking about?"

"Come on," my father snorted. "I know that nanny of yours taught you that kung fu chop suey."

I took a deeper slug of sangria than I had planned to while I formulated a reply. During thousands of hours and over a period of sixteen years, Wu Tie Mei passed to me a good grasp of Chinese history, a useful everyday philosophy entirely absent from my Western schooling, and exquisite martial training; a blend of many famous styles. She also shared the principles of Chinese medicine, always making clear that to be a martial artist— as opposed to a thug—one had to equally adept at hurting and healing, to be fully ready and able to undo any harm inflicted. She taught me that in China last names come first, that her given name, Tie Mei, meant Iron Plum Blossom, and she taught me to be sensitive to the delicate interplay of opposing forces in the world, the male and female, the hard and the soft, the lean times and the full. She taught me values I didn't get anywhere else—compassion and justice among them—but most important, she taught me the difference between right and wrong.

"Nanny," I said. "Is that all you think she was?"

"You two thought you were fooling me all those years."

I wondered how he could know about the training. I was certain she'd never told him, and the two of us had been so careful; I couldn't imagine he had seen us. At first I kept my mouth shut because I was in awe of the knowledge, bowled over by the moves. Later, I honored the confidence because we both feared my father would dismiss her if he found out.

"She helped me with my school lessons, if that's what you mean."

"You loved her and you were loyal to her, but you're a grown-up now. You don't have to lie for her anymore."

"I'm not lying for her," I said. "I'd have never made medical school without her."

And in truth I have kept my pact with Wu Tie Mei all these years, not merely to honor her memory, but because I have come to realize how miserable the lowest common denominator of human exchange really is. Alone at night, and sleepless as always, I watch television news, and too many of the victims of gunshots, car accidents, and domestic outbursts end up on my table, where I become intimately acquainted with their shattered spines, severed nerves, crushed heads, and useless limbs. I know violence all right, and I know how to keep my counsel.

My father picked an orange out of his wine glass and sucked the meat off the rind. "Fine," he said. "Have it your way. But your mother's in heaven and she hears your lies."

The reference to being watched made me long to tell him about Wu Tie Mei's visit that morning. I turned away and watched a big Latin family come in, the little girls dressed primly in lace, the boys in tiny dark suits. I wondered what people had thought of our little family when I was the age of those boys, my father, the petite Chinese woman, and me.

"A patient died on my table this morning," I said.

"Spare me the morbid talk. I'm surrounded by *alte kakkers*."

"You're just there because you're too lazy to cook and clean up after yourself."

"Hymie Grossman had a stroke today, right in the middle of a hand of bridge at lunchtime. Sixty-two years old and we don't know if he's going to make it."

"My patient was a little boy. The parents said he fell off his bike, but that's not what happened. Somebody beat him with a pipe."

"A pipe?"

"A pipe, a wrench, something hard."

"This world," he said. "There are times I wish I could leave it already."

"Don't be in such a rush," I said. "You've got plenty of living to do."

An army of waiters pushed three of the tables near us together for the giant family. They sat down, and their chattering made me grin.

"You need a barber," my father said, rumpling my dark hair. "Ponytails went out with the hippies."

"When I'm your age I'll cut it short."

"When you're my age you'll put in your teeth in the morning and pray it doesn't rain because of what the low pressure does to your elbows."

"The boy was Russian. The way the mother dresses and the father comes on, I make them Mafiya. I'm thinking of making a police report."

"Stay away from gangsters."

"The kid's brain was bashed in. The law says I have to report abuse. Anyway, it'll all come out in the autopsy. The cops will get involved after that."

"Just stay clear of the Mafiya. Promise me that."

"Sure," I said.

Our waitress showed up with black-bean soup for two.

"My darling wife, Helen, died twenty-six years ago," my father told her, sprinkling his bowl with onions. "You never smelled such sweet breath, may she rest in peace. You never saw such an angelic face."

The way she smiled, I could see the waitress didn't understand a word of English, not my father's heavily accented English at least, barely softened at all by decades of absence from Russia.

Cuban white bread came with dinner. It was crispy at the crust, doughy in the middle. My father covered his with butter. I dipped mine in my soup.

"You still know any Russian people?" I asked. "Someone who could check on this guy Petrossov for me?"

He looked up at me, startled.

"Petrossov?"

"What, you've heard of him?"

"It's not an unusual name," he shrugged.

"Where did you hear about him?"

For two full decades my father owned Pearl's Suits and Ties, a men's clothing business on Miracle Mile in the wealthy Miami community of Coral Gables, where I grew up. He provided fine tailoring, sold silk shirts and leather accessories, Italian suits of 140-point wool. As both he and his customers got older, he also offered a line of elastic waist slacks he kept in the back and never put in the window.

"I didn't say I heard about him," my father shook his head.

There was no pursuing this, I'd learned that much. When my father shut up, he shut up. He was more stubborn than a boulder, more opinion-ated than a priest, more judgmental than a gas gauge, tighter around a roll of dollars than a thick gauge rubber band.

"I miss Tie Mei as much as I miss Helen," I said.

"Soup's good," he grunted.

"You can say you miss her. It doesn't diminish what you had with Helen."

"You sound angry when you call your mother by her name like that."

"I'm not angry. People die. In a way, I got to have two moms. "

"Bullshit you're not angry," my father said. "I got news for you."

Once again, I almost told him about seeing Tie Mei at the hospital, about how she still smelled like almonds, about how her body still looked tight and fit and strong, about how her skin still had the glow which would have gone so well with the name Pearl if my father had done the right thing and given it to her.

"You should have married her," I said.

"If you got more sleep you wouldn't talk about things you don't understand."

I wanted to argue. The little taste of sangria might have been at fault. "I understand plenty," I said.

"You get some sleep, your thinking will clear."

"I inherited your insomnia."

"So now it's my fault? You work too much, you can't relax, you drink too much tea. Take a pill, for God's sake. You're a doctor."

My father isn't so good at taking blame. He's a dodger, which I attribute to growing up in a communist country where blame was shared, rewards were few, and power and money distributed themselves along the most cynical of lines.

"I'm not blaming you, I'm blaming your genes. There's no fault involved. And caffeine doesn't juice me that way."

At the long table next to us, the children fell on the steaming hot bread like starving dogs.

"You're a doctor," my dad said. "Take a sleeping pill."

"There's poison in pills," I said. "And no long-term cure."

"Listen, Zee, I'm getting married."

Later, I thought he might have deliberately waited until my mouth was full of black beans, but whether he did or not, I sprayed them across the paper tablecloth in surprise. It took time for my coughing to stop. Through it all, my father just watched me, his arms folded across his chest.

"All I've got is a big-shot son who works night and day," he said when I was finished. "I'm all alone and I've got life left in me—you said that yourself."

"You've got Grandpa too."

"Don't even speak his name."

"Does he know about your plans?"

"I said don't speak his name."

The waitress came again, and I gave her an order for fish in garlic sauce. My father ordered a Cuban sandwich, layers of cold cuts and cheese on a roll.

"So who is she?" I asked when I was ready.

"You remember Rachel."

"The knish baker?"

"She's a real estate agent. Her baking has to do with exactly nothing."

"It sure can't hurt."

"She's very proud you're a doctor."

"You showed me a picture of her once. She was wearing a taupe pantsuit."

"All that time I had the store, and now you've got a nose for clothes?"

"Does she have children?" I asked.

"She has a condo with an ocean view."

"So that's what this is about? Waterfront property?"

"I'll pretend I didn't hear that. You've got a new brother coming. A new sister, too."

"Can't you just live together?"

"Why should we?"

I thought about that question, and I couldn't come up with a good answer.

"So you break this news to me on Mom's birthday?"

He took a long draught of sangria. "When Rachel was a toddler, she went to the concentration camp at Belsen with her parents. The Nazis tattooed a number on her forearm. She knows how important it is not to waste time. She just wants to be happy. I want the same."

I couldn't help noticing his beatific look when he talked about her. It so surprised and compelled me that I totally forgot to tell him that I had finally had confirmation of life after death; I'd seen a human soul that morning.

It had wings.

4

So much of my life is the night. Sleeping, time goes by quickly, broken only by a somnambulant trip to the bathroom followed by a dull stumble back into bed. Not sleeping; time slows to a crawl. Redolent of secret flowers, the night fills with the sounds of insects at industry. Deepened, it renders endlessly subtle shades of black, all faces necessarily cloaked. I had a bulging moon as my companion that night, and also Drum Mountain White Cloud for tea. I acquired a taste for the world's second most popular drink back when puberty took me. My father is right that the caffeine doesn't help me sleep, but it doesn't keep me awake either; that is the job of an ill-defined disorder that not one of my colleagues has ever been able to diagnose, a riot of neurotransmitters that keep me constantly alert.

I live in a place called Hillsboro Shores, the only place in Broward County where houses rather than condominiums preside over the beach. My house is not on the sand, but I hold it in view, not bad considering I am still paying off medical school debt. I can also see the Hillsboro Lighthouse, the oldest working beacon in the state. The rotating beam flashed by, revealing a slice of platinum tide between the beach houses across the street and then, an instant later, the sage green walls of my home, along with the color festival in my front yard; the orange flower of a Geiger tree, the deep purple of calla lilies, the pale green of silver buttonwood, the dark green of Arabian jasmine leaves, and the gentle white gardenia flowers.

I went downstairs to begin my practice, not medicine—although Tie Mei did teach me to soothe sprains and bruises with herbs, and to dispel chronic health challenges with long acupuncture needles—but the art of death and destruction, a delicate meeting of harmony and havoc. Within bamboo walls, beside a Chinese-style gazebo, protected by Fu dog statues, and shielded from aerial view by a trellis the length of a freight car, I commenced my routine as I always did, with the ancient qigong set known as Eight Pieces of Brocade, a series of movements that bring the entire musculature to bear, even the small soldiers, and stimulate all the energy meridians in a way that can wake even the dead.

After stretching with the help of some wood and stone props, I took up my teacher's old straight sword, precisely the kind of weapon I had asked Jordan Jones to make for me, but smaller of course, a woman's blade, dainty in the hand but fast as a harried wasp. Wu Tie Mei is with me every moment I wield it, and there are times I swear I can feel her presence in the steel. My early lessons were with a wooden sword she kept under her bed for me. Sword practice involved prescribed movements of ancient and formal sequences. When I got better, we would spar and she would use a live blade. Once I stumbled and she cut me on the arm. I told my father it was a jungle gym accident, and he took me to the hospital for a tetanus shot. Wu Tie Mei didn't know it, but I practiced in empty college classrooms as well, and even in my gross anatomy lab in medical school, where mute cadavers were my only audience. It was only with the greatest restraint that I did not practice cutting on them.

I have no sparring partner now, but traditional Chinese weapons like staffs, spears, poles, and swords have become so familiar to me that I don't always do prescribed forms anymore. Increasingly, I cut and thrust unpredictably, flicking, pointing and slicing my way through air thick with ocean mist.

Lately, I have become aware her sword is wrong for me, which is why I commissioned a new one. The handle is too dainty and the balance is off a bit in my hand. In truth, the problem is the blade is lonesome for its mistress and will never dance for anyone again the way it had danced for her. I love the sword, but it's not mine.

I sat down in the mulched ground, helped a gecko off my leg, and thought about why it was that my father was getting married again while I was thirty and still single. I thought about Jordan. As lovely and quirky as she was, she would interest me even if she didn't share my passion for steel. Working all the time and keeping to myself, I didn't have many friends. I'd been a slave to my pager for too long. I needed to start thinking about myself.

As if on cue, the pager buzzed. Such seeming coincidence happens often, and as much as I resented this particular interruption, I generally regard the connection between interior and exterior worlds to be a sign of living clearly on a true and correct path. Sometimes, I have merely to think of a person and he or she calls. Often, I have what I think is a novel idea and read it in a newspaper the next day. Frequently, I have an epiphany or sudden insight, only to hear a stranger making the same observation. Quantum physics explains this, tiny energies around tiny particles, but I prefer to think that somehow all my martial arts work has given me the kind of subtle precognitive ability that is always there, so long as I can get my mind quiet enough to recognize it.

I went inside, threw a towel around my neck to ease the bite of the air conditioner, and called the hospital. It was another trauma case, not a child this time but a young man of twenty-six. I fired up the Triumph and drove back in, still sweating from my workout. The patient had a bandage covering one side of his head, and he was intubated.

Roan Cole was back at the dials.

"You again," I said.

"Ain't it a bitch?" he grinned.

"What's it been, nine hours?"

"Feels like nine minutes."

"Who have we here?"

"Gunshot to the head. Gangbanger. Just a kid."

The lead nurse was a young woman named Monica Dietrich. She did a nice job prepping the wound, cleaning out the bits of bone to make a clear field, retracting flesh from the ragged, burned hole.

"Doesn't look like he liked himself very much," I said, taking the burns for the powder that collects at the end of a gun barrel.

"I thought the same thing," said Roan, "but the word is it was a strip club shootout, not a suicide attempt."

"Isn't that lovely," said Monica.

Roan told her she smelled like strawberries. He didn't say it in a kind way.

"Hair conditioner," said Monica. "No time to rinse when the page came through."

"I think it freshens up the place," I said.

I turned my attention to my patient. The bullet had entered at an oblique upward angle. A couple of inches higher and to the back would have taken it right through the soft depression at the temporal fossa and into the brain, generally a fatal wound even with what I recognized to be a small caliber round. As it was, the CT scan showed that the lead had been stopped by the zygomatic bone. The patient would live, although obliteration of part of the facial nerve and the end of the maxillary branch of the trigeminal would leave him with paralysis and prone to the kind of sinus headache that would make him wish he had died.

"He came in cursing," Roan said. "Completely awake but with a bullet in his skull. Can you believe it?"

"So they caught the shooter?"

"I think the cops are still chasing him around."

I leaned in for a closer look at the MRI. I wanted to make sure there were no line cracks in the bone, that no fragments managed to get into the dura mater, the thickest of the protective bands around the skull and the one through which venous channels bring brain blood back down to the heart. The last thing I wanted was to pull the bullet free and light up another bleeder. Seeing no penetration, I got hold of the bullet with a pair of small forceps.

Although thoracic and orthopedic surgeons sometimes have to put their back into their work to beat the body's thick, long bones, brain surgery always requires a delicate touch. My martial arts training always has an effect on the proceedings, because if there is one recurring theme to the physical training I received from Wu Tie Mei, it's that when any one part of the body moves, the rest of the body moves with it.

"Think of your body as a bag of interlocking gears," she was wont to remind me. "If you turn any one wheel, all the rest turn with it." When I was a teenager and suddenly became aware of motorcycles and cars, she used a different analogy: "An opponent's force is the engine for your transmission. All you need to do is be sensitive enough to use that force against him."

Whenever I took hold of anything with forceps, I tried to sense which direction it wanted to go, and to help it go there by sinking, relaxing, bending my knees, dropping my elbows, and letting my instrument go where it would. I did that with the bullet in the gangbanger's head, feeling which way it wanted to move, and it popped out easily, with no insult to the trigeminal nerve.

".32 caliber," Roan sniffed.

Most anesthesiologists are content to watch their patient's vitals, but Roan has a real taste for forensic detail, a dark side of the guy that is not really so unusual among docs who put people to sleep for a living. It might be this dark side that gives me the feeling Roan and I belong together, that we are connected in ways beyond the professional.

"You missed your calling as a medical examiner," I said.

"Pocket automatic pistol," Roan went on, emboldened. "Could be a revolver too, but it's unlikely unless it was an old Smith & Wesson. The caliber used to be popular for the I-frame Terrier model, but that was before the .38 came along. There's a magnum version that the new Smiths can handle, Brazilian Taurus weapons too, but if that were a magnum blast the bone would never have stopped it. Nowadays it's mostly automatic rounds anyway, 9 millimeters and .40 calibers."

"Good to know," I said. "We can tell him all about it when he wakes up."

"They shoot each other faster than we can patch them up. Can't change the world, I guess."

I nodded in agreement, but all I could think about was Wu Tie Mei's warning that my world was about to change dramatically.

5

Given the choice between a life of contemplation punctuated by moments of frantic action, or a life of frantic action punctuated by moments of contemplation, I prefer the former; but by the time I was clear of Broward Samaritan Hospital, the sun was coming up and it was almost time to go to work again.

I keep a consulting office in Lauderdale-By-The-Sea, in an old strip mall between the ocean and the Intracoastal Waterway. I rent the space, but I've been trying to buy it from my landlord, Joe Montefiore, an overweight chain-smoker from Brooklyn, who has become a minor real estate mogul as a result of the never-ending surge in water-view prices. Joe was out at the ficus hedge with a hose and a cigarette. He gave me a nod when I rode up.

"Early to work, ain't ya, Doc?"

"Got some paperwork to do."

"Too much chocolate maybe?"

"Seems I'm getting a reputation," I smiled.

"Amazing to be able to eat that much chocolate and stay as lean as you are."

"The dark stuff is almost sugarless. That's the secret."

"Yeah, well I didn't sleep much either," he squinted at the eastern sky and shaded his eyes with his hand. "Venus is in transit. She's going across the sun, and these celestial events affect us; don't think they don't. We're part of a bigger system, see? Cosmic energies are at work, stuff flying in from all quarters of the universe, landing here, saturating us. It's a quantum thing, like an alien star drive."

"Sure it is," I said. "Everything's quantum."

"Take for example those little coincidences you talk about. You imagine an object or event and it appears or happens."

"What, you've decided to sell me the building?"

He laughed a great horsy laugh. "You know I'll just piss the money away," he said. "Go out of me just like the water out of this hose. I'm too old to be rich. Just going to stay where I am, that's what I'm going to do."

"You can't take it with you," I said.

"I'm sure going to try."

"Well, don't spray my shoes with that hose, okay? A man can't look neat if his shoes look beat."

Joe reached down and turned off the tap, then stared at me. "My dad used to say that."

"Mine still does."

"Your shoes do look pretty good for a guy who rides a bike."

"I like my shoes polished. Maybe I'll get over it someday, maybe I won't."

"Don't go thinking things like that matter, Doc," Joe said, starting up the water again. "And by the way, the leprechaun is here, so you ain't the early bird who got the worm."

He meant Travis Bailey, a very short man who prefers the term "little person." Medically a midget as opposed to any other kind of dwarf, Travis is properly physically proportioned and every part of him functions just fine. Forty-four years old, he lives in an apartment in the three-story condo across Oakland Park Boulevard, and comes into the office every day to do my books and appointments, and file insurance forms too. He's been working for me since I took a tumor out of his spine when I was an intern at Jackson Memorial Hospital, freeing him from a wheelchair he never thought he'd leave.

"What's on tap today, Travis?" I asked after he told me good morning.

He glanced at the computer screen on his desk, seemed to see nothing sufficiently worth mentioning to answer my question.

"I had a hot date last night," he said.

"The girl from the car wash?"

"Wow. You remember I told you about her?"

"Brazilian, legs like a polo pony, muscle tone you fear will squeeze you to a happy death."

"Forget all that," he said. "Her name's Marta. She was a lawyer in Brazil. Well, maybe not a lawyer, but a legal assistant. Anyway, it's all about her mind."

"Of course it is."

"Anywhere else in the world, a foreign professional degree is meaningful, but not here, not in the U.S. of A."

"The law varies geographically, according to culture," I said, putting my helmet and jacket down on the counter. "You can understand why she'd have to learn how to practice in Florida."

"But a car wash," he shook his head. "It's degrading."

"Help her find a better job then."

"Speaking of that, I was wondering if you thought she might lend a hand here."

"I'm not sure what help the office needs, Travis."

"I'm swamped and Kellie is, too," he said, referring to Kellie Fleming, my physician's assistant. "Sometimes she can't get specimens to the lab on time, run errands, and also get the filing done."

I've seen Travis get his heart broken time and again. He may be small, but he is handsome and surprisingly athletic. Some women find him curiously appealing. They treat him like a doll, discover he is a man with a complete set of urges and ambitions, and then back off from the particular challenges of a relationship with someone four feet tall.

"Why don't we talk about it again in a few weeks? That way you can get a chance to know Marta better and decide if having her here is a good idea or if she'll just distract you from your work."

"You don't think we'll last."

"I'd like nothing better than to see you happy. Just think about what I've said, okay?"

We spent the next ninety minutes filling out insurance forms. Putting profit before patient, insurance companies design these forms so as to trip us up on some detail so they don't have to pay. Since it is often in a patient's best interest to omit a certain detail and include another, these forms require the type of attention that gives me a terrible headache. After that, we reviewed my journal subscriptions and decided which to continue and which to drop, then evaluated solicitations for business, answered three consulting requests, and cleared up notes I had made in patient charts that neither Travis nor Kellie could read because when I haven't slept for a week or so, my handwriting becomes especially illegible.

At length, Travis produced a letter from the Drug Enforcement

Administration. It maintained that routine monitoring of pharmacies in my area indicated I was prescribing an unusually high number of opioid analgesics for my patients.

"They obviously don't understand your caseload," said Travis.

"It's easier to frame a doctor as a pusher than to hunt down real crooks on the street."

"You don't want to pick a fight with the Feds," he said. "Maybe we could tone down the scripts, eliminate refills, and decrease the number of pills per order?"

The way he said it implied he had experience on the wrong side of the law. I knew very little about his career before he came under my knife. Kellie suggested to me one time that he must be an ex-convict because he could get so tough so quickly, and because he was tight-lipped about his past. I have never wanted to violate Travis's privacy, or his hard-won trust, by looking into it.

"Just because a thing's against the law doesn't mean it's wrong," I said.

He raised his eyebrows.

"There's morality and there's legality," I went on. "Sometimes they're one and the same, sometimes they're not."

"And who are you to judge?" Travis asked in a conversational way.

Martial artists develop their own laws through the necessarily careful study of the natural laws guiding the world. Because lawgivers and enforcers alike are rarely free of political influence, an intuitive sense of justice that transcends any particular time in history or spot on the globe, is one of a martial artist's primary responsibilities.

"If I have to think about it, I stay within the letter of the law," I answered slowly. "Mostly, I know right and wrong immediately."

"And the DEA is wrong?"

"I understand the needs of my patients better than any DEA agent does; better than some congressman, some attorney, some lobbyist or judge. I became a doctor to help people, and I'm going to continue giving my patients whatever relief they need."

Travis nodded as if he was satisfied with my answer, but I could see he was worried about the ramifications. I thought about saying more, but instead I changed clothes and prepared for my first patient.

Kellie was waiting for me outside the examination room. She is as large as Travis is small, with the rosy-cheeked, bright-eyed kind of beauty that grows from the inside out. She grew up as a ward of the state, but despite being shuttled between foster homes, has retained great sensitivity and is an unerring judge of character.

"Who do we have?" I asked.

"New patient: Woman, 27. She complains of low back pain. Her internist says spinal stenosis. Tell you the truth, she gives me the willies."

"How so?" I asked.

"You'll see." She pushed me through the door.

The patient's chart called her Gloria Brownfield of Bayview Drive in Fort Lauderdale, a ritzy subdivision of waterfront homes. She was thin and blonde and wore too much makeup. Her purple nail polish caught my eye, as did the size of the diamond on her finger. She moved as stiffly as a cricket.

"I can't sleep at night," she said.

"I know the feeling. Show me exactly where it hurts."

She clutched her paper robe tightly to her and pointed at her lumbar spine.

"My family doctor says my spine is closing in on me."

What that doctor obviously had not explained is that our notion of what constitutes a normal spinal canal broadens daily as we see more and more pain-free patients with severely deformed spines right alongside suffering folks whose spines show no abnormality at all.

"Is the pain worse when you're sitting or standing or lying down?"

"Lying down," she said. "I don't sleep at all."

"And if you're on your feet for a while, say at the grocery store?"

"That's the worst."

I asked her to move this way and that, comparing my findings to the films I had.

"Can you touch your toes?" I asked.

She tried, and when she did, her blue paper gown fell forward and I caught a glimpse of her belly.

"Were you in an automobile accident?"

She shook her head.

"Would you drop the gown, please? I need to examine you fully."

"I'm all right."

"If that were true, I don't believe you would be here. Please let me examine you, Gloria."

She shook her head.

I drew back and crossed my arms. A doctor in a white coat standing in front of a patient in a paper gown commands great power. Some doctors wield this power gently, sparingly, reluctantly, and only to good effect, others abuse it on a regular basis. I suppose I stand somewhere in the middle.

"If I can't look, I can't help," I said gently.

"The pain's on my back not my front," she insisted. "There's nothing to see."

I could have told her that sooner or later someone was going to see what she was afraid to show, and it was better it be a doctor than a policeman or a coroner. Instead, I simply sat down on the examination table beside her. We stayed like that, not moving, barely breathing, not saying a word, until finally she shrugged her shoulders forward and let the gown slip fall to the floor.

The area between her navel and her upper pubis was a patchwork of burns: some were fresh and oozing; others were dried and scaly; others had healed long ago, but bore a complete core and corona. I tried to suppress my horror, tried to still myself from recoiling, but she was watching me and I'm not that fine an actor. Her gaze dropped to the floor.

This was the second time I had seen this kind of awful cigarette work on human flesh. The first time was when I was a pubescent boy and I accidentally walked in on Tie Mei in the bathtub. My teacher shared our home, but her personal habits were a dark and unexplored planet to me, information just beyond the edge of my solar system. I never knew exactly where she went on her free days, nor had I ever seen her toilette. She was private, elegant, and classy; in some ways an open book, in others a total mystery. Rather than staring at her breasts as any boy might, my attention was commanded by the line of burns along her inner thigh.

Later, while I huddled in my room, Tie Mei came and talked to me. She told me that she had been trapped and tortured by Mao's Red Guards during that infamous period of history known as China's Cultural Revolution. She told me that Mao always had it in for martial artists, as

30

they have been, throughout history, bulwarks against state-sponsored terror of any kind.

While Wu Tie Mei sprinkled history, philosophy, and tradition liberally on her teaching, I didn't really understand the lofty social role of the true martial artist until I saw my teacher's burns. I remember that in the months afterward, I approached my secret training with a new zeal, deepened by the stories my father told me about life in Russia under the Communists, about pogroms and other persecutions against the Jews, and, of course, about the Holocaust. I fantasized that my place in society would be determined by my personal skills. I like to think that as a surgeon, I've made that dream come true.

"What happened here, Gloria?" I asked when I could speak clearly.

She licked her lips; her mouth was as dry as mine.

"I don't wear clothes much at home," she said. "Sometimes I spatter myself with cooking oil at the stove."

"Cooking oil," I repeated. I thought about Rafik Petrossov beaten and dead on my operating table, and, of course, I thought of my teacher. I know my face colored.

"That's right."

"You don't do this to yourself on purpose, do you, Gloria?"

"No!"

Her response was intense and immediate and convincing. She had been expecting questions, but not that one.

"If you need my help, this would be a good time to ask for it," I said.

She blinked and looked away. "Are you going to operate?"

"Not without trying other things first."

"I've tried other things. My husband doesn't like me taking strong painkillers. He says they make me a space cadet. He's not wrong. Those pills help the pain, but they confuse me. They're hard on my digestion, too."

"You mean they constipate you?"

She blushed, and then nodded.

"How long have you been with your husband, Gloria?"

"Six years."

"His name?"

"Spenser."

"And what does Spenser do for a living?"

"He's in construction."

"Good field in this real estate market. Now tell me, have you considered yoga?"

"You've seen me move. I can hardly bend."

"Yoga helps flexibility."

"I've tried physical therapy."

"For some people, yoga works better. All right, lie down now. I'm going to do a little treatment on your back."

"I wasn't expecting any procedures today," she said, dark dots of perspiration suddenly appearing on her gown.

"Just acupuncture," I said, helping her lie on the table. "You might feel a little pinch, but that's all."

The law required that I tap the needles out of little plastic guide tubes. It's a hygiene issue. There is a lot more hepatitis in China than there needs to be and the state doesn't want that problem here. All the same, Tie Mei eschewed the untraditional tubes. When she taught me, the needle went straight from my fingers, first into folded paper, then into gauze, cotton, fruit peels, and, finally, raw chicken. In the years since, I've learned to adapt.

I chose *Hou Xi*, Back Ravine, on her right hand, *Shen Mai*, Extending Vessel, on her ankle, *Lie Que*, Broken Sequence, near her elbow, *Zhao Hai*, Shining Sea, along her midline near her navel, and finally *Shen Men*, Spirit Gate, in her ear to relieve her pain and calm her mood.

"Ouch," she said. "That last one feels heavy."

"That means it's working."

The Chinese believe that the body is suffused by a vital energy called "qi," which perfuses the body via channels called meridians. Qi has no direct analog in Western medicine. Some scientists define it as low-frequency vibration, bioelectric power, DNA resonance, or merely circulation. I know qi exists because I can feel it coursing through me during my martial practice, and, of course, when I treat patients.

"I'm going to leave the needles in for about twenty minutes," I told Gloria. "If you're uncomfortable, just call us. I'm going to turn the lights down so you can relax and take a nap."

I gave her hand a reassuring squeeze and went to my consulting room to try and clear my head.

I had seen cruelty and ugliness before, but for some reason, this particular insult, combined with what I had seen in the poor Russian boy, created an alchemical change inside me. I could only feel outrage. I could see Mr. Spenser Brownfield and Mr. Vlexei Petrossov. I had the uncanny sense that my life would come down to this moment, that it had all been building toward something that was at once unthinkable and familiar as my own heartbeat.

It was as if someone old and familiar was knocking at my door.

6

Most clubs in South Florida are built on acres of reclaimed swampland and feature manicured lawns, fountains, columns, and porticoes. The Fort Lauderdale Yacht Club, by contrast, is no more than a couple of low wooden buildings served by a parking lot of broken seashells and hidden at the back of a residential neighborhood. Dr. John Khalsa was waiting for me in the lobby. He clucked disapprovingly at my motorcycle helmet. He was my department chairman at the hospital, but administrative duties were not what made him conservative. He was a political animal through and through, long and lean with a tennis player's legs and arms. He was reputed to be a good foot surgeon, but I'd never even seen him in greens. As far as I knew, all he owned was a pair of knife-creased khakis and a navy blazer with nautical buttons. He liked speedboats, and he had a fast one out back, a cigarette as low in the water as he was, with a big engine and sharp at the bow.

"Have a drink," he said, after taking me to a table in the club dining room. "I happen to know you're not on call."

"No drinking when I'm on the bike," I said.

"You should sell that thing before you get killed or worse."

"Maybe when I can afford a speedboat," I said.

"You're in the most lucrative field in medicine. You could have a boat anytime you like."

Khalsa lacks even the tiniest hint of the singsong cadence you hear in people just over from India. His family has been here two generations and he loves nothing more than to flaunt his heritage; eating steak is the least of it. A consummate politician, he has the Southland's social scene all figured out. Not only is he chairman of the Department of Surgery, he's on the hospital district's Board of Regents, his wife is a Daughter of the American Revolution, and he's a member of the Rotary Club. I wouldn't be surprised if he ran for state office, maybe sooner than later.

"I have some debts to settle first," I said. "Anyway, sailboats are more my speed."

A waiter appeared, and Khalsa ordered a Bloody Mary extra hot. I asked for a crab salad, Khalsa for a petit filet.

"Sailboats are romantic," he said when the waiter retired. "But they're such a pain in the ass."

"More than any other money pit on the water?"

"There's the damn keel and all that rigging. Besides, when it comes right down to it, you have to go where the wind takes you."

"Sometimes the wind knows best."

"You can't get where you want to go in a sailboat, Zee."

"The wind worked for Columbus."

"He got here by accident, and sailboats are crazy slow."

"Anything worth doing is worth doing slowly," I countered, thinking of all the times Tie Mei had put me through my paces at a microscopic pace, examining my alignment, testing my strength and balance in every direction like a sculptress finessing some kind of moveable marble.

Khalsa grinned at me. "If you brought that credo to the O.R. I'd have to fire you. Fortunately, when it comes to the scalpel, you're a jet ski, not a schooner."

"I'd say I'm more of a ketch."

"I know a few nurses who think so."

"Oh, for God's sake. I just think sailing and surgery go together. They both require careful preparation and the ability to handle the unexpected when it happens."

"You are pompous beyond imagination. Oh, have I hurt the golden boy's feelings?"

"I'm not pompous, John. I just take my job seriously; people's lives in my hands and all that."

"When you were four years old, you promised your dying mother a doctor for a son. I've heard the legend," he said sarcastically.

"At least I went to medical school to help people, not to angle my way into public office."

"Fuck you, Zee."

"No, fuck you, John."

Before things could get any worse, the waiter brought soda crackers and iced tea. I picked at my food and tried some breathing techniques. Seemingly unfazed by our argument, Khalsa ate with undisguised gusto. He didn't get around to the subject of Rafik Petrossov until we were done with our appetizers and our main courses arrived.

"So what happened with the boy's neck?" he inquired lightly.

"The scalpel slipped."

"Don't say that ever again, all right?"

"I was startled. I saw an apparition in the room: a bird, maybe a butterfly. It was white with wings."

"Wings? Did you catch it? Did anyone else see it?"

The waiter came by with the dessert cart. I desperately craved the tang of Trinidad cacao, but I ordered hot tea instead of the chocolate mousse. Khalsa chose carrot cake.

"What's the difference?" I asked. "The boy was already dead."

"The difference is you had a bleeder. And we don't know he was already dead."

"I know," I said. "Autopsy should prove it."

"The parents don't want one," he said. "Thank God."

"Now isn't that just perfect."

"Yes, it is. They're content to let things lie."

"Let them lie?" I pushed myself back from the table. "Of course they want to let things lie. They beat the kid, or they're protecting whoever did! That boy no more fell off his bicycle than I came down to earth in a flying saucer. Did you speak to Roan Cole about the spine?"

"I did, and he backs you up, says the kid was basically DOA. He also says you are wound pretty tight about this."

"So maybe I am. Let's get the medical examiner involved and find out if I have a reason."

"I told you the parents won't have it."

"Do it anyway."

Khalsa sighed. "I've met with the father, Zee. He's preparing to file suit. If I push on the autopsy, we'll have lawyers so far up our ass we won't be able to shit for a year."

"So what, you cave?"

"Cave? I'm covering for you here, doctor. The last thing I need to see is an attitude."

"Next thing we know, Petrossov will be making a donation to the hospital."

"Don't be an ass."

"I'm going to speak to the M.E.," I said.

"No, you're not."

I stared at him. There was a bright vein shaped like a tree upside down running through the middle of his forehead. I'd never noticed it before, but it pulsed like flashing neon now.

"I get it," I said. "I mean how could I have been so thick? You've already made the deal, haven't you? You're just cluing me in after the fact."

"It's not a deal, Zee. It's an agreement, and a simple one. We don't talk to the authorities about the injuries; he doesn't file malpractice against you."

"Let him file it," I said. "I'm going to the cops."

He struck a pose, elbows on the table, gaze fixed right past me and out to the water like a U.S. Marine with a thousand-yard stare. "We've had a bad year in the O.R.," he said. "Our stats are down, costs are up, and the administration is reaching for cuts. You're a talented surgeon, maybe the best we have…."

"But you'll throw me to the wolves if I don't play ball."

"You killed the man's son, Doctor. You bled him out, let's not forget that."

"I saw the kid's soul," I said. "It flew up into the light like some flapping white bird. That was my butterfly. That's why I slipped up. Because I saw it go."

Khalsa sat back and folded his arms. His carrot cake appeared. He let it stand.

"You need a vacation," he said. "Everyone talks about how you never sleep. You're pushing yourself too hard. Let this thing with the boy blow over. Take a break from surgery for a while if you need to. Do a little expert testimony. It's high-paying work."

"It's whoring. And I don't need a break."

Khalsa took a bite of his cake, chewed, swallowed, took another bite, ran his tongue over his lower lip, dabbed his mouth daintily with his napkin.

"You're off the boy, Zee. Pretend you never saw him. No cops, no calls, no contact with the parents. If you don't like it, you're out of a job."

I stood up. I'd had enough of John Khalsa.

"One more thing," he said. "Nothing about white birds or butterflies. You hear me? No talking about souls going for the light. Not if you ever want to operate in South Florida again."

7

After lunch, I went back to the office and saw two more patients. I got an e-mail message that the gang boy with the bullet in his head was walking and talking and nearly fully recovered, but my beeper stayed quiet for the rest of the day. Usually it brays, so I figured this was Khalsa underscoring his point, keeping me clear of the duty roster. Every patient knows that a doctor's ego can run amok. God-players that we are, surgeons are most at risk. What most folks don't realize is that such swelling of character is compensation for years of institutionalized degradation: medical school hazing, the sleep-deprivation torture of internship, and the slavery of residency. Despite the arrogance so many doctors exude, the truth is it takes years to replace the self-esteem that medical education obliterates. Khalsa's insults, and his threats, weren't helping me with mine.

Still smarting from the meeting, I passed Gloria Brownfield's house on my way home. It was in the low-rent quarter of up-market Coral Ridge Isles, meaning there were fixed bridges between the Intracoastal Waterway and the canals behind the homes. The Brownfield's was battle-ship gray and in greater disrepair than others around it, and I took the rotting roof and the peeling paint as signposts of the owner's internal decay. Still, as inauspicious as it was, the structure filled me with the uneasy sense I was moving toward something old and familiar, but not yet clear.

Puzzled, I rode up and down the beach for a few hours, stopped for some tea, and watched summer tourists in Speedos and bikinis blister on the sand. After half an hour of that, I went home and dialed Jordan Jones.

"It's Xenon Pearl."

"Hello. Look I'm just on my way out. May I call you back?"

"Hot date?"

"One can hope."

"Why put your faith in chance when you can see me?"

"Kind of last minute, doctor."

"I know, and I'm sorry. Everyone seems to need a neurosurgeon lately. Anyway, I've been thinking about you."

"That's nice. Please try again, okay?"

"I will, and if you find yourself free, I'm always up late."

I gave her my cell number, and decided to work out. I selected a ten-foot spear with a Chinese waxwood staff two inches in diameter. The wood had been white when Wu Tie Mei gave it to me, but years worth of sweat had darkened it, making it denser, heavier, more resistant to breakage, and a valued weapon overall.

The moon had been turgid and bright the night before, but it was just a dark sliver now, and one had to take its spherical shape on faith. The lighthouse beam passed overhead, and like so many times before, I used it as a metronome, changing positions only when it passed over me, relishing the energy flowing through my body as I assumed each new posture.

Tie Mei called the spear the soul of the Chinese martial arts, and claimed the movements she taught me were her family's secret form. I never learned much about her family, and had little hope of doing so as Wu is a common Chinese name. Some day I will go to China and learn what I can about my teacher, but a burgeoning medical career has a momentum hard to overcome, and so far my surgical schedule, and financial commitments, have kept me stateside.

My body was relaxed, but the movements were still explosive and there was as much water in the air as there was in the sea that June night in South Florida. I sweated, I moved, I parried, thrusted, blocked and jumped, pretending the tropical fruit trees I'd planted back there—the mango, sapodilla, and loquats—were foes. When I had completed the sequence, I ran through it again, and then a third time. Then I sat in the hot tub and let the jets work out the knots.

The bamboo waved gently over me. Clouds scudded past. I closed my eyes and set my breathing to a meditative pace. As I did, Gloria Brownfield's face crept in from stage left, unwanted and unannounced. I imagined her screams when the cigarette touched her flesh, and the sound rent my quiet inner world. In my mind's eye I could see her husband right behind her. I saw his nose was slightly askew, his hands bulged with veins, and a hemangioma peeped just past his collar on the right side of his neck. The tableau began to move then, and I saw Spenser look right at me, and raise his hands in horror. I saw my teacher's sword rise and fall, and when its work was done, Spenser's mouth dropped open, revealing where his dental work was porcelain, and where it was gold.

I jerked to my feet, splashing water out of the tub. Wu Tie Mei stood beside me.

"These visions," she said, waving a hand draped in the red silk of a matching, loose-fitting pants suit.

"Yes?"

"You've always had them."

"The last one was the day before you died. I was an undergraduate."

"You saw me die," she said. "You saw my daggers come out too late, the bullets passing them in the air."

"Stop," I said. "How can you know what I saw?"

"You saw what happened to my face."

"I don't want this," I said, sliding back down into the tub. "I don't want this at all."

"You used to foresee events when we worked together as imperial guards. You had them when you were a monk in the northern provinces, and I was your acolyte. You had them when I was a ferryman in Guangling, and you were my wife."

"Oh no," I said. "Not your wife."

"You were a demon with the fighting fan then," she said, laughing. "I remember how you would twirl it under a sliver moon while I carried bags of rice in from the boat. You always liked a slim moon for its cover, the friend of a warrior that kind of moon is, letting you see where you're going, but not letting others see you."

I ducked down into the tub and put my head under the water. I listened to the roar of the jets and the cacophony of the bubbles. Was my teacher really speaking to me from beyond the grave? I didn't know much about ghosts, other than that the legendary ghost hunter Zhong Qui was busy fighting them through most of Chinese history. I wondered whether her crazy talk was purely a product my crazy mind. I felt any firm sense of reality slip away, and if not for my screaming lungs, I would have stayed all night in the deafening quiet of the tub.

When I came out, she was still there. "It is essential you remember your lives," she said. "Without that memory, you're doomed to repeat your lessons."

"How do I do that?"

"The meditation I taught you."

"I meditate every day. I don't remember any other life."

"You have to go deeper. You are a fearsome warrior no matter what skin you wear, no matter the shape of your eyes; it's time to give up the scalpel."

"The hell it is," I said hotly.

"It's an exercise in denial, and worse than that, it's using force against force and flying in the face of nature. It's a law of the universe. You can't change what you are."

"I'm a doctor. And the way things look right now, I'm a schizo-phrenic doctor."

"So long as you hold the scalpel, you deny your true self."

"So long as I hold the scalpel, I know I have at least a shred of sanity left."

"Your visions always come true. You are going to cut the man who burned his wife."

"The only way I'll cut him is if he comes into my operating room on a gurney."

"I'm telling you to cut him now."

I jumped out of the tub and ran into the house, hot droplets sliding down my legs. I wanted to get away from her, and so I retreated deeper and deeper into the orderly bosom of my house. I caught sight of myself in the polished red lacquer of one of the old Chinese apothecary chests I keep in every room. The chests are from my father's old house; some are painted, some are fashioned from wood stained darkly and decorated with carved flowers and beasts. Dad did not live neatly, and Tie Mei was always trying to clean up. At some point, she convinced him the chests were antiques with investment potential, and he purchased eight of them. Two days later, his house was transformed, everything put neatly in each chest's twenty or thirty drawers. Now they hold my own curiosities, odds and ends, and tools, keeping things orderly as a hedge against precisely the kind of passion of mind chasing me now.

I moved on to my full-length, cherry-framed bedroom mirror. I have mirrors all over the place. They function to redirect or counter earth energies according to the principles of Chinese geomancy, feng shui. I tried to recognize myself there, but there was something new about my face, an old familiar streak. It wasn't in my features exactly, but in something else; my eyes, perhaps, or the way I held my head.

Wu Tie Mei appeared in the mirror beside me.

8

"Get away from me," I said.

She frowned, and I felt a pang of fear. The loving memories I had of my teacher were true-blue and full, but she had been a stern mistress, and there had never been any denying her. It occurred to me right then that my father was right, I don't know everything, and maybe there had been more complexity to the life they shared under his roof than I would ever know or understand.

"That's how you talk to me?"

"I'm not a vigilante," I said. "I'll call the police on him."

"Warriors don't ask others to do the necessary work," she said. "You think you fulfill your purpose by striking trees with your weapon? You think that's why I spent half my life teaching you? So you could pick fruit with a spear?"

"I became what you wanted me to be."

"You became what your mother wanted you to be."

"You can't seriously expect me to go punish a man with a sword. This is the twenty-first century—America, not China."

"Do your work. It has to be done. Applying justice is nothing to be ashamed of, and nobody who deserves what they get is going to call the police on you."

"This is crazy," I said. "I'm having some kind of nightmare."

"You're depressed," she said.

"I know depression. I'm not depressed."

"If you're not depressed, how can you know depression? You talk like a woman who says she knows what it is to have a penis."

"That's ridiculous."

"You're always alone. You're exhausted, and you don't sleep. Has it occurred to you to ask why?"

"I work long hours. I never know when they'll call."

"You lie waiting for those calls because you feel like a nobody without them."

"I am nobody without them."

Of course, that lousy admission just lent power to her words.

"Go now," she said. "Go do your real work. When you return, meditate and recapture yourself. You're lost. This is the only way back home."

I got dressed in front of her; that's how angry and terrified I was. I dropped the towel and slipped into black jeans and a black t-shirt. I put on a pair of low sneakers with dark tops and dark soles. I wrapped Wu Tie Mei's sword in a towel, went out to my motorcycle, and used rubber straps to fasten it crosswise to the top of the saddlebags. I peeked out the window, saw the street was clear, pushed the bike out of the garage, and let it roll down the slightly inclined driveway so nobody would hear me leave. I waited to hit the starter until I was half a block away.

If someone had stopped and asked me where I was going, I don't think I would have been able to speak. Full of my teacher's exhortations and life-changing revelations, I drove south along A1A, the beach road, anonymous in my helmet, hunkered down. A night flier, heavy and ripe, hit my visor with a thud. I reached Commercial Boulevard, turned west to Bayview, and rode right straight to the Brownfield's house and parked behind the hedges. I went straight for the door at the back of the garage, found a brass handle there, turned it with both hands until I felt the tongue shift in the receiver, then shouldered it open easily and without a sound.

That's how quickly it all unfolded: automatically, as if I wore some kind of homing device. I went past an electric mower and two bicycles; his, an expensive lightweight, hers, a beach clunker decorated with rust. Breaking and entering, moving to rewrite a future that Gloria had no doubt deemed inevitable, I was precisely the natural warrior Wu Tie Mei claimed I was, and that terrified me.

I went into the hallway, walking on toes. I got through the pantry and the kitchen and the living room and then checked bedroom doors for guests or children, not wanting to surprise any innocents, not wanting to leave any unnecessary nightmares in my wake. I found an empty guest room, and then a linen closet. A face towel fell and unfurled. I left it, following the sound of snoring, opening a third door to find that it was Gloria making the noise, not Spenser.

She slept in a fetal position, her back to the wall. Her hair was splayed out and she looked pretty. Her eyelids were open a crack. My mother, Helen, used to sleep like that, as if she were watching one world while engaged in another, and I often wonder whether my problems with sleep come from some undiagnosed sleeping disorder I inherited from her. Still, the sight made me feel uneasy, and I spent more time than I should have watching Gloria, and remembering.

I found Spenser in the next room. He was bare-chested and in jockey shorts, leaning forward enthusiastically to Internet porn, working the keys for different views. He didn't notice me until I showed up as a shadow on his screen, the devil in the dots. I stopped dead at the sight of the hemangioma on his neck, a regular mulberry. It was precisely as I had seen it in my vision, down to the tiniest, grainy detail. I might have stayed frozen indefinitely, might even have turned away in confusion at seeing my vision so clearly manifest, if he hadn't sensed me, turned and raised his hands to either defend or attack.

In my hands, my teacher's blade did its work. Indeed, the violence unfolded precisely as I had foreseen it. I took the little red hemangioma berry off like the surgeon I was, separating it from his flesh with the first stroke. Invariably such anomalies are highly vascularized, and this one was too. It bled in a red shout, soaking his shoulder in seconds.

My second cut was lower, taking him just under the nipple, making the kind of line a thoracic surgeon makes when starting a flap or going in for a pacemaker, raising a piece of beef. Spenser was a lean man and looked like he could move, but the action was so instantaneous he didn't even have time to work up an expression. There would be no look on his face for me to relive, nothing to burn itself into my memory, but the surgical field itself.

I leaned forward then, and spoke into Spenser's ear. "Not one more cigarette touches your wife."

He looked up, his chin trembling. I brought my blade up to his throat. I had the strong desire to finish it, to run him through right there. The need was so strong that just for a moment, a tiny, barely recognizable instant, I saw something of myself in a previous life, a forearm only, darker and thicker than the one I have now holding a sword dripping blood.

"I cut, therefore I am," I said.

"What?"

I tickled his neck with my blade, and felt the rasp of his beard. "This was a yard accident," I said calmly. "You were using your electric mower late and it caught on a wire, and you bent down for a look, and the blade ate you. One word about me, one word about what really happened, and every newspaper reporter in town will be looking into your private life. After that, I'll return to send you to hell. Are we clear?"

He looked down, saw what I had done, and started to cry. I speared the bloody little nugget on the floor and brought it right up to his nose. "Are we clear?"

He managed a nod; his hand went to his neck. I wiped my teacher's blade off on his shorts—long, slow, deliberate strokes—and then I walked out.

My cell phone rang before I even reached the garage. "Doctor Pearl," I answered, ever so softly.

"You haven't turned in yet, have you?" asked Jordan Jones.

"Actually, I've never been more awake."

9

She was at a seaside bar quite close to my house. She wanted me to come by for a drink.

"I'm a little busy right now," I said as I slung a leg over my bike.

"You said I could call you late. Where are you, anyway? Why are you whispering?"

I started my bike, and drove a block down the road, holding the phone to my ear with my shoulder,

"How about now?"

"Sounds like you're in a hurricane. Listen, are you coming or not?"

I worried I smelled bad and had bloodstains on me. More than that, I was afraid I might suddenly laugh or cry. I didn't feel in control of myself. If Wu Tie Mei was right about rediscovering the real me, why did everything feel so uncertain? "I'm feeling a bit off," I said.

"Maybe a little company would help."

"It might take me a little while to get there," I said.

"Well, I don't want to wait too long. The date didn't end well. He had a few and he wanted to kiss me. I said no and he got forceful. I took out my knife."

"You took out your knife?"

"I didn't cut him or anything. He backed off right away. The bartender laughed at him, though. You know how some guys are about losing face. I think he's still outside and I'm worried he might come back."

"I'm just out on my motorcycle," I said. "I'm not dressed like much."

"That explains the wind noise. Come take me for a ride."

I told her yes and hung up. I looked in the bike mirror. My hair was plastered flat with sweat and, even though my shirt was black, I could see stains around my collar and around my armpits, too. My teacher's sword needed a good cleaning, should have had more than a wipe before I put it back in the scabbard. There would be DNA evidence in that scabbard,

I thought; blood stains. And if the sword itself were ever to be the same, it would be only after I had sterilized it in an autoclave to remove every one of Spenser Brownfield's proteins.

I was a hurricane of conflicting passions. I trembled at the thought of what I'd done; I lost strength in my arms; I had trouble with the handle-bars. My big bike veered toward the sidewalk and it was only with great effort that I brought it back to the crown of the road. My whole body ached. My belly felt like a giant bubble, expanding to the bursting point. I was ashamed, but I was also exhilarated.

I heard an ambulance coming from Federal Highway behind me, to the west, in the direction of the hospital where I worked. I figured it was on account of my handiwork. Experience told me the patient would need thirty stitches per side, plus five more at the neck. My mind raced through one rationalization after another, trying to link—in some acceptable way—the cutting I had just done with the cutting I did every day. Maybe I hadn't become a surgeon because of how my teacher had died, but because I had lacked the courage to become a warrior. Maybe the two professions were less different in kind than degree. After all, hadn't I beaten back Spenser's disease with a big blade just as surely as I used a small one to restore voluntary control of a retired colonel's bladder, ease the agony of a young volleyball player's herniated disc, release the pressure of a radio announcer's spinal swelling, and remove the embolism strangling the cerebellum of a temporarily paralyzed concert violinist?

One aspect of neurosurgery is that even the surgeon can never be entirely certain of the outcome. The brain and the spinal cord together represented a strange and complex universe where the unexpected is commonplace and the typical is often elusive. In the same way that I did-n't know for sure if a paraplegic patient would walk again after I made repairs, I couldn't be sure if, in view of his obviously flawed character, Spenser would not be galvanized to new lows of depravity by what I had done to him. I couldn't say for certain that he wouldn't start his own line of rationalizing, his own version of spin, and seek revenge for what I had done to him through more violent acts of his own. All the same, I felt that I had helped Gloria. I couldn't imagine he would touch her again.

That was something.

I rode home as quickly as possible, showered in record time, stroked the sword with a rag soaked in camellia oil, dressed in casual clothes, stuck on a spare helmet and came out of the garage. Halfway to the restaurant, a police cruiser pulled in behind me from a side street. I felt my mouth go to cotton waiting for his lights to come on, but he turned off a moment later.

Jordan was at the bar, all elbows around a big pink tropical drink that matched the tank top she wore over tight jeans. I hadn't seen this much of her before, and she was, in all her parts, better than good. I said so, and then asked the bartender for a beer.

"You probably shouldn't drink and ride," she said.

"I never do, and I'll stop after one."

"You took your time," she said. "But I'm glad you came."

"I didn't see your guy out there. Nobody loitering I mean."

"Take a sip of this. Schnapps, rum, pink lemonade. I call it a Gibbous Moon."

"Gibbous is a medical term, you know, pertaining to a spinal cord turned backward."

"Also means more than half-full. I never finish these drinks."

"Very literary. I thought I'd find you romancing some high-end vodka."

"Too yuppie," she said. "I make swords, I don't decorate salons."

"The two of us and our ripostes."

"At least you're not dull."

"The worst possible word for us both."

We laughed as we had that first day at her home. It was a tremendous relief. I hadn't realized how tense my entire body had become. I remembered the last time I'd seen her smile, how wonderful it was, how it transformed her face. Suddenly everything felt light and easy. I had no sword in my hands, there was no blood in sight, some guy was doing a poor Jimmy Buffett imitation in the corner, but his audience, liquored up and loose, was uncritical. It was late night, it was summertime, people were happy. Maybe everything would be all right now. Maybe what I knew I had done would somehow dissolve into mystery.

"Show me your knife," I said.

She got a sly look on her, and reached for her waist. The blade was tucked inside her pants with a clip, not in a pocket and not in a sheath.

It was a folding knife, but it came open with an automatic snap and she moved it to my belly and held it there.

"Don't tell me you made that."

"I bought it. I don't know anything about these mechanisms."

"Doesn't look like a woman's blade," I said, thinking of my sword against Spenser Brownfield's chin.

"You've been hanging around the wrong kind of woman."

I took it from her hand and closed it and slipped it gently back into her pants. Then I kissed her.

She pulled away at first, but I followed, and this time she didn't pull away. I tasted the pink lemonade.

"Well," she said when she could.

"I know how you feel about kissing, but I'm just so glad to see you."

She took a long pull off her Gibbous Moon and turned back to me.

"You have no idea how I feel about kissing," she said and then kissed me again.

It was even better this time. I tasted the Schnapps, but also something warm and inviting, something that stirred an old, familiar feeling. I wondered if Jordan had been with me before, had run the wheel of reincarnation sometime, somewhere, as my mother, or daughter, my friend, teacher, partner, or simply my lover.

Somebody shouted at us to get a room. Out of the corner of my eye, I saw the bartender freshen our napkins. Wu Tie Mei taught me there are five levels of the self, and as I fell deeper into the kiss, I could feel and see at least three of them. There was Zee kissing Jordan. There was another Zee watching Zee kiss Jordan. There was another Zee watching Zee watching Zee kissing Jordan. Two more like that, at least, but I lost track of myself melting into her. I wanted to give in to the experience utterly, to be the kiss rather than watch it.

"Hoo," she said when we parted.

"Hoo squared."

We looked at each other until the looking became too much to bear.

"I was a swimmer in college," she said, resuming her Gibbous Moon.

"Where did you go?"

"I wanted to stay close to home, so I went up to the University of Florida in Gainesville. But my real school was my father's forge. I knew that even back then."

"And what's this about swimming?"

"I thought you might want to take a dip."

The restaurant had lights shining on the beach. Folks were fishing from a pier no more than a stone's throw away. Flashes of phosphorescence broke the monotony of the waves.

"Little crowded, don't you think?"

"You're a private person, is that it?"

"With a house by a private beach. What say we go there and swim?"

So we went. I tried to pay her bar tab, but she wouldn't let me. She was high, but not that high, and she managed to hold on just fine behind me on the bike. She didn't complain about the spare helmet either, even though I knew that it was too big on her, could see it slipping into a tilt when she turned her head.

The last person to use that lid had been a nurse I'd dated. There are doctors who date only nurses, and nurses who become nurses just to marry a doctor. This particular nurse had found me wanting. It was in no way, shape, or form enough for her that I was a neurosurgeon. She wanted me to be warmer with her, to open up more quickly, to take her into my life. After two months of seeing each other, she still had not seen more than my front yard. I don't share secrets easily, so she had not seen my weapons or my practice garden. We slept together, but at her place. She had pushed me on this, and I'd pushed back. At the time, I'd figured I just needed to get to know her better, to trust her. I told her that the women in my life have made a habit of leaving me too soon. In retrospect, although that was true, the meat of it was that she just wasn't right for me.

"This is so great," Jordan shouted into my ear, making a wide gesture with her hand, taking in the subtropical night.

"I've got déjà vu. Feels like we've done it in another life. On a horse, maybe, dashing across the steppe."

"The steppe?"

"Just a feeling," I said.

"So you believe we come back?"

"Maybe, I'm not sure."

I didn't want to say any more. I rode all the way to the house bound up in the realization that my private life had on this night become my secret life. I had no idea how I was going to deal with all that. I stifled a groan at the prospect.

"I never even knew this neighborhood was here," Jordan said as I turned east off A1A.

"That's the beauty of it," I said. "In front of your face, but you don't see it."

Just like me, I almost added. Scalpel by day, sword by night.

I grabbed a towel from inside the front door. I keep a stack there, on top of a temple table, just for the beach. Jordan wanted to come in.

"Let's get to the water first," I said, worried that Tie Mei might be waiting with some commentary about the night's adventure, a fear that stayed with me as we crossed the street and went through the gate to the beach.

Much as she seemed to always find me in some state of undress, there was no sign of Tie Mei as Jordan and I took the boardwalk over the sea oats and the dunes, those bulwarks against storm surge erosion, the last hope for expensive houses in the sand. Perhaps, I reasoned, I was not in the right frame of mind to receive her.

"Sharks feed at night you know," Jordan said, slipping out of her sandals.

"Actually, they feed at dusk and at dawn."

"What about the opening scene of Jaws, the girl clinging to the buoy?"

"A movie," I said.

We were alone on the sand. An airplane blinked overhead. A lone fishing boat made its way seaward through the Hillsboro Inlet. Yellow hazard tape on posts demarcating turtle nests fluttered in the wind.

"I love that there are eggs here," I said. "Life, just starting out."

"I think it's wonderful that you love that," she said.

She dropped her tank top. Her nipples were small and dark, her breasts sloped downward like tears; her skin was the blue of her veins in the light of the sea. At her invitation, I gave her jeans a tug down low. They came off, and she stood in the moonlight, naked but for panties. She had an athlete's body, elegantly proportioned, a flesh-and-blood statement of personal priorities and discipline. Her thighs bulged with muscle and her fingertips twitched. I made a move to hold her, but she stepped backward, taunting me with her toned, long torso, beckoning and walking and walking and beckoning until she was in the ocean up to her ankles and then up to her shins. I saw a small tattoo at Ming Men, a point at the base of her spine known as Heaven's Gate, and also as the source of all the body's power.

"Nice body art," I said as I stripped and followed.

"The scales of judgment," she said. "My father chose it. It's not big but there's a lot of detail in it. Took hours to do."

After watching her endure the burning slag in her glove, I didn't bother to ask her about the pain.

"Your father chose it?"

"I was a teenager. I was hell-bent on getting a tattoo. My dad went with me and recommended it because he said if I was going to live with a symbol forever it should have eternal meaning."

"Sounds like a guy with his eye on the big picture," I said.

"You said it," she said, wading out.

"Anyway, it's beautiful."

"You're tall without your clothes on."

"It's my shadow."

"There is no shadow, Xenon. It's nighttime."

I wanted to tell her shadows are everywhere, but instead I dove in the water to be with her. The southern Atlantic is a bathtub in summer, the temperature closer to ninety degrees than eighty, especially right at the littoral. There is the scent of brine, but there is also a persistent meniscus of marine diesel and also a fine film of high-octane fuel left by jet skis.

"Have you ever noticed how Florida cleans herself before dawn?" Jordan asked me, scissor kicking gently in a path parallel to shore, holding my hand lightly with hers. "All these dirty things happen during the day, and then at night the rain comes and the wind picks up and the plants make oxygen and the whole place renews."

I thought of all the plants in her house, wondered if she kept her greenhouse to purify her world while she slept. I wondered if I would sleep tonight, if having done Tie Mei's bidding would bring me the peace she'd intimated it would.

"That's a great way to look at things," I said.

I pulled myself gently toward her, put my arm around her waist, let my hand rest on her flat belly. We lay bobbing as one, the sea creating a hundred little crashes between her flesh and my flesh as the waves came in and pulled out again. She ran her toe along my leg.

"I don't know what I expect for us, but I find myself hoping for a lot," I said.

She kicked herself vertical and took my face in her hands.

"Me too," she said, her lips inches from mine.

"Let's not rush," I said. "I want to, but I don't think we should."

"I fear you may be too good to be true," she said, biting her lip.

"Good might not be the best word for me."

We got out and lay down on the sand, side by side. "Let's stay here until the sun comes up," she said, wrapping up in a towel and lying down beside me.

"All right."

So we held hands, twin cocoons linked only by fingers. Things, I realized, were happening more than fast enough.

Gulls came, then sandpipers and crabs, then finally the light.

10

The Old Testament recounts that after Moses died, Joshua led the Jews into the Promised Land. Twelve tribes arose—named for the sons of Jacob—and God collectively renamed them "Israel." Ten of the twelve tribes were later assimilated during the Assyrian conquest, gaining fame in history as the ten lost tribes. 2000 years later, a group of Jews migrated from Persia to Song Dynasty China, and settled in the metropolis of Kaifeng, at the terminus of the Silk Road. More than 800 years later, there was still a Jewish community in that august city, practicing the old rites, holding the original beliefs of the Hebrew people. Wu Tie Mei's own great grandparents prayed in the Kaifeng temple, and she always insisted that these far-flung and forgotten Jews were the real lost tribe.

I'm sure that if Tie Mei had not been of Jewish extraction, my father would never have let her raise me. It's not that he had any feelings about Chinese people. The only ones he knew were waiters in restaurants. He accepted there were things about Tie Mei he did not know—an understatement, I know—but her faith was his faith and that was enough for him. He himself has not always been strictly observant, but he has strong opinions about mixing Gentile with Jew.

Rachel, of course, was Jewish, and my father arranged for me to meet his bride-to-be and her adult children at Sunday brunch at the Biltmore Hotel in Coral Gables. It was an extravagant venue, but he felt it was an important occasion. A celebration of two families becoming one, he told me on the phone.

I guess he chose the Biltmore because it was only a few blocks from his old store. He couldn't afford to live in the Gables anymore, but he'd had countless drinks at the hotel's bar and as many lunches at the restaurant, so he probably felt comfortable there.

The day was a blast furnace by eleven. I rode down, sweating all the way. No matter: the hotel was so cool, the sweat turned to salt on my neck in seconds. The group was already there, at a round table in the back, one chair empty. Dad had started in on the smoked salmon; everyone else had better manners.

Rachel turned out to be a slender redhead with pretty features. Fit and toned, she looked maybe five years younger than my father. "I'm Mom number two," she said, taking my hand.

I almost said number three, but I saw a look forming on my father's face so I embraced her instead and gave her a nice kiss on the cheek. "I'm so happy for you both. Dad's good fortune never ceases to amaze me."

"You're right, Asher, he is a charming boy," Rachel smiled.

Her daughter came up to greet me. Wanda Berkowitz was a larger-than-life woman with a strong grip and a sculpted face. "A doctor in the family at last," she cried.

I turned to meet her brother, Martin. He was a good 6'3", a hulking guy whose tie couldn't find the center of his neck. He took me in, saw me taking him in too, figured out I was wondering how these two Gullivers could have come from such a willowy mom.

"My father was six foot five and he weighed two eighty," he said without my asking. "An NYPD detective."

Fleetingly, I wondered if he and I had shared another turn of the reincarnation wheel; in fact, I wondered it about all my new family members.

"You and your sister live in New York?" I asked him.

"Oh no. We're down here with Mom now," Wanda replied. "I'm a detective with the Broward Sheriff's Office Strategic Investigative Division. Martin's a reporter for the Miami Herald."

"I hear you practice Chinese kung fu," Martin said.

"Never have. That's just a strange rumor rooted in my dad's fantasy life."

"I bet you're just modest. I do Krav Maga, Israeli self-defense. Very tough, very street-oriented."

"It's just so great that you're a brain surgeon," Rachel clapped her hands.

My father walked over, smiling as if to say: Look, she's bragging about you already. The waiter came by. We all told him we would have the buffet, except for Rachel, who ordered an egg-white omelet with spinach and wheat toast, dry.

"That's how she stays so thin," said my father.

"You're so young to be cutting brains," said Wanda.

"You're young to be carrying a gun."

"Law enforcement is a young person's game."

I was newly wary of cops, but I liked Wanda anyway. I liked Martin, too. I suddenly felt that maybe late was better than never when it came to having siblings. I mentioned the thought aloud, and the ice broke. After that, I asked Wanda about her dad.

Her face lit up at the mention of him. "He made assistant chief on drug interdictions. There was a particularly famous harbor sting, half a ton of cocaine."

"He was also in on the subway vigilante case," Martin put in. "Remember that guy? It was in all the papers. He would board the subway and fumble with bills and drip jewelry until some dumb schmuck tried to rob him and then he'd shoot 'em dead."

"The world could use more vigilantes," my father said, a piece of bagel coming out of his mouth. "We should be more like the Israelis. They don't take any guff from anybody."

"Israel has become a terrible place, Asher," Rachel said. "You don't want this country to become like that, with killing and blowing up children."

I moved over to the cheese blintzes, took two, and drizzled them with raspberry sauce.

"Speaking of killing, what do you know about the Russian mob?" I asked Wanda as casually as I could.

"We have regular briefings on them. They're very active. Of course they play second fiddle to radical Moslem groups. What's your interest?"

"Strictly professional. I've come across a couple in my work."

"Patients?"

"And their relatives."

"Be very careful. They make the Italians look tame. Modern Russia is a criminal state. Police mean nothing; the law means nothing. The rape of Russian resources after Yeltsin was the greatest theft in the history of the world, and the rapists rode all that money right out of the country. We've got our share of Redfellas here in Miami."

"Redfellas," I said. "I hadn't heard that term."

"They're in prostitution, extortion, drugs, gambling. You name it.

It's a terrible crowd—armed, technically and financially savvy, and internationally connected. They are more ruthless, more senselessly violent than any other group in organized crime."

"Heard the name Petrossov?"

Wanda rolled her eyes.

"The worst of a bad lot," she said. "We love them for a particularly vicious nightclub massacre, but we just can't get the evidence. Not only that, but we know they are bringing young girls in from Siberia. They put the pretty ones in their strip clubs and the rest out on the street. Can't prove it so far. We rescue the girls and promise the moon, but they're too scared to squeak."

"How about some dessert?" Rachel asked brightly.

We all went up to the far end of the buffet. I saw Martin go for fresh fruit and my father do the same. Rachel had some espresso-flavored cake, but a slice as narrow as a budgie perch. Wanda and I stopped in front of the mango cheesecake. Close to her, I recognized cheap orange blossom perfume. Somehow, on her it smelled good.

"I shouldn't do this," she said. "I war with my weight."

"Oh go ahead and splurge. You don't gain a brother every day. And the truth is I can't resist chocolate either, especially if it's bitter and strong."

"I'm stuck on the milky stuff. You're really nice. I wasn't sure how I'd feel about the marriage. We all miss my dad so much."

"They're good together," I said.

"Don't let mom's size fool you," Wanda shook her head. "She's tough."

"She better be."

"And you must be, too, a doctor who practices kung fu."

"In my dreams, maybe, after a late night movie."

"Your father said you'd say that. Says you lie because you're modest."

"He lies because he isn't."

"He says you actually practice with swords."

"I suppose a scalpel is a tiny sword."

"I ask because the duty sergeant talked about a strange case at roll-call this morning. An emergency room doc phoned it in last night. Patient said he'd had a lawnmower accident, but the doctor said the wounds looked like they'd been done by some kind of long knife."

I dropped my cake right then, and stumbled to make it look like I had tripped. I kept my shaking hands busy cleaning up the floor. Wanda noticed.

"You all right?"

"This is why I don't drink coffee when I work—makes my hands shake."

"I was just wondering if you would know a sword cut if you saw one?"

"Brain surgeons don't treat stab wounds much, that's more a trauma specialty. What happened to the guy?"

"He won't be taking his shirt off at the beach, but he's alive. Staying with his story, too."

I took a lick of icing. "So maybe it really was the lawnmower."

"Oh, it's obvious he's lying. But if no charges are filed we have to let it go."

"It stops there? No medical examiner?"

"Not unless more victims show up."

A busboy came and picked up my cake. I cut myself another slice.

"Look at how he eats," my father pointed at my plate when we got back to the table. "They don't teach nutrition in medical school, I can tell you that much."

Rachel slapped my father's hand. "What he eats is not your business."

Wanda gave me an I-told-you-she-was-tough look.

Despite everything, the crazy bunch got a chuckle out of me.

11

On Monday, my pager was still quiet. I called to check in and make sure I wasn't missing anything, and got Vicky Sanchez on the line.

"Khalsa's taken me off the roster, hasn't he?" I asked.

"I'm sorry, Zee."

"Exactly what did he say?"

"That you need a rest."

"But that's not all the buzz, is it?"

"People are talking about the Russian boy."

"Roan knows the boy was gone coming in."

"It's not Roan you've got to convince."

After I hung up, I didn't know what to do with myself. Tie Mei was right. I drew my sense of self directly from my scalpel, and was at the mercy of people around me. More than that, my teacher had me thinking more and more about reincarnation. If I came back, that had to mean others did too, and I couldn't help but try to identify the recurring players on my personal stage. Was Khalsa someone I had tangled with before? Had Roan watched my back a thousand years ago in some Chinese battle with barbarians? How could I know if this was all true? How reliable, in short, was the source?

I believe Wu Tie Mei made some mistakes in how she conducted affairs with my father, and although I may not ever know for sure, she may have missed an opportunity there. Certainly, I know he loved her in his own way; his dearth of commentary on the subject is the surest clue. She also seems to have erred in her final battle, although the details are vague; I wonder whether she hadn't performed precisely the role she was meant for on that fateful day, no matter how badly it had broken my heart. In short, she was a magnificent woman who made few mistakes and never intentionally led me astray. If she says I'm the reincarnation of a powerful Chinese warrior, perhaps I am. The most compelling affirmation of her reincarnation claim is in the curious calm I feel whenever I think about what I had done to Spenser Brownfield. I might be at the beck and call of others as a surgeon, but as a warrior, I am my own man.

So I put Spenser out of my mind, and poor dead Rafik, too—who had he been in my previous go-rounds, I wondered—and went to the garage to work on the vintage BMW motorcycle I'd picked up out of the Miami Herald classifieds. It was dented and rusted and in rough mechanical shape, but it was the same model my father had ridden as a young man, and in combination with it's Teutonic simplicity and low production numbers, that made it an intoxicating find. I'd been waiting to start restoring it, and this seemed the perfect time.

I removed the front wheel and saw that the disk brake needed polishing. I loosened the fork legs and pulled them out of the clamp at the top of the handlebars. I took the seat off and was amazed to find the original factory tool kit, wrapped in a vinyl sleeve and jammed into a plastic tray. Old tool kits are highly prized. Hard to explain, but true. I speculated that this one might be worth more than I paid for the entire bike. Gingerly, I removed it from the tray and was all set to open it when a flash of color caught my eye.

It was a photograph. The emulsion had become tacky from the heat and there were scratches on the surface, along with dents the shape of a screwdriver and a sparkplug wrench. Still, I could see Tie Mei smiling at the camera, her arm around me, tugging me close to her hip. I was wearing an old red Donald Duck sweater, and looked to be about six years old. I sat down hard on the garage floor, lost in a rush of recollections, amazed that my father's old bike, his exact one, had come back to me. Later, I would realize the odds were not really so slim, that the bike had merely stayed in the neighborhood, but at the time, the coincidence made me feel the world was really much smaller than it seemed.

I found two more pictures behind the first. The second image showed Tie Mei and me again. My head was thrown back in laughter as she tickled me, smiling. I tended to remember her in jeans or a sundress, but here she wore a Mao pantsuit and a single long braid of her thick black hair down her back, a somber but pretty woman with an unlined face. I had forgotten how Chinese she looked when she came to us, how exotic, delicate, and porcelain white.

The last picture was a headshot of Tie Mei against the front door of our old house. Perhaps it was because she looked so entirely small and ordinary that I was suddenly overcome with anxiety. Sweat pricked on my brow, and I felt my low back grow hot and my belly grow cold.

Reincarnation? A fearsome warrior?

I had just gone out and cut an unarmed man with my sword. He hadn't even tried to fight back. There was nothing fearsome about me.

My panic deepened. I wasn't used to this! I was the coolest hand in the O.R., the man everyone turned to for my icy nerves, but here I was undone by my own crazed actions, and the supernatural ravings of the shade of a woman dead ten years.

I paced the garage, trying to calm down, but the walls of the garage seemed to close in on me until all I could do was leave. I put the photographs aside, got on the Triumph, and rode to my office. It took a monumental effort to watch the traffic around me, and fight the cold terror inside.

A strange woman greeted me at the reception desk.

"Can I help you?" she asked.

By her soft treatment of consonants, I figured her for Travis's Brazilian friend, Marta, the woman he suggested might help out around the office.

"I'm Dr. Pearl," I said mildly. "And this is where I work."

"Meet Marta Bilbao," said Travis, jumping up from behind the file cabinet. "She's here on a trial basis."

Marta offered her hand, and I saw she had been sitting on telephone books. She was a polo pony all right, maybe an inch shorter than Travis himself.

My eyes arched in the little man's direction. "I thought we were going to wait on this."

"These patients need follow-up," Marta said, handing me a thin stack of files. "I've marked those who have already had procedures with green tabs and those who are due for surgery in red."

Travis laced his fingers through hers, but way down low, as if he didn't want me to notice. "I didn't think you'd be in today," he said. "We don't have anything on the schedule."

Having Marta working the desk was a minor change, but in my state of mind, I found myself craving the safe and familiar, so I retreated to my consulting room. Such quarters should be designed to put patients at ease, but instead they are usually a doctor's panegyric, containing testimonial letters, diplomas, a bit of medical art, a plant in the corner, and a big desk that emphasizes power, authority, and distance from the patient. My own desk was small and set off to the side. A four-fold Chinese screen showed water buffalos carrying farmers through a stream, and gave depth to the room, but the centerpiece was a trio of chairs, because patients so often bring a spouse to meet the man who will bare their brain.

Bird's-nest ferns graced the corners and a vaporizer produced mist against the back wall for mood. Classical music played soothingly in the background, although sometimes when I was alone, I chose the blues. It was Travis' assignment to make sure there were always fresh flowers on the desk, and that morning there were gardenias nestled amongst their dark, dark leaves.

I put my face forward, and let the petals brush my nose. I inhaled the rich scent and tried to slow time to a pace where I could see dust witches growing by simple aggregation, where I could see sunbeams make their spectacular journey from source to earth, where I could see back and forth in time, and thereby learn that little Rafik was my former war commander, or that his father had been a village pimp.

I was in the aftermath of panic, and safe at my desk. A combination of wonderment and exhaustion washed over me, and I slept.

12

It had been less than two days, but I felt like an alien in the operating room. Roan was off-call, and an anesthesiologist I knew only slightly was on the job, an older man with a rough haircut and skin so white he looked out of place in South Florida. His name was Bill Prince and he worked only two days a week. The story was he'd retired and then come back after the bubble burst and his stock portfolio went away. He had a son-in-law in college and a daughter who broke code for the navy. He seemed cool toward me, but maybe I was putting that in myself, worried as I was about the word on Rafik.

"Cessna Golden Eagle," said Prince. "Twin engines, retractable landing gear, pressurized cabin and this guy Cartwright slams it into the drink off Boca Raton. He was alone in the plane. Some people on the beach said there was a giant croc in the water."

"You mean an alligator?"

"No, an American crocodile, probably up from the Everglades. Sometimes they come up this far, lost or adventuring, who knows. It's rare, but I've heard of it happening. This poor bastard was low on his approach to the Boca airport and must have seen the beast in the water, done a double take, and forgot to look up. Ten more yards and he would have been on the beach, props chopping up sunbathers and all that. As it is, the wheels were down and the reef grabbed them hard, the nose went under, and the plane did a half-somersault underwater. A lifeguard pulled him out."

If it had been Roan in the room rather than Bill Prince, I would have been treated to some reference to life in the fast lane followed by a soliloquy about the similarities between air disasters and motorcycle crashes.

"Bad luck," I said. "He married?"

Vicky Sanchez was at the sponges and instruments. "Divorced," she told me. "But his fifteen-year-old boy is outside."

I could see the pain on her face. Vicky was especially sensitive to anything do with children. Two years earlier, she lost her only child, an eight-year-old girl, to childhood leukemia.

"Has anybody spoken with him?" I asked.

"Dr. Khalsa said you should handle it."

I couldn't make out from her tone whether she meant the boss wanted me to face another child in some kind of twisted morality play, or whether he thought I was the only one qualified to give a prognosis.

There was no time to figure it out.

"The bone-man's waiting," said Prince, meaning that a maxillofacial surgeon was on-call to rebuild the pilot's face once I had his life-threatening brain injuries under control.

Vicky shaved Cartwright as best she could, but there were patches just too rough to run a clipper over. The result was a patchwork mosaic of dark clumps, osseous tissue, white dura, and gristle that looked as if it might be from what was left of his nose. While Prince monitored Cartwright's uptake of Desflurane sleep gas, his expired CO_2, his blood pressure, the oxygen saturation in his tissues, and of course his heart rate, I went to work arranging the skull bones.

The process of moving them gently back into position along the suture lines was a martial arts exercise all its own. Wu Tie Mei always told me that to label a thing was to separate from it. Labels lead to prejudice, she said. And on a deeper level, they lead to a disconnection, a sense of you and other that gets in the way of total engagement. For this reason, she never gave her martial style a name. She didn't want me to compare what she taught me to other styles, and more importantly, she wanted me to integrate my style into my thinking, my movement, and my being.

Nameless though it remains, I can't help but think that, while I have seen echoes of what she taught in Japanese swordsmanship; Thai kick-boxing, Aikido, and of course many variations of Chinese kung fu, from Hung Gar and Shaolin to Baguazhang, most of all, however, it resembles original taijiquan; not because she taught me to move slowly, but because the Taoist principles she talked about were to be found there. One of these was sensitivity. Tie Mei was so sensitive; she could trap a fly on her arm. The fly has to push off with its legs to get into the air, she told me, and the moment it did she moved away slightly so the fly had nothing to push against. I remember watching, fascinated, as the trapped fly, in utter futility, moved back and forth along her arm looking for somewhere, anywhere, from which to leap into the air.

I used that sensitivity in teasing Cartwright's skull bones into place. While Vicky gently picked stray bits off the surgical field, I put my fingertips on the bones and silently asked them where they wanted to go. I sought the tiniest tendency in any direction, the subtlest possible inclination, and then I helped the bone get there. I concentrated on the damage around the paracentral sulcus and lobule, and in due course everything lined up.

Had the impact been farther forward, Cartwright would have been rendered a vegetable; the way things were, the prognosis was unclear. When the jigsaw puzzle was approximately reassembled, I took a look at the scan. Typically, when the forehead is penetrated or crushed there is damage to the frontal lobe, but Cartwright showed an odd kind of impact injury; there was massive bleeding across the top of the brain, probably the result of shearing contact with the windshield or instrument panel.

Way back in the last century, a physician named Wilder Penfield mapped the brain. He discovered that many functions, including the sense of self, are shared by many different sections of the brain. The man whose gray matter I held in my gloves might be doomed, but he might also emerge with some abilities and sense of self intact, might even gain, by neurological reassignment, a new ability to count cards or sing on key. As I worked, I hoped for the best. Anybody who starts a career in neurosurgery already a pessimist is going to wind up sucking down a combination of pills so irrevocably devastating that not even his most talented colleagues can save him.

Vicky shook her head. "He's got no chance."

"He can hear you," I said. "And you're wrong, he's going to be fine."

We had mannitol and steroids going in the IV drip to keep the pilot's blood from swelling, but even so the brain was bulging against the damaged bones at the top of his cranium.

"Sure he is," Prince laughed sarcastically.

I raised my gloved hands, index fingers up, like a conductor.

"I mean it," I said. "He's going to be perfect."

The vigilante inside me was back at the wheel, although the sword was nowhere to be seen. It was scalpel all the way. I felt a huge surge of energy, less the result of injustice than the need to battle entropy, the tendency of the universe toward maximum disorder. I did not want this man to fall apart. I would not let it happen. I worked at the feverish pace Khalsa had referred to when he said I was a jet ski in the O.R. It was all Ms. Sanchez could do to keep up with the little slices and stitches I made: here, there, gathering tissue together, pulling it apart. Retractors and clamps appeared and disappeared. I tossed blood-soaked sponges into the tray. I used a few screws where they were absolutely necessary. Gradually the pilot's head began to look human.

"Pearl cheats the angel of death one more time," Prince shook his head admiringly.

"The angel had his chance when the plane went down. I'm not cutting him any slack."

"Cutting," clucked Vicky Sanchez.

For all my efforts, there was a moment when things got dicey, when despite my best efforts Cartwright took a turn for the worse. Nothing showed on the monitor—perhaps it was a smell or a subtle sound or some kind of energetic aura—but I detected the change even though both Prince and the redoubtable Ms. Sanchez did not.

"What's the patient's name?" I asked.

"Hugh," said Vicky.

I took Cartwright's hand in mine.

"Stay with me, Hugh," I said in a voice so loud Prince nearly fell back off his chair. "I'm doing everything I can to keep you here, but I need a sign you want to stay. Your boy is out there. Give me some good news to share with him. Do that for me, will you?"

Any anesthesiologist will tell you that a patient under the gas cannot move. It's impossible, they say: there is no motor function. I waited a long time, during which I had the odd but distinct sensation Cartwright was thinking things through. Eventually, however, he twitched. It was a tiny tick, just a finger, but Vicky noticed it and Prince did, too.

I took it as vindication for my theory about hearing things while asleep.

"Fight for it then!" I shouted.

Vicky gently caressed the remains of his forehead. Prince made some adjustment, probably to send poor Hugh further into orbit. I stitched the top of his skull back together, using the skin to hold the bones. The plastic surgeons would have their chance with him—I doubted he would recognize himself—but my day was done and the work rang true.

I went out to talk to the son. He had a cell phone tucked into the pocket of his flowered beach shirt and a skateboard under his arm, but despite the surfer duds he radiated self-possession, defiance, class and pride at a time most kids his age would have been either macho and angry and hard or one big quivering lip.

"What's your name?" I asked.

"Orson Cartwright."

"I'm Doctor Pearl. Your dad is alive, but it's going to be touch and go for a while. Can he count on you?"

"Sure."

"Great," I said.

"Can I count on you?"

It was a perfect question, but it didn't add up from a teenager.

"I did my best work in there," I said. "The other folks around here will keep doing the same, but the truth of it is, the ball is in your dad's court right now."

"He's the world's best dad."

"That much I can tell," I said, guessing that with such a classy boy, Hugh Cartwright probably really was the bomb.

13

On my way home, I stopped off to see the Petrossovs. Rafik's hospital file put their home in Idylwild, a wealthy community at the end of Las Olas Boulevard in Fort Lauderdale. Las Olas is a tourist street, a thorough-fare ripe with opportunity for folks to buy goods they don't need with money they don't have. Galleries sell paintings allegedly created by great masters but actually churned out by minimum-wage immigrants in a factory in south Miami-Dade County; curio shops sell stone animals carved in Africa for a dollar and on sale here for two hundred; vendors hawk Chinese dragon kites, and snooty shops sell Italian sofas actually sewn in Mexico. You can eat pizza baked by Cuban chefs on Las Olas, and Cuban food prepared by Brazilian ones. A person in search of a cup of coffee on Las Olas has many vendors to choose from, and although I am devoted to my tea, I must admit that Las Olas' coffee rules the town.

The entrance to Idylwild was free and open, but access to the Petrossov compound was not. I pulled my bike up to a steel gate and spoke into a box to gain admission.

"Yes?"

Even on that lonely word, the Russian accent was heavy.

"Dr. Pearl to see Mr. Petrossov," I said.

"Mr. Petrossov is unavailable."

"Mrs. Petrossov, then."

"Take off your helmet."

I complied. A camera on top of the concrete post whirred as it took me in.

"Wait," came the command.

My sword hand itched at the curtness of the command, but the gate slid open a moment later. The camera monitored my progress onto the circular drive and up to the front of the house. I was about to ring the doorbell, when it opened.

The Petrossov home had an open floor plan, affording a view straight through to the water. A low, sleek, vintage race boat was docked out back, enormous engines exposed, black hull with a teak deck. A powerfully built butler in dark pants and a white serving jacket attended me. He smelled like pipe tobacco.

"This way," he said.

I saw another man walking along the dock, all in black, carrying a rifle. I heard other voices, low and guttural, coming from different parts of the house. The butler asked me to sit down in the living room, on a couch upholstered in fine gold brocade. I did so, but carefully so as not to stain the fabric with the sweat from my hot ride. Looking down at the area rug, flowers and leaves in paisley tones, I rued my boots.

Overall, the décor was nineteenth-century French. Russia has always had the particular problem of being neither Europe nor Asia. Despite a devotion to Rodina, the motherland, that helped the poor starve to death without complaining too much, middle-and-upper class Russians—the so called intelligentsia—have had a romance with the trappings of European culture since the 17th century reign of Tsar Peter the Great.

Vlexei's thin, ultrafine Breguet wristwatch should have tipped me to his tastes at the hospital, but the artwork and Europhile décor surprised me anyway. Of course the grandest vision of all was Mrs. Petrossov. She swept into the room wearing a broad-brimmed sun hat and a black caftan, despite the heat. Her makeup was perfectly invisible, and she looked at me and made a big job of blinking. At first I thought she was having problems with her contact lenses, but then I realized she was squeezing back tears. A little girl stood by her side.

I rose to greet her and she extended a hand bejeweled with a grape-size princess cut diamond of startling brilliance.

"Doctor," she said.

"Mrs. Petrossov. I'm very sorry to intrude."

"I'm sure you're not intruding. And please call me Natalya."

"How are you holding up?"

"What can I say? The days come and go; it's light and then it's dark."

Now that I was there, I realized I didn't know what to say. I wondered whether it had been a mistake to come.

"And who is this young lady?" I asked.

"Forgive me. Doctor Pearl, my daughter, Galina. Galina, this is the doctor who tried to save your brother's life."

"A pleasure," Galina said.

The syntax was incongruous from a girl who couldn't have been more than eight. Made in her mother's image, her dark hair was bobbed all the way around. Being a man who sometimes cuts faces, I noticed she would grow up to have her father's bad chin and also his tiny ears. She was dressed in patent leather and frills: straight out of Tolstoy if not for the cell phone clipped to her waist. I suddenly felt I knew her, and wondered if this was reincarnation recognition at work again.

"I'm very, very sorry about Rafik," I said.

"My dad says you didn't try very hard to save him."

That felt like a kick in the groin.

"The truth is I did; but he was in very bad shape when he came to my hospital."

"You must be sad that he died."

"Very sad," I said.

"He wanted to live. He always told me about all the things he wanted to do. His room is a mess and he had a girlfriend at school even though Mommy says he didn't."

"Nobody wants to die," I said.

"Suffering people do," Galina said.

I stared at her. The butler shifted his weight from one leg to the other.

"May I offer you a drink?" Natalya interrupted. "Iced tea with strawberry jam?"

"Sounds lovely," I said.

I don't know how the order was conveyed, but I got the clear sense tea was on the way. We sat quietly for a few seconds. I tried to relax.

"That's a magnificent Pisarro."

"Thank you."

"And the Monet is amazing. The Renoir—it's an original, isn't it?"

"Of course," said Natalya. "I'm glad you like it. Renoir rejected the Impressionists, you know. He alone among them understood the proper use of black."

"He learned from the Italians," Galina added. "He was inspired by the Mannerists."

I stared at the little girl for the second time. "I had no idea," I managed.

Tea appeared. I worked hard to resist the feeling that I had time-traveled back to imperial days. I paid close attention to my movements. I didn't want to break anything in the room.

"Ask for canapés," said Galina. "My mom makes them fresh. Some are sweet and some are savory. If you have some, I can too."

Natalya almost smiled. "Galina goes to school in England during the year," she said.

"How about I try these famous canapés?" I said.

"Oh, thank you," the little girl clapped her hands.

"I came to pay my respects," I told Natalya. "And to ask you to reconsider an autopsy on Rafik's body. I'm told you won't allow the hospital to perform one."

"Jewish people bury their loved ones at once," she answered.

I made some kind of surprised sound.

"You didn't know we were Jewish?"

I spread my hands.

"There are many Jews in my husband's line of work," she explained.

"What line is that, exactly?"

The conversation caught the butler's attention. He moved closer. There must have been some house rule about where he could step, because Natalya stopped speaking and looked down very pointedly at the shoe. She kept her gaze on it until it withdrew to the edge of the area rug.

"He doesn't like me to talk about his business. Nor does he wish me to discuss Rafik's body with you or anyone else. I'm afraid he made himself quite clear."

The canapés appeared. Like the tea, there was a little bustle about them at the doorway, but they ended up in the butler's hands and then on the coffee table before me. As Galina suggested, they were both sweet and savory, little zakuski, Russian finger food: meats on crackers, smoked fish, caviar, tiny custard cups, cheeses both hard and runny, some fruit bits, all on toothpicks with foil flourishes—yellow, green and blue. I tried a little triangle of toast with caviar.

"Delicious," I said.

Natalya took a little custard.

"There are things we could learn from an autopsy," I ventured. "They might help the next little boy."

"Raffy really loved his bicycle," Galina said.

"Will I be able to see Mr. Petrossov?"

The butler stepped in. "Mr. Petrossov is detained," he said.

"I can wait," I said.

Natalya touched my arm. "Chazov has a bad temper," she said. "Probably, you shouldn't talk to him."

"I'm going to dance," said Galina. She moved to the center of the room, put her little patent leather shoes together. She pirouetted once, very close to me, and when she did I noticed finger-shaped bruises on her upper arms, and bigger, deeper ones—some purple and some, already healing to yellow—at the tops of her thighs, visible only as her little skirt flew up. She noticed that I saw them, and a desperate, imploring look crossed her face. It was gone in an instant, but that was long enough for my throat to close down.

"What was Rafik's girlfriend's name?" I asked her.

"Galina has ballet Tuesdays and Thursdays. It's time for her to go," said Chazov, and then he had his hands on her shoulders and he was moving her away toward a dark door.

14

Right down the street from the multimillion dollar Performing Arts Center is a little park honoring Major William Lauderdale, who built a fort at the mouth of the New River as part of the federal government's unsuccessful campaign against the Seminole Indians. Condo towers rise to the east of the park, but just to the northwest is a slice of old Florida known as Sailboat Bend. Bougainvillea reign supreme, followed by live oaks and banyans, their crowns touching to shade the streets, their trunks thick with climbing philodendron vines. The area has been fashionable and it has been a slum and it is now on the way to being fashionable again. The variety of architecture along its streets is limitless, but there is no more ramshackle dwelling there than the gingerbread cottage of my maternal grandfather, the octogenarian, freethinking poet, and former rabbi, Lou Rappoport.

His house has survived the attention of lower social elements and more than a few hurricanes, drawing sustenance directly from his will. The wood slats have been painted bright blue for as long as I can remember, and the door has always been fire engine red. The single-car garage droops and the white window frames are cracked, the glass taped in one or two places. The roof is shedding terracotta shingles, which fall to the lawn and grow mold, standing like chipped sentinels to warn off golems, anti-Semites, and other forms of bad juju.

I rang the bell—more precisely I hit the old glass Coca-Cola bottle with a heavy fork the way the note by the door suggested. When nobody answered, I peered in a few windows. A schnauzer barked on the sidewalk behind me and the woman walking him shot me a dirty look.

I discovered Grandpa Lou in the back garden, prostrate before a stone Buddha, chanting rhythmically while running meditation beads through his gnarled fingers. He looked up at me, but only for a moment, then put his head back down on the ground.

"I've got a rusalka in the fountain," he said. "Go see."

Some water tinkled after drenching ferns in the corner, and I went for a look. The garden was overgrown, so weedy and full that I had to fight my way through. When I got there, all I saw was green water.

"You've got algae, anyway," I said. "And maybe some minnows."

He stood up. "She didn't speak to you then. Probably she thinks you need to let your beard come in."

Grandpa Lou's beard was sure in—I couldn't remember when it had not been—full and white and clean.

"My Russian's pretty good but I don't remember that word," I said.

"A rusalka is a drowned virgin who sings for men's souls. In the north, rusalki were ugly and mean and just tried to rope you in and drown you when you went by. My little girlfriend over there is the southern kind, like they have around the Danube, wrapped in a misty dress and all sloe-eyed with high cheekbones. She sings to make even my brittle bones quiver."

I couldn't remember ever having seen him around a woman who made his bones quiver, maybe not around any woman at all. Grandpa Lou had divorced my grandmother when my mother died, and she moved back up to New York. I knew my grandma was alive, but I had little other news of her. My mother's death had left her heart too tender for contact, at least that's what my father always said. It was, in any case, clear that she felt that her entire life lost purpose with my mother gone, perhaps even that it had all been one fifty-year-long mistake.

"What's it been, six months since I've seen you?"

It might have been closer to a year. He stood, and we embraced. I could feel his breastbone through my shirt, and sensed how frail he had become. He cupped my cheeks in his hands while he looked at me. His sky-blue eyes were still as clear and bright as when he had held forth in Hebrew for his reform congregation.

Grandpa Lou abandoned the pulpit the day my mother died. Some people claimed to have seen it coming, claimed he had been making mystical references to the confluence of East and West for years, moving in the direction of some sort of Asian monism—Taoism perhaps, or Zen. Personally, I saw it the way my father saw it, which was that when my mother died Grandpa Lou simply lost his faith.

"If you were still a rabbi, I'd have bad things to confess."

"Rabbis don't take confessions, but grandfathers do."

Unexpectedly, I began to cry. I felt safe there in his yard—that is probably why my tears flowed so fast and warm. Grandpa Lou was as likely to fend off the arm of the law with his own skinny radius as he was to raise a stave to heaven—in the fashion of Moses—to win me a reprieve at Judgment Day.

"Tell me again about when you went to jail," I said.

"Jail was better then. From what I hear, you don't want to go now."

"But you went for what you knew was right?"

"You know it," he said, clumsily stroking my hair. "The communists were destroying Korea and that was wrong; but I'm not a man who can kill. After jail, I could still live with myself, with your grandmother, in this old house. If I had shot people dead, things would have been different."

Of course, Tie Mei had me looking at everyone differently now, and I did wonder for a moment whether Grandpa Lou was part of my reincarnation cycle, but more than that, I wondered what he would think of me if he knew how I had changed since last he saw me, and whether he would still love me so much if he knew what he did not.

"Any new poetry?" I asked, wiping my eyes to try and keep from crying.

"I've been too busy fighting termites. I paid to have a big orange balloon put around the place. Paid to have all the air pumped out while I went into town for some incense."

"That's what I smell."

"Sandalwood from India. It cleanses the spirit. After all the bugs were dead, I went out, got some wood and borrowed a ladder from the lady next door. She's an accountant. You can imagine the negotiations. I had to sign a waiver in case I fell off and died. That's how decrepit she thinks I am, although she never offered to help. I put up the two-by-sixes myself, lifted them all through the hole in the ceiling, and nailed the plywood in. It was hot up there, I can tell you."

"You should have called me. I would have done it for you."

"You fix brains, not boards. You would have paid for someone else to do it while I sat in the garden. I wouldn't even have seen you."

"You should have called my father, then."

"I haven't talked to him in years."

"Easy to fix."

"According to whom? Our contract is over. Done. Paid up and torn up and forgotten."

"Come on. There's no contract. It's not a business we're talking about; he's your son-in-law. He hasn't forgotten you, and you haven't forgotten him. If you had, you wouldn't be so mad."

"Talk about something else."

"All right. Can I borrow your Volvo?"

"You came over for my car?"

"I came to see you. Maybe you'll take the drive with me. There are a few things I have to move and I could use the company."

He got the keys from a hook by the kitchen door and we went into the garage. I admired his handiwork. It was the best part of the house, now. There were political posters dating back to Martin Luther King on the wall, and a signed album by Frank Sinatra. There was a cot at the back. Suddenly I understood he was living out there; I felt immensely sad.

"The termites did that much damage?"

"They told me maybe heavy pieces would fall on me while I slept."

"I'll send some guys here to rebuild the place for you."

"I knew you'd say that. I'll get to it. I don't want you to spend your money. You think I'm talking like a martyr, but I really don't mind. There's a door to the garden and I still watch TV inside; the bathroom works fine; the big fan I installed up above in the crawlspace makes a nice breeze, even soothes me at night with its buzzing. Anyway I don't sleep much."

"We are some bunch of sleepers in this family," I said.

"I'm not as bad as you Pearls. You get the night crazies from your father's side."

"The night crazies," I said. "You have no idea."

The cream-colored Volvo was 25 years old, but it looked showroom new. There was plastic over the seats and the dashboard and all the switches and knobs glowed with love and polish. Grandpa Lou was fastidious about it in a way that I could not find evidenced anywhere else in his life. Even so, he let me drive, and I think he did that so he could watch me. The cross-town ride took only 15 minutes, but he stared at me the whole time as if he were looking for my mother.

"She's going to call the police," he said. "She already filed a couple of complaints."

"Who is this woman you keep talking about?"

"I told you. She's the accountant across the street. She came to get her stepladder, saw what she saw, and now she wants my house condemned. I explained I'm on a fixed income. I explained I'm getting the repairs done as fast as I can. She doesn't care. Doctors are moving in, she tells me. Lawyers too."

"What exactly does she want you to do?"

"Move out so somebody can tear the house down. They're building mansions on every corner. She wants the neighborhood to look up-market. She's a real estate speculator. Her house is not a home; it's an investment vehicle."

"People make real money in real estate," I said. "There's nothing wrong with that."

"I remember when Sailboat Bend was special. I remember when it was a real community, when people cared about each other. Things are different around here now."

I had never talked about finances with Grandpa Lou. I had no idea what he had or did not have in the bank. I couldn't imagine that an ex-rabbi who had done jail time as a conscientious objector had much of an investment portfolio. "Maybe it's time to consider cashing out and moving to a condo," I said.

"You think I should move just because some woman is hell bent on making me miserable and getting me out of the neighborhood? You think that's a reason to move? I've lived my whole adult life in that house. I raised your mother in that house, loved your grandmother and wrote my sermons in that house. I'm not moving to some condo to die because some yuppie puts on the screws. Besides, what would my water witch do out there all alone, my darling rusalka?"

"What do you think about reincarnation?" I asked him casually.

"What, you're religious now?"

"I've got a friend who believes in it."

Grandpa Lou shrugged. "Jews believed in it in the early days.

Christians believed too. Early Christians, the Gnostics, believed in the preexistence of the soul, and they had a whole set of teachings that came out of near death experiences, about what you could expect when you died. The organized church got rid of them as heretics, so you don't hear much about this anymore. The Tibetan Buddhists have the teachings, too. They train their monks to go into a near-death meditation state, make an investigation, and come back to teach people how to die so as not to be reincarnated as a cockroach, but to come back advantageously and progress toward enlightenment and the state of a free soul. They say there's a limbo place called the bardo, where you wait for your next life assignment. You could read all about it in the *Tibetan Book Of The Dead.*"

"They figure all that out through meditation?"

Grandpa Lou shrugged. "That's what they say. There's nothing like direct experience to convince a person that something is true. Personally, I don't believe any of that shit, but the older I get, the more attractive I find the idea that it's not all over when I go. I'd like to believe in heaven, but I'm afraid I don't believe that either. I might believe in hell though. I figure it might be a place where you get attached to things and then they're taken from you, where the people you love die before you do or won't talk to you anymore, where you know you're going to die and you see it coming and you can't do anything about it and you have to live like that: a place where you are almost always alone. Sound familiar?"

I wanted to tell him it wasn't so bad, but I couldn't. When we stopped at a light, I reached over and hugged him. "We need to spend more time together," I said. "You're not alone."

"You say that," he smiled sadly. "But you're a busy man, a bigshot. You don't have time for me, and we both know it."

"I'll make time," I said fiercely.

When we got to Hillsboro Shores, Grandpa Lou got out to smell the wind. He stood by the side of the car, inhaling the ocean. "A place this beautiful, you could almost believe in God," he said.

We went inside. I made him some Dragon Well green tea, deep and aromatic, the leaves as tight as pine needles. After that, I offered him chocolate from a place in New York City that makes each square as fastidiously as he used to make little boats out of walnut shells to set sail in the storm drains after a summer rain. He ate a couple, then watched as I carried my weapons out to the car: my staff, my teacher's sword, my spear, my broadsword, and the 30 lb, 7-foot Chinese halberd known as a *guan dao*. He watched as I opened every closet and cabinet and checked boxes and baskets and closets for any clue that I practiced martial arts, any incriminating link to my training and my new mission, to what I had done and what I was sure to do again. Through all that, he uttered not one single word. Grandpa Lou was a man who had learned the consequences of questions.

"The Chinese were good to the Jews," he said when we were finally back on the road. "Nobody else is, you know. Oh, they talk about Holland. They talk about how the Dutch hid our people from Hitler. There are good seeds everywhere, and bad seeds too, but as a nation, as a government, the Chinese have never wronged us."

He and my grandmother had been active in their Jewish rights crusade back in the 1960s, had helped oppressed Jews throughout the world, including Jews from China, from Shanghai, fleeing Mao. My grandparents were the ones who had scooped up my nanny when she came in with a bunch of Asian refugees and taken her to my parents' house, recommending her for the maid's job that eventually became so much more.

"You're thinking about Tie Mei, aren't you?" I asked him.

"I remember the first time I saw her. She was getting off the boat at the Port of Miami. Her heritage showed in every step. Even in China, Jews put an emphasis on education, on Torah study. She had such a proud bearing—the cheekbones of a queen. Honestly, she glided more than walked."

"My father should have treated her better," I said.

"Your father should have treated a lot of people better."

"He's getting married again," I said as we pulled back into his driveway.

Grandpa Lou looked startled by the news, and, as he often did, kept his counsel for as long as it took to help me bring my things into his house: the weapons, the books on Chinese medicine and history and kung fu, the practice clothes—flat black slippers, pants with specially gusseted crotch. Inside, I piled everything on the sofa in the back room under the window. While he used the bathroom, I climbed the stepladder for a look at the attic in hopes of gauging the condition of the house. Although I smelled mold and saw some moisture around the ducts, things appeared better than I expected. The old beams were sound and strong, with neither warps nor bows and none of the little piles of dust one sees beneath termite drills. Best I could tell, they had another fifty years left in them.

The old man came out of the bathroom with his zipper still open. He offered me a photograph. I took it and looked down at my mother's young, happy, expectant face, her hand touching the belly in which I, the future brain surgeon and vigilante, was visibly growing.

"You're flying low," I said, gesturing at his trousers.

"My moods come in cycles these days," he replied. "Tomorrow I'll probably wake up high as a kite."

15

The next morning, I went to work on the spinal cord of a Miami Dolphin fullback referred by Franks, the orthopedic man. Jake Derringer was twenty-four years old and 240 pounds. His back was as broad as a snowfield, and peppered by freckles that looked like alpine villages lost in the peaks and valleys of his enormous latissumus dorsi. After consuming a case of beer, two teammates thought it would be fun to throw Jake into his swimming pool; one bruiser headed north and the other headed south, and the resulting torque separated Derringer's lumbar column, forcing the extrusion of disc material. Rushed to Broward Samaritan Hospital by ambulance, Derringer had no feeling in his legs, couldn't stand, and was crying buckets from the pain.

Roan Cole helped him to sleep, and I got started.

"I hear you're pushing for an autopsy on the Russian kid," he said.

Immediately, I thought of Galina's bruises, and her desperate look. "Khalsa's furious, but yes. I called the morgue last night."

"The parents are fighting it."

"Of course they are."

Roan rubbed one eye with the edge of his smock. "I'm behind you on this, don't think I'm not, but you know the father's some kind of goon."

"Organized crime boss, from what I can tell."

"A goon, like I said."

"If the hospital blocks me, I'm going to the cops."

Roan nodded. "Do what you have to do. I've got your back."

I wondered in how many other lives he had looked out for me, and how many times I'd looked out for him. Something flashed through my head, an image of a forest in winter, tall, dry, empty trees, but it was gone before I got a bead on it, and I wouldn't have trusted it even if it had been crystal clear. Wu Tie Mei's contentions were really starting to get to me.

"I'd do the same for you," I told Roan.

"I know."

I approached Derringer's problem by cutting vertically along his paraspinal muscles. I wouldn't be anywhere near this million-dollar body if the hospital's top back specialist hadn't been on safari in Kenya. I found the problem right away: the rubbery material from the disk had spilled out of the donut between the vertebrae, an erupting mushroom along the column. To repair it, I had to remove the disc and fuse the spinal bones above and below it. It would have been a relatively routine procedure if the stakes hadn't been so high. Experience taught me that people contended unpredictably with newly imposed physical limitations. The injury could be a career-ender for Derringer, and of course I was worried I might slip up as I had with the Russian boy.

Still, there was no flight of soul that day, and no slip of the knife either. The operation went so flawlessly that at the last minute I decided not to fuse the bone, but rather opt for a less radical cleanup. The decision would give the athlete maximum mobility, but he would have to be very careful at first and follow the instructions of his therapist to the letter.

"Risky," said Roan, shaking his head. "If it doesn't go well, or if he re-injures it, the team will sue your ass right out of the state. I'd be conservative right now if I were you."

"Forget hospital politics. This guy's a young pro. He should have maximum range of motion."

Roan shook his head, but Monica the nurse gave me an encouraging nod, and I did the surgery the way I thought best. I closed Derringer up and said a little prayer the gamble would pay off.

After I showered, I stuck my head in to see how the pilot, Hugh Cartwright, was doing. He was still in intensive care, and had yet to regain consciousness. His son, Orson, sat beside his father's bed working a Gameboy like a slot machine.

"How you holding up?" I asked.

"I'll be okay if he'll be okay."

"Do you believe in praying?"

"Isn't that a bad thing for a doctor to ask?"

"Not at all. All doctors pray, they just don't admit it."

"You're saying he's gone, aren't you?"

"The longer he stays in a coma, the less likely it is he'll wake up. On the other hand, sometimes people stay out a long time and then make a surprise recovery. Even the experts who write books about coma don't really know much about it. Mostly it's the brain's way of taking the time it needs to heal."

"Can he hear us right now?"

"Most people don't think so, but I do. I think you should put the toy away and read to him. Take a break. When you come back, bring his favorite book. Read it close to his ear. Tell him all the things you wished you had told him before the accident, the secrets you kept from him, how much you love him, all of it. Can't hurt and it could help."

"Remind him of what he's missing, huh?" he asked, blinking back a tear.

"You're a good kid," I said.

In the hallway, I found myself wondering where Cartwright's mind had gone, and what he was thinking. I wondered if he was in what some Buddhists call the bardo, trying to decide whether to stay in his body or die, weighing the options, seeing if a better choice for the next round came along. I also wondered whether he was one of my reincarnation partners, whether, indeed, all the folks who went under my knife had previous connections to me. It was a fascinating thought, and it made me want to be a better surgeon.

A week ago, I wouldn't have had any such thoughts. Now, of course, I had taken up my sword in the night and cut up a stranger just as my father married into a family of cops. More than that, I was headed for a major collision with my hospital, and with a crime boss I was sure had murdered one child and was beating the other.

I rode home, put on some sweats, and went out back, resolved to find some answers in meditation. The meditation techniques I knew were not designed to provide answers about life after death, but rather to complement my martial art training. The way Tie Mei explained it, her style of meditation did for the mind what the movements she taught me did for the body; it prepared my psyche to accept the changes the movements created in much the way one would till the soil before planting seeds.

I put my arms out as if I were hugging a tree, touched my tongue to the roof of my mouth in the familiar, comfortable spot behind my front teeth, and set to relaxing deeply and dropping my center of gravity. In that position, I concentrated on my hands until I felt the qi flow there, a technique to increase my manual sensitivity and augment my surgical technique. After that, I tried to free my mind, to set all delusions and worry aside, and to roam as freely as I could through time and space and causation and dimensions, looking for some kind of sign that I had been a warrior in multiple lifetimes and was here to be a warrior again.

What I came up with was that I was headed for a whole boatload of suffering. My sacrifice came to me like a cork popping up into a stormy sea. If I followed my teacher's orders—or the orders of some revenant my mind created to look and sound and smell like my teacher—I was headed for utter self-destruction. Everything I had worked for since my under-graduate days was at stake: the generous living, the respect of my commu-nity, the opportunity to help people in need, the sense of purpose with a tangible result, all of it.

I groaned out loud as images of Spenser Brownfield's terrified visage came back to me again. I opened my eyes and cried out for Tie Mei, but all I got was a little echo off the tall board-on-board fence around my yard. Giving up on meditation is something I am loathe to do; the disci-pline of the practice is one of my central personal tenets, but it was just too damn painful to be me right then.

"I was better off before!" I shouted. "At least I could deal with that pain."

I waited for an answer, daring her to show up and refute me, but she didn't. I went up to my bedroom and tried to sleep, but it was still daytime, and the insistent light of the Florida summer crept in around the edge of the blinds and conspired with my disquiet to keep me awake. I passed the balance of the afternoon sweating in front of *Star Trek* re-runs on top of rumpled sheets, but I found no succor.

16

When the sun finally eased down, I got on my bike and rode to see Jordan Jones. In her driveway, I stood listening to the cooling of Triumph's cylinders. I was there a long time, long enough for Jordan to stick her head out the door.

"Well, hello. How long have you been here?"

"The sword needs to be shorter," I said.

"You came here to tell me that?"

"I've been thinking about it. I didn't want you to get too far into it and then have it be wrong."

She had on blue jeans and a rust-colored tank top. She wore no make-up, and I could see fine lines on her face, by her eyes and in the crescent between her mouth and nose. I hadn't noticed them before. They made her look more beautiful. There was a crinkle on her left upper eyelash. She sat down on the doorstep, and her jeans stretched in a wonderful way.

"What's the traditionally correct length?" she asked.

"Did you just wake up?" I asked.

"Why, do I look bad?"

"I've got special considerations. About the sword, I mean. And no, you look great."

"This art I do is all about intention," she frowned. "There's no other reason to forge a blade in this day and age. I have to put consciousness and pride into the work, and because it's a tool, I have to know its purpose. That's critical, in case you're not following my feelings on the subject. My swords vibrate, not just with the resonant frequency of steel, but with my vision, the way I execute it. Every sword is the embodiment of my hard work, sweat, sense of proportion, balance, weight, and line. I forge the same way the Japanese masters did, those folks who you told me spent forty days just getting ready for the forge. It's genetic, that sense of purpose. I got it from my father. He made blades as a way of taking a stand against impermanence. He thought art was more important than anything. Expressed in steel and kept from the rain, passion lasts forever. This is my work we're talking about, so if my intuition is right and you plan some hijinks with one of my blades—and really, Xenon, that's the vibe I'm getting—then we had better have a heart-to-heart right now."

I couldn't think how to answer her challenge. What could I do, tell her I was increasingly convinced I was a reincarnated warrior whose job it was to go out and cut people at night?

"Hijinks?" I joked. "Now there's a word."

"I'm not kidding, Zee."

I recognized Jordan's intuitiveness for her own version of my precognitive visions. I liked her for following her hunch. I decided I couldn't lie to her, so I'd have to give her a piece of the truth. "I take my sword as seriously as you do," I said. "It's an expression of who and what I am. I just wanted to ask you to keep the length shorter than the width of my motorcycle saddlebags so that if I take it with me somewhere it won't be clipped in tight traffic."

"Take it with you where?"

"Anywhere I like. To practice."

She put her hands on her hips.

"Hey, you know what I notice? You always talk about your father. Why don't you tell me about your mom?"

She pulled her knife out of her jeans and waved it at me. "Change the subject on me again and I'll cut you."

"Length is length. I explained my reason."

She gave me the stink eye and waited for me to crack. I held fast.

"All right," she said at last. "My mother moved to a condo in Boca Raton after my dad died. I see her every week. Are you coming inside or not?"

"Maybe if you put the knife down."

She grinned and flicked it closed. I followed her into her bedroom. I hadn't seen it before. It was simple and painted blue. The metal four-poster bed and matching candelabrum were obviously Jordan's work. Frilly things, pink ribbons, a lacy bra, panties, a baby T, lay crumpled atop it. A small aquarium bubbled in the corner and a mural-size photograph of a submarine nearly covered one wall. She saw me looking at it.

"That was my grandfather's boat," she said. "He was an engineer in the Navy. The way he told it, he used to crawl inside the space beside the electric motors and press his ear against the cold plates of the hull. His shipmates thought he had a gift because he always managed to squeeze a few more knots or a few more hours out of impossibly stressed engines. They had no idea his real gift was in his communication with steel. I think it was a quantum sharing of elemental carbon."

"You know about quantum physics?"

"I may not be a doctor, Zee, but that doesn't mean I don't have an education."

"I didn't mean anything by that. It's just not something people talk about very often."

"Yeah, well I'm not people, I'm Jordan."

I took a deep breath. "So the gift with metal runs in the family, huh?"

"Why do you think I'm telling you this? My grandfather could read the contour of the ocean floor simply by pressing his ear to the bottom of the boat. He told me he often fell asleep listening to the whales. Steel was his only real companion in WWII. The captain knew about his talent. He asked my grandfather for help in the heat of battle."

"What kind of help?"

She shrugged. "What the sea bottom looked like, if there were reefs or rocks that would damage the hull, if other subs were down there, hiding from the sonar. His boat had great victories at sea, but my grandfather never took credit for any of that, said it was a secret he had with the captain. He loved his engine room so much he didn't even want to see the sky. When the boat broke the surface, he stayed down in his hole. When he visited us, he would spend all day in my father's shop. He even slept in there on a lawn chair, with a blanket."

"Grandfathers," I said. "They sleep in the strangest places. Mine's moved into his garage."

I stepped over to her aquarium and bent down for a look. I didn't see any fish. There was a little clay pagoda in there, a decorative trinket red and green and yellow and gold.

"Empty?" I said.

"There's an electric eel inside the Chinese temple."

She tapped on the glass and a drab creature came out of hiding, mottled and brown with short whiskers and tiny eyes. "Once a week, I give it goldfish," she said. "The amazing thing is the way the little fish wants to die."

"I doubt it wants to."

"But it does. It can sense the eel, and for a while it avoids the pagoda. After a while, though, almost as if it has been screwing up the courage, it makes a sudden, mad dash for the hole, and zap, it's all over."

"Like it's looking for release."

"Just like that. All of life is waiting for the end, isn't it, Zee? The question is what you do while you're waiting. I think there's a contract between predator and prey. The two understand each other, are even willing to make sacrifice when they see there is no way out. I think the tango between the strong and the weak is nature's most glorious dance."

"How about the tango between the strong and the strong?"

"I know where you're going with that. Just when I was thinking how nice it was to tell you things, you give a quip worthy of an utterly average man."

"Ouch," I said. "Please, tell me some more."

She sat down on the bed and curled her feet up under her. "When I was a kid, my sister, Noreen Rae, went missing," she said. "I pray she's alive but she's probably dead. Not knowing for sure is the hardest part. My father left her in the car one day when he went out to get some oil for the milling machine. Less than five minutes, to hear him tell it. It was summer, so he kept the engine running with the keys in the ignition outside the hardware store. He had a spare set, did it all the time, so she'd stay cool."

"How old was she?"

"I was seven and she was five. It was twenty years ago."

I sat down on the bed beside her. She scooted over to make room for me.

"He came out of the hardware store. Then what?"

"She was gone. The car was gone. It was a Ford Fairlane station wagon, the kind with fake wood panels on the side. My father called it a Woody. He liked it for its size and even after it started falling apart he kept it going. He was mechanical, like my Grandpa Lyman."

"What did the police say?"

"They interviewed Dad for hours. Mom too. But they never did find the car. We were all hysterical, and it went on for days and days and then for weeks and weeks. They talked about it all night long, the two of them, and one of my uncles came and two of my aunts and my grandparents. The house was Grand Central Station, but it didn't make a damn bit of difference. They thought I was asleep but I heard them talking. My father tortured himself by speculating Noreen was in the hands of some perverted killer. My mother put her fingers in her ears when he talked about it. She just cried and cried and kept saying she was sure the kidnapper was just some woman who desperately wanted a child but couldn't have one. Dad was all for facing the nitty gritty all the time, but Mom was always into denial. She simply could not bear the idea anything bad could ever happen to her baby, so she pretended that it was all for the best. Years later I heard her talking to one of my cousins on the phone. She said she'd dreamt Noreen was living in a castle in Europe with all kinds of dresses and diamond earrings to wear, even a tiara. My cousin didn't say anything. You know how family is."

"Don't have a big one," I said. "I was an only child and spent most of my childhood with my nanny."

Jordan twirled a lock of dark hair around her finger. "My mother didn't leave the house until my father died, they stayed legally married, but I never saw her touch him after that, or allow him to touch her. Of course I wish he was still around, but in some ways my father lived longer than he should have—there was so much suffering at the end."

"I'm sorry," I said.

She turned to kiss me, then wrapped around me and held me tight. We kissed some more, content at first with the comfort of touch, but pretty soon we had our clothes off.

There was no part of her I did not explore, no smell of her I did not inhale as if each breath were my last. She allowed all that, seeing how I cherished pleasing her, and rewarded me by pleasing me back. I found surcease from the preoccupations that had taken me as prey ever since I picked up my teacher's sword against a man's flesh.

"I'm not going to give you up easily," she said at the end.

"Who said anything about giving anyone up?"

"You've got a head full of ideas, I can tell that about you, Zee. This is just my way of saying I'm planning to stick around."

I looked at the ceiling. I could see little stars there, decals like in a child's room. I reached over and turned off the light. After a moment, I could see them glowing.

"Thirty and married to his work, that's what you're thinking," I said.

"Thirty and busy and pretty good-looking, I figure you must have a history. Is there anybody else in the picture I should know about?"

"Nobody," I said. "But I come with certain risks."

"Risks I can handle. Other women, I'm not up for that. So you're sure there's no one else?"

I almost said Wu Tie Mei.

17

The next night, I entered Sailboat Bend through Riverside Park. Crossing the New River on one of the last swiveling drawbridges left in the state of Florida, I fantasized the superstructure suddenly let loose and began to spin. I grew dizzy at the idea. I imagined the ground dropping away as my bike and I spiraled up and away with only my teacher's sword to protect us. I wondered where my trip might lead if I actually managed to do it. Perhaps Rafik Petrossov was up there waiting for me, wondering if I was going to get his sister out of that waterfront prison just three miles down the road.

Live oaks and banyans make their own weather in summer, the result of the humid air trapped under the canopies. I felt the meteorological crackle as I rode north from the bridge. A Jewish doctor with Russian forebears and shot through with Chinese culture, I still felt a cracker's connection to the south. I wished there was more Spanish moss in South Florida, wished there were more old Florida neighborhoods like Sailboat Bend into which a man could disappear.

I rode past the market up near the top of Las Olas, a mustard yellow building with a blue roof. A couple of homeless people leaned against the newspaper dispenser under the overhang. They appeared to be sleeping, but even so, I pulled in the clutch and coasted almost silently past so as not to get their attention. Any random recollection could, at some future date, turn into a testimony that could bring me down.

I parked alongside my grandfather's house, opened the side gate and crept through. I moved past the Buddha and past the little fountain, blowing a kiss to the rusalka, that soul-stealing water nymph. I stopped outside the back room, jimmied the window, reached in and brought up my teacher's sword from the couch.

It was only a few steps to the accountant's house but I took the trouble to approach from the far side. I didn't want any connection made between what was about to happen, and dear Lou Rappoport. Crouching low in the flowerbed by a riot of hibiscus, I slipped on a pair of surgical gloves I had pocketed at the hospital, and became what I had become.

I attacked the garage window with the same front kick I had practiced thousands of times under Tie Mei's watchful eye and thousands of times since she died, but the door, built to meet hurricane codes, would not give. Chagrined, I made a quick circuit of the house. Around back, by the little papaya-shaped swimming pool, I found a set of wet footprints beside French doors slightly ajar. I shoved my flashlight into my pocket and cautiously followed them inside.

The place smelled like paint, and I could see Grandpa Lou was right about the owner's ambitions for the property. The sitting room screamed Tuscan country mansion; there were sconces on the wall, wrought iron to match the front gate, and a long, narrow table bearing a crystal bowl of potpourri. I opened a woman's briefcase sitting on the coffee table, and perused the papers inside, from which I learned that Olivia Spode was vice president of finance for a major communications company.

I pulled the sword from the leather sheath strapped to my back, and followed the wet footprints on the hardwood floor. I peered into the master bedroom. It was empty, but a gooseneck reading lamp glowed by the bed. The footprints led to Olivia's open kitchen.

The woman who wouldn't leave my grandfather alone stood by the counter with her back to me, wearing only a cabernet teddy. On the countertop before her were boxes of fancy chocolate: tiny truffles, downsized petit fours, glowing golden sticks of candied orange coated in the darkest of European dark, cherries soaked in grappa and coated in white chocolate—not chocolate at all, being devoid of cacao—and of course, the hazelnut surprise.

Perhaps she sensed my salivary glands kick in. Maybe she heard my sweat hit the floor. Either way, Olivia jumped when she caught sight of me.

"You're binging," I declared.

"No!" she gasped, looking wildly around. "I swear I'm not. There's more to me than chocolate. I give money to starving children and endangered owls."

How quick she was to justify herself. Something told me I had not met her before, that she was not one of the recurring characters in my cycle of lives. I might have told her that I had a little addiction to the seductive cacao bean myself, that even in these bizarre and dangerous circumstances it was all I could do not to sample her wares. Instead, I whirled my blade overhead and brought it whistling through her delicacies, passing just inches above the countertop, vivisecting her pleasures. The gooey fillings spattered, as bits of crisp outer layer passed through the air on their way to making stains on the cupboards, the tile backsplash, the granite countertop, and on the concrete floor. She gasped, and I brought the blade up to her face, still dripping sweetly.

"Stand still," I said.

"What are you going to do?"

"I'm going to cut you."

"No," she whimpered. Tears came to her eyes. She started to shake. I felt a draft inside me, a wavering of conviction. I thought of my grandfather, of how her complaints, her focus on money and her lack of compassion toward the old man had forced him to live in his garage.

"Yes," I said.

"But why?"

"Because somebody has to balance the scales."

She stared at me. I found it difficult to breathe. "What scales?" she demanded.

"Someone has to look out for those who can't defend themselves. Someone has to keep score. Now keep still. That's it; freeze. Don't even blink."

She tried, I'll give her that, and it was enough for me to bring my sword up like an oversized scalpel and make a cut my surgical staff would have applauded. She closed her eyes at the approach of my blade, and then opened them again as the steel wind passed. She saw her eyebrows flutter down in a shower of tiny hairs. Her fingers flew up to the smooth skin, and she made a sound in her throat like she might be sick.

"Before they grow all the way back in, I want you to put your house on the market," I said.

"You want me to sell my house?"

"Take the first offer, and leave the neighborhood."

"The first offer?"

That simple repetition brought me down from the lofty world of the reincarnated warrior enacting vigilante justice. I felt disgusted. "I've got a sword to your neck and you're worried about top dollar?"

"Can I wait a month? The market's going up...."

"Unbelievable!" I shouted. "Put the house up in the morning and sell it! And not one word to anyone that I was here. If you describe me to a friend or the police, I'll come back and finish what I started and the next cut won't be cosmetic. Do you believe me?"

She looked down at the blade, which was vibrating with my anger. The only muscles in her face that seemed to be working were the ones directing her eyeballs. Everything else was either paralyzed or twitching. "Yes," she said.

I left her nodding and shaking, and retraced my steps to the bathroom. I used the French doors for an exit and closed them behind me. Outside, I cleaned my steel on the dewy grass, wiped it dry with my shirt, returned it to its sheath, and lowered it carefully through the window and back onto the couch in my grandfather's peaceful little old house. I was just about to mount my Triumph when Wu Tie Mei appeared.

She shimmered in the now-familiar way, occupying a borderland between memory and substance, this time wearing a long, peach-colored, formal gown.

"I feel like a bully," I said. "She was just in the kitchen making love to some chocolate."

"That bothers you? Five hundred years ago you chopped off the head of a man making love to his wife."

"What did he do?"

"You have to start remembering."

I leaned my bike over onto its kickstand and looked furtively around. I felt certain Olivia would not call the police, but there was always a chance I was wrong.

"Believe me, I've tried to remember," I said.

"No. You've tried to test what I say. You've tried to conjure an idea into reality; to put to the test what you fear is just a theory. That's not trying to remember at all."

"The important thing is she won't bother my grandfather anymore."

"Of course that's the important thing. You did what you had to do to protect your family. I'm sure she's grateful. I would have taken her nose."

"Grateful? I doubt it," I said.

"You would be surprised how grateful survivors feel after a brush with violence. It's much the same with captors and captives; after a time, if you treat a captive well, he comes to thank you for it. Do you remember how you were in the Qin Shihuangdi's dungeon?"

"What?"

"The tyrant who unified China; the Duke of Qin. Tell me you don't remember the Burning of the Books."

A car cruised by, slowing to look at me. It was all I could do not to jump out into the street, flag him down, and ask him if he could see the Chinese woman in the formal gown standing by my bike. I turned away instead, not wanting anybody able to put me in front of Olivia Spode's house.

"I don't know what you're talking about."

"Mao wasn't the first Chinese ruler to try to erase the past to quiet criticism. Shihuangdi lived 2,200 years earlier, and he was even more of a tyrant. You didn't like him at all. You were a doctor then too, and you spoke up against the loss of medical treatises."

"I was a doctor thousands of years ago?"

"And you were in jail, which I know you're worried about here. You do what you have to do, just like you always did."

"And you? Were you there with me?"

"How do you think I know what happened."

"You were in jail too?"

"I was your jailer," she laughed softly. "I was there when you and four hundred others were burned alive."

I started my Triumph, and donned my helmet. "I told you, I don't know how to remember the details of someone else's life."

"You remember what you had for lunch yesterday," she said. "Maybe you're trying too hard."

Trying too hard was one of her usual charges. I'd love a dollar for every time she told me I was trying too hard with my punches, trying too hard with my kicks, moving my weapon with too much heavy effort, over-thinking my opponent's moves in my desire to forestall them.

I gunned the throttle and moved quickly away into the night. Glancing in my rearview mirror, I saw her peach-colored gown still fluttering by the road.

18

Two days later, on a humid morning, I did Parkinson's surgery on a 50-year-old Cuban man whose daughter had four times taken him to a Santeria priest for an exorcism requiring goat blood and feathers. After the procedure, I drove home. A police car was waiting in my driveway. I dismounted and walked to the driver's window.

My stepsister to-be watched me approach using the side mirror. She got out when I drew close and gave me a cross between a handshake and a hug. We were in that strange time, Wanda and I, when each and every greeting was an exploration.

"What a nice surprise," I said, my heart a storm and a gale.

"Just popped by to say hello."

She was wearing a cream blouse and a skirt with pinstripes that did a job of toning down her bulk. I could see a shoulder holster past the buttons. I invited her into the house, thanking all stars I'd moved the weapons. She looked around casually, the way any visitor might, but I sensed she wasn't missing a trick.

"These armoires are beautiful," she said. "Are they antiques?"

"Most of them, yes. That one over there by the kitchen is a reproduction. There's another new one upstairs. The old ones came from my dad's house."

"And the artwork?"

"I buy what I like and try not to overpay. If it ends up being valuable down the road, all the better."

"Own nothing that isn't beautiful or useful."

"That's it."

"No swords?"

"My father's fantasy because I once had a Chinese nanny."

"But you like to read about them," she answered, reaching into the wooden rice bucket I used for magazines and waving a recent kung fu rag in the air, the address tag clearly visible along with a fearsome guy holding twin broadswords aloft.

"Doctors and their journals," I smiled, furious at myself for leaving it there.

"You think it's macho to keep quiet about that stuff, don't you? Maybe you can teach me some moves some day. Hey, how about taking a ride with me? You're not on call, are you?"

To calm my nerves, I brought along a couple of pieces of Porcelana chocolate: hazelnut, with white chocolate icing. I sat up front with her, and we shared the chocolate with a few grunts and licks. She kept the air in her car very, very cold. The radio crackled on and on. I heard a lot of code numbers I didn't understand, and Wanda translated them for me. I learned that cops often don't know where they are going and need to be given directions.

"You know how to handle a gun?" she asked after we had driven a few miles.

I put my hand on the windshield. Somehow, the magic of cop glass kept even the sun of summer from getting through. "No swords, no guns," I said.

"Ever been to Markham Park?"

"Out on the edge of the Everglades?"

"That's the place. I'm taking you to a target range there."

"And why might that be?" I asked, shifting in my seat.

"Sibling bonding. Despite what you say, I figure you have your weapons and I have mine."

"I'm not one for loud noises."

She patted my cheek. "Don't worry, I'll protect your delicate ears."

We made the run down I-95 and then turned west on I-595. Wanda exited just before Alligator Alley, the road that heads over to Naples and Florida's west coast. Five minutes later we were in the park. She tried to pay the range fee, but the man behind the counter waved her patrol car past. We went outside to the firing line. A long tin roof kept the sun off the line of twenty shooters, all grizzled middle-aged men but for a husband, wife, and their two teenage children taking turns at the trigger. Someone gave orders over a loudspeaker, a set of instructions pertaining to how weapons were to be handled and where people could and could not walk.

Wanda taped targets to a piece of metal-framed cardboard, and handed me a pair of plastic safety glasses.

"For flying shells and spits of powder," she said.

"Remember, I want to be able to hear a butterfly pass wind when I'm eighty."

"Ya big baby," she grinned, passing over a pair of headphones.

Next, she introduced the guns, starting with a stainless steel revolver. "This is my favorite: simple, reliable, and newly upgraded with an eight-shot cylinder. Note the rubber grips for your million-dollar hands. I've loaded it with .38 wadcutters for nice, clean holes on the paper. This one here is a Sig-Sauer .45 auto. It shoots these hollow points, which make a real mess when they hit flesh."

"Good to hear."

"Say, I've been thinking about swords since the slasher case. They're different than guns, aren't they? With a sword, everything is visceral. No pun intended, but it takes a cool customer to make his point with a blade. He's got to get close and dirty, bloody even, and there may be a struggle involved. There's personal risk. The sword could miss its target, be wrestled from his grasp and used against him. With a gun, the victim doesn't even have to see his killer. A sniper can take someone out from a thousand yards away, that's ten football fields. There's hygiene to the distance. Handguns like these aren't much good past twenty feet, but that's still way past slashing range."

"Any new lawnmower victims?" I asked casually.

She nodded. "Funny you should ask. We actually think there was another attack, although we're not sure. We have a witness who saw someone with a sword break into a lady's house in Sailboat Bend. So, an officer rings her doorbell and asks if she's seen a prowler. She's very nervous. She says no. The officer gets suspicious, thinks maybe the guy is still hiding in the house. He searches and finds nothing. He does notice, however, that someone has shaved off the woman's eyebrows."

"Her eyebrows?" I said.

"Right. Gave her an eyebrow job. All the same, she won't file a report. We send a police artist out there, offer to do a drawing, the woman denies everything, says she plucks her brows to make her eyes look bigger. Now I can tell you, every woman with a heavy brow does a little plucking, but this woman is shaved clean. Officer on the job figures she's scared shitless the guy will come back and cut her throat."

"He must be terrifying," I said. "What do you think he wanted with the woman?"

"Robbery, maybe. She may have caught him in the act and he threatened her."

"Maybe she had it coming."

Wanda stopped and looked at me.

"Had what coming? An eyebrow job?"

"Some kind of street justice. Who knows?"

"Street justice? This is just some lady living alone in an old house. She has a corporate job. What we have here is some whacko dancing around with a knife; a fetishist of some kind. We see everything, Zee. You wouldn't believe the freaks and weirdos out there."

"I probably wouldn't," I shrugged, and then, just to emphasize my dispassion, I slapped on the protective headphones she gave me, squeezed the trigger, and hit a bull's eye.

"Hey, I thought you'd never shot a gun before."

"Beginner's luck. So are you going to catch the guy?"

"Not unless the lady comes forth with a description."

Wu Tie Mei claimed people who had it coming didn't call the authorities. I hoped Olivia's measure of just desserts was up to my teacher's lofty standard. I wasn't the least bit sure she knew why I had come, and deeply doubted the way she had treated Grandpa Lou would ever cross her mind. I was counting on her fear, pure and simple, and I had to hope it grew, not faded, with every passing day.

Wanda put some big holes in a target printed with a picture of Osama Bin Laden. When she was done, she talked to me about ballistics. She explained about hydroshock, the way a big bullet stops someone better than a small bullet by creating a standing wave in the body's ocean. My next shots were off the mark, and Wanda used the clock theory of bullet placement to analyze what I was doing with my body.

"When the rounds go high and to the left like that, you're flinching in anticipation of the blast," she said. "Try to relax."

She gave me her big girl's gun to try. The .45 left me with sore fingers and a tingling wrist and, all told, a new respect for my sister-to-be: for her strength, for her smarts, her sense of fair play, and her loyalty to family. I offered to buy her lunch when we were done, but she said she had cop business to do, so she took me back home.

Alone again, I walked to the local convenience store for some cold juice. Out in the parking lot, I popped the top off the bottle and took a cool slug of passion fruit and mango. A navy blue Lincoln Town Car with blacked-out windows pulled into the parking lot beside me. It stayed there for a moment, the air conditioner roaring. I took another sip of juice. All the car's doors flew open at the same time, and four men in dark suits and sunglasses poured out. My martial alarm started chiming when they headed for me rather than the front door of the shop. I dropped the bottle on the ground just as the first man went for my legs in a tackle.

Wu Tie Mei trained me to handle the bum's rush, but as I got bigger, it was not something we practiced. Nobody had tackled me in a very long time. I put both hands on the man's torso, but lightly, right under the armpits. Resisting the temptation to grab—grabbing creates an energy bridge on which traffic can flow both ways—I followed the way he rose and turned as he closed in, and in so doing lifted him up and off his feet. Surprised, he went spiraling into the side of the building behind me as I stepped out of the way.

It was a nice maneuver, but it didn't stop the man behind me from climbing my back like a monkey. He outweighed me by at least 30 lbs, and he dragged me back with an arm around my neck. I dropped my chin and turned into the soft spot on the inside of his elbow just to keep my airway patent, but by that time the downed man was back up and the other two guys were on me too, batting at my head and pummeling me in the kidneys and the gut. I lashed out with one foot and took a boot in the balls for my trouble. Twisting and lashing out with my hands, trying to find anything and everything to grab onto or hit, I went down, a bright constellation behind my eyes.

I took a couple of kicks to the ribs and one to the chin. One of the men crouched right down there on the pavement so his face was next to mine.

It was Petrossov's butler, Chazov.

"I'd like to kill you," he said in that nasal, accented voice of his.

"Show up in Idylwild again and I will."

Then the man who had rushed me, some nameless goon in Petrossov's army, unzipped his fly and made himself comfortable all over my head.

19

Trying not to show her disgust, a woman with a baby carriage helped me to my feet.

"I'm a doctor," I said, as though that made it all right to be bleeding and soaked in another man's urine.

The shopkeeper came out, surveyed the sea of broken glass, and asked me unenthusiastically if I wanted him to call the police.

"No," I said, fighting an intense wave of nausea from the groin kick. "I live around the corner. I'll just walk home."

"Oh thank you," the man gushed. "I am Pakistani. Homeland Security will think I'm a terrorist and take me away."

I staggered out of sight behind a stand of trees, then doubled over and vomited. My knees shook. I wiped my chin, and my hand came away bloody. I made the two-block walk back to my house slowly, trying to disassociate myself from the pain by looking at the whitecaps and tracking the pelicans in their orbit over the waves.

At my house, I went to the bathroom. There was a tinge of blood in my urine. I gathered what I needed and went to the couch to treat myself. I opened a bottle of vodka. A gift from a grateful patient, it was allegedly brewed with water from Baikal, back in the days when the lake was a symbol of the nurturing motherland, a crisp, clean, bottomless well of beauty and strength. I rinsed my mouth with a taste, then used a touch of it on a washcloth to clean the gouge on my chin, and the miraculously tiny cuts on my hands. I poured another glass, mixed blood and qi-moving herbs, frankincense, myrrh, and *dang gui* into the liquid, and took a big swallow. I followed that with a tablet of arnica, which is a homeopathic remedy, not a Chinese one, and stuck myself with three acupuncture needles, two in the ear—shen men to settle me down, a kidney point to support organ healing—and ling ku, between my thumb and forefinger, for the pain. Last, but not least, I applied a liberal splash of Wu Tie Mei's *dit da jow*, a topical, healing linament I make from twenty-six different herbs.

Hard core practitioners of traditional Chinese medicine don't use ice, but despite the arguments against it, I believe that has more to do with the fact it simply wasn't available in the old days. Anyway, in my life east meets west, so I keep a few packs in the freezer. The older I get, the more often I use them. Tie Mei took the long, slow view to training. She never pushed so hard or quickly that body parts were bruised or broken. She taught me to build up the body not tear it down, to change the set point of strength and stretches by gradually familiarizing muscles and tendons to her rigorous training regimen. The pace of my life is faster now, and, of course, I lack her patient tutelage. I push myself harder, train in frenzied episodes, and feel sore more often than I did.

I took another drink. I noticed that the bottle, which had been full, was half gone. The irony of Russian succor for Russian pain did not escape me. I fumbled with the remote control, clicked on the television set, saw a few minutes of the news. Raw, drunk, vulnerable, and weepy, I felt redeemed by my pain. I took solace in the notion that it was the warrior's lot to be busted up as well as do the busting. If I really was my old self, reborn, I had been through this before.

Wu Tie Mei appeared on the other side of the coffee table, wearing a dark skirt and blouse. She sank down into her favorite chair, the solid ebony rocker I brought from my father's house. I waited for the chair to move as proof of her material existence—she was always vibrating and swaying, even in meditation, said it was her qi bouncing around inside like water sloshing inside a teapot—but I didn't trust my drunken eyes for an accurate report.

"Go ahead and tell me that was only the latest in a long string of beatings," I slurred.

"You still don't remember?"

"Remember what? It's all I can do to force myself to believe you're real. I've thought about committing myself for observation, I really have."

"Observation?"

"Mental illness."

"Trying too hard never gets you what you want. You have to relax and allow the images to come to you. Relaxation is the key to everything, you know that."

"I remember everything about you," I said. "I remember every moment we spent together."

"Do you remember your life as a court calligrapher for the emperor, Taizong?" she asked.

"And when was this?"

"Taizong died in 649 A.D."

"Tang dynasty?"

"So you do remember. Very good."

"I don't remember the emperor, I remember the dynasty dates. You drilled them into me, if you recall."

She sighed theatrically, stood and glided over to the window. "History treats Taizong kindly, but the truth was he had a terrible temper. You made a mistake on a scroll, smeared the ink with the arm of your robe if I remember it right, and the court eunuchs beat you within an inch of your life."

I knocked the bottle of vodka over, tried to pick it up, and left a puddle on the floor.

"I was beaten by eunuchs?"

"Using waxwood sticks and a flail. You never talked straight after that; they did something to your lip. You remained a good calligrapher, though."

"Was I always Chinese?"

"Don't be stupid. You're not Chinese now."

"What else was I?"

"A Dutch housepainter, a Balinese wood carver, other places, other lives."

"I was a wood carver?"

"You're good with your hands. Certain traits carry through."

"Were you one of the eunuchs who beat me?"

"Are you suggesting I was a eunuch?"

I grinned. I might have drooled on the couch. "Not suggesting, just asking."

"Ask something else."

"Am I going to get beaten up again?"

"You should be telling me how you're going to get revenge," Tie Mei responded tartly. "You can't let a beating like that go unpunished, particularly when it happens in public. You are *ding liang zhu.*"

"The finest, strongest wood," I translated.

She nodded. "The supporting beam of the house: the person on whom everyone else depends. That's your character."

"There's more to me than that."

"But that's the best you are. You need to find the men who beat you."

I struggled to sit up. "For revenge, I know. Look, I'd like to think the reincarnation cycle has an endpoint: enlightenment, freedom from the physical plane, whatever it is. I hate the idea I have to keep cutting and getting my ass kicked and getting my ass kicked and cutting some more."

"Drinking is good for you. Do it more often."

"You want me to drink more often?"

"Get drunk once in a while. Just stay off your motorcycle."

"Speaking of revenge, tell me who killed you."

I don't know how or why that question slipped in—maybe it was because I had wanted to know since I first saw her again, and of course my tongue was loose and my thinking less than clear. In any case, she faded away without answering, and I went down into a rough sleep, tossing and turning, and feeling the occasional twinge when my kidneys rubbed the edge of the couch, or when my face slipped off the pillow.

When I awoke, I was still drunk, but less so, still sore, but less so. I could find no trace of the glass cuts on my hand, and wondered if I had dreamt them along with my teacher, or whether she had healed them as a gift. It was drizzling, but I got on my bike anyway, and rode to Jordan's place.

By the time I arrived, enough cold water had worked past the seams to bring me thoroughly back to sober. I rang the bell. Her Subaru was in the driveway, but she didn't answer. I went around to the back and knocked on the screen door but still there was no response. I made my way to the side of the garage, and tapped on the blacked-out window. A moment later, Jordan slid it open.

She wore her welder's goggles and her apron. I took off my helmet. Her smile disappeared. She shoved the billet onto her workbench and nearly came through the window to get to me.

"Zee!" she cried when she saw my face. "Are you all right?"

"Nothing broken, anyway" I said, trying a smile.

A moment later she was fluttering around me like a moth, touching me here and there. "You fell off your bike in the rain, didn't you?"

The question made it so easy for me to lie. "Can't even tell from looking at the bike," I said. "I caught it on the way down."

"You weren't wearing your helmet."

"It was just a quick trip down along the beach."

"You've been drinking," she said. "You said you don't do that, but you do; this time and that night at the bar with me."

"Just lately," I said.

I could see her wheels turning and see a new flicker of uncertainty about me, a fresh and previously absent dose of reservation. It hurt, but was weaker than my desire to keep her from the truth.

"What am I supposed to make of that?"

"People have cycles," I said. "Men and women both. And it's not necessarily a sign of illness. If we were at the top of our form all the time, we'd just suddenly drop dead. Ups need correction with downs, and vice-versa. It's normal—more than that, it's desirable."

It was a good speech, and it was all true and straight out of Chinese medicine, but of course it had nothing to do with what was happening.

She nodded slowly, as if trying to convince herself to buy it. "You're the doctor," she said. "What do you need?"

"I think you know."

"Not when you're drunk," she said.

"I'm not that drunk anymore. I just had a taste for the pain."

"Had a taste. That's a drunk talking, even if you're sober now. Hand over your bike keys."

I did as she requested. She took my hand and led me into the house. I went down in an easy chair and she disappeared into the garage, coming back a few minutes later.

"How's this for length?" she asked, proffering what was obviously the beginning of my new sword. There was no handle on it, although the tang was clear and strong, and no edge, or finish either. Even so, I took it in my hand and moved it slowly through the air.

"Don't be too critical," she said. "The balance will change when I put the guard and wood on, and it will lose some steel in the final grind."

I bent it gently by putting the dull point into the carpet and applying some weight. It came quickly and easily alive, a thirty-inch tapered spring. It was thicker in cross-section than my teacher's sword, and it made a better line off the end of my wrist. Hefting it, I felt a thrill. "Perfect," I said, imagining the new blade across the back of the Thruxton.

"The Damascus pattern will come out when I polish the blade," Jordan said. "There are 13,122 layers there, although you can't see them."

I wondered how many layers were in Tie Mei's sword. I never asked and she never told me. I handed it back.

"I'll make the blade black if you like, with etching. I already know it's my best work to date. All those layers help it bend the way it does and also give it a microscopic saw-tooth edge. You'll be amazed at how it cuts."

"What a woman you are."

She eased the blade gently out of my hands. "Take a shower, Casanova. I'll have some toast and aspirin waiting."

I gave a drunken salute.

"And Zee? Never show up drunk again."

20

I felt all the worse the next morning, because I knew precisely what was transpiring inside my pounding braincase. I could visualize the dead neurons waiting to be scavenged. I imagined the tipsy terpsichore of neurotransmitters running wildly amok, coloring my sensorium and affecting my cognition. Still, I was thinking clearly enough to get to the hospital and make my way to patient records, where I requested a copy of the scans that had been done on Rafik Petrossov when he had first been admitted to the hospital. A fifty-ish clerk named Gutierrez did the search while I tapped my foot. The hospital is on the way to an all-electronic system, but for now it's paper, with audit control so there is a signature record of who looks at what.

"What's up with your chin?" Gutierrez asked when he came back.

"The hiccups came on while I was shaving."

"That's a good one. Anyway, we got no Petrossov here."

"Sure you do," I said. "Kid came into the ER barely more than a week ago with trauma. Had scans from head to toe."

"Maybe you got the name wrong. Kids especially, they can use the mother's name sometimes if the parents are divorced. Were drugs involved? Junkies use nicknames and lie about everything."

"He didn't have a chance to lie. He died on my table."

"When a big-shot doc comes down here, it's always on account of malpractice."

"I'm no big shot."

"I've heard of you, so I guess you are. But I got no Petrossov here, not Rafik, not any other. This is the first time I got no news to share with a guy like you. Usually if you have to ask, you don't want to see the chart. You follow?"

My next stop was Khalsa's office. "Nice work on Jake Derringer," he said when I walked in. "The kid is wowing them in rehab already. You've made a lot of football fans very happy."

"I don't know that fusing him would have been a career-ender, but no way it would have left him as limber. Differences like that count at his level."

"Good call. What happened to your face?"

"Random act of violence with a golf putter."

"You don't golf."

"Every day's a fresh start. Where's Rafik Petrossov's chart?"

"I beg your pardon?"

"The kid's chart. Where is it?"

"Down in Records with the rest of the charts, not that I want you poking around his case. I told you to stay off it and I meant it."

"The chart is missing. The clerk down there says he's never even heard the name. You want to tell me what's going on?"

"I haven't a clue."

"I think you do."

Khalsa started to vibrate. He stood up.

"Are you aware that your confrontational style is objectionable? No, it's worse than that. It's offensive."

"There is no record of Rafik Petrossov in this hospital. I find that offensive."

The vibrations dropped in frequency, but not much in amplitude. "I don't know anything about his records," he said. " They should be there."

"CT scans, MRIs, PET scans. They're all missing."

"I'll look into it."

"Will you?"

"I just said I would."

"Thank you."

"This doesn't mean I've changed my position, Zee. Just let the case lie."

"No problem."

"And by the way, that pilot you did the other day is awake and talking."

21

An on-line business profile informed me that Hugh Cartwright grew up in Chicago, moved to New York and started selling aircraft parts. Headquartered in Queens, he serviced commercial planes at both Kennedy and LaGuardia airports. Because he couldn't get enough of flying, he also gave lessons at the Marine Air Terminal using a single-engine, 4-seater Cessna, a few steps down from the pressurized, twin engine 8-passenger Golden Eagle he crashed into the drink off Boca Raton. Cartwright was such an accomplished pilot, he transported mortally ill patients from outlying areas to major medical centers, flew volunteer search-and-rescue for the Coast Guard, and carried live transplant organs from donors to recipients. Nobody knew the reason he went down, and in all likelihood they never would because when he woke up, he did not remember crashing. More than that, he did not remember being Hugh Cartwright.

His boy, Orson, met me at the door outside his private hospital room. He was wild-eyed and distraught, not at all the cool and collected kid who'd played a video game next to his comatose father's bed.

"He doesn't know me," he said without preamble. "He doesn't recognize my mom's picture. He doesn't even know he owns a business. Guess all that whispering you suggested didn't help."

"Has your Mom been here?"

"They're divorced. She moved to Coeur D'Alene."

"Be good if she came to see him. Sometimes a loved one's touch really helps."

"Yeah, well he's had that all along. I've been sitting right next to him holding his hand. Anyway, she's with another guy now. They've got horses. I got a card from her on Christmas."

"How old are you, Orson?"

"Just turned fifteen."

"And where are you staying?"

"I got an aunt. She's crazy into orchids, but she's okay. Lives way west in Delray Beach. East Naples, I call it. Friggin' swamp out there. I can't stand the place in the summer heat. She and her husband have an exotic plant nursery called Bird's Nest Tropicals. The only thing nesting there is the two of them, oh, and maybe coral snakes; I've seen more than a couple of those. My aunt and uncle are lovebirds. They make goo-goo eyes at each other all day, and water plants that look like lobster claws hanging from a tree. I hardly see them. I don't know how they make a living, I really don't. I think my Dad gives them money."

"They going to take you to school when it starts up?"

"We haven't really gotten that far," Orson answered. "I was thinking Dad would be okay by then."

He followed me in to see his father. The first thing I did was the first thing I always do with a neuro patient—I looked carefully into his eyes. Cartwright's were clear and sharp beneath the bandages, and from the way his hand flitted to the tube in his nose he was aware enough of the support he was getting to be irritated by it, no doubt feeling the urethral catheter, and wondering about the function of his legs. He watched me when I walked in, rubbed his wrist gingerly where the IV went in, and looked at Orson so blankly I was sure he pierced the boy's heart.

"Mr. Cartwright," I said.

"That's what they tell me."

"I'm Doctor Pearl. I helped put you back together after your plane went down."

"He's the brain surgeon who saved you," Orson kicked in.

"Lots of people worked on you, sir," I said. "It was a team effort."

"I don't remember anything," Hugh said. "I wish I knew what you were talking about."

"Head injury often results in amnesia," I said. "Often the memory loss is temporary, sometimes it is permanent, sometimes it comes back in a rush, more often it reassembles a jigsaw puzzle that has been scattered, a piece here, a piece there as an outline begins to form. Would you like to tell me what you do remember?"

Orson turned away as his father furrowed what was left of his brow. The plastic surgeons had done a nice job of creating a forehead out of the skull pizza I pieced together in my efforts to preserve his brain, but the guy still looked like Frankenstein.

"Light blue's my favorite color," he said.

"I would call you a cup half-full kind of guy. Would I be right?"

"Sure."

"Tell me your favorite tunes."

I have a theory about music. It has to do with imprinting, a concept coined by the great animal behaviorist Konrad Lorenz. Lorenz noticed that when baby ducks hatched and saw him before they saw their mother, they followed him around instead of her. He concluded that the brain is open to certain input at certain times. I believe the music we hear between the ages of twelve and twenty is the music we will love forever, the music we will always associate with emotion, experience, the deepest parts of life and love.

"Grateful Dead," he said.

"American Beauty," I countered, thinking to use Cartwright's favorite songs as a way into his memory.

"Casey Jones you better watch your speed," he giggled.

It was heartbreaking to see a face like that smile, but it was elating, too: the most beautiful, horrible thing I had seen all day.

22

I was in my examination room palpating the occiput of a flirtatious nonagenarian named Henrietta Zakowski, when Travis burst in to give me the glad news that an agent with the Drug Enforcement Administration was in the waiting room.

"I pegged him right off the bat," said Travis. "You can always tell by the shoes."

"That's a stunning cliché," I said.

"Maybe, but it's true."

"Scuffed shoes are a sign of low self-esteem," Mrs. Zakowski winked. "Yours are always shiny and you look handsome even with that cut on your chin."

"Mrs. Zakowski needs a boyfriend," I smiled at Travis.

The old lady reached out for my hand. "Don't be silly," she said. "I've got you."

"It's not the shine, it's the rubber," said Travis. "They make 'em dressier these days—wingtips and oxblood and all the rest—but they're still cop-shoes on the bottom."

Mrs. Zakowski was sure she had a tumor in her neck. I was equally certain it was a muscle spasm. I massaged the site a little bit to bring in the circulation, then deftly stuck a needle into the knot.

"Try to relax here for a few minutes while I go speak with the gentleman. Would you do that?"

She gave me a winning smile, showing some of the best dentures I'd ever seen. Travis followed me into the waiting room.

The agent wore a gray suit and a southern drawl. I asked him about his previous assignment. "El Paso," he said.

I imagined him driving a 4x4 across the desert trying to head off some pregnant teenager trying to make the States. It was one of my visions, maybe just an instinct, but he had brutish hands and he twisted them as we talked.

"You here about the opioid analgesics I write?"

"Sure am."

He had a briefcase with him, and he bent to open it. When he did, I saw the big automatic pistol tucked under his arm. "You have good luck with the Sig?" I asked.

"You like guns, doctor?"

"Shot one once, heard an opinion or two. Let's say I know as much about guns as you know about pain management."

His jaw went tight, causing a couple of fingers worth of space between his collar and his neck. "Now that I've met you, I have a certain feeling about your license," he said. "So I'll be watching you, your scripts, your clientele."

"Patients, not clients: people in pain. Maybe there are bad docs out there pushing drugs for dollars. I'm not one. I'm concerned with the far bigger problem of folks living and dying in agony because they can't get the relief they need."

"These are some prescription guidelines," he said, shoving a sheaf of informational material into my hands. "They're here to help you make informed decisions about giving patients access to prescription drugs."

I was tempted to go off on the whole damn drug war, on what our failed drug policy has done to the South American continent, on the connections between the Golden Triangle and highly dubious foreign policies. I wanted to tell him we would be better off spending money on hip TV programs that educated kids on how quickly drugs ruin lives. "Thanks for dropping by," I said instead.

He walked toward the door at a slow saunter, surveyed the office, and made a big job of looking Travis up and down.

"Dickweed," said Travis, the moment he was gone.

"Ah, but you didn't say it to his face."

"Neither did you."

I saw four more patients after that, and then checked the O.R. schedule. When I saw I wasn't on it, I had Travis look up the address of Bird's Nest Tropicals. Young Orson Cartwright had found himself a little spot in the back of my head, so I took a ride out west to see him. The seat hurt my groin where the Russian thug had kicked me.

The place was in West Delray Beach, off Atlantic Boulevard, in an area known for nurseries and swamp mansions built for the benefit of real estate rubes. I found Orson flying a model airplane.

"Don't they make a muffler for that thing?" I asked.

"My father crashed on my birthday," he said. "This was supposed to be my present. I found it in his closet. He always keeps things for me in there."

"You fly it really well."

"The physics of flying are the physics of flying," he informed me, guiding the toy through a series of barrel rolls. "Doesn't matter if the wingspan is five feet or forty-five. There is lift and there is drag and there are thermoclines, pressure gradients, turbulence, and trim."

"Your aunt and uncle don't mind you scaring customers off with the noise?"

"Sure they mind," he grinned. "But I promised to cut the throttle at the first sign of a customer. Been flying for two hours now with no reason to land."

"How's your dad today?"

"Greatest piece of broccoli in town," he said.

I studied him closely. He was a willowy kid, built a bit longer and lighter than I was, but that difference might change in ten years. He moved with a certain spare grace, as if he were unconsciously trying to get the most out of all his movements, to use the least energy to accomplish each and every physical task. It was an instinct I had too, one Tie Mei had recognized in me, and one of the reasons she chose to teach me what she did.

"Land the plane and we'll talk," I told him.

He set it down just the way I've seen man o' war birds come down, with their giant wingspans and hollow, dainty bones. It taxied across the driveway and stopped at our feet. Up close I saw it was a triplane based on an old German Fokker from World War One.

"Stable at low speeds," he said. "That's why the Red Baron tore up the skies with one. Made such a reliable shooting platform for his guns."

"You know a lot about airplanes."

"My dad likes to tell me stuff. Back when he was my dad, you know."

"Punch me," I said.

He blinked.

"Excuse me?"

"Throw a punch at me."

"Are you kidding? You're my dad's brain doctor. I'd never hit you."

"You're not going to hurt me."

"Actually, I'm pretty quick," he said.

And I could see he was, that he had that ropy developing strength of the adolescent and the natural squint of the martial artist, an ability to focus that gives the fighter the advantage of being able to take in an opponent in his entirety, to not get suckered by a feint or undone by a one-two combination.

"Bad boy in the schoolyard, are you?" I asked.

"You could say that."

"Go for my belly if it makes you more comfortable. I don't use it much when I operate."

He stared at me for a long second. I was counting on the gameness I saw rising in him, the little twitching smile. He put down the airplane control. "You know this is awfully strange."

"I won't tell anyone."

"You don't have some sadist thing going, do you? Beating up on kids?"

"Not even a little."

"Masochist then? Want me to open up that cut on your face so you can feel the pain all over again?"

"Not that either."

Less than a second later, his foot, not his fist, was on tight trajectory toward me. I stepped obliquely toward him, parried his leg at the knee, and pulled gently upward. He went down flailing like a bronco, but not before I tapped his nose with my fist. He was up quickly, dust on his pants.

"Hey," he said, panting a little. "What the hell kind of fighting was that?"

"It's called mind boxing," I said. "*Shing-yi ch'uan* in Chinese. It's one of a few kung fu styles I practice."

"Kung fu?" he asked, incredulously.

"Want to learn it?"

"You know a school?"

"I can teach you."

"But you're a doctor."

"That too."

"Cool," he said. "I mean definitely cool."

"We'll begin at the hospital when you come and visit your dad. When he's out, we'll meet somewhere else. I'm not going to lie to you and tell you it'll come quick. You've got good reflexes and you're smart, but it's still years of work and tough changes to your thinking on top of that. Still, it will help you in places other than the schoolyard, help with dealing with anger, give you some patience."

"I've got patience."

"Maybe you do, but you've got anger too."

"Tell me you wouldn't be angry if your dad went veggie overnight?"

"See what I mean? And by the way, your dad is no vegetable. He's still your dad, just fighting a battle inside his head right now. If he has to learn everything about his life all over again then he'll do that. The training I'm offering will help you keep your cool while you help him."

He appeared to be considering it, but I knew he was formulating a plan. A moment later he launched a flurry that began with a decreasing radius roundhouse, the kind of punch that comes tucked tight and from behind like a drawn sword. I blocked it softly as it came into my ear and followed the circle he started, spiraling in on him so I wound up right at his center line, his blow rendered useless, my elbow deep enough in his throat to set him coughing.

Tie Mei had told me about kids like Orson, guys who wouldn't believe anything until they tested it for themselves, felt it themselves, challenged and were beaten. She said I was one of them.

"It doesn't take much to cut off a person's air supply," I said. "If you want to play with a technique, press on the side of the neck. You'll get dizzy quickly. If you've got a stick or a blunt instrument and want to send a guy to hell in a hurry, you can strike hard right at the trachea for the non-reversable option."

This time he looked a little scared. Tie Mei had scared me plenty of times. I remember how hard her dainty feet were, ironwood against my temple. I also remembered all the times I had tried to trick her with sudden attacks, only to find myself twisted brutally to the ground at her feet. Untrained people put a lot of stock in so-called masters who throw their opponents a great distance. Serious fighters know to keep opponents close, preferably on the ground at their feet.

"You have a lot of students?" Orson asked, gently easing away.

"You're it," I said. "My very first."

"You a black belt?"

"Chinese martial arts don't have belts," I said. "This is traditional, original training, not a health-club thing, not a strip-mall kid's school either. It's not about looking good; it's about getting the job done. It's not the stuff on TV; it's real, gritty, homegrown, and powerful. It will change your body and your mind, change your priorities, the way you look at others, rock your world. It's the real deal, Orson. My teacher was from China, and she studied her whole life."

"Why don't you send me to her?"

"I would, but she's dead."

"So why pick me?"

"When the teacher is ready, the student will appear. That's what they say, anyway."

He picked up his little airplane and carefully tucked it under his arm. "It's funny," he said. "Sometimes I feel like I was a kung fu master in another life."

"You can't deny your true self," I said. "I'm learning that, and you will too."

23

I invited Jordan to go with me to my father's wedding. This surprised everyone, me most of all. Surprised or not, she was the belle-of-the-ball in a yellow sundress that came just to the knee. The thin straps of it on her bare shoulders caught my heart between beats.

"Inviting me here cancels out the showing up drunk thing," she said. "But only just."

"So you keep score," I said.

"Past experience and all that."

"I've got no problem with booze," I said.

"With temper, then, getting in a fight and then giving me some bullshit about a road accident. You told me you caught your motorcycle on the way down. You actually said that."

"I lost self-control on account of an issue at work. That happens sometimes, not often, but it does."

"I keep getting a message that this is only part of the story. Call it woman's intuition. Maybe you should trust me, did you ever think of that?"

"You're at my father's wedding," I said.

"And happy to be. But I'm still armed."

"You're not."

"For your eyes only," she said, flashing her skirt up to reveal her little knife in a sheath strapped to her upper thigh.

"Call me strange, but that might be the sexiest thing I've ever seen in my life."

"You're strange," she smiled.

The festivities were held at Bonnet House, an old Fort Lauderdale estate set against a saltwater wetland and a jungle of mangrove trees. There was a seashell museum and an orchid collection as well as a colony of squirrel monkeys cavorting outside. As Dad and Rachel drew together under the traditional Jewish chuppa, my brain filled with noise, medical trivia mostly, but also of Petrossov's daughter, Galina. I wondered how long she had. I wondered what was holding up my autopsy request. I wondered if Khalsa really was looking into Rafik's missing medical records, or if he was already eating out of the Mafiya palm.

"Your pheromones slay me," I whispered in Jordan's ear.

"Will you be quiet?"

"No, really. It's a good thing I'm doing the boxy British suit thing today, otherwise I'd embarrass myself."

"You're a child, honest to God."

"Is that a child's lump you see?"

"Your father is talking Hebrew, Zee. Don't you want to hear it? And will you stop sniffing me?"

"I can't help myself."

"You need to shut up now. See, the rabbi is staring at you. I don't know much about rabbis, but he doesn't look happy."

"Rabbis never look happy. There hasn't been a happy rabbi since the Holocaust. Oh, they laugh all right, but every laugh ends in a sigh."

"You're Jewish, aren't you?"

"That's how I know. There's a joyous part to Judaism, an optimistic, engaged, funny, warm and wonderful dimension. I just don't see enough of it."

"Now the rabbi's staring at me."

"All men stare at you. You're irresistible."

"Now Rachel's looking at you, Zee. And your new sister Wanda looks like she wants to arrest you."

That did it. I took my nose away from her neck and gazed at my father. It had been decades since I had seen that happy, goofy look on his face. Perhaps the last time was when Tie Mei fixed his sore back or maybe when, immediately following a discourse on the Chinese medical benefits of cashews, she fed him one, putting her fingers to his mouth.

"You may now share your vows," announced the rabbi.

"I vow to bake knishes at least once a week," said Rachel. "And never to use store-bought dough."

"I vow to eat everything she cooks without complaint, even when it falls short of her knishes, as all other food in the world is bound to do," said my father.

"I vow to love him very close to as much as I love my children, but a lot more often."

"Great," muttered Rachel's son, Martin.

"I vow to never turn from her, even if it means showing pain," my dad went on.

"I vow never to keep a secret from him," Rachel continued, "even if it reveals me."

"I vow to wear pants with a belt instead of an elastic waist, at least when I'm out in public, although this one I'm not happy about," said my dad.

"I vow to wear the pink g-string until he gets tired of it."

"For God's sake," Martin grumbled again.

"Who is that guy?" Jordan wanted to know.

"Her son. He's a newspaper reporter."

"This is the greatest wedding I've ever seen," she whispered, "and not because of Rachel's chiffon dress and not because of the violin music and not because of the orchids either."

"I vow to do my little elf dance upon request," said my father.

Wanda jumped a little when my father did the traditional Jewish wine glass stomp. Probably she took it for a gunshot. I smiled at her reaction and Jordan caught it.

"She's cute, your new sister. In a butch kind of way."

"I like her."

"Have you thought about asking her out?"

"Stop it."

"She's not really your sister, so it wouldn't technically be incest."

"Will you stop it?"

"No, really. I mean she's attractive and you two have so much in common."

"Not interested," I said. "Why would I want her when I have you?"

"That's an excellent point, but you are lying. And do you know how I know you're lying?"

"Enlighten me."

"I know you are lying because you have a penis."

The rabbi pronounced Asher and Rachel man and wife just then, and asked God to protect them with his strength and nourish their union with his love. The crowd, about forty people, most of whom I did not know, rose and applauded. A few folks hooted and hollered. I gave both my father and Rachel a hug.

"Do I see a tear in the doctor's eye?" said Rachel.

"That was beautiful, you guys. Congratulations, Dad. Worth waiting for, I'd say. Now what's this about dancing like an elf?"

"It's this little wiggle he does," Rachel began.

"Never mind!" my father interrupted.

I filled the moment by introducing Jordan.

"What a beauty she is!" said Rachel.

"You're the beauty," Jordan smiled. "That's such a fabulous dress."

"If you think she dresses well, wait until you taste her cooking," said Dad.

Jordan asked to be introduced to Wanda.

"Just don't tell her you make swords. Come up with another answer if she asks."

"What's that about?"

"Some criminal is carving people up around Broward County. She'll pester you for blade details, call and interrupt your forging, won't give you a moment's peace. She keeps dropping by my house with questions because the guy's so medically meticulous with his slicing."

"All right, I won't mention anything."

She moved off looking a bit conflicted. I didn't think of myself as a liar, but I had a long history of secrets, beginning with hiding my childhood training. Now, after a long period of quiescence, the secrets had started again and I felt lousy about it.

I went over to Martin.

"What do you know about Russian gangsters?"

He smiled at me, squeezed my shoulder with his big hand. "You sure have a one-track mind. Didn't we talk about this at brunch that day?"

"There's just this problem I'm having with a gangster," I said. "He beat up his son and the boy died on my table."

"So the Russian issue is professional."

"The guy's name is Vlexei Petrossov. The way he lives, he must be some kind of a don."

"You've been to his house?" Martin looked at me with a new glint in his eyes.

"I dropped by to express my condolences."

"How can a doctor get a hard-on for a mobster?"

"Easy, when the mobster beats his kid and then brings him to the hospital a bag of broken bones. Do you think you can help me? Poke around in the files a bit, talk to someone at the paper?"

He thought for a moment. "There's a born again reporter from Charleston three offices down from me. He thinks he's on a mission from God, and follows the mob like a bloodhound. He gets death threats and changes pool cars like underwear. They screen his mail downstairs with an X-ray."

"Might be a guy to ask," I said.

"For my new brother, I'll sniff around."

Wanda came up right then and put her arms around both of us. "Your girlfriend's a doll," she said.

"I inflated her right before the party."

"And she says such nice things about you."

"My turn to meet her," said Martin, disengaging to head Jordan's way.

The caterers had followed Rachel's recipes well. After tasting the buckwheat and potato knishes, along with the beet soup and the cabbage rolls, I figured my father had made one of the smartest moves of his life. Martin poured Jordan some champagne, and I turned to talk to Wanda.

"Do you have connections with the medical examiner?" I asked her.

"Why, you need a doctor to sew up your chin?"

"You're funny."

"I heard you asking Martin about Petrossov. Tell me the cut on your chin has nothing to do with him; those are the words I need to hear."

"So many rounds fired and she still has the ears of a deer. Forget Petrossov. I fell down on my bike."

Wanda took my arm and guided me to the pastries. I hung back from the table. "It's amazing you look so good," I said. "If my mom baked like that I'd weigh 500 pounds."

"It ain't easy being me, Zee. That's only the edge of it. Look, I'm glad you just fell off your bike. Petrossov is well known to us."

"Well known how?"

"Let's just say many law enforcement agencies are interested in his business."

I couldn't stand it anymore. I broke down and took one of the chocolate desserts—a soufflé. I didn't expect much; it's hard to bake anything good for so many people, and a soufflé—which depends on critical control of oven temperature and delicate, just-so timing—is nearly impossible *en masse*. To my amazement, the dessert was crisp on the edges, just like it should be, not burned and not gooey either, and the chocolate inside was light, fluffy, and consistent. More than that, it was dark chocolate, slightly bitter, not too sweet, and of good quality. I resolved to spend some time around my new step-mother's kitchen, and I looked forward to discussing the finer points of chocolate with her.

"Wow, what a soufflé!" I said after I'd put about half the dessert down. "Look, Wanda. Petrossov beat his kid to death and the boy ended up on my operating table. It's not something I can let go. I owe the kid, for more reasons than I can explain."

"If that's true, you should order an autopsy. In the meantime, steer clear of him. I don't want to see anything bad happen to you. You're family."

"I tried to get an autopsy but he threatened a malpractice suit. He intimidated my chief, and now all records of the kid have vanished from the hospital. If we exhume the body we'll find he died of multiple injuries that could not, as the parents claimed, have come from falling off a bicycle."

"Both parents had the same story?"

"As far as I know," I said.

"They usually don't. Mothers protect their children, but they don't always do the same for their husbands. I'd say you're out of your depth here. Let the pros handle this one."

"The pros aren't on it; that's exactly the problem."

"So press for that autopsy."

"I've tried," I said, finishing the last bite and carefully considering taking the last remaining soufflé on the tray. "Maybe I have to try harder."

"I'm not telling you to do that. You're diving into a real cesspool here, Zee. He's even worse than I've told you."

"The kid died with my scalpel in his neck, you get that? It happened right on my table. I can't ignore that. I can't call it someone else's problem. The longer I stay on the sidelines the more worms feast on his little body. You see what I mean?"

Wanda turned away from the spread without taking a single dessert. I marveled at her willpower.

"I suppose you could make a complaint," she said. "Since you were witness to the injury."

"I should have done that already," I said. "I got a bit behind wrestling with a few changes and ideas."

Just then, Jordan charged over, Martin in tow. "Did you taste this food?" she gasped.

"And Rachel's more than just a great cook and a beautiful bride," I smiled. "There is, after all, the pink g-string."

"You had to remind me," Martin shook his head sadly. "You just couldn't let it lie."

24

Wu Tie Mei materialized between the water buffalos on the Chinese screen in my office as if stepping out of a mountain stream with a rainbow in her hair. Indeed she was clad in peasant dress of the period, perhaps Sui dynasty, gold in color because the paint on the screen was gold against a black lacquer background. A farmer's hat over a cotton top and pants framed her elegant face.

"They ridicule you," she said without preamble.

I put down my paperwork. "What? Who ridicules me?"

"The Russians."

"You're in touch with the Russians now?"

"Of your world, I know only you. But I'm certain they ridicule you, because they beat you and you sit here with a pen in your hand. This is the action of a mole, not a warrior."

"A mole?"

"A blind little animal who ignores the world in favor of chasing grubs underground. That's what you do, rooting around under the dirty illusion of how badly you are needed by your patients, hiding from your true calling."

"I didn't know they had moles in China."

"They have them. And they have them in Florida, too, because I'm looking at one."

"What do you want me to do?" I sighed.

"Torture them. Take your sword and kill them."

"I can't go to Petrossov's house again," I said. "If I show up, they'll shoot me at the gate, drag me in, and claim it was self-defense."

"Find the man who beat you and show yourself a warrior," she said. "Why do I have to tell you this over and over again?"

"You always said I was a slow learner."

"You were a fast learner. I said what I said to keep you humble."

"And now?"

"Now you are a mole. How can you let this stand? They beat you and you do nothing?"

"I think you're just angry because Dad is getting married."

"Asher? Is he well?"

"How can you not know how he is? How can you not know what's happening? If you're a figment of my imagination, you have to know what I know."

"If I were in your imagination, you would know what I know," Tie Mei responded tartly. "And as for the marriage, I pity the poor woman."

There was a knock on the door.

"One minute," I called.

"I need your signature on some papers," Travis said, beginning to open the door.

Mainly because I trust my staff implicitly and have trained them well, I don't have a strict policy on a closed consulting-room door. This time, however, I leapt from my desk and jammed my foot against the door.

"I'm not doing nothing!" I whispered to my teacher. "I'm filing a complaint with the police."

"I'm filing a complaint with you. You're an embarrassment to your soul."

Travis worked the door. "Doctor P? Are you all right?"

"I'm an embarrassment to my soul?" I repeated. "How can that be? My soul is me, isn't it?"

"I beg your pardon?" Travis said through the door. "Your soul?"

I let him in after that; I had to. All I could do was trust that my teacher would vanish. As it was, when I turned around, she was holding still, astride one of the buffalo as if she had always been in the painting. Travis seemed not to notice, but I couldn't say if it was because she blended in so well, she wasn't really there, or perhaps because only I could see her.

"I was dreaming," I said. "Fell asleep at the desk. What did you say?"

Travis frowned, trying to figure out why he hadn't been able to open the door.

"Never mind," he answered. "I know it's been a big week, your father getting married and all. You're no great sleeper under the best of circumstances. Go home and go to bed. It's almost the end of the day anyway, and Thursdays tend to drag."

"What do you need signed?" I asked.

He gave me some insurance files, and a DEA form with dosing guidelines. I signed them, my mind awhirl with an idea. When he went out again, I went on-line and looked up ballet schools in Fort Lauderdale. I found several downtown, but only one close to Idylwild. I got on my bike and rode over.

It was the word Thursday that did it. Petrossov's butler, Chazov, had said Galina took ballet lessons on Tuesdays and Thursdays. I parked in the alley beside the school, and walked quietly around and looked in the parking lot. There were cars there, but no blacked-out Lincoln. I went into the school and asked if I could watch the class.

"I have a little girl who's desperate for lessons," I told the young woman at the front, a thin, freckled, ballerina in a purple leotard. "We live close by and I've heard this place is great."

Inside, girls from 5 to 15 were lined up along the ballet barre, but Galina Petrossov was not among them. An elderly woman in loose clothes and a scarf was walking back and forth, tapping them on the back and knees, encouraging them toward better posture.

"Excuse me," I said, in Russian.

The woman turned to look at me, put her finger to her lips, and went back to work. I couldn't make out if she understood me or not, so I went out to the front.

"Is the teacher Russian?" I asked.

"No, she's from New York."

"I thought there was a Russian ballet teacher around here," I said, working on a wing and a prayer.

The young woman thought for a moment. "There's a former Bolshoi Ballet choreographer in Victoria Park; he teaches out of his house."

"That's the man I'm looking for. Would you happen to have his address?"

She frowned. "He doesn't take new students. I mean, from what I hear, you have to know somebody."

"Perhaps I could swing by and see if there's anyone there I know."

The girl shrugged. "I'll draw you a map," she said. "I can't pronounce his name, but I know where he lives."

I took the map and got back on my bike. I was there within minutes. The ballet master lived in an old house marked only by the fresh new paint on the trellis out front. Flowers bent inward at the walkway. There were several vehicles by the curb. One of them was a blacked-out Lincoln Town Car. I rode by quickly, made a turn, went around the block, and parked. I left my helmet locked to the bike, and walked quickly to the car.

There were two men in the front seat, but neither man was Chazov. I guessed the butler, or another man, was inside with Galina.

There was no question in my mind both men were armed. Coming straight from the office, I was not. I picked the angle of approach least likely to be visible in the rearview mirrors, crouched down low, and ran to the back of the car. I took a pen from my pocket and began tapping the exhaust pipe with it, expecting the noise to go right through the system and manifest in the driveshaft well, right under the console.

I kept tapping until I heard the passenger door open. I watched underneath the car as the thug came around his side. When his shoes reached the end, I pushed off the bumper and took him down. I needed to get it over with quickly and I did, using a hard ridge-hand to the pressure point in his neck. He saw it coming and tried to bob away, but the blow landed, and he went down.

Pressure point training is controversial stuff in the martial arts. There are exhibition fighters who swear by it, and ground-fighting grapplers who relish it, too. There is no doubt there are many points that produce anything from pain and nausea to unconsciousness and long-term damage, but Wu Tie Mei eschewed using them, believing that in the heat of battle it can be hard to find points unless you are making a surprise attack.

Knowing the other man would be out of the car any moment, I crept around to his door, and stayed low and under his mirror. He checked it, saw nothing, and opened his door.

"Dmitri?" he said.

I slammed the door as hard as I could into his knees. It wasn't enough. There was padding on the door and he was standing at a safe angle, so he went down but without damage and came up again, a pistol in his hand.

I've become more aware of pistols since shooting with Wanda. This is not a good thing, because whereas before I would have only noticed that the weapon was in hand, I now spent a precious extra second taking note of the size and brand. That instant lost me the advantage, and I could only duck down as he squeezed off a shot.

The round flew past my head. He stuck his arm over the top of the window to be able to draw a bead on me, and when he did, I grabbed the pistol, threading my thumb through the trigger guard and clasping the slide so he couldn't fire. Then I locked his arm against the door.

My teacher was the mistress of joint locking, an absolute human tornado, able to manipulate an opponent's body in three-dimensional ways I'd never dreamed possible. I vividly remember the feeling of being brought hard to my knees by the most excruciating pain in my wrists, elbows and shoulders, and I remember the joy of learning how to execute the techniques, too. Despite her proficiency, however, my teacher cautioned against relying on locking in a combat situation. "It's only a first move, not a last one," she said. "If you do it right, you disconnect your opponent from the ground, rob him of his root, and leave him open to the real attack."

By real attack she meant a deadly strike: a kick or a punch. I levered the Russian over the car door, recognizing him as the one who had kicked me in the balls.

"I remember you," I said.

"Fuck your mother," he told me in Russian.

"Both my mothers are dead," I answered, and brought my elbow up hard and fast under his chin.

I took his gun, dropped the magazine, cleared the round as Wanda had shown me to do, and lobbed it across the street and into a neighboring fountain. I was in a mood, then, so I returned the favor he had so graciously done me, using the instep of my foot while propping his unconscious body against the car. Each time I kicked him, he jerked, but quietly. Frankly, I wished for the pleasure of a little more moaning.

Dmitri was starting to wake up. I broke two of his ribs with my elbows, getting into a short-distance rhythm with my strikes, contracting my own ribcage and rotating my middle, what the Chinese call the dantian, making my strikes decidedly vicious. A middle-aged man in jogging shoes turned the corner, caught sight of me, and actually began to run backward.

I went down the walkway to the house. Music was coming from inside, but faintly. I tried the door and found it locked. I rang the doorbell. A woman with close-cropped red hair opened it.

"I'm here for Galina Petrossov," I said. "Fire drill."

"Fire drill?" she said with a heavy accent. Her teeth were perfect, meaning she had to have been a performer back in Russia.

"Very dangerous," I said. "Her father sent me."

She seemed not to trust her English then, and held up a finger. I stepped to the side of the door and waited. A moment later, the third bodyguard appeared. He stuck his head out the door, and I hit him as hard as I could with a rising roundhouse kick.

He shook it off. My foot hurt from where it had hit his chin. He was the biggest of the Town Car gang, the man who had jumped on my back. Heavy, and layered with the kind of hard muscle that comes from physical work, not from the gym, he went off on me with hands like rocks. He swung an uppercut, but he was slow, and I saw it coming, slipped my head out of the way, and stepped back, greeting the blow with the kind of block Tie Mei had made me practice ten thousand times: a light movement, so delicate the big gorilla didn't even feel it. I followed his arm on its intended trajectory, encouraging it upward and upward until he was taken off balance by his own momentum and found himself reaching for the sky as if trying to catch a Frisbee.

It happened more quickly than it takes to tell it. In an instant he was up on his toes, and leaning forward. I wrapped around the arm like a snake climbing a tree and brought him around in a great spiral, up and up and then down and forward, until he came down with his face right into my knee.

His face wasn't pretty to start with, pockmarked and thick around the lower jaw, but I pushed his nose in so when he sputtered blood, bits of cartilage were actually blown out. As a neurosurgeon, I found it curiously fascinating to think of how difficult the repair would be. Deciding it might not be hard enough, I bent and put an elbow hard and fast into his temporomandibular joint.

"Three guys to cover one little girl and you'll still be sucking breakfast through a straw for a month," I whispered into his ear. "Your boss must really be paranoid about his kid. Wonder why that is. And say, when you give Chazov my compliments, you'll have to do it with a pen and paper."

I didn't wait around to see Galina. I didn't want her to know this side of me. I hoofed it back to my bike, thinking how crude the exchange had been, how much less precise and satisfying it was to pummel people with hands and feet than to make surgical precise cuts with a good sword. Even so, I figured Wu Tie Mei would approve.

"How was that?" I cried out loud as I ran. "Satisfied?"

I was sure she could hear me.

25

Upon close examination, petite Janis Wilcox could have played the part of a budding monster in a turn-of-the-century silent film, one of those black-and-white masterpieces that achieve mood and menace through shadows and angles and the frank, up-front revelation of the bizarre elements of the mundane. Janis' primary care physician in Pembroke Pines referred her to me pursuant to her complaint that she had outgrown her sun hat.

"It's straw with a cotton band of happy tropical flowers," Janis pouted. "I got it on a Caribbean cruise with my last boyfriend and it kind of makes me think of him. We broke up when he went to Iraq. I didn't think I could deal with that sort of long-distance relationship. Please don't think me heartless; he's not in the combat zone or anything. He runs an Army radio substation over there. Anyway, I like to pamper my skin and this hat has good shade. It just doesn't fit me anymore, even though I've cut my hair."

I could sympathize. While I am extremely sensitive to the shadows and shadings of natural light, I have a thing about sun damage to my own skin, courtesy of Tie Mei, who was a tireless advocate of sunscreen, floppy lids and long-sleeve shirts. South Florida beach culture notwithstanding, she counseled staying out of the sun completely. In China, dark skin is a sign of the low, agricultural masses, while pale skin is the color of privilege.

The Pembroke Pines general practitioner had a pretty good idea what was going on. He ran an endocrine panel, identified unusual levels of pituitary hormone, and sent Janis my way.

A quick MRI revealed the trouble. Kellie was in the room with us and held Janis' hand as I explained the problem.

"You have a pituitary adenoma," I said.

"Cancer," Janis whispered.

"It's a tumor," I said, "but it's not malignant and it's not life-threatening. Right now it's about the size of a pinhead. It occupies the master gland that controls many bodily functions, including how fast you grow. Your hat is too small because your head is growing. Other parts of you are too, thickening and enlarging. I'm sure you've noticed the changes in your fingers, your ears, your lips and brow. The longer we leave the tumor where it is, the worse all that will get."

"I know what you're saying," she blinked back tears. "I'm going to be a freak."

She could in fact end up looking like one—disproportionate nose, overgrown jaw and brow—but only if we let the process run amok.

"That's not going to happen, because we're going to take it out," I said. "This is not the kind of tumor that threatens other body systems, but nonetheless it needs to go. I recommend you do the surgery immediately."

Immediately turned out to be two days after my father's wedding. Janis' operation was the last procedure of the day. Sometimes these adenomas have rapid effects, and it seemed Janis' nose and brow showed overgrowth that had not been visible when I'd last seen her. I said this to Roan, who had his back to me while fiddling with her endotracheal tube.

When he turned to answer, I saw a pair of plum-sized shiners on him.

"Go out drinking last night?" I asked.

Vicky Sanchez was with us, and she shot me a look. Roan's temper doesn't mix well with booze.

"No, I did not go out drinking last night."

"So how come the Rocky Raccoon?"

"You're so subtle and kind."

"Girlfriend whack you with a tennis racket?"

"Keep going."

"Sleepwalk into a wall?"

"I had an altercation over a canine, all right?"

The procedure called for me to enter the air-filled sphenoid sinus, just beneath the sella turcica, the cavity that houses the pituitary gland. I made an incision in Janis' gum, and employed intraoperative fluoroscopy to see where I was going. Roan had a catheter in Janis' thecal sac, a bulging of the lumbar spine, and he pumped air in to blow up the whole area and give me a clearer view of the tumor. Then I began the excision. The tumor was just below the part of the brain known as the optic chiasm. If I went up just a little too far, I could blind Janis. Lateral to the tumor were the carotid arteries. If I nicked one of those, Janis could have a stroke, she could bleed, or worst of all she could develop an aneurysm, a weakening of the arterial wall that could paralyze or kill her without warning.

"I always wonder what makes someone grow cancer," Vicky mused while I worked. After the death of her daughter, Vicky had been silent about kids. Lately she had started to chatter, remembering things, details from her child's short life. "Maybe she has unresolved anger issues, or feels dissatisfied with her size. Maybe someone insulted her when she was small; maybe just a remark or jibe, and she carried a wound about it right into adulthood. Children can be so cruel. Probably she got cancer because she wanted to grow."

"Oh for God's sake," said Roan.

I wasn't so quick to dismiss Vicky's rumination. The training Wu Tie Mei gave me in Chinese medicine left me with a broader horizon than most of my allopathic colleagues, more willing to accept the nuanced connection between body and mind. On some level it made perfect sense to me that a brain long irritated by negative emotions could grow a tumor.

"You going to get a rabies vaccine?" I asked Roan.

"The dog didn't touch me, okay?"

"Human bites are the dirtiest of all." I goaded him. "Did you start antibiotics?"

"Lay off," said Roan.

Vicky chuckled as she disposed of a blood-soaked piece of gauze.

"Why don't you just tell us the whole story," I said. "It'll be easier and cleaner that way, save me pushing and prodding and sniffing around. Janis here will appreciate it too, because once the mystery is revealed I'll be better able to concentrate on my work."

Roan took a step back from his dials, pinched his nose gently between his thumb and forefinger, and sighed. "I was jogging, okay? This asswipe was going the other way, covering the sidewalk with the leash. I swerved onto the street to avoid the dog. A garbage truck was coming by. The mirror nearly whacked me. I yelled at the guy, he yelled back."

"A street fight," I said. "Best anesthesiologist in Broward County and you're still mixing it up in public."

"If I were a diplomat, I wouldn't put people to sleep for a living."

Vicky's smile crinkled her facemask. I finished removing Janis' tumor and surveyed the area carefully. I was satisfied I had all of it, that there was not even the tiniest remnant left. Everything looked good.

"The jerk had twenty feet of lead out on the mutt," said Roan. "I wasn't the only one he pushed off the sidewalk. I saw half-dozen women cross the street. I like dogs. I never say a cruel word to a dog. It was an attitude thing, that's all, and I was nice about it."

"Nice how?"

"I just said maybe he could keep his dog on a tighter lead and share the sidewalk. Maybe I didn't say it that nicely, but I didn't yell or shoot him the finger or anything."

"Big fellow?" I asked.

"Huge. Harley Davidson tattoos, bulging biceps sticking out of his vest, little mirrored sunglasses, shaved head, the whole deal."

"Who threw the first punch?"

"I got pushed into the gutter, see? When I got up I was pretty filthy. He was already halfway down the block, so I followed him."

"What about the dog?" Vicky interrupted.

"The dog didn't even look at me."

"So then what happened?" I asked.

"He went into a bar. I went in after him. I grabbed his shoulder and tried to turn him around. That's when he hit me."

"And then?"

By way of answer, Roan pulled down his mask so I could see the rest of his face. His upper lip was torn and had been stitched up by hands far less skillful than my own.

"Ouch," I said.

"What kind of a dog was it?" Vicky asked.

"Never mind."

"Rottweiler?" I asked.

"How about we close this lady up and get her off the gas?" Roan said.

"Bullmastiff?" I ventured.

"I picture a Rhodesian Ridgeback," said Vicky. "They're tough but they're in the sight hound group, which makes them fierce hunters. I know this. I go to dog shows sometimes. Whippets are in the same group, and greyhounds, which are awful to hares, and Borzois, which were bred to hunt wolves."

"Chihuahua," muttered Roan as I began to close the operating field.

"Most doctors are white collar as well as white coat," Vicky said. "They drive nice cars and make lots of money and they belong to clubs and they play golf and tennis. They're educated; they have class, they don't crawl into bars and scrap in the middle of the day. Hello. Did you just say Chihuahua?"

"I wasn't scrapping over a dog," Roan growled. "I was challenging a man on principle."

"What principle would that be?"

"Let's just say I was born evil and leave it there."

"Drinking?"

"About to start," he smiled ruefully.

"Nobody is born evil," Vicky put in. "And there is no Satan. Evil just lives inside us as an option, a choice, and you can do with it what you will. Anybody can."

26

Rather than admit I was still addictively buzzing on the energy of combat, let's just say I wanted to see the scene of Roan's crime. The bar was a blues joint over on Federal Highway, north of Sunrise Boulevard. Roan often ducked in after work to hear live music. Once I made sure that Janis was stable, I went down to the place myself, just to satisfy a certain itch.

The décor was nothing special, but the music was unexpectedly good. A couple of homely guys did the peanuts and pours, while an auburn-haired singer worked the mike. A cardboard tri-fold on the tip table identified her as "Emma the Dilemma." She kept half her face hidden with the curtain of her hair and her lively fingers flew over the piano. Her piano work could have been better but her voice was strong and unique, a cross between Norah Jones and Koko Taylor, with a little Diana Krall thrown in. I put twenty bucks in her jar and asked about a big biker with a small dog. She touched her cheek self-consciously. I saw acne scars beneath her makeup.

"Only one guy like that comes in here. We call him Big Steve. He chains the dog to his vest when he rides. We're not supposed to allow animals in here, but nobody's got the balls to tell him."

"I like him already," I said. "Except that he beat up my friend."

"The guy who came in off the street after him last night?"

"That's the one."

"That wasn't pretty. Your friend's no genius for hassling Steve."

"You think the big guy will come in tonight?"

"Stick around and find out."

To encourage me in that direction, she played some music more my tempo: *Help a Good Girl Go Bad, Something Inside Me* and finally *Queen Bee*, the last with a look that said she'd like to sting me.

"You're a doctor aren't you?" she asked me after finishing the set.

"What gives it away?"

"Your cheap watch doesn't match the twenty you put in the jar. Plus you talk like you have an education. I had a part-time boyfriend down at Jackson Memorial in Miami. He did my lips for me. He wore a watch like that too. Bet you're a surgeon, huh? Can't leave a nice timepiece in the O.R. locker?"

"It hurts me to learn I'm such an open book."

The way she smiled at me, I could tell she didn't realize I meant it.

The bar filled up when darkness fell. I kept nursing club soda and lime and wondering whether there would be violence here tonight, or whether Petrossov was waiting for me at my house. I wondered why Tie Mei hadn't said anything about the Russian crime lord, whether she could see into my life and tell me which of my personal intersections was with a repeat customer. By the third bottle of club soda, I was beginning to suspect Tie Mei didn't know those things any better than I did. It occurred to me once again that her shade was some sort of schizoid manifestation of my subconscious mind.

Big Steve arrived just after ten. His Harley was his calling card, pipes with drilled baffles and the idle set so low that over and over again the engine would seem to die and then catch. This, I have learned from some guys at the Triumph shop, is the mark of a certain proud school of motorcycle engine tuners. He shut it off after making his point and came into the bar.

He wore a vest of distressed leather right against his skin, the buttons little skulls. I'd seen it all before, the shades, the swagger, the chain threaded through the belt loops in his pants, all but the dog. It really was a cute thing, not the grizzled canine version of its owner that I'd expected, but a fresh-faced little pup: fawn-and-white with buggy eyes and a pink tongue. I was fascinated by the notion it had somehow displaced Roan Cole from the sidewalk.

I bent down to pet it. Most Chihuahuas I meet are rough customers, but this one licked my hand and went left and right with its tail and showed me white teeth, in a smile that said her owner brushed them.

"Your Triumph outside?" he asked me.

"Sure is. Say. This is a nice dog. You, on the other hand, are one ugly motherfucker."

I figured I had to plunge in. I had wasted all my small talk on the piano player.

He blinked at me. "At least you like Luna," he said.

"She smells good; you smell bad."

"I get it. You're a cop."

"No sir."

"Undercover."

"I'm just some guy calling you a dumb fucking ape."

He put the dog down.

"You're packing heat," he said. "You're a psycho and you're packing heat."

I was keeping my voice low, not wanting to spread the joy, but he wasn't, so we had an audience pretty quickly, body language telling the story.

"Not armed," I said, spreading my hands.

"A Baker Act then," said Big Steve, curling and uncurling his hands as he called me clinically insane.

"Saner than most, not as sane as some."

"So it's a dare."

"No dare."

Watching me, Steve reached for a few peanuts, tilted his head back and popped them down his throat.

"Insurance? Looking for free plastic surgery?"

"You're good," I said. "You should be a lawyer."

"Bingo."

"You're kidding."

"Personal injury," he said with a little smile. "But I can't represent you against me, if you see what I mean."

"You're the one who is going to need your own services."

The dog looked expectantly up at his face, her little haunches quivering.

"People wonder how come she does what she's told," said Steve. "I always give them the same answer. If you were three pounds and your master went two fifty-five, what would you do?"

"You hurt a friend of mine last night."

"Aha. So that's what this is about."

"The way I heard it, it was over the dog."

"They always blame it on poor Luna."

"You gave him a pair of shiners."

"That would be the skinny fuck who made fun of her rhinestone collar and didn't like her long leash. He actually followed me in here."

"You're the one that looks rabid and dumb," I said, just not finding it in me to insult the dog. "You're the one who needs dipping for fleas."

He came up off the barstool. "You're working this pretty hard," he said.

"Small dog, small dick. That's what they say."

That was the quip that turned it. Big Steve started to chuckle. The chuckle turned to a guffaw. The way he was bent over made me start laughing too. He wiped a tear from his eye. "Buy you a drink?" he asked.

Deflated, grinning, and disgusted with myself deep down, I said yes, but only to another club soda. He ordered Bourbon.

"I don't booze and ride," I explained. "Mostly I drink tea. Full of antioxidants, gives me energy, fights cancer—all that."

"I should be as smart as you. Look, I'm sorry about your buddy. But you gotta know he's got a mouth on him and no sense at all."

"That's my man," I said.

"And you really came looking for a fight?"

"It's been happening lately."

He looked at me curiously. "What's been happening lately?"

"I crave violence," I said.

"Oh boy. You got a history?"

The question gave me a lump in my throat. I flagged down the bartender, and ordered a single-malt Scotch, neat.

"I got Abelour, I got Oban, I got Lagavulin," the bartender told me.

"Lagavulin," I said.

"Stuff tastes like smoked bacon," said Big Steve.

"I like it."

"Yeah? What happened to not drinking when you're riding?"

"I got bigger questions."

"Slamming into a phone pole drunk has a way of commanding your attention," said Steve.

"You're drinking Bourbon and your bike is outside."

That kept him quiet, for a moment. "So, you got priors?" he asked me at last.

"You're asking if I've ever been locked up?"

"That's right."

"Not in this life."

"I see."

"Why, you think I might need your services?"

"I'm a good lawyer," he said. "Plus, a bar's a good place to offload on a stranger."

I slugged the Scotch down and ordered another. The calluses on Big Steve's elbows told me he was used to using them. I was glad I hadn't fought him. The bartender showed up almost immediately with my drink. Lagavulin's expensive stuff. I guessed they didn't sell that much of it. Steve kept staring at me expectantly.

"I get visions," I said. "They tell me to do things."

"Violent things?"

"Yes."

"You act on these instructions?"

"Sometimes."

He put one huge finger in his drink and stirred the ice around. "Seen a shrink?" he asked, in a neutral tone.

"No."

"You act like something's bugging you, eating you up inside. You want to talk about it?"

The words of a stranger, that's what it took. I stared at him, plucked my phone out of my pocket, and dialed my new sister.

"Xenon, what a nice surprise."

"I want to file the complaint against that Russian bastard."

"I knew this was coming. Is there anything I can do to change your mind?"

"No."

"Are you all right? You sound a little loose."

"I'm fine. Can you help me with the paperwork?"

"I'm on a burglary call right now. I'll have someone meet you at the front desk of the station."

I took down the second drink in one swallow, and reached for my helmet.

"Maybe you should wait a little bit before you ride," said Steve.

"I'm going to the police station."

"Then you should definitely wait."

"It's all about what's eating me," I said.

He touched me lightly on the shoulder, nodded, and paid for my drinks.

"Be careful," he said.

27

I woke up the next morning with the profound satisfaction of someone who has finally screwed up the courage to do what they needed to do. I knew Petrossov's house would be crawling with cops, and I imagined policeman riffling through the dead boy's things, questioning the staff, looking for evidence and clues. For a doctor to report that a child was beaten to death was something law enforcement could not ignore, no matter what federal investigations might be cooking, no matter whether racketeering or money laundering charges were in the works.

Straight out of bed, I checked for surveillance. Sure enough there was a car parked on the grass in the empty lot across the street. For a moment I thought Wanda might have sent a unit to watch over me, but there was no spotlight by the driver mirror, the hubcaps were wrong, and the windows were blacked out. When I saw the pile of cigarette butts by the driver's door, I had a pretty good idea Petrossov was sending me a message.

The game being afoot, I thought it a perfect time to finally accept Jake Derringer's invitation to a cruise. Grateful that I had saved his back and maybe his career, Jake had left a flurry of messages asking me to one thing or another. I asked Jordan along, and was glad I did. Jake and his girlfriend, Tawny, met us on his 52-foot Hatteras, a sporting yacht with a blue hull, a sleek, streamlined superstructure, and a nice tanning deck out back. Jordan took to the ride like she was born to it, which I had to explain to Jake she was not.

"She sure is a world-class beauty," he said admiring Jordan stretched out in the sun.

"I think so."

"And you met her where?"

"Just in the course of things."

"You say she makes blades?"

"Following her bliss," I said. "And her father's lead. It's a family affair."

"I didn't even know people made swords anymore," he said, unconsciously touching his sacrum with a big, rough palm. "That's the great thing about America. You can do anything you want, as long as you don't bother anybody."

"That second part depends on ethics," I said. "Mostly those seem in short supply."

"You mean morals?" Derringer shrugged. "Just some learned ideas. Science and technology are going to change what's right and wrong faster than one of her knives can cut a throat. Before long, we're going to redefine what it means to be human."

"How's that?"

"We're replacing flesh with spare parts. They're already doing titanium hip joints. Knees too. More and more of us will evolve past flesh. At what point, do you suppose, do we stop being real? When both knees are nylon? When both hips are titanium? When the stomach is a synthetic filter? When the heart is plastic? Before the end of your career you'll be operating on silicon brains."

"Fantasy," I said. "Science fiction."

"You don't like science fiction?"

"As a boy I did. I wanted to speed up the present to get to the future. I wanted to see what was to come. I look at life differently now. Everything in the universe winds down. It's the Second Law of Thermodynamics, the tendency toward minimal energy states, toward disorganization and chaos. Ever since the Big Bang everything blows apart, slows down, quiets down. Life is the sole exception. It's the leaf caught in a little eddy in the big river, the kind you see when you're fishing, going counter to the flow. I don't like science fiction as much as I used to because nothing the human mind can come up with is as endlessly interesting to me as life itself, the one flaw in that otherwise perfect rule, the one little rebellious current in that universal river. It's fantastic, really."

Derringer steered delicately around a smaller boat that was ogling a mansion built along the Intracoastal. "I don't fish," he said. "But I can tell you the future is now. Brain scans are happening. Functional MRIs tell market researchers what is saleable and cool. Merchandisers use them in my business already. Pretty soon they'll evaluate brains and spines and tell you exactly where to cut, and the patient will actually think differently after you are done."

"When it happens, it happens. I'll have a new skill set to learn; I'll become even more of a handyman than I am right now. Speaking of spines, how is yours feeling?"

"Just perfect, thanks to you. My trainer told me you chose an unorthodox technique. I appreciate it."

"I was cutting close to the cord," I said. "That always carries certain risks. But realistically, I don't think there was a big downside and I wanted you to have all your flexibility and strength for the game."

"You saved me pain, and you might have saved my career," he said. "I won't forget it."

"They'll be other lives, other careers."

"Other lives?" he looked at me. "You believe that?"

"I think so," I said. "I've seen some things lately. It makes sense to me that the motivating force that gives the frank finger to a universal law should just keep on ticking, body after body, life after life."

"Reincarnation?"

"If you consider the past and the future as one, it doesn't seem so strange. Then, a soul is just one constant part of a broader landscape not broken up by our what you call learned ideas. It's all one continuum."

"A brain doc who believes in the soul. Who would believe it?"

We went out to sea through the Hillsboro Inlet, a natural exit perilous for small boats because of the current and challenging even for a big craft like the Hatteras. Derringer was a good captain for such a young guy, and soon we were cruising south along the shoreline. His girlfriend, Tawny, sunned herself up front with Jordan, but they both came to the stern when the swells started to break over the bow.

"It's so cool that Jordan works with steel," Tawny said. "Powerful and feminine at the same time."

"Tawny has been telling me about the plight of the Hopi Indians on Black Mesa in Arizona," said Jordan. "Do you know they have to walk miles with buckets for water because we've diverted their spring water to wash coal?"

"It's all the result of a short-sighted energy policy," said Tawny.

"She's a theoretical physics major at Florida Atlantic University," said Derringer, smiling as if this were merely a pretty girl's quirk. "She works on string theory."

"Endless parallel universes," I said. "Do you think string theory explains ghosts?"

"Why, have you seen any?" Tawny grinned at me. She was a tall blonde, built like a fashion model, with a braid halfway down her back.

"My dead stepmother came to visit me recently."

"Aha!" Derringer rolled his eyes. "So this is what started all that shit about reincarnation."

Jordan looked at me. I hadn't mentioned my conversation with the shade of Wu Tie Mei.

"Wicked stepmother or good stepmother?" Tawny asked.

"I shouldn't call her that," I said. "She and my father were never legally wed, but she was definitely good."

"Zee has a real stepmother now, though," said Jordan. "We went to his father's wedding a few days ago."

"Congratulations," said Derringer. "Hey, how about some kayak surfing?"

"Never tried it," I said.

"It's very Zen. Just you and the ocean."

His little plastic boat was under a tarp. Derringer tossed it in the water and handed me a paddle. I swam out and put a leg over and managed to maneuver in close to the surf line. The women were watching, so I tried not to tip. Even so, the first couple of breakers took me out and I came up sputtering. Derringer hooted from the bridge and I climbed back on and got more serious about timing my attacks on the swells.

Because my father is afraid of the ocean and because Tie Mei eschewed the sun, I never got much beach time growing up, and even less time in the water. Aboard the little kayak, I concentrated on applying my martial sensitivity to reading the movement of the water, and keeping my equilibrium. In Tie Mei's martial system, the word for equilibrium is wuji, which refers to the state of infinite potential—not of nothingness or emptiness, as it is sometimes translated—the state of the universe before it was organized into the opposing forces yin and yang. In the west, this idea is expressed as the biblical ether, the constellation of infinite possibilities present before God created the heavens and the earth. To stay in wuji is to stay in a perfectly relaxed and clear-minded state, one I had certainly not been in since Rafik Petrossov died on my table, and since Tie Mei returned as a phantasm to goad me to violence.

In the Chinese medical model, wuji is also connected to health. In this ideal state, qi flows unimpeded through the body's acupuncture channels, properly nourishing the vital organs, the skin, brain, and extremities. This requires a certain body alignment. Maintaining this perfect physical alignment is the core idea of Tie Mei's martial art, and the way in which it differs from any other system I know.

"Concentrate on your own wuji, and the fight will take care of itself," she said. "Respond to what is coming your way not with a plan for your opponent's destruction, but with one for your own salvation. If, in preserving yourself, you happen to smash someone's head open, that's their problem, not yours. You were merely staying on your feet, calm and unhurt."

Cruel as this self-centered approach may be, it is stunningly effective, and great at teaching balance to boot. Sitting on top of the kayak, I applied her lessons. Treating the waves as my opponents, I approached them in wuji. Jordan cheered me on and I made a good run of a five-foot wave, carving down the side of it, nearly falling off but holding the bow at just the right angle so that I could stay abreast of the curl, treating the paddle as a monk's staff, and used my hips to control the boat.

My concentration was so complete I did not even hear the sound of the approaching vintage powerboat until Jordan shouted a warning.

I turned just in time to see Vlexei Petrossov at the wheel, and Chazov his butler beside him. The engines screamed as the prow closed in, black and sharp and fast. I paddled frantically, but the kayak was hopelessly outmatched. The speedboat's bow wave came in. I rode it obliquely, narrowly avoiding being rammed. Petrossov worked the wheel. I saw the name Miss America X on the stern of the boat. Out of the corner of my eye I saw Jake Derringer try to position the Hatteras between us, but there was no time.

Miss America X came back around. I heard Jordan scream. This time when the bow came in I dove free of the kayak and kicked furiously downward. The wooden hull passed above me like a foaming green dragon, the keel barely inches from my head. The kayak split in half. I felt the churning of the wake, and the propellers brushed me with bubbles. I was disoriented, flailing, kicking and gasping. Salt burned my throat and nose.

I struggled to find the way up, but the boat turned on a dime and Petrossov had it on top of me again before I could surface. I willed myself not to breathe, waited for the hull to pass over, and managed to get only one arm out of the water before he spun around for a third pass. I had to go down again or die, and when I did, my need to breathe overcame my will, and all I had to breathe was salt water.

Perhaps, if I had seen the attack coming, I could have prepared with a deep, deep breath. As it was, I began to drown. The pain was indescribable. My lungs turned to fire, and the world grew dim around me, closing like the aperture on a camera lens. I didn't see my life flash before me, didn't see Wu Tie Mei or Helen, my mother.

In the face of so little oxygen, my heart began an arrhythmic beating. I felt it worming around in my chest as if looking for something, expanding and contract wildly against the confines of the pericardium. My panic was indescribable, so much so that when I saw Jordan's long, lithe body stroking down toward me through the churned-up green water, I felt a wave of gratitude simply at not having to die alone.

28

"These voices, they started after your patient had a near-death experience?"

I regarded Diomedes Ramirez across the coffee table in his office. A spare and elegant man with an aquiline nose and relaxed air, Diomedes is the kind of guy who looks good in expensive clothes. More important than that, he is the best psychiatrist in Broward County.

"It's actually only one voice, and it started before the patient nearly drowned."

"You're sure? Near death experiences often cause a feeling of being connected to something larger than you. That kind of connection could be misconstrued as a voice."

"He said it started weeks before the drowning."

"I thought you said the patient was a woman."

"She is. She started hearing the voice about ten days ago."

"I see. And she came to you for what?"

"She's got Parkinson's. Her neurologist is thinking about installing an electronic implant to control her tremors."

"They work like a cardiac pacemaker, right?"

"About like that," I said, shifting in my chair.

"And she just happened to mention hearing a voice?"

"She wondered if the implant would stop it."

"Who is talking to her?"

"A dead relative, an aunt."

"You're not giving me much to go on," Diomedes shrugged. "Do you have a full history?"

"There's no mental illness in the family, as far as she knows."

"How far back?"

"To her grandparents, at least. Look, she says the voice is as clear as yours or mine. There's a visual hallucination that goes with it.

This brought the psychiatrist forward in his chair. "A visual halluci-nation?"

"The aunt comes to visit her. She shows up at odd times, and says things that are very clear and convincing. The ghost even dresses according to the period."

Diomedes's office was perfectly neutral, a studied blend of calming colors: beige tweed for the couch, friendly, pale green paint on one wall, pastoral paintings done in oil, one Tiffany lamp, along with full-spectrum fluorescent bulbs in the ceiling fixture. I could see how someone who loathed himself less than I did—someone whose life was not growing more and more out-of-control and desperate—might be appeased by the décor.

"The voice belongs to a ghost?"

"That's just it," I said, unable to stay seated any longer. "It seems like a ghost, in the sense that it just seems to materialize, but it walks and talks and doesn't float or anything."

"It doesn't float," Diomedes said. "Well, that's good. Can the ah, patient, touch the ghost?"

I made a quick circuit of the office, which felt smaller by the minute. I picked up a framed photograph of Diomedes shaking hands with the governor of Florida, read the governor's signature, then put the photo back down. "She tries," I said. "But there doesn't seem to be any substance there, although the ghost does have the dead aunt's smell."

"Why don't you sit down, Zee?"

I took my seat. I found my legs moving in and out at the knees.

"Can I get you anything? A glass of water?"

"Thanks. I'm all right."

"This patient means a lot to you."

"I find the case disturbing."

Diomedes studied his tie for a moment. It was blue, with little gold horseshoes on it. "You said something about the smell."

"The aunt smelled like almonds," I said. "It was just her skin smell."

"Not perfume?"

"No."

"And you said something about being dressed for the period."

"She comes back from different periods of history."

It was Diomedes's turn to rise. He went to the window, pulled the gauzy curtains aside, and looked out across the boulevard. We were on the ground floor, and I saw a fire engine go by. A palm tree bent low to a gust of wind.

"This ghost has a sense of history?"

"Just tell me what you think, Diomedes."

He let the curtain drop, and returned to his leather chair. "Visual and auditory hallucinations are signs diagnostic of schizophrenia; you don't need me to tell you that. Tell me, is the patient degrading in all walks of life?"

"Not at all. She's functioning perfectly. Even has a new romance going, and is doing great work."

"She works?"

"As a librarian."

Diomedes smiled. "How does one do great work as a librarian?"

"Helps people with research, keeps the catalog up to date? I don't know, Diomedes, I'm a neurosurgeon. She says the visions and voice are as clear and real to her as you and me."

"Could be schizophrenia, but I'm putting my money on PTSD."

"Post traumatic stress disorder? From the drowning, you mean?"

"If the condition predates it, the drowning may have been a suicide attempt. There was probably an earlier, precipitating event."

I felt the sudden and overpowering need to urinate. Ever since Jordan pulled me from the water, my bladder had acted like a treacherous and unreliable accomplice, sounding its warning bell at the most inopportune times.

"I need the toilet," I said.

I closed myself in the bathroom, sat down on commode, and bit my hand while I relieved myself. My teeth made deep marks in my finger. I wanted to scream or cry. I flushed and washed my hands. I had risked everything I had worked for and yearned for, on the say-so of a hallucination, and now I had nearly died at the hands of a Russian crime boss. Maybe Diomedes was right. Maybe I had killed Rafik by mistake and was twisting myself because of it. I remembered how Tie Mei had told me deformities of body were nothing compared to deformities of mind.

When I came back into the room, Diomedes was writing notes on a yellow legal pad, using an imposing black fountain pen. "You mentioned the ghost appears to her at odd intervals. Is there anything to link those times?"

"What do you mean?"

"Sometimes, but not always, schizophrenic events have a trigger. I just wondered when you had seen the ghost."

"The first time was in the locker room at the hospital. The second time she came when I was in the hot tub outside. Another time, I was stretched out drunk on the couch."

"Are you drinking?" Diomedes asked, not blinking an eye at having broken through my fiction of an ailing patient.

"Not much."

"But you were drunk."

"She, the patient, was drunk that one time, yes."

"And only that time?"

"Maybe she's been drinking more lately."

"A history of alcohol abuse in the family?"

"No."

"What about recreational drugs? Traumatic events?"

"There may be things she's not telling me."

Diomedes creased the paper he'd been writing on, folded it back and forth, and then ripped it off. The sound of the paper tearing was deafening. He crumpled it up and threw it into the trash.

"The bathroom, and the tub private places. Was the patient naked when the ghost appeared?"

"I don't know."

"Did the patient have sexual feelings for this ghost, this aunt?"

"Sexual feelings? No, not that."

"You're sure?"

"I'm sure."

"The patient, is she about your size and weight."

"Yes. A big woman."

"Let's try Geodon, 40mg twice a day, with food."

Geodon was a new antipsychotic drug. I knew it had stimulating effects.

"She has trouble sleeping," I said.

"Then try 2mg a day of Risperidol."

"Makes you fuzzy, doesn't it?"

"Better choice if she has trouble sleeping."

"She can't be fuzzy at work," I said.

"At the library?"

"If she puts a book in the wrong place, it's lost forever."

"Do the Geodon, then. Might keep her up, but it should get rid of the visions. Try it for the short term, Zee, but get the woman into therapy as soon as possible. You.... she has to get to the bottom of this if she's going to feel better."

"Thank you," I said.

Diomedes clasped me by the shoulder. "Page me anytime, if you need to talk again, all right."

"Sure."

"Will you put my card in your wallet?"

"Of course," I said.

29

"You mean there was someone in the water? How perfectly dreadful to hear."

According to Wanda Berkowitz, those were Petrossov's words when confronted with Jake Derringer's report of the attack. He admitted vaguely remembering my name, said that in his time of mourning the "technicians" who had attended his dying son had become a blur to him. He denied following me, denied giving orders that I be beaten, denied running my kayak over with his speedboat.

"You could press charges," Wanda told me on the phone. "There were witnesses, after all."

"He has as many on his side. They'll just say they were moving at speed and never saw me. It will make my interest in his son's death seem more like a personal issue and give it less weight at the hospital. I'm pretty sure he wants to make me look like a paranoid with a chip on my shoulder. I'm just going to press the autopsy request."

"It's completely outrageous!" Jordan cried, when I called to fill her in. "Can they get away with this?"

When I recounted the episode to John Khalsa, he seemed less clearly on my side.

"Miss America X?" he frowned. "Are you sure?"

"It's Petrossov's boat," I said. "I saw it at his house. There were three witnesses on the boat."

"You weren't admitted for the drowning?"

"I was pulled out just in time. My girlfriend did mouth-to-mouth. I came back. She stayed with me all night. I didn't want to go to the ER."

"You're a doctor," he said, taking a sip of what looked and smelled, even from across the room, like single malt Scotch. "A surgeon, for Christ's sake. Top of the heap, Master of the antiseptic universe. What are you doing at some mob bosses' house?"

"So you admit he's a mobster."

He sauntered over to his credenza and poured himself a Dr. Brown's Celray. "Miss America X was Garfield Wood's boat," he said. "The speedboat king they called the Gray Fox. The guy was a maniac. He ran Golden Cup Races on the Detroit River and won them: the Harmsworth Trophy, too. In 1921, he raced a speed train called the Havana Special from Miami to New York in one of his fast boats. Won by twelve minutes. He liked airplanes and was convinced airplane engines were more reliable than boat engines and put out more power, too. His hulls were the fastest nearly a hundred years ago, and Miss America X was the best of them. If I remember right it was good for one hundred and twenty-five miles per hour with a couple thousand horses worth of twelve-cylinder Packard engines. Madman's dream, they called it, but the thing flew over water."

"Well, Petrossov owns it."

"If that's true, he would never take it out on the ocean."

"He does and he did."

"It's invaluable," said Khalsa. "I can't even tell you what it's worth."

"He doesn't deny owning the boat or having driven it. He just says he never saw me in the water. I'm going to bring the fucker down. It's as simple as that."

"There's nothing simple about any of this. You should hear yourself. What kind of doctor talks like you talk?"

"Doctor is what I do," I said. "Not what I am."

"Ah," said Khalsa, looking at me through the golden bubbles of his soda pop. "That's where the trouble lies."

I left his office and went out to the parking lot behind the hospital. Orson Cartwright was waiting there, examining my yellow Thruxton. "You're late," he said.

I had forgotten about my appointment with the boy, set up before the day I drowned. I no longer felt up to taking on a student. How could a crazy man teach a child? He would do well to stay away from me, that's what I was thinking.

And then I caught the expectant, trusting, excited look in his eye.

"Here's how it works. If I'm late, you wait. If I'm later than that, you wait longer."

"Fine," he said, putting his hands up in submission. "Whatever. No offense, okay?"

I found us a place next to a trash dumpster, out of sight, in an alley. There was a cardboard box on the ground marked "sharps." I moved it.

"Do the hospital people know you do this?" he asked.

"The real warrior keeps his skill to himself. Attacks can happen anytime, seemingly for no reason at all."

"Anyone ever tell you, you're paranoid?"

I thought of Diomedes's comments on schizophrenia. Orson must have seen my face. "I'm only kidding," he said.

"This is South Florida. Grandmothers carry guns in the glove compartments of their cars here."

"So this is about grandmothers?"

"It's about being ready for the unexpected, and about building health and strength. But really we want to learn to keep our cool, to understand ourselves and the world more deeply, and to be tough enough to be gentle."

"Yeah," Orson nodded. "That's just what I was thinking."

We started with Chinese splits. Common knowledge has it that the inside of the groin limits flexibility, but it's actually tension in the outside, abductors of the hip—what Tie Mei called the *kwa*—that make low stretches hard.

"Ouch," said Orson as I helped him down into the posture, spreading his feet wider and wider, lowering him to the ground.

"Stretch is twenty percent in your legs, eighty percent in your mind," I said.

"My mind is saying my body hurts."

"Your mind believes your body is a torso with arms sticking out the top and legs sticking out the bottom. Big mistake. The spine is the only hard piece connecting the top and bottom halves of you; the truth is you've got two separate entities to work with, limited only by that bony link. Your top half can do one thing while your bottom half does another, just the way you can learn to chew gum and walk at the same time. Realizing this is very freeing. It opens up a whole world of new possibilities."

"Like finding out your father doesn't really care what you do," said Orson.

"Sure he does. He just doesn't remember that yet."

"What about you? Who cares if you're happy?"

"I have family," I said. "And a lady called Wu Tie Mei; maybe another woman too."

"Wu Tie Mei is the teacher who died, right? How can she care about you?"

It was only with the greatest effort that I avoided saying she came to me in psychotic episodes. "Good question. But I know she does," I answered.

"So the other woman is your girlfriend, right? I bet she's hot."

"Sizzling," I said.

I put my hands on his shoulders and pushed him deeper into the stretch, then set him up for pushups on the hot asphalt. "This will build your chest and toughen your hands," I said.

"Your hands don't look so tough. I don't even see any calluses."

"I have to keep them sensitive so I can feel what the brains are thinking before I cut them."

"That's your secret, isn't it; surgical kung fu?"

"If I have a secret it is that I treat gravity like a powerful uncle who always gets his way, but with whom you can negotiate. In the end gravity gets us all, but you can affect how you go down to him and when. You can also offer opponents up as bribes or sacrifices to buy you a little more time, or a little gentler treatment in gravity's hands."

"A sacrifice to Uncle Gravity," Orson laughed. "I like that."

"If you get out of the way, gravity will take the bad guy down. You can count on it."

"Any other words of wisdom?"

"Diet is important. Eat less sugar. It'll help your acne."

"I heard that's not true."

"According to Chinese medicine, sugar is a hot food, and pimples are signs your system is overheated."

"Overheated?" Orson looked doubtful.

"It's a way of describing our metabolism, and the energetic properties of food."

"So you do Chinese medicine?"

"It's part of martial arts training. We need to be able to fix what we break. It happens there's a famous story about food heating someone to death."

"Tell me," said Orson.

"Thousands of years ago, there was a tyrannical Chinese emperor who was known for his ruthlessness. He killed anyone who plotted against him. One of his most powerful opponents was a minister who suffered from boils; think of it as acne times ten. The emperor sent him an elaborately prepared duck. A dozen cooks delivered it, and set it up with a beautiful service. When they uncovered it with a flourish, the minister fainted. Duck is very hot, and the emperor had chosen it deliberately to overwhelm the man's system. It was a death sentence, and the minister got the message. Forced to eat it, he died the next day."

"How do you know all this stuff?"

Orson's admiration was a tonic. Teaching him made me feel I was worth something, that I had a contribution worth making, that I wasn't just a violent nut-job who was lucky he hadn't done worse than mark up a wife beater and intimidate a greedy lady into selling her house.

"School," I said. "Lots and lots of school. So you've learned to stay away from duck. Avoid chicken, too, and spicy sauces. Eat beef, lots of lightly cooked vegetables, and plenty of fruit. As you start to balance your system, your attitude and moods will even out, and your acne will fade."

I worked Orson to the point where he couldn't lift a leg. I did the exercises right along with him, and they made me feel better, too. The medication Diomedes Ramirez prescribed for me gave me a dry mouth and a jumpy stomach, and the energy work inherent in the stances balanced my system, and took the edge off those complaints. When Orson was a cooked egg, I sent him packing and went home. I found a package from my new stepbrother, Martin, leaning against the door.

Martin had prepared a short history of the Russian mob for me: background for one of the stories his investigative colleague had run. I had less interest in the subject than when I'd asked about it. I was determined to avoid any further contact with Petrossov. I was starting to accept the idea that seeing Rafik's flying white soul had merely been the first sign of my impending psychotic break.

Martin's package made fascinating reading nonetheless. From it, I learned organized crime in Russia was as old as some of my father's stories, maybe even as old as my grandfather's water nymphs. Jews had been involved for centuries because so few avenues for making a living were open to them. Educated and intellectually inclined, they turned their brains to crime and joined the so-called *vor v zakonye*, a fraternal order of elite criminals dating back to the time of the tsars.

In the modern era, Martin's material related that mob activity could be traced to the Russian Revolution. Recruited to the cause, crooks taught Lenin's gangs to rob banks to raise money. After World War II was over, all collaborators were killed by the *vors* in a series of prison wars, and a new criminal dynasty was established. Vlexei Petrossov was that dynasty's American heir apparent. His father had been a *vor*, and his father's father before that. Martin had attached a hand-written note to the end of the report:

> "This guy's whole universe is twisted up like a pretzel. You're more likely to grasp how a hyena thinks than to understand him. Steer clear. You're family now. I don't want to write your obit."

Petrossov was behind me now. Rafik was dead and Galina would have to fend for herself. I was not going to ruin my life on the say-so of a hallucination, no matter how much it resembled my dear and departed teacher. I was a neurosurgeon. I had a life. That was my final decision.

I slept fitfully and dreamt ceaselessly about Russia's prison wars. Images of toilets dug from the frozen ground flashed through my head, along with visions of knife fights over scraps of food, cigarette-scarred flesh like poor Gloria Brownfield's, and, of course, children beaten to a pulp and then shaken like rag dolls in the hot mouths of Siberian tigers. I woke up as early as the sun, and called Jordan.

"I've had nightmares all night," I said.

"Drowning?"

"I wish you were here."

"I'll be over a little later."

"What time? I have to go to work."

"You're softer lately," she said. "I kind of like the new you."

30

Jordan rang the doorbell an hour later.

"That's your new boat," she said, pointing to a long and elegant craft strapped to the top of her Subaru. "I read up on near-death experiences on the Internet. The consensus is you've got to confront your fear to get over it, to go right back to the source of your trauma. I ordered this one from Maine, priority trucking. I must have gone through five hundred boat reviews. This is a modified Greenland style kayak, like the Eskimo's use, but faster. You work the rudder with the foot pedals, and those hatches are for stowing gear."

"I can't accept this," I said.

She frowned. "Can't accept it?"

"It's too lavish a gift. At least let me pay you for it."

She touched my face. "You're such a moron. I don't know whether to kiss you or cut you."

"Kiss me," I said.

She did. One thing led to another.

"I thought you had to go to work," she murmured into my neck.

"I can't exactly go like this."

"The solution will only be temporary. The condition will return."

"That's a chance I'll have to take."

I took the chance, and it was a gamble well played. Afterward, I went off to work.

"There's a lady here to see you," Travis told me as I came in the side door. "Won't take no for an answer, seems like it's personal. She's making a scene in the waiting room."

Before I could ask her name, Emma the Dilemma burst into my consulting room. She was breathing hard, and her red ringlets were frothy and dripping from the rain outside.

"You're a hard man to find," she said. "I had to go by two hospitals and describe you before anyone would even give me your name. Fortunately, there aren't that many neurosurgeons with a ponytail."

"Sad, but true," I said. "How can I help you?"

"I'm here because you seemed so nice at the bar," she said.

Travis shot me a worried look. I led Emma into my consulting room.

"You know high-up people, right? You're connected?"

"Start at the beginning," I said.

She started to cry. I waited for her to compose herself. Finally, after a few wracking sobs, she began. "I work a gig at an all-night bookstore. I went to the bathroom to fix my face but I couldn't find my tortoiseshell lipstick holder. I played the blues bar earlier and thought I might have left it there. Around four in the morning, I went back to check."

"So late?"

"There's this new girl working late-nights and I didn't want to step on her toes. She's got boobs, I'll give her that, and the way she sings she's lucky she does."

"So what happened?" I asked, eager to get to my patients.

"I looked in the ladies' room and it wasn't there. I had ducked into the kitchen earlier for a snack and so I checked there too. I was down on my hands and knees searching that disgusting greasy floor when I saw Simba's size thirteen feet. He's the owner. He had the propane tank pulled away from the wall and he was fiddling with some wires and a battery and a jar. There was a pipe on the ground beside him. You don't have to know anything to figure out what he was doing."

"I'm sorry. What am I missing here?"

"He blew the place up."

"What?"

"It's a hole in the ground, Doc. People died."

"You're saying the owner blew up his own bar? Have you gone to the police?"

"I came to you instead."

"You need to go to the police."

Emma shook her head. "The police are not an option. I do things. I did things. They're always looking for me, the cops are."

"What kind of things did you do?"

"Take a wild guess."

I looked at the weary desperation in her profile and could imagine a few transgressions. "Whatever it is, I bet they'll forgive you if you help them with this."

"Ha, and ha again," she said. "Maybe you're smart in your world but you don't know mine. Trust me when I tell you that the police are not going to hear anything from me."

"You could make an anonymous tip."

"They'd trace me. They'd find me. They've done it before."

"So you want me to tell them? They're going to ask me how I know."

"You'll turn me into a suspect if you tell them," she said. "I'm a felon. I used to be Simba's girl. They'll spin some bullshit; watch if they don't."

"So this is an act of conscience?" I asked. I was feeling my way slowly through the exchange, worried I was on loose footing. I was a roiling nest of conflicting emotions myself: medication or no medication. Even though I wasn't having visions anymore, I didn't trust myself to pass judgment on someone else's actions.

"I want to keep performing," she went on. "Simba gave me a break even though he was always after me to get my face and tits done. I wanted to keep singing there, Doc. I wanted to get discovered, not torch the place."

If she was acting, she deserved applause. I didn't offer any.

"I'll have to think about this," I said.

She looked hard at me. "I remember you being more decisive."

"That was night, this is day."

"So that's it?"

I nodded.

She stood up and walked around my consulting room, pacing fast as if she were on uppers. She looked at the photographs on my wall.

"Who are these people?"

"My family."

"This?"

"My mother. She died when I was four. Look, I need to get back to work."

"And this Chinese lady?"

"My nanny."

"You have more pictures of her than your mom."

"She was around longer."

"And this?"

"My grandfather."

"And this is your grandma?"

"That's right."

"These are nice," she said, still looking at the pictures. "Big Steve died in the blast. The little dog, too."

I had been twirling around in my chair, tracking her, not sure what she was going to do. That stopped me cold. I thought about the gruff, tough lawyer and his Chihuahua dog and I felt a hollow forming inside.

"That little Luna was the only female in the state of Florida who could eat those ribs and stay skinny," Emma shook her head. "Steve was in there three days a week holding her on his lap and feeding her those ribs. There was nothing left of the bike except the headlight, a chrome thing. I found it stuck in the bottom of the barber pole across the street when I went to check out the scene."

"You found a piece of Steve's motorcycle across the street?"

She nodded. "I took it home. It's stupid, I know. Sentimental. I don't even know his last name."

I stood up. "You have an address for this Mr. Simba?"

She took up a pen and paper.

"Simba's his first name, George is his last. This is where he lives. Nice place on the ocean."

She leaned over and kissed my cheek gently. Her lips were hot. They left a burn.

"Keep singing, Emma," I said. "You're a world-beater."

She gave me a heartbreaking smile. "It makes sense that you're a brain doctor," she said. "Honest to God it does."

And then she was gone.

31

The Fort Lauderdale blast killed eleven people, and left nothing at the site but the building's concrete slab. According to the newspaper article I read on my couch Saturday morning, arson investigators allowed only that a spark created a devastating fuel/air explosion. In a sidebar interview, Mr. Simba George claimed he had recently contracted for a new propane tank—the better to make more Cajun ribs. The installer, a 20-year veteran installer who denied any wrongdoing, was said to be under a suicide watch in the wake of the disaster.

The bodies were sufficiently vaporized to require identification by dental records. One victim was a little girl sent by her mother to bring her daddy home from a bender. Although she had a different face entirely, her haircut reminded me of Natalya and Galina Petrossov's bob. Another photograph showed a bystander holding up a beer stein that had miraculously landed unbroken across the street. I resolved to make a donation to Chihuahua rescue in Luna's honor.

The paper carried Simba's comments. He was shocked. He was devastated. He had been the proprietor since taking the bar over from his father, who had run it most of his life. Simba's grandfather had played Delta blues on the bar's little stage. The nephew of Robert Johnson had played there, along with Mississippi John Hurt. One time Muddy Waters had stopped in for a jam while visiting a relative in town.

Simba said his life would never be the same. He said his livelihood was gone, his connection to his roots destroyed; and his love of good music and drink devastated beyond repair. He claimed he didn't know where he would go or what he would do next, how he would live with the tragedy, the loss, the memories.

Diomedes's drugs kept me cool while I read all about it. I found myself thinking about the boat Jordan had bought me, and whether I'd be able to force myself to try paddling it. I thought about anything and everything that didn't have to do with being a Chinese warrior reborn, or having been beaten with a flail by angry eunuchs in some ancient imperial court. The drug gave me a shield against Tie Mei. There hadn't been a peep from her.

"I should poison you with mushrooms, you ungrateful dog. I've done it before, you know. When you cuckolded me."

The sound of my teacher's voice made me leap off the couch. She wore a blood-red robe, and looked angrier than I'd ever seen her.

"What?" I said dropping the newspaper and feeling my mouth go dry.

"You're polluting yourself with drugs, you dumb camel. You're denying your teacher, your destiny, and yourself. That's enough, isn't it? I'm going to give you the beating you deserve."

"You're not real," I said. "I'm thinking you are a manifestation of post traumatic stress. I might have killed the Russian boy."

"You know you didn't."

"I'm talking to myself here. You simply cannot be real."

"Not real?" she fumed, closing in. "I'll show you not real."

She pulled a three-section staff out of her robe and closed in on me. I've always found the weapon imprecise and unreliable, but Wu Tie Mei had none of my limitations. Three two-foot pieces of wood linked by two short stretches of chain, it is fast and flexible and she used it to great effect.

"The mind can convince the body of anything," I said. "People can be scared to death. Religious trances can bring on stigmata."

She flicked the staff out. I felt a sting on my cheek. She flicked it again, I put up my hands, and I felt a hard rap on my knuckle.

"I'm just trying to say I'm worried I might be nuts," I said.

She came at me again, and this time I grabbed for the weapon. I watched it pass through my forearm, but my wrist turned red and began to swell almost immediately.

"The drugs have made you slow," she said, obviously disgusted. "And you're getting a pot belly. Have you noticed that little bulge? You never had that. You haven't been training, that's for sure. You've got stretch marks on your legs."

"I don't have stretch marks," I said. "I've only taken a week off."

She flicked the staff out again. I tried to dodge it, and tripped over the coffee table.

"You're clumsy and slow. Why do you still go through these slothful, debauched phases? Don't you remember your fight with Wang on Wudang Mountain?"

"Wang?"

"Ming dynasty. So recent! Tell me you've forgotten that."

"I don't know any Wang."

She whirled the staff impatiently. "Petrossov is Wang. He's always hovering around. Do you remember how he bashed your head on that rock in the snow, then held you out over the edge and dropped you off? The fight wouldn't have gone on so long if you hadn't been drunk. Took a fall off a cliff to sober you up."

"I fell off a cliff?"

"There was a ledge, lucky for you. Not that Wang knew it."

"And where were you? Did you try to help me?"

"I was a nine year old boy. There was nothing I could do. I watched the whole thing from the monastery on the peak."

"So what do you want?" I asked wearily.

"The same thing I always want. To see you a warrior."

"I'm going to rest this weekend."

"A man committed murder. Go do something about it."

"I drowned. I nearly died. And don't tell me I survived drowning before. What? What does that face mean?"

"Drowning," she said.

"I was pulled out. My heart had nearly stopped."

"The last time, it did."

I stared at her. "I drowned?"

"You weren't the only one. China's Sorrow made a flood."

"The Yellow River? I drowned in the Yellow River?"

"I tried to save you."

I pulled Diomedes's card out of my wallet. "You need to go now," I said.

"You've let my sword rust," she sighed.

And with that she was gone. No fading, no floating away, just an image gone the way an image does if you turn off the TV, except no TV images can cause a wrist to swell.

I rode my motorcycle to my grandfather's house. When I got there, I noticed with pleasure that Olivia had a *For Sale* sign in her front yard, and that my grandfather had repainted his house and had a stack of new tiles on the roof. He wasn't home, but the back door was unlocked. I retrieved Tie Mei's sword, and sure enough found flecks of rust where the scabbard met the guard. I sat looking at it for a while, then wiped it. There was a baseball cap from a seed company sitting on the windowsill. I stuffed the hat in my pocket and got back onto my bike.

The engine buzzed, but I barely heard it. The tires ran with the road, but I scarcely felt them. Traffic lights turned and glowed but I did not consciously register their color. I made my way east to Federal Highway and then turned south. I went down through the tunnel at Las Olas, and rode on past Hollywood to Hallandale Beach, where I found Simba's building, an old, run down condo past that Art Deco fusion of soaring arches and concrete and glass called the new Diplomat Hotel.

There was a directory and buzzer. I made note of the apartment number but beat the lock with a credit card. I put on the baseball cap and kept my face low even though I didn't see any security cameras. I took the elevator high up, and went to Simba's door. I stood there for a moment. Intuition told me he was home, and if Tie Mei taught me anything, it was to trust my intuition.

I rang the bell.

"Yes?" the deep voice came from inside.

"Maintenance. I need to reset the switch. It'll only take a moment."

"Switch? What switch?"

"The hypergarburator rheostat. So you're not billed too much."

"I got no idea what you just said," Simba grumbled as he unbolted the door.

When I saw him, I understood that Emma was right to refer to herself as the dilemma. She forgot to mention things. She didn't think things through. Simba George was a giant. He might have been Shaquille O'Neal's brother. He was a hugely muscled black man and he wasn't happy to see me.

"What are you staring at?" he snapped.

"That little girl didn't have to die," I said. "The other ten people didn't either."

He started to slam the door but I blocked it with my foot. I brought the sword up from behind my back. I did it fast, and I put the point to his throat. "A witness saw what you did."

He swallowed. "If there was a witness, don't you think I'd be in jail?"

"The witness didn't talk to the police. The witness talked to me."

"And who the fuck are you, Bruce Lee?"

While I bet Simba clearly understood Sig-Sauer, Glock, Smith & Wesson, Colt, and Heckler & Koch; he seemed not to speak sharp steel. I drove the point in a little deeper, starting a warm trickling line down his throat.

"You put a pipe bomb by the gas tank," I said.

"You got the wrong story. An installer was there. That tank was new. The man did bad work."

I pushed him backward into the apartment, closing the door behind me with my foot. He moved well, taking angles like a skater.

"If there was a leak, someone would have smelled gas. Eleven human beings died, and you killed them."

I was waiting for him to protest. I was expecting him to try and clear his name. Instead, his face twisted up.

"I tried to make a go of my daddy's business, I really did," he said. "I hired real talent, and used name-brand liquor in the well. I served good food, too. What did I get for it? Mortgage goes up, insurance goes up and those fucking drunks squeeze me for two-fers."

"You could have set the timer to blow at night when it was empty."

"I got nothing more to say to you."

I moved the blade and opened the wound. He put his hand up, tried to grab the blade, got cut and let go.

"I used dried pinto beans in a mayo jar, okay?" he whispered. "I poured in some water and covered them with a piece of foil. The beans absorbed the water and moved the foil up to touch a couple of wires. I got the idea from the Internet. It was supposed to take two hours. I couldn't go back to check on it 'cause it could have blown anytime."

"Tell it to the dead."

"A bunch of mid-day-drinking-losers. Town's the better since they all got blown to hell."

"Little girl too?"

"She would have just grown up to be a drunk like her dad. That defect runs in families. Now put that thing down and let's talk. I'll pay whatever it takes to make you see things my way."

I said nothing.

"That place needed blowing up," he pleaded. "The place and everyone in it. That whole life needed blowing up. Don't you see?"

That was when he kicked me. If his foot had met my kneecap the way he intended, I would never again have walked without a cane. As it was, he only grazed my shin. I went down on all fours, my sword still in my hand. He jumped on top. For a long moment he was a horse riding a man, his weight bearing so fearfully down I thought my spine would crack.

"How's it feel to be on the bottom, boy?" he roared, tugging at my cap while working an obscene pelvic thrust into my back.

It wasn't the physical humiliation that did it for me; it was being called boy. I remembered when I was a boy with a sword. My father thought I was in Little League. He never went to a game, so he had no way of knowing that Tie Mei dressed me for baseball and took a bat and ball and put it in her little car and drove me to a park called Matteson Hammock, in Coral Gables, down by the water. All manner of trees grew there, gumbo-limbos and banyans, sea grapes, mangroves, even rubbers with their big, soft leaves. We put in hours of cutting practice. I felled a five inch sapling one day, sliced it clean through with one cut. Tie Mei was unimpressed. But when I took a free-floating leaf in half, severed it along the vein in a most perfect line, she was nearly moved to tears. That cut, she said, showed the softness she was after, the ability to relax and flow like water, the ability to overcome even big strong men not by meeting force with force, but by following the spiraling power of nature.

Strong as a stevedore, Simba closed his hard hands around my neck. My own hands, soft and sensitive from years of wielding the scalpel, locked his in place as I dropped and rolled, twisting his elbow until he was forced to release me.

I stood to face him. He raised his thick fist. A perfect silence grew between us like a glass wall, a mixture of tension and concentration. When at last his strike came forward, I guided Tie Mei's blade through the soft tissue at the bottom of his shoulder joint. I felt no resistance at all, but I did hear a strange hiss. Completely severed, Simba's arm fell to the carpet; the index finger beckoned to me once and then froze.

Simba's jaw dropped. His mouth worked. He wanted to speak but he couldn't. He got up just enough to clear me and then toppled over in shock, pumping a jet of blood from his arm.

Even if his eyes and brain had been working normally, I don't think he would have seen Wu Tie Mei float in off the balcony, grinning a grin that was not devilish, but rather relieved. Her expression was relaxed and happy, and it seemed to me she looked younger than she had appeared to me previously.

"Is this what you want me to be?" I asked her.

"What?" Simba groaned.

"You are what you have always been, an instrument of something bigger than yourself."

"I'm going to die," Simba interrupted, staring at his arm. His voice was suddenly matter-of-fact. "I'm going to bleed to death while a lunatic talks to thin air."

"Scalpel and sword have become the same to me," I said.

"Yes!" she smiled. "Now remember your past lives. That's the way out. That's what you're looking for."

Behind her, a summer tempest danced over the open ocean. Static charges from the storm made snakes of her hair. The lightning show might have been a spotlight; the thunderclaps might have been applause. To this fanfare, she drifted away.

Simba tried to sit up. "Are you the devil come to get my soul? Look, I'm sorry about the little girl, all right? I didn't know a kid would be there."

"I need a belt to tie off your arm," I said.

He pointed to the bedroom with the only hand he had.

Through the door, I found a sea of packed suitcases, some still open. One contained thirty pairs of shoes. I stared at them. Innocent people died, including a guy who could have become my friend, and this son of a bitch had thirty pairs of shoes packed. I felt my temper rise. Bile came into my throat. Everything in my visual field sharpened and glowed. I found a belt and brought it back. Simba was looking at me with something like eagerness in his eyes. It might have been an eagerness to live, but it might have been an eagerness to die. I thought about what Jordan had said about predator and prey the night we looked at her aquarium.

I put the belt around the stump at Simba's shoulder. There was barely enough tissue protruding to give a purchase, but I managed to cinch it tight.

"It doesn't hurt," he said wonderingly.

"It will. You're in shock."

I picked up the telephone, and dialed 911.

"Not the devil. Some kind of avenging angel," Simba said, his eyes wide.

"Ask for help," I said. "Don't say anything else."

"My name is Simba George. My arm has been amputated and I am bleeding," he whispered into the receiver.

I hung up the phone. "I've got friends on the force," I said. "Say one word to the cops, and my witness goes to the newspapers. Spill your guts and I'll be chopping them up with my blade. Are we clear?"

"Crystal," he whispered.

I walked to the door, then immediately turned around and came back. I knew the miracles of modern surgery. I didn't want anyone reattaching that arm. I picked it up by the thick, muscular wrist and walked to the balcony. I wound up the pitch and let the flesh fly.

Simba howled.

32

Sitting alone in my consulting room, I contemplated the bottle of antipsychotic pills. Tie Mei had come despite them, so there was no point in taking them anymore. I could go round and round in my head about PTSD and schizophrenia, could hold an endless internal debate about reincarnation and ghosts, but the fact was someone had killed Rafik Petrossov, and that someone was not me. I hadn't broken his bones, I hadn't crushed his organs, I hadn't sent him to the emergency room and on to the operating theater. Petrossov's attacks on me were real, whether or not, in some far off time and place, he had been a fellow named Wang.

I had to find a way to live with myself, and so far the best solution was the truce I'd proposed with my teacher. I'd do what she said I was born to do, if she would allow me to find balance. The process felt like growth to me, and if it provided an exit door from the endless cycle of birth and death—a passageway to enlightenment or salvation—I was all for it.

The decision to embrace the new role fit with the model of nature my teacher had awakened in me before she was a ghost, back when I was a little boy, when rather than exhorting me to rediscover my spiritual core, she was simply tried to reveal the true workings of the world. There were patterns and cycles everywhere, she told me: ebbs and flows and rhythms and beats. For the last quarter century, I secretly practiced and refined my skills; the period of quiet nurturing was over; the time for action was nigh. The Simba Georges of the world had a new upwelling of justice to contend with, and it was positively disarming.

A knock on the window behind me brought me back to ground, and I parted the blinds for a look. Gloria Brownfield stood peering in. I released the locks and slid the frame open.

"Nobody answered the door," she said.

"The office isn't open yet."

"I saw the glow of the light. I had to see you."

"Come around to the front."

"Can't I just climb in?"

Letting her in through the window would require removing the screen. Any Floridian knows that once you bend a screen to take it out of a window frame, it never again fits flush. "I can be at the door in a minute," I said.

"I want to come in this way."

So I bent the screen and let her in. She seemed remarkably agile, a far cry from the stiff, wasted woman who had visited my office the first time.

"How's your pain?" I asked. "How do you feel?"

She smoothed her skirt and looked up at me fresh-faced.

"The help you gave me was a miracle. That's why I'm here."

A breeze came through the open window and it brought me a strong whiff of her perfume.

"Would you like some tea?" I asked, suddenly aware of how close she was standing.

"I understand some things I didn't understand before," she said. Her previously timid, disconnected way of talking had given way to clear diction.

"How about some chocolate?"

"Nothing hurts anymore."

"Pain occurs in the brain," I said. "It often requires an organic stimulus, in your case a narrowed spinal canal, but how that stimulus is interpreted determines what you perceive."

"No brain no pain," she smiled.

"I couldn't have said it better."

"It was my marriage, not my back that was the problem. Specifically, it was my husband."

"You're off all meds, aren't you?"

"My husband isn't beating me any more. I think you know that."

"I was afraid he was abusing you," I said. "I'm so glad you've resolved it. Are you getting counseling?"

"Don't do this," she said.

"I'm sorry?"

"Don't act as if you didn't do what you did. It was really hard for me to come here."

"I can't imagine what you're talking about," I said.

She was close now. I could feel her breath on my throat.

"You cut him," she said. "You came in the night to save me."

"Ms. Brownfield," I said.

"Gloria."

"Gloria, grateful patients sometimes fixate on their doctor. It's like the Stockholm syndrome for kidnapping victims."

She put her finger on my lips. "He said you used a sword. He was crying when he told me. He wanted me to forgive him. I told him to go straight to hell."

"My tool is a scalpel," I said.

"Shh," she said. "I know it was you. Nobody else saw what you saw. Nobody else knows what you know. I kept it from everyone. I even kept it from myself."

Perspiration grew on her upper lip. I felt helpless at the rush of thoughts I was having, what this could mean for my forays into the night, the way she could complicate my life.

"You've got this wrong," I said.

"He's gone now: moved to Vermont. He has a sister there. All he could talk about was how he wanted to live someplace where there were autumn leaves and winter snow. I saw him pack long johns. He never took off his shirt."

She backed me up to the desk. I tried to push her away. Her lips brushed mine, and I smelled mint on her breath. "I'll do anything for you," she said. "You could come live with me. He left me the house. I'm starting all over again and I'm free."

"I'm awfully flattered, but there is somebody else," I said.

The telephone rang. Gloria tried to stop me, but I snatched it up.

"Working early, huh?" Wanda Berkowitz' voice came over the line. "I tried you at home."

"Not any earlier than you, it sounds like."

"See the morning news?"

"No."

"The vigilante struck again. The guy with the sword."

"Tell me about my complaints against Petrossov instead. And what about my autopsy request? What can possibly take this long?"

A lynx on my desk, Gloria began unbuttoning her blouse.

"I don't know anything about the autopsy. Your complaints are in the system. Law enforcement has a complex relationship with Petrossov. Cases like this have to be built without holes."

"I'm a doctor," I said as Gloria stripped. "My testimony should count."

"A doctor whose department chairman says has a grudge against Russians. I know, because I called him."

"Don't be silly. My own father's from Russia."

"Maybe that's why. Family passions are strongest. Every cop learns that on the first domestic violence call."

"No history of that for me," I said.

Gloria reached behind her back to unclasp her bra.

"You told your colleagues you saw the boy's soul fly off like a bird," said Wanda.

"Khalsa told you that?"

"Not me, Zee. This isn't my case. Petrossov has attorneys."

Bare breasted, Gloria slipped out of her skirt. She wore a g-string to match her brassiere. I picked her clothes off the floor and handed them back to her with a gentle shake of my head.

"Wanda, listen," I said.

"No, you listen. The vigilante cut off a guy's arm."

"His arm?"

"Yes, Zee, his arm. Guy owned some Fort Lauderdale bar that blew up. You'd see both stories on the news, if you watched it. The local PD suspect arson, and think a victim's relative attacked him for revenge. The Sheriff's Office is not buying that though, on account of the fact that the perp used a sword."

Dropping her clothes again, Gloria pressed her bare flesh against me. Through my shirt, I could feel the tough ridge of her burns.

"Don't," I said.

"Don't what? Tell you about the sword? The guy cuts with medical precision, brother. Our forensics men say he has an intimate knowledge of anatomy. He knows how a shoulder is constructed, and how to strike between the hard parts. We've checked with a few local martial arts instructors and they all agree that kind of training doesn't take place anymore, at least not around here. They say nobody has that kind of sword skills these days."

"The whole thing sounds farfetched," I said.

"We're thinking now that he has an addiction to violence: an obsession with the avenging role. We're working for a DNA match."

Gloria put her tongue into my ear.

"Sounds like you've got a lot of folks on the case," I said.

"This case is more important than the previous ones. You see, the victim bled out before he got to the hospital."

Wanda's words did not register right away. "He what?"

"He died, Xenon. This is a homicide investigation now."

Finding air to breathe was tough, and when I did it had a certain choking smell. Gloria reached down to my trousers. I pushed her away so hard she went to the ground with a whimper. Her sad look said this was just the latest in a long line of shoves.

"Homicide?" I managed.

"A murder case. Zee, why didn't you didn't tell me you made a mistake during surgery and that Petrossov threatened you and the hospital with a malpractice suit?"

My tongue was cotton. "What does that have to do with anything?"

"It just makes me wonder what else you haven't told me."

Huddling away from me, Gloria began to put on her clothes.

"I'm sure there are lots of things, Wanda. We've only just met. So I slipped up on an incision. The boy was a goner before he even hit the table, and I'm telling you he was beaten."

"It was a hit-and-run. Witnesses saw a minivan hit the bike."

"Then Petrossov bought them."

"I'm afraid for you, Zee. Truly I am."

"I have to hang up," I said.

After I did, Gloria smoothed out her hair.

"I was an idiot to come here," she said. "I thought you were different. I was wrong."

An uncontrollable pain washed over me: fear, guilt, and regret. I yearned to tell this burned woman everything.

But I didn't. A long moment passed, and then I heard Travis come in the front door and set about moving chairs and sprucing up the place.

Just outside, Joe Montefiore was watering the swale, grunting and humming some old tunes he'd learned from his Italian grandmother back in Brooklyn. Gloria let herself out the window.

Joe pretended not to notice, but after she was gone, he peered in through the glass and gave me a lascivious wink that left me feeling sick.

33

I went off to the hospital, a murderer. Denny DeBroussard was my first patient. Denny fought in the World War I, saw the trenches and smelled mustard gas, heard the drone of biplanes above, and single-handedly downed a German observation blimp by hitting its hydrogen airbag with a lucky shot from his Enfield rifle.

He saw the truth go marching on," said his 84-year-old daughter, Anita.

"Your father is how old?"

"104. He fell out of bed—at least that's what the people at the home say. I don't believe them. I think they treat him poorly. It breaks my heart, him being demented and all, but there's not a thing I can do about it. I'm on social security, and his veteran benefits aren't much."

Roan stood with me, ready to prep Denny for surgery. "He's got a subdural hematoma," he said.

Hematomas are pools of blood. This one was right on top of his brain. They usually come from a blow to the head. The nurses had taken Denny's teeth out, and his mouth sagged down into his chin. He was silent, unresponsive, and seemed in a sad trance, although in demented patients it is sometimes difficult to separate the effects of age and depression from the consequences of an acute injury to the brain.

"I'm sorry I've kept you waiting so long," I told Anita. "I had an emergency at the office and just couldn't get here sooner."

"Poppy gets the apology, not me. He's such a glorious man, a wonderful dancer, a loving father, a harpist who could make angels trip lightly down."

"He plays the harp?"

"He did," Anita smiled.

"Good. We could use more angels around here," said Roan.

Anita glared at him. "Make fun if you like, but a church full of people saw them appear, with wings, when Daddy played."

182

"Doctor Cole meant only the best," I said, kicking Roan's instep.

The operating rooms are in a circle around the main service desk. It took us a few minutes to get to the neuro room. Vicky Sanchez was already setting up my work area.

"You gotta ease up on family," I said, taking Roan aside.

"I don't want to live to a hundred and four."

"I'm sure nobody around here wants you to, but Anita is depending on us. Good studies show that prayer makes a difference. It wouldn't hurt to give her a little hope, would it?"

"That's why I put people to sleep for a living; I just don't have your gift for gab."

Armando, the floor janitor stuck his head in the door. I went to him.

"I brought this toy for Doctor Cole," he said. "A patient left it in his room. Push this button and the little plastic box swears a blue streak."

The scans were waiting for me on the light board. I looked at the damage. The fluid covered more than half of Denny's brain.

"You think he fell or what?" Vicky asked me.

"Patient this old, he'd probably be on Coumadin even if he hadn't had bypass surgery. It wouldn't take much of a tap on the head to get him started bleeding."

Coumadin is the brand name for warfarin sodium. In essence it is rat poison; it thins the blood and makes bruising easy.

"Are you going in with a burr hole?" she asked.

"The lesion is too big. I'm going to make a flap in the bone so I can take a look around."

The orderlies wheeled Denny in past the fifteen other carts in the room. People think operating rooms are austere; in fact they are cluttered and bear the marks of those who work them. Roan's, for example, bears the familiar black and yellow Batman oval, and a bumper sticker for Arrogant Bastard Ale. Vicky helped roll Denny onto the O.R. table. Roan put him out with the fast-acting narcotic Diprovan. Then, when I was ready to start, he changed the gas mixture to pure oxygen: a little trick to saturate his tissues and buy us a few extra minutes should Denny stop breathing. Roan gave the rubber ventilator bag a couple of squeezes and turned on the automatic ventilator.

I shaved off Denny's hair with a clipper and put it in a plastic bag.

It's policy that a patient's hair belongs to him, perhaps arising from the superstitious belief that spirit lurks there, or energetic essence—or at very least virility. Vicky covered his legs with a disposable heating blanket, checked the compression stockings around his legs and stroked his feet.

"That elbow needs padding," I pointed to Denny's right arm.

Under anesthesia the body isn't able to shift away from potentially damaging positions. Damage to the ulnar nerve in the elbow is one of the most common grounds for post-surgical problems, and lawsuits against surgeons.

I used a blue marker to map out the size and shape of the door I wanted to cut in Denny's skull. Lay people don't know this, but each brain looks different to the trained eye. The pattern of arteries, veins, gyri and sulci is as unique as a fingerprint. I have a habit of mentally preparing for what I'm going to see, because surprise is not a positive experience for a neurosurgeon on the job. Roan handed over a hypodermic so I could give a local at the site of incision and we could keep Denny's slumber light.

"Plug me in," I told Vicky. "Let's get this show on the road."

She hooked up my fiber optic light and lit up Denny's skin. I draped the field and made the first cut, penetrating the skin and then the galea, the layer Native Americans used to take as a scalp. I clamped off the edges to reduce the bleeding. I eased loose the temporalis muscle after that, and peeled all the tissue back, securing it with towel clamps.

I went through the bone with a rounded drill bill so as not to accidentally go too deep, and then used the fluted blade of what amounted to a tiny hacksaw, cutting quickly through the skull, following the marks I had made with my pen. I handed Vicky the flap of bone. She wrapped it in saline-soaked gauze, as Denny DeBroussard's brain met the open air for the first time.

What happened next might or might not have had to do with withdrawal from Diomedes's antipsychotic script, and it might or might not have had to do with the life-changing experience of suddenly being a murderer, of moving from the arena of talk, fantasy, and philosophy, to blood and guts, and life and death. It might also have to do as much with Denny as it did with me, or been the consequences of the intersection of our particular transmissions and receptions.

Whatever the explanation, I was suddenly hit with a memory that didn't belong to me, yet was as strong and clear as my visions of my teacher's shade. Even though I stood in a South Florida operating room with a team of professionals by my side, I was suddenly Denny, in bed, making love with a young brunette. The vision, like the augury I had before removing Spenser Brownfield's hemangioma, was full of intimate, sensuous cues. I sniffed the warm aroma of my lover's hair, while an old-style Victrola blared scratchy jazz. An elevated train rumbled by outside the window. As ecstasy came, my lover's feet locked out, toes pointed up. I rose up like a wave. I heard myself groan in Denny's young, strong voice.

"Oh!" I cried.

"Zee."

Roan's voice floated down from the ceiling. The brunette continued to move beneath me with her eyes closed. I looked around wildly. The jazz fell off key.

"Zee!"

And just like that, I was back in the O.R. Vicky looked deliberately away, but Roan stared at me. He would never tell anyone he had seen me lose touch. Doctors stick up for each other; it's an inviolable code.

"I forgot to tell you something," I said, casting desperately around for a way to cover what had just happened.

"What might that be?"

"Your big bald buddy with the Chihuahua, he burned to death when that bar went down in flames."

Roan looked confused. "What are you talking about?"

"The place blew up. It's all gone, down to the last barstool."

"When did this happen?" he blinked, suddenly not sure who was losing touch, him or me.

"A day or two back."

"I saw that fire on the news," Vicky said, eager to put my apparent fugue behind her.

"I've been on twenty-four seven," Roan muttered. "I'm dead on my feet and out of the loop."

Before I could give them any more detail, Denny made another bid for my attention, and I was back with the brunette, but in the hospital this time. The sheets were bloody, and a set of old fluorescent ceiling lights buzzed. A fresh placenta spilled out of a stainless steel tray on a bedside table. Baby Anita cried in her swaddling clothes. I clapped for joy at the wonderful sound; I felt so proud.

"Zee," Roan said again.

"I could see how Denny called down angels," I said coming back to the present.

"Doctor?" said Vicky.

"Nothing is forever," I said. "Don't ever think that it is."

"Could I know what's going on here?" asked Vicky.

I knew that a third episode would be one too many. I wouldn't be able to brush it off. There would be consequences with my colleagues if Denny took me again. Hearing seemed a dominant sense to Denny, and I needed to raise my auditory barrier so he couldn't break through it.

"Music," I said to Roan.

He hooked my iPod to the boom box on top of his cart. The strains of Steve Miller Band's The Joker filled the room. The pounding bass served as a filter, and I went back to work, hoping it would hold.

The layer of fibrous tissue that contains the brain is called the dura mater. I could see the swollen mass of the hematoma pulsing beneath it with each beat of the heart. The movement was more visible than usual because of the quantity of blood drawn to the injury.

"It took one hell of a bump to do this," Vicky murmured.

I began to excise the pathological wall of capillaries Denny's body had erected to wall off the injury. I used cautery calipers to burn the small vessels closed and reduce bleeding. Vicky continuously irrigated the surgical field with sterile saline, and kept suction going. We filled bag after disposable bag with fluid from Denny's brain. Roan kept his eye on the monitor, constantly evaluating Denny's vital signs, his level of consciousness, the level of the various drugs in his system, how much air was getting through.

The procedure was essentially a clean-up job. When it was done, I covered the brain again with the opaque curtain of the dura, and stitched it back in place using permanent silk thread. Denny's tissues were not as pliable as when he fought at the Battle of Verdun or listened to a radio broadcast of the Wright Brother's successful flight. Little gaps developed around my stitches. When I was in school we used the dura from cadavers for the job, but it turned out that fatal viruses like Mad Cow Disease hid inside the transplanted tissue. These days I used a cellulose sponge, which in time would be reabsorbed.

The iPod treated us to Bob Dylan's "Idiot Wind" as Vicky began to clean up. I put Denny's skull flap back in place and used a kit of small plates and screws to attach it. Relieved that I had avoided another episode, I was just closing the shaven skin over the bone when John Khalsa stuck his head in the operating room door.

"May I see you a minute?"

"Little busy right now," I said, gesturing at Denny on the table.

"Looks from here like you're done."

Some surgeons do a continuous suture, because it is faster and smoother to the touch. Even though it takes longer, I favor the interrupted style because it doesn't unravel. Very deliberately, I did six more individual stitches, closing up Denny's head. I gathered the thread together, snipped all the ends off in one cut. Then, and only then, I went to the door.

"What do you need?" I asked my boss.

"The police are raising the Petrossov boy's bones."

"Thank God."

"Did you have anything to do with it?"

"I certainly hope so," I said.

"You hope so?"

"That's right."

"Then go update your resume."

34

Throughout my childhood, Wu Tie Mei drew freely from Jewish, Taoist, and Buddhist sources to nourish my religious beliefs. In typical, practical, Chinese fashion, she saw such a synthesis as necessary and natural, and cited examples from history: the combination of wild and woolly Taoism with the socially responsible teachings of Confucius, the successful importation of Buddhism from India, the way Christianity and Islam grew out of Judaism and the works of the Gnostics. As I matured, I came to regard Taoism as a guide to the how of life, and sought answers to the why of life in Jewish and Buddhist doctrine.

In the short time since the transit of Rafik Petrossov's soul, my belief system had become much more complicated. For one thing, I now definitely believed in life after death. Since Wu Tie Mei's reappearance, I also believed in ghosts. To top it off, I was seriously entertaining the idea I was a Chinese warrior come back to life. I had been comforted by the promise of moving in the right karmic direction, but the death of Simba George shook me deeply. I felt terribly guilty. More, I was terrified I would be caught, tried, and jailed. Last but not least, I worried that despite the fact I hadn't intended murder, I might still be doomed to return as a cockroach.

When I closed my eyes, Simba appeared. Waving his arm around, he joined Wu Tie Mei, Jordan Jones, Orson Cartwright, Gloria Brownfield, little Rafik Petrossov, and my birth mother, Helen. This army of souls also intruded when I tried to sleep, and hovered at the periphery of my visual field as I rode my motorcycle to lunch at my father's new residence, Rachel Pearl's Miami Beach condominium.

Rachel set lunch out on the balcony. The light was beautiful despite the midday sun, softened by the moisture in the air the way it can be in South Florida on days so humid even porcelain sweats. I sat down and began the conversation by asking her where a child of rich Fort Lauderdale parents was most likely to attend private school.

"Pine Crest," she said.

Ignoring the soup and brisket of beef, my father reached over and helped himself to a big slice of poppy-seed cake.

"Look at the oinker," said Rachel.

"Why don't you wait on that, Dad?"

"I'm still on my honeymoon."

"You know he doesn't exercise," Rachel confided.

My father drew himself up. "Of course I exercise."

"Shuffling cards doesn't count," his new wife put in.

"Dad used to be very athletic," I told her. "He rode horses back in Russia. He had a regular street gang back in Lvov."

"Horses," Rachel sniffed. "Motorcycles, more like it."

My father leaned back and made an expansive gesture toward the salubrious view, which for me recalled nothing so much as the sight of Simba George's arm sailing off the balcony to leave bloody streaks on the sand below.

"Motorcycles," my father sneered.

"He feigns disdain but the truth is otherwise," I said.

"They're dangerous," he shook his head.

"So you ride along the beach on Sundays," said Rachel. "I can't imagine such low speeds are dangerous. How romantic it would be! Here, have some more brisket."

"Thank you. And Dad? If you eat any more of that cake you'll get high on poppies and drift off dreaming of winter among the larch trees and of a rainbow on the frost."

"A poet and a doctor," said Rachel."

"Since you love me so much, can I ask you to call Pine Crest for me?"

"Whatever for?" she blinked.

"A young boy died on my operating table," I said. "In his last waking moment he asked that I tell his girlfriend how much he loved her. I promised I would, but I never did get her name. Perhaps if you call pretending to be the boy's grandmother, it would go easier than getting into a medical conversation."

"What a conscience," said Rachel. "That cinches it, Asher. I should have married your son."

"He's not easygoing like I am," said my father, heading for the living room. "He makes judgements about everything. Living with him is no picnic. Anyway, I'm going to watch the baseball game."

"He wants me to get a big screen TV," she said when he was gone. "I told him I'd buy him a good pair of walking shoes instead."

Listening to her on the telephone, I decided she could easily talk my father into becoming a marathon runner. The deceptive web she wove around Pine Crest's dean of students was a work of sheer genius. Rafik had been named for her own grandfather, she confided breathlessly, and she was in possession of a small locket that bore his initials. She knew that the boy favored a girl at school and she wanted the girl to have the piece so that her grandson would always be remembered.

"I'm in awe," I said when she hung up and wrote down the girl's name and number.

"You owe me a ride on your motorcycle," she smiled.

On TV, the bases were loaded. Dad didn't even notice when I left. I called Rafik's girlfriend, Bimini, when I got downstairs to my bike. I had a line worked out in case one of her parents answered, but I got lucky and the girl herself picked up on the fourth ring.

"My name is Xenon Pearl," I said. "I'm the doctor who tried to save Rafik's life."

There was a silence so long I had time to think about John Khalsa. I wondered if he was interviewing anyone for my job.

"I guess you're not too good at what you do," Bimini said at last.

"I wish I were better."

"Why are you calling me?"

"I'd like to meet you."

"What for? Rafik's dead."

"I have some questions about him."

"What kind of questions?"

"I don't think his death was an accident," I said.

"Of course it wasn't."

"Will you talk to me about him?" I asked.

Bimini treated me to another long silence. "I'll meet you for ice cream," she said at last. "You're buying. And hurry. I'm supposed to be grounded. If my mom finds me gone, she'll eat me alive."

35

The ice cream parlor Bimini identified was in Wilton Manners, a Lauderdale suburb increasingly popular with the gay community. It was forty minutes away, but I got in the left lane hunkered down behind the windshield, cranked the throttle open, and made impossible time. I took off my helmet, shook out my hair, settled the bike onto its side stand and went through the door.

Fifties music was playing. A full wall mural showed air crash victims Richie Valens, Buddy Holly, and the Big Bopper crooning and strumming guitars under a great white, Vegas moon. There were jukeboxes in the booths and an endless bar next to ice cream in bins beneath frosty glass and red leatherette barstools held up by chrome pedestals. The tabletops reminded me of my grandfather's kitchen: pure 1975 Formica. I identified Bimini at once. She was sitting alone in a booth at the back, a skateboard on the seat beside her.

"No way you're a doctor," she said when I slid in across from her.

I took out my hospital ID and slid it across the table. "It's nice to meet you too."

"Surgery," she read.

"Brains and spines," I said.

"Oh yeah? How can you be a brain doctor and ride a motorcycle? Are you thick or something?"

"I get that a lot."

"And the haircut? They let doctors wear long hair like that?"

"I wear a paper cap when I'm working."

"What kind of a name is Xenon?"

"You can call me Zee."

"Yeah? You're kinda hot, you know that, Zee?"

She had a blonde ponytail and a pierced tongue and about five hundred studs in her ears, nose and lips. Her clothes looked like she'd taken them off a homeless woman. In ten more years and with a new wardrobe, she might be hot too.

"Good to hear," I said.

"Before I talk to you anymore, I need a banana split. I like chocolate chip mint ice cream, butterscotch syrup and rainbow sprinkles."

"Coming up," I said, and moved off to the counter.

She said nothing until the first bite was in her mouth. After that, she said a lot. "Do you know the difference between the *via negativa* and the *via affirmativa*?" she asked.

I took a few chocolate sprinkles from the rainbow and put them on my tongue. "How old are you?" I asked.

"Old enough to have read Alan Watts."

"Come on. I can't believe that."

"Old enough to have smoked pot, too."

"Oh boy."

"Oh boy what, Doctor I-ride-a-motorcycle-even-though-I-work-on-brains?"

"Two paths to enlightenment," I said. "The first through long practice, the second through instant realization."

She nodded. I stared at her nose.

"Quit looking at me like that."

"I like your freckles. You're older than he was, aren't you?"

"So what? You didn't know him. It wasn't an age thing. He was incredible. My parents hated him because of his family."

"I'd like to hear more," I said.

"You're weird to call me, you know that, right?"

"You're not the first person to say that."

She smiled. "I'm fourteen," she said. "But it wouldn't have mattered if I was sixteen. Raffy was the coolest and the sharpest kid at school. Everybody knew that. He was going to be another Rasputin. That's why they killed him."

"I need a chocolate shake," I said, moving off to get one.

"It figures you'd do chocolate," she said when I came back. "It's totally addicting to the brain."

"You said someone killed Rafik."

"I also said he was going to be another Rasputin. Do you even know who that is?"

"Mystical monk and advisor to the last Russian tsar," I said.

"Advisor to his wife, actually. The tsarina."

"Rasputin went into trances. A prince shot him in the snow."

Bimini nodded and took a huge bite of the mint ice cream. Some of it dribbled down her chin. She caught it with an anteater's tongue, showing me a silver stud shaped like a large screw. "That's movie stuff," she said. "What's really interesting is that he had visions. He saw the future and had conversations with God. He knew he was going to die."

"Are you talking about Rasputin or Rafik Petrossov?"

"Both, I guess. Raffy had influence on the people around him."

"I've met a lot of special people lately. I'd say he was one of them."

"Raffy was powerful, for a kid. We had ESP. He could send me messages with his mind."

"Me too," I said.

"I'm not kidding."

"I'm not either, although he was in really bad shape when he got to me."

She pushed her ice cream away. "Oversharing," she said.

"Do you have any idea who killed him?"

"You ever watch TV cop shows?"

"Not much."

"You read mystery novels?" she pursued.

"When I find time."

"Great, a doctor who doesn't have time to read. What about thrillers in the theater? You see those?"

"What's your point?"

"Anybody who watches TV knows that when a kid gets hurt, ninety percent of the time it's someone close to him that does the hurting."

"His parents say it was a hit-and-run."

"Sure they do. Listen, you say you two had a connection. Did he say anything about me?"

"Right at the end he told me you were the only one who understood him. He said you were plugged in."

"Plugged in?" she repeated. "He said that?"

"Totally."

She suddenly looked like she was going to cry. She pushed her ice cream away with a shove. I caught it before it hit the floor, cupping it in my hand so I didn't spill a drop. The medication was leaving my system, and I was moving better. Maybe it was the desire to redeem myself after Simba's murder. I couldn't take anything slow anymore, not even casual movement. Everything counted now, and it was all somehow martial.

"Good reflexes," she said.

"I was wicked at dodgeball."

"You know what he meant by plugged in, don't you?" she said. "He was talking about the stream, the matrix, the river of consciousness."

"You can't be fourteen."

"Everyone says that."

"Was his sister plugged in too?"

"Galina? She takes ballet, for God's sake. She doesn't know anything. Raffy loved her the way I love my pet hamster."

"I met Galina. She seemed nice."

"Everybody's nice," she said. "Until they're not. Do I have any ice cream on my face? Any sign of food at all?"

"You're clean."

"His parents said he fell while riding his bike."

She laughed out loud at that one. "Right. He was better with that bike than you are with brains. He did twirls and jumps and ledges and tricks."

"Did you see him argue with his parents a lot?"

"Argue? You don't argue with a big-time criminal. You know that's what his old man is, right? Big-time as in he's a monster."

"I didn't know you knew that."

"Everyone at school knows. But Raffy loved him anyway. He was mystical and he was special, but he was no match for dear old dad. Life is well and truly fucked up, I'll tell you that, Dr. Zee-who-for-sure-has-secret-plans-of-his-own."

I scribbled my address and phone numbers on a napkin and handed them to her. "No secret plans," I said lightly. "I'm just trying to find out what really happened. If you think of anything else I should know, call me."

"I think you should go back to medical school," she said. "That way, maybe you can save the next kid."

36

Wanda swung by my house again the next morning. "Got time to take a ride?" she asked.

"My wrist still hurts from shooting that cannon of yours."

"I'm sure your wrist has been through hell lately."

I tried to read between the lines. Her curiosity made me more and more nervous. If she suspected me of swordplay, I wondered why she hadn't taken me in for formal questioning. "What's that supposed to mean?" I asked.

"I just figure wielding those blades must lead to strain and injury, carpal tunnel, whatever."

"The scalpel is the tool of my trade."

"The scalpel. Yeah. That's what I meant."

"So where are we off to?"

"Broward County Main Jail."

I knew everything depended upon how well I controlled my reaction. "A little sightseeing?"

"I figured it would be good for you to see what happens to violent offenders."

We had an odd little dance going. Wanda didn't know what I knew, and I didn't know what she knew, so we moved, eyes on each other, but not touching. Perhaps she figured there couldn't be that many swordsmen with medical skills out there—perhaps she just wanted to get to know me better. Perhaps it was a gambit with no downside for her; perhaps it was a test of nerve for me.

Inside the jail building, she talked her way past a captain downstairs by telling him I was a doctor here for an interview at the infirmary. Then she took me eight floors up to the top of the building. Squinting through the slit windows I could just make out the Andrews Avenue drawbridge. I could see the New River, too, the same water I crossed on my way to my grandfather's house. Straining in the other direction, Riverwalk came into view, a shopping center built for its views and still chasing customers after being open for nearly ten years.

"They tore down eleven historic buildings to erect that nightmare," Wanda said when she saw me looking. "There was plenty of energy in those old buildings, and now it's turned to bad juju for the place, bad karma."

"You believe in karma?"

"You can't be a cop and not believe it," she said. "Everyone in this jail had it coming from this life or another."

"You buy reincarnation too? How did that happen?"

"I learned it on the street. You have to believe people come back. There are too many coincidences otherwise, too many repetitions of the same acts of violence and kindness, the same seemingly impossibly unique twists of character."

"You think people keep their essential traits down through the ages?" She looked at me curiously.

"Way I understand it, you learn the lessons you need to learn until you're all done learning."

Down the hallway I could see the prisoners clearly through the Plexiglas cell walls. Most ignored us; a few licked their lips and made obscene gestures at Wanda. She brushed a lock of hair from her forehead in a very feminine gesture.

"What do you have to do to earn one of these lovely solitary cells?" I asked.

"Some folks get to jail and figure they've got nothing to lose. They don't understand the system, aren't aware they have a good chance for parole simply because we're overcrowded. Figuring their lives are all done, they give in to the urge to rape a cellmate or stick a fork in a rival's throat. That's when they end up in here. Of course, bad behavior isn't the only route to solitary. Bad cops get put in here for their own protection— there's nothing an inmate loves better than to torture the cop who put him away—and so do certain special visitors."

"What makes a visitor special?"

"Psychopaths who are a threat to the prison community," she said. "I imagine that would include the occasional martial arts whiz. Of course, most martial arts guys give themselves away with grunts and stances, and so cops just shoot 'em."

"Sometimes meeting violence with violence is the only way," I said.

"Practical," she said, keeping her eyes on me, "but not necessarily legal."

"There's legal and there's just," I said. "Sometimes they are one and the same, sometimes they aren't."

"The law is the servant of justice."

"Should be," I said. "I'm not so sure it is."

"People do violence out of a desire to survive," she said.

"They also do it out of passion, greed, anger, hatred, and lust."

She stopped walking. "And then there are those who think they've got justice figured out," she said. "You know, the guy who sees a million injustices and then just wakes up one day and figures it's his job to even the score."

"I would figure the system would appreciate some help."

She stepped closer to me, so close I could feel her breath on my face.

"No system is perfect," she said. "Every cop knows that even if we gave everyone a nice beach house like yours and free food for life, there would always be some peckerhead who wanted to beat his wife. Still, it's better to have a system than a free for all. Without a system, there are no checks and balances. Without a system, everyone's a vigilante."

"This place stinks," I said.

Wanda shrugged. "Nervous sweat, full toilets, disinfectant. You get used to it. It's worst up here, a little bit better one floor down where they keep the sex offenders, a little bit better than that on the floor below that, where they put the armed robbers, muggers, murderers, and assault artists."

"Assault artists," I said. "I like that."

"Of course you do. Now let's keep up your cover and go see some patients."

We took the elevator down to the third floor infirmary. Wanda introduced me to the staff doctor, a thin, hyperactive, nervous woman named Martinsson. She reminded me of a darker Gloria Brownfield, and seemed impressed by my credentials. The male nurse assisting her was a Guamanian Chamoru named Limitiaco. He had tattoos below his ears and looked like he could wrestle a Boeing 747 to the ground. Me being a neurosurgeon didn't seem to impress him at all.

"We only have three patients right now," Martinsson said. "All of them put themselves here."

"Self-mutilations," said Wanda. "Some lunatics don't feel pain. That's why I carry a big gun."

"There's a very particular neuropathology to these violent offenders," Martinsson went on. "They really do have a sensory deficit. Their insensible world is hell to them. They hurt themselves to escape it."

"Cutting themselves up is better than feeling nothing," Limitiaco put in. "Least that's what they say. Seeing what they do to themselves, I'm not so sure."

The first patient was a Cuban gangster who had repeatedly and purposely slammed his cell door on his ankle.

"He'll never walk straight again," said Martinsson.

The Cuban was sleeping, but fitfully. He turned, and lost something from his pocket. I picked it up.

"His tracking card," said Wanda. "Any time a prisoner is moved, he has to carry it with him."

"What's that red thing stuck to it?"

"A bingo sticker. It means he has AIDS. Kinda changes the way the deputies deal with him, makes them alert to scratches and bites."

I had operated on any number of AIDS patients. Despite the gloves and the goggles and the filters and other precautions, it was always nerve-racking. Even so, I wasn't one of those doctors who turned AIDS patients away.

I moved to see the patient in the second bed. He was a black man with short hair going gray at the temples. His features were distinguished. He might have been a college professor. He was awake, but he wouldn't look at me.

"I'm Dr. Pearl," I said.

"Jewel of a guy, I'm sure," he said, staring at the ceiling.

"Never heard that one before."

"This is Mister Doorite," said Limitiaco. "Real name, not nickname, although I haven't seen him do a damn thing right, yet."

"His gut's a hardware store," Martinsson added. "These killers do that sometimes. They eat whatever they can get their hands on, looking to get sick. The administration here thinks it's because they want to come here to the infirmary, as if it was some kind of palace down here. Nobody seems to understand these are suicide attempts."

"More violent offenders kill themselves than are put to death by the criminal justice system," Wanda said. "Sadly, the same is true of cops."

"The sex offenders are the worst," said Martinsson. "Sometimes they shove pens up the urethra, use the tubes to administer ink, soap, solvents, anything they can get their hands on. They end up with bladder infections, kidney failure and death. Sometimes we have to amputate the penis, which is what they're after in the first place. When they ingest foreign items we don't usually operate unless there is a threat of intestinal perforation. That's why Mr. Doorite is here. We had to go in and remove the single-edged razor blades he ate."

"Where did he get razor blades?" asked Wanda.

Martinsson shrugged. "From someone in the physical plant, presumably in return for sexual favors. We don't know who his connection was, but we'll figure it out. Some members of the support staff here get carried away with the prison black market and make a fortune. We catch them all in the end. We performed the surgery laparoscopically. He should be out of here in three days."

In response to that news, Doorite glared at her.

"Why did you do that to yourself?" I asked him.

"I choked an old lady to death behind the church and took her donation money. When I had her throat in my hands, I felt alive. I swallow blades: I feel alive again. Nothing in between, see? No life in all that time."

Listening to him, I realized I had felt that for a long time before Rafik flew away on me, and a long time before Tie Mei came back. Between surgeries, I was a dead man keeping his body sharp. Now, with my new activities and a better understanding of who I was, I could keep the intervals shorter, and even forgive myself for murder.

"Are you all right?" Wanda asked, stepping close to me again.

"Sure," I said. "Sad story, that's all."

The third prisoner cleared his throat. He was unkempt and wore a five o'clock shadow. He fidgeted with his sheets, kneading them and then dropping them away. His fingers were long and his hands were bursting with veins.

"That is Mister Ferdman," Limitiaco said. "He is with us on account of a seizure he induced by swallowing a roach trap."

"Doorite did it because he got tired of waiting for that guy with the sword," Ferdman said.

"What guy is that?" I asked.

"He means the vigilante," Martinsson explained. "The word came in from the street, and now all the inmates are talking about him. Mister Ferdman is off to the Federal Pen in the morning: death row for the rape and murder of four coeds on Fort Lauderdale Beach last year."

"You remember the Spring Break Murders, don't you?" Wanda added. "They happened down the beach from your house."

"That vigilante is God's angel calling," said Ferdman. "No matter what you do he'll come and cut you up. Most guys in here want him more than a boatload of pussy."

"I need to get going now," I said. "I'm supposed to be on call."

We said our goodbyes and got in the elevator. "Medical examiner's report came in," said Wanda. "Seems he agrees with you. He thinks Rafik Petrossov was beaten to death."

"Of course he was. Why did you wait so long to tell me?"

"I was getting to it."

"So will you arrest his parents now?"

"He may have been beaten, but we don't know by whom. We need evidence."

"Evidence," I repeated. "The kid's a sack of busted bones."

"Trust the system," said Wanda. "It's the best you can do."

37

I rode back to Grandpa Lou's and got him to give me a lift home with all my weapons. I didn't see much point in hiding them anymore. Wanda had her convictions and I had my enemies and it wouldn't do to face them empty-handed. When I got to the house, I saw the word "Sold" diagonally pasted across Olivia Spode's real estate shingle.

"She's probably smart," remarked Grandpa Lou. "The market is still rising, but one good storm or another rise in interest rates could cool things down."

"Only a fool waits for top dollar," I said.

"Why take the weapons home?"

"Roofer around and all that. They'll be fine. Coast is clear at home now."

I waited through the night, thinking that because of the medical examiner's report, the stalemate between me and Khalsa would somehow break and I would be put back on the duty roster. Unable to sleep, I kept a vigil around my home, waiting for Petrossov's dogs. The medical report would stir them, too.

Jordan showed up for a visit, and I was suddenly desperate for all the time I could get with her before things started to explode.

"You paddle your new boat yet?"

"I'm a bit crazy, but I'll get to it."

"Glad to see me?"

"You have no idea."

"Tell me."

"Gladder than a rose about the rain," I said.

"Not bad, but you can do better."

"Gladder than a wave at the tug of the moon."

"Getting better," she grinned

"Gladder than a racehorse at the twitch of a crop."

"How did I know whips were going to creep into the conversation?"

"I'm kinked and I can't help it," I said.

We stayed in each other's arms for a while, under the dew from the big Banyan tree in my front yard. A jogger went by, wiped his glasses when he saw us, took a better look and smiled. A young girl on a bicycle followed after that, pulled by a Malamute, the kind of dog that spends a Florida summer on top of an air conditioning vent dreaming of the Arctic.

"I'm kind of fired," I said.

"I beg your pardon?"

"As in I lost my job. Argument with the powers that be."

"This isn't about drinking, is it, Zee?"

"Drinking? God no. I haven't touched a drop lately. I told you, that's not my problem. It's politics. I'll work it out."

"If you've got time off, come away with me. There's a hammer-in a couple of hours north of here. We'll have a great time."

I decided yes in about two seconds flat. I took a quick shower, threw some clothes in a duffel and we were off. When we got to the turnpike it was still lit by headlights. As she drove, Jordan explained that a hammer-in was a gathering of bladesmiths.

"They happen all over the country," she said. "Arkansas has a big one, and Tannehill Park, Georgia has another. I used to go all the time with my father. This will be the first time I've screwed up the courage to go without him. As a fan of sharp steel, I promise you'll have a great time."

We hit a rest stop and shared a sticky cinnamon bun for breakfast. An hour later, we were in Lake Wales, a small town just west of the spine of the state. The event was at someone's farm. Pickup trucks were trickling in. There was dust on every surface and soot in the air.

"Gas forges make that whooshing roar you hear," Jordan said happily. "Coal forges make the dust."

She took me around. Vendors were setting up small tents and lean-tos, placing their wares on tables in the grass, or laying them out in the back of pick-up trucks. I'd been expecting knives and swords, but what I saw instead were smithing and forging supplies.

"There's an informal show at the end," Jordan said. "Most folks here are members of the American Blademaker's Guild. They come to share ideas and to learn. There are a couple of competitions. If you do well, you get points toward a national cutting championship."

By early afternoon at least a hundred people had shown up. There were "NO ALCOHOL" signs all over the place, but I was suspicious of the clear liquid in Mason jars I saw folks carrying.

"Moonshine," Jordan grinned. "This is the South, a world away from the tourist camp called South Florida."

Power hammers started up, air hammers too, and of course the distinctive clang of a hand hammer hitting hot steel and anvil, a sound like no other. The party got noisier. I heard the ring of steel on anvils. We went to watch a forging presentation. Even without knowing anything about the subject, I could see the presenter was a master smith. He greeted Jordan, catching her eye right in the middle of the seminar.

"Jones!" he bellowed.

Jordan blushed. There were a few people in the crowd who seemed to see her for the first time. Simultaneously, I seemed to see them for the first time as well. What I had previously taken for a crowd of grizzly mountain men, now looked to be doctors, businessmen and lawyers relaxing to engage a hobby alongside full-time blade makers who in another era and another culture would have been artisans revered by emperors and kings. There was expertise, there was money, and there were also some tight-lipped people struggling to break into the club.

"I used to have long hair," Jordan whispered to me. "That's why they don't know me. And maybe my jeans weren't so tight."

"For those bozos out there who haven't figured it out, this is Thaddeus Jones' little girl," the master smith announced.

It was as if someone had turned on a switch. I hadn't realized what a reputation Jordan's father enjoyed. The group swarmed around her, taking attention away from the master smith's demonstration. There were lots of questions about how Thaddeus died, and I felt badly when Jordan admitted it had been from cancer, that he had gone slowly and painfully. He had spent his very last living last hours at the forge, Jordan told them, and she had found his body beside it. The master smith broke off his presentation and came over.

"You can't know how much we all miss your dad," he said.

"Oh yes I can."

"A man like him should have had a better end."

"He weighed ninety pounds when the cancer finally took him," she said.

"Jordan's taken over his shop," I said. "She's making swords herself now."

This was the critical moment. There were no other female makers there. I saw glances and I saw nods but no smart remarks were forthcoming. A few of the men asked if she had brought any work.

"You'll see it at the cutting competition," she said.

After that, the men were avuncular. One fellow told me I had better treat her right or answer to him. I quaked in a suitably cowed fashion and mumbled and groveled a bit. I broke bits off of a very bitter, dark, Venezuelan chocolate bar in my pocket, and snuck them when nobody was looking. We took in a couple of short seminars, one on the construction of the folding knife, another on art knife design. It was beautiful to see Jordan blossom in her element. A couple of times she jumped in with a pointer about forging, slipping on a leather apron and showing her dexterity in handling glowing steel.

There was a party planned for that evening but the weather soured and a storm moved in. We helped a couple of guys secure a tent. Some others climbed into their trucks to sleep. We went off to a motel on the outskirts of town.

The storm passed, but our lovemaking that night was one long tropical fever. We threw bedclothes around, overturned the coffee table, trashed a pair of lamps, twisted the mattress off its frame, caused two pieces of hanging artwork to fall, tangled up the queen bedclothes until they looked no bigger than a face towel, and finally lay giggling and panting in the semi-darkness. Someone lit an M-80 in the motel parking lot.

"Fireworks," Jordan panted, climbing on top of me. "How perfect."

Suddenly, she had her knife out. I can't even say I saw where it came from. Perhaps she had it hiding under the pillow. She held it to my throat. I felt my mouth go dry.

"For some reason, I bet you can get out of this tight spot," she said.

"What makes you think I want to," I bluffed.

"What's this? Shrinkage? Don't tell me the tough guy is scared?"

She made a tiny cut at the base of my neck. I felt the blood seep out. She darted forward and took it off with a quick lick. She searched my eyes. "Too kinky for you?"

I pushed my head back into the bed, momentarily making a space between my flesh and the blade, then grabbed her knife hand, trapping the blade in place. I rotated her wrist in three dimensions, creating a painful lock, and slowly applied pressure. She tried to wriggle out of it by following the circle I was making, a surprisingly good strategy for a beginner. Her tongue came out in pain, but she didn't yield. I pressed harder. She came up onto her knees and used her thighs to fight the lock, twisting her torso. I followed her twist until I had the knife up and away, then around and between her breasts.

"Don't cut me there," she panted.

"I wouldn't dream of it."

I took the knife with my other hand, closed it, and tossed it onto the floor. She rolled forward and put her legs around my neck to choke me. I forced my hands up between her legs, and wedged my way out of her sweet place.

She jumped off the bed after that, but rather than going for the knife, she put her dukes up. I went for the prize. She shot one after the other, a roundhouse and an uppercut, and was quick enough to graze my ear as I feinted and dodged until finally bowling her over. She went limp as if to submit, but the moment I loosened my grip on her wrists, she was at me again, using her knees against my abdominals. I listened to her breathing, figuring to wear her out, but she was fit and she kept going much longer than I expected. Finally, I started to laugh.

"You think that's funny?" she said, suddenly exploding against me again.

She caught me unaware and I got an elbow up into my chin for my trouble. I heard the squeal of enamel as my teeth clashed, barely missing my tongue. Roughly, I turned her over, yanked her toward me, and made my case.

She started to gasp as I thrust, and then the gasp became cries, and then a shudder. Slowly, she slid off me.

"Beg for mercy," she grinned.

"Please, no more."

She rubbed a breast against my lips.

"I can't hear you."

"Please, don't do that some more."

She giggled.

"Wow," I said. "That knife bit was a first. Not for you, I bet."

"I'll never tell. But you were nice. You controlled yourself and didn't hurt me."

"You're too tough for me, is why."

She gave me a long, deep kiss. "I wish my father could have met you," she said wistfully. "I've been thinking about him a lot. People really respected him. I know your background is in the Chinese arts, but his connection to Japan was incredible. He used to tell me the story of the Battle of Sekigahara, about the warring lords and the rise of the shogun. After the Country At War Period the code of the Samurai deepened. It grew to be about more than fighting for your lord. Samurai became intellectuals. They were expected to learn poetry and art and history and letters. The code they developed became Dad's own. It held loyalty and honor in the highest regard, but also the concept of balance. Nobody lived by his principles the way he did. Nobody outside of Japan made swords that way either."

"The idea of balance came from China," I said. "Social responsibility came from Confucius, and yin/yang theory from the *Book of Changes*, the *I-Ching*. The Taoist sage Lao Tzu talked constantly about the harmonious interplay of opposing forces."

"That's a good description of the way Dad made swords," she said. "I wish there was a single one left to show you, but he sold them to pay bills just as fast as he could forge. I used to ask him to put one aside but he always said his next sword was his best sword. He didn't get attached to them. It was all about the process for him."

"Neurosurgery is like that," I covered her hands with my own. "People think that outcome is everything, but focusing on the outcome you want is not the best way to achieve it. You put your heart and soul into the job at hand and pay attention to the details. Those details can make the difference in a patient's IQ points after recovery, in gait and coordination, also in whether the patient keeps or loses memories. The work is delicate; but in important ways it is also its own reward."

"You had your heart and soul into saving that Russian boy, didn't you?"

"He died quickly," I said. "My strongest feelings developed after the fact, when I had time to fully understand what his potential was, what the world had lost, and what I had really witnessed in the O.R."

"Is it possible you let suffering get to you too much?"

"It's not something I can control. I'm just wired that way. I saved turtles from the road when I was a kid, stepped on limping ants to put them out of misery, took a raccoon to the vet and risked rabies to do it, always read the looks on the faces of the people around me and knew they were sad even though they tried to hide it. There's sadness everywhere, it's the human condition, awareness of the passage of time, of what we're going to lose, of the fact we're going to die. I used to lie awake at night angry at God, even yelling up at him for making people sick."

"Your mother," Jordan said gently.

"Yes; but not just her."

"But you stepped on the ant. That doesn't fit with the rest."

"If I could have done ant surgery, I would have. Using my shoe was the best I could do."

"I notice your shoes are always shined."

"Yeah, I've got a thing about that."

"So much caring can run you down. You have to care for yourself as well."

"You wouldn't say that if Rafik was your kid," I said. "Nowhere is it written that I am in any way more important than my patients."

"You are to me," she sighed.

We cuddled. I wanted to tell her that my way of caring for myself was to care for others. Instead I reached up and stroked her hair. Delicately, I traced the bones of her skull with my fingers. I wanted to know every detail of her, to commit the sutures and curves of her to permanent and indelible memory. A little later, while she napped, I did a circuit of the parking lot performing Bear Walking, a Taoist technique to restore seminal essence, *jing*, through stimulation of the kidneys, and breathing, and intention. The techniques were effective, as were certain other things I have come to practice and to know.

She wrapped her heels around me when I returned, locking them at the middle of my back. "Sleep now," she giggled. "You're going to need your strength in the morning."

I smiled and drifted off into a rare deep sleep. In slumberland, I met Thaddeus Jones; he liked me despite my dark secret, maybe because he could see into my heart.

38

Later that night, a noise in the parking lot woke me. I turned on the bathroom light and let it play gently over Jordan's sleeping form. I found that by opening and closing the door, I could moderate the glow and create mysterious avenues of darkness around the bed. Gazing at Jordan's lovely body stretched out in the bed, I had the stunning realization that the short piece of life I had already lived with her was better than any romance in my dreams.

"Don't you have anything better to do?" she asked, a few hours later, when I sat on the closed commode and watched her shave her long legs in the shower.

"Absolutely not."

She rolled her eyes then, and again when I watched her apply her makeup: the flick and dab of lipstick, the application of base powder, eyeliner and mascara. She thought her strong, straight eyebrows made her look masculine, and she plucked them with a vengeance. "I've never let anyone sit where you're sitting," she said.

"I'm honored. Watching you is a huge turn-on."

"You're crazy. And by the way, I watched you too. You say you hardly sleep, but you didn't seem to have any problem last night."

We ate some stale rolls and drank some bad coffee at motel reception, then drove back to the event.

"It's the start of the cutting competition," she said. "Knives only, no swords, but I play anyway because the points make my reputation and my reputation sells blades."

She showed me a Bowie she'd made, a reproduction of an antique blade made by one Daniel Searles, and presented by Resin Bowie to Colonel Fowler at the Alamo. The overall shape was that of a large kitchen knife, but Jordan's Damascus was beyond glorious, with a rainbow pattern of wavy lines running the length of the blade and a handle of dark and lustrous African Mpingo decorated by row after row of meticulously placed silver pins. I'd never seen anything so soulfully perfect—perfection is so often without that elusive dimension—and I said so.

"My father showed me how to make the temper lines," she said. "Looking good isn't enough for the cutting test though, all nine inches of the blade have to cut."

"Are you going to cut with it yourself?"

"The competition requires it. You bring it; you sling it. Those are the rules."

I loved the way Jordan handled the knife. The hundreds of hours she had spent on it showed in every one of her movements. She knew exactly where the balance point was, because she'd held it through so many delicate stages. She knew the blade's sharpness precisely, because she had coaxed it from the steel.

The competition was held inside a big white tent, and comprised several standard requirements and a couple of wild cards thrown in. The first requirement was to cut through a length of one-inch thick dangling hemp. The rope dangled freely, and it had to be severed in a single cut. Jordan was ninth out of twelve people in the competition. It started to rain as her turn came up, and the constant thrumming of the downpour filtered out the ambient noise. The hall was free of human sounds save for the cutting strokes, and I heard her blade go cleanly through the hemp.

The second test required hacking a 2x4 in half; the best time took it. Jordan struggled a little more with that one. Each time she came down on the wood her expression was fiercer. It didn't go as easily for her as Simba's arm had for me, and by the end of the round, she was ranked fourth.

The third standard test was to chop a can of Coca Cola in half with a single stroke. The can was half full and sitting on a table. Knocking it off or spilling the contents was a disqualification. Two contestants went down on this one. Jordan stayed in, kept her rank, and gave a whoop when she did it.

The judges announced the first of the two wild-card challenges. A ping-pong ball was placed on the table.

"One stroke to cut it in half. If the ball is crushed or rolls off the table, you're disqualified," announced one of the judges, the smith who had introduced Jordan to the crowd the day before.

The little plastic orb defeated five out of the first eight contestants who tried it.

"I'm not sure how to do this," Jordan frowned.

"The trick is to be fast," I told her. "Measure the stroke a few times for accuracy, but be careful not to touch it when you do. Slice, but don't chop. If you chop it will flatten. If you slice, it will divide. Once you have the trajectory, just pretend it isn't there, and make your cut."

The contestant before her mashed the ball, and they put out a fresh one for Jordan. I saw beads of sweat on her brow, and an expression that said she was running through my suggestions. "A guy who cuts brains for a living should know how to cut anything, right?"

"Here's what you need to understand about cutting. It's not about violence, it's about facilitation; it's not about imposing your will on something, it's about helping molecules spontaneously divide. When you do this right, you're working at the level of atomic bonds. It's quantum; see? Your intention affects your target through the medium of your sword, and encourages the bonds to surrender. Maybe it's the carbon we share with steel that makes it such a good transmitter. Maybe that's why a good sword, the right sword, feels special to us. Anyway, it doesn't matter how it works; it just matters that it does. Without intention, cutting is more difficult because you're using sheer power; with intention, every cut is a seduction."

She stared at me. "You've really thought this through."

"Not thought. Felt. Lived. Experienced. I've cut through a thousand lifetimes."

"What? What does that mean."

I flushed. I felt something strange in my blood, moving through the vessels like an alien liquid. "I don't know. Nothing. Just remember what I said."

"I'm helping molecules spontaneously divide," she said.

"It's your mantra."

With that, she turned her attention from me to the ball.

"Divide," I heard her whisper, as she took her stroke.

The ball fell apart so effortlessly there was no visible edge. I could tell the judges were impressed. I wasn't. I understood Jordan's skill.

The gooseneck straw was the next wild card. Plastic, it was placed in a hole in the table. The test was to slice it in half above the flexible portion of the straw, one cut, no second chances. The first guy sent the whole straw flying and was disqualified. The second contender made the cut, but the straw was left dangling by a thread. The connection was almost invisibly tenuous, and the judges argued with each other but disqualified the attempt in the end. The only remaining contestants were Jordan and a blonde Viking with a fifty-inch chest. Both of them dissected the straw without a hitch.

"The next wild card to decide the winner," one of the other judges announced.

They had in mind for Jordan and the Viking to cut a wet t-shirt hanging from a hook. As before, the requirement was to cut it through in one stroke. Jordan looked upset at the assignment. We stepped outside for a pow-wow.

"It's wet," she told me quietly. "I've never cut anything wet before."

"The water makes it heavy," I said. "It's actually easier than if it were dry."

"But the wet shirt will grab the blade."

"Just remember to slice," I said. "Use your hips to decrease the radius of the cut as you go. It's a martial arts technique based on proper rotation of the dantian, the hip area. None of these guys will know it."

The rain flattened her hair against her head. Her beautiful bones stood out in relief. I could smell moonshine in the night.

"I'm not sure I can do that."

"Exaggerate the motion by pulling the handle toward you. If you've done it right, you'll bring your wrist almost to your navel at the end. Try it in the air."

She looked at her blade and then back at me, then flicked it out so smoothly we both saw a raindrop split. The judge inside called her name over the loudspeaker and she went inside with a confident smile. The Viking was using a curved blade, almost a kukri. The shape of his blade did much to make every cut a slice, and when he completed his try successfully, the crowd whooped it up. A few die-hards clandestinely raised Mason jars in tribute. Someone belted out a harmonica tune.

All was silent when Jordan went up, quiet when a fresh shirt was hung. She reached out, felt the shirt between her fingers, drew back, set her stance, pulled back her knife and shook her hips to loosen them.

She cut with a cry. It didn't sound like her. Half the shirt fell to the ground.

The bladesmiths clapped in thunderous, rhythmic applause. There might have been a thousand people in the tent. There might have been ten thousand. "Jor-dan, Jor-dan," they cried.

"The next test is the last," the judge announced. "If there is no clear winner, we will declare a tie."

The challenge was to slice a feather, and it was a challenge indeed.

"I wish you could do this one for me," Jordan told me.

"Stay with your slice. Be a human corkscrew."

She looked at me blankly. I put my hands on her hips.

"Spiral down as you cut," I said, pressing down on her hips to turn her. "That's the way to get the cleanest slice. The corkscrew is a spiral, and the spiral is nature's answer to every question."

"I understand the slice, but you've lost me with the corkscrew."

"When the screw enters the cork it has to go in straight to avoid hitting the neck of the bottle, right?"

She nodded.

"Great. Now I'm talking about your body here, not the blade. I need you to stand as straight as the corkscrew, so don't bend at the back."

"All right."

"Now, to engage the threads, the corkscrew has to turn, not just press. You follow me?"

She showed me that she did by turning her waist,

"Yes. Now, to avoid simply making a divot in the cork, you have to push down on the corkscrew as you turn it."

"Like this?" she asked, turning and bending her knees.

"Yes, but the turning and the sinking have to happen simultaneously. That way, your slice will have a vertical dimension, which in turn will stop the edge of your blade from pushing the feather out of the way."

Her eyes widened. "I think I see what you're saying."

I moved her through the spiral again, pressing and turning, and then again, until she mastered the movement.

A moment later, the Viking made his cut, but left the feather intact.

The crowd grew very quiet. Jordan signaled she was ready. The judge blew the feather out of his hand. It floated in the air for what seemed like a six-day work week. Finally, Jordan aimed and cut.

The blade met the feather, and for a long moment, it wasn't clear what had happened. Then two little specks of down appeared over Jordan's head. They glowed like little embers in the lantern light and then began floating down.

The audience let loose, making an earthquake in the ground. Jordan turned to me, elated.

"I love you," I called, but the crowd loved her too, and they drowned me out.

39

Any true martial art is a ladder. On the first rung, you gain physical strength and flexibility. When you reach the second rung, you learn to breathe, and begin to cultivate qi, that life force that keeps you young and empowers you to best pathogens and stave off the degenerative diseases of aging. Special abilities manifest at the third rung, including: healing powers, killing powers, invulnerabilities, clairvoyance, sexual dynamism and more. You refine your character on the fourth rung, and when you reach the fifth your insight is such that you grasp your role in the universe, and the fundamental nature of being.

Although high-level martial practice has more to do with experiencing heaven than kicking like hell, Tie Mei told me there are no angels, there is no floating, bearded God, and there are no pleasure palaces. She said heaven is found inside each of us, and flows from defeating our demons and appreciating the sublime beauty of the universe. In this blissful state, she said, you lose judgments, preferences, ambition, and romantic or utopian ideals.

I had achieved the third rung with a lifetime of hard work, but my feelings for Jordan Jones made me want to jump right off the ladder. Just thinking about her brought sharp pangs of joy. I had a strong sense that whatever happened next in my life mattered less because I had achieved the kind of romantic connection of which most folks only dream.

Back home, that conviction stayed with me while I unpacked my clothes and did the laundry. It stayed with me while I checked for phone messages—there were none—and it stayed with me while I emptied the dishwasher, put Robert Lockwood Blues on the stereo, made my favorite Gunpowder green tea, and sat down in the living room to eat a small piece of dark chocolate. It was not until I had that particular view of the room, a view about four feet high, that I realized a stranger had been in my home.

Roan and I have often discussed my seemingly prescient ability to sense surgical disaster before it occurs. We speculate that my eye might be sensitive to microscopic changes in the color of vessels, or to shifts in the pattern of movement that is always occurring in the brain as the cerebrospinal fluid ebbs and flows. Just then—halfway through my chocolate—I detected a series of subtle clues. Sickened, I spit the chocolate into the sink.

I opened the drawers in my Chinese chests to check for theft, gingerly using a tissue on the handles so as not to violate fingerprints. Precision comes with my job, so although I don't commit every knickknack to memory, I do tend to lay things out in rows, making disorder obvious. What I saw was that although nothing had been taken, an inventory had been made. Someone had defeated my expensive alarm system, and I wondered if it had been Wanda Berkowitz come to substantiate her hunch, or merely Vlexei Petrossov sending me another signal.

I went upstairs and looked through my clothes. I keep my shirts in one place and my trousers in another, my suits and neckties all in their assigned spots along the line. At first glance I saw that one of my favorite sports jackets, an English box-cut blazer, was hanging alone amid my pants. Starting with those whose wear patterns showed they were my favorites, I inspected every pair of my shoes for the kind of boobytraps I've seen in scary movies—a scorpion, superglue, a little pool of acid. I checked between the sheets of my futon bed, and went through my herbs and acupuncture needles too. Finding nothing, I went through my medicine chest.

Finally, as an afterthought, I made a quick check of the garage.

The moment I opened the door, I received the intruder's message loud and clear. My beautiful Triumph lay like an overturned turtle. Every inch of the machine had been ravaged, as if by a hailstorm. The dents were deep and numerous, irregular but everywhere. More than that, the handlebars had been twisted, the gauges smashed, the switchgear splintered, the tires slashed. All lines had been cut and the floor of the garage was pungent with gasoline, oil, and brake fluid. In a day when most motorcycle engines are housed beneath a plastic fairing and a mesh of hoses and clamps, the Thruxton's polished aluminum cases are especially beautiful; sadly, they had not been spared. The cooling fins on both cylinders bent in. Even the frame had been assaulted below the seat, back near the rear wheel.

I sat down on the garage floor. I reached out and touched what was left of the bike. Any motorcyclist will tell you the bond between machine and rider is more intimate than the feelings one has for a car or perhaps any other mechanical thing. My bond was all the deeper for having put nearly 50,000 miles on the bike in the two years I had owned it. I felt a numb rage come on.

In response, I did what my teacher taught me to do: I folded my hands in my lap, crossed my legs, and tried to breathe myself into a meditative trance. I searched for the tiny hint I'd felt at the hammer-in with Jordan, that strange circulating feeling that might have been the first stirrings of past life memory. I saw it out on the outer edge of my consciousness, but no matter how hard I tried to swim to it, fly to it, reach for it or run to it, I couldn't get there, couldn't grasp the edges and bring it in.

Frustrated, but with perspective and priorities restored, I turned my attention to my dad's old BMW. The frame and forks had been refinished, and newly trued wheels sat beside repainted fenders, gas tank, and boxes of original, hard-to-find engine parts. Everything was new and shiny, but hours and hours of assembly were required.

I cleaned up the floor and got to it. I worked on and on into the night. At one point I took a break and found my back stiff and my knees sore. I splashed cold water on my face, brought a stool into the garage from the house and went back to it. Fury had given way to an obsessive kind of energy. During long brain surgeries, the passage of time eluded me; during this long motorcycle assembly, time bowed out as well.

Sucking down tea—always hot, never cold—I rebuilt the Italian Del'Orto carburetors—all other old BMW models used German Bings— and replaced wheel bearings. Hour after hour, working at an insane, frenzied pace, I applied decals, ran new wires, put in new fuses, cleaned bushings and freshened gaskets. I fitted a new seat and replaced every bulb on the bike, even the tiny ones that lit the refinished speedometer dial. I hooked up a set of aftermarket stainless steel exhaust pipes—they cost a fortune, but the originals would rust in a heartbeat here by the beach—and also installed stainless steel nuts and bolts throughout. I used a bicycle pump to inflate the new tires, filled the gleaming gas tank from a can in the corner, gave the chrome cap one last buff with my elbow, and opened the garage door. I started the engine and used a vacuum gauge to synchronize the carburetors. Feeling slightly disloyal to the beaten carcass of the Thruxton, I rode the old bike out into the night.

Goosebumps grew on my arms. I learned later that a cold front had come through, part of a complex weather system developing around the hurricane that was all the talk on the news channels. In summer, a cold front in Florida means the temperature might dip below eighty at night.

The bike's engine was still tight from the rebuild, but it felt better with every mile. Riding helped clear my head. I knew I had to report the vandalism, and I hoped Wanda wouldn't learn about it, at least not right away. Heading north on the beach road I went through the lowlands of Hillsboro Mile, where some of the most expensive houses in the nation sit on the sea, and where the Intracoastal Waterway swells up over the road in storms. I inhaled the intoxicating aromas of night-blooming jasmine, and frangipani, and wondered why I was alone on the road until I saw the first rays of the sun and realized I'd worked the night through.

At Delray Beach, I ducked into a café just shy of Atlantic Avenue in hopes of a croissant or a muffin, but the bleary-eyed waiters were just putting out the tables and told me they wouldn't be serving for an hour.

I took off again. I rode fast, then slow, slow, then fast, encouraging the fresh piston rings to set. My eyes watered in the wind. I wanted to reach out and lick the ocean with my tongue. The sun drifted upward, buoyed by expectant clouds, but the dawn was an unnerving rust color, probably because of the hurricane that forecasters predicted was coming our way. Tie Mei had told me that the first light of morning determined the day's weather. My crazy work schedule combined with insomnia conspired to give me a gift of many sunrises, and through the years I learned she was right.

Not five blocks north of the café, Roan Cole and I passed on the road. He was in his Hummer. I saw him before he saw me; no doubt he didn't recognize the old bike. I looped around and hailed him. He pulled over.

"What are you doing out so early?" I asked.

"Coming to see you. Why don't you answer your phone?"

"I'm not on call and I've been busy."

He put his flashers on, got out and walked over to me. I put the kickstand down and leaned the bike. He put his hands on my shoulders.

"Hugh Cartwright hung himself last night. The police found his journal. Seems like his memory was coming back. I don't think his airplane wreck was an accident. Seems he couldn't get over losing his wife to some rancher in Montana."

"Idaho," I said.

But all I was thinking about was Orson.

40

The Cartwright home was on the Intracoastal Waterway, inside a ritzy Boca Raton development called Royal Palm, which up until ten or fifteen years ago had not allowed Jews. There is no topic more eagerly bandied about than the relative merit of local communities—unless it is the fact that Baby Boomers are driving up the price of Florida real estate as they slide all the way down the eastern seaboard to escape the cold edge of winter—but nobody would deny Royal Palm was at or near the top.

The house was coral-colored, with cream window trim, gables, columns, gargoyles, balustrades, wrought iron, and just about every other styling cue that contractors—I wouldn't grace them by calling them architects—could throw at a building to make it look expensive.

Roan pulled into the driveway with me, and we parked behind two police cars. At first he wanted to join me inside, but reading Orson's body language through the picture window at the front of the house, I thought it was better if I went in alone. The boy was in the midst of a standoff with police over the diary. They didn't think he should see it. He thought the same about them. His expression was wild. I could smell his fear five feet away. I saw his hands and his feet and they were calloused in an impossibly short time: red too, the knuckles bleeding in some places. I realized he had been practicing what I taught him, and from the looks of it he had been practicing a lot.

"No, you cannot have the diary," Orson stormed.

"You're a minor," a Boca PD sergeant said gently. "You can't hold this. We need it as evidence."

I came up slowly and spoke Orson's name gently before putting my hand on his arm.

"You made him do it!" he shrieked, lashing out at me hard. "You fucked up his brain!"

I didn't try to argue the point; I just pulled him in and held him against me. He kicked my insteps and flailed against my back and still I held him in some combination of a lockdown and a hug. I looked at the officer over the top of Orson's head.

"I'm Hugh's neurosurgeon," I said. "I worked on him after the crash."

"Surgery's not going to save him this time," said the sergeant. "Guess all these open beams were just too much of a temptation."

It was an insensitive thing to say in front of Orson, but more than that, I felt it missed the mark. The way I see suicide, it's all about options. We're born with a constellation of them. Everything is open to us. At the moment we emerge blinking and wailing, we have the potential to let our godliness shine through, or lend Satan a pair of legs. Each day after that first one, though, various forces whittle down our options. Relatives can be responsible, as can friends. The messages of media, both subliminal and overt, can diminish us, as can peer pressure, the harsh words of a teacher, or the back of a father's hand. Socioeconomic reality takes hold, pride and prejudice sink in, the harsh lessons of genetic limitations manifest, and the world in our eye grows smaller and smaller. Most of us are left living a life that is less than we had hoped it would be. Some find our choices reduced to two, ending it or continuing in terrible pain. Nobody had mentioned to poor Hugh Cartwright—a man who had obviously rediscovered his own misery in the form of a diary from another time—that there was a different way of looking at things.

I let Orson go. He pushed away from me, both raw hands on my chest, his mouth a silent symphony.

"I'd like to see the diary," I said to the sergeant.

Orson went to the staircase and sat on the bottom step, his face in his hands.

"I'm not sure I can show it," he said.

"I'm the man's doctor."

"It's evidence."

"Your colleagues will be calling me, you know that, don't you? They will be asking me to render an opinion on Mister Cartwright's state of mind."

"His state of mind was pretty obvious."

I saw Orson wince.

"My father taught me that there are more horses' asses in this world than there are horses," I said. "You're living proof he was right. Now where's the fucking diary?"

The cop handed me an evidence bag and a pair of plastic gloves.

"No prints on the book, hotshot," he said.

I went to a bench by a bay window, sat down, and started to read.

The handwritten book went back nearly two years. The entries from before the airplane wreck were progressively morose. There were frequent references to Orson: to what a terrific kid he was, to how he deserved a better father. There were peripheral references to Hugh's business dealings, which were not going so well. Most of all, there were musings about Orson's mother. Diana had left him after fourteen years of marriage. There were twenty years between them, and Hugh had been quick to see the writing on the wall. He mused about her affair with a shoe salesman at Burdine's department store, referred to having tracked her there and watched them disappear together into an inventory closet. He tortured himself with a description of how flat the young lover's stomach was, and how not one hair on the young man's head was gray.

The more I read, the more apparent it became that Hugh had thought about his son incessantly. Orson was the one and only reason he had stayed married to his philandering spouse. There were more affairs detailed, including a lesbian liaison with the sturdily build woman who changed the fluids on Diana's roadster Benz. It wasn't being the older cuckold of a young wife that drove him to the bullet, but bipolar mood swings that had him forgiving her one day, and raging against her the next.

I didn't need psychiatric training to understand what an intricate system of weights and counterweights maintained Hugh Cartwright's equilibrium. Brain damage had ruined that delicate balance, and rediscovering his pain upon finding the journal had made life unbearable. I wondered whether therapy that allowed him to express his anger would have helped. I felt doubly sad knowing that the right medication probably would have made a big difference.

The sergeant tapped his foot impatiently. Orson remained huddled on the stairs.

"I want to see the body," I said.

"Knock yourself out," he said, gesturing at the staircase. "But do it now. We're about to take it to the morgue."

"Him, not it," Orson snapped.

The boy made no move to accompany me, and I was glad for that. Upstairs, I followed the rising smell of the body. It had only been a few hours, but death bacteria were already hard at work and molds were too. Gas was being produced. Unmistakable odors were forming.

Hugh's skull was still clean and tight where I had sewn it, and the maxillofacial man had done nice work, but his neck was creased, and his eyes bulged, and he was stiff in the extremities. I was sure that Roan was wrong about Hugh intending the airplane crash. Everything I read in his journal suggested that right up until the pain was more than he could bear, Hugh Cartwright cared about other people at least as much as he cared about himself. Crashing an airplane posed a risk to the general populace. Hanging himself from a beam did not.

He had been able to look angry at the very end. Like doctors over the millennia, and friends and relatives too, I wondered what had gone through his mind at the moment he died. There was no medical role left for me other than to tell him good-bye.

I did so, and then went downstairs to face his son.

41

Orson looked so frail and angry and frankly Lilliputian, I didn't have the heart to leave him alone. The big house was deafening in its stillness. We sat together quietly for a time until he finally stood up.

"I have to do something," he said. "I have to move. I can't just sit here like this. It hurts too much."

"There's a storm coming," I said. "Let's put up the shutters."

"We don't have shutters. All the windows are impact-proof glass."

"We can bring in the patio furniture," I said. "And turn off the pool pump so it doesn't suck debris into the filters."

"Should we fill the bathtubs in case we run out of water? Dad always did that. He liked to be prepared."

"The six cases of water in the garage should be enough, but we can fill the tubs if you like."

We went for the patio furniture first.

"Where do you suppose Dad is right now?" Orson asked, hefting a table. "Did he go to hell for what he did?"

"There are all sorts of theories about life after death," I said. "I'm suspicious of all of them."

"I think it's all over when we die."

"I used to," I said. "Now I don't."

"Why? What happened?" he asked, pushing the table through French doors and coming back out for a chaise.

"I've read the writings of some Tibetan monks. They train for years to get to the brink of death and then yank themselves back at the very last minute to report what they've seen. The reports are remarkably consistent, and speak of paths with forks in them, waiting rooms for souls, and of course the occupation of fresh bodies. All the monks seem to have the same experience, and they all agree on the choices one should make so as not to reincarnate as a cockroach. Of all speculation about death, theirs compels me the most because it is based on experience."

"But they don't actually die."

"That's right. And the common experience they report may simply be a function of brain chemistry—of the degradation of the system at the end."

I went looking for the pool pump. He showed me where it was, and I found the off switch.

"My science teacher says reincarnation is nonsense," he told me.

"I'm sure he's equally popular with the academic set and with the religious right," I smiled. "But what scientists seem to ignore is that all we can do is rely on our senses and the machines we build to augment them. I don't believe they will ever find the answer to all the mysteries of the universe; in fact I find the very idea preposterously arrogant. We're too dumb and small to grasp it all, too limited by our cerebral architecture and by the constraints of language. Still, I believe that by combining the logic of science with the power of meditative intuition, we can learn a lot."

"Do you meditate?"

"As much as possible.

"My father didn't. He didn't believe in reincarnation either."

We got the rest of the chairs inside and began filling the house's four bathtubs, starting with the one by the guest bedroom downstairs. "Reincarnation is a tough one," I said. "Mostly because it puts responsibility for our lives right on our own shoulders. There's a law describing how that works. It's called karma."

"Karma like Buddha karma?"

"That's right. Actions have consequences, and they tally up for you or against you."

"How can you know about Buddha if you're a fighter?"

"Some of the greatest fighters the world has ever seen were Buddhist monks."

Orson turned the spray down so it didn't splash out of the tub. "I thought Buddha was all about non-violence," he said. "I read in religion class he taught it was better to die yourself than hurt another living creature."

"Buddha didn't say that at all. He said we should strive not to hurt any sentient creature, but that guy was a realist above all else. He saw poverty and suffering every day, and war plenty of times. He was a savvy politician; he kept close to powerful rulers, and understood sometimes people just have to do what they have to do to survive. What he asked of us was that we do everything in our power to avoid violence, and if we had to use it, he asked us to conduct ourselves with as much compassion as possible. The great Chinese sage Lao Tzu asked the same thing. In fact, he said violence was a sign our hard work had failed, and that whether we win or lose we should mourn that we couldn't do better."

We finished that tub and went on to the one upstairs. I carefully avoided the scene of the hanging. Orson pretended not to notice.

"So you don't know whether Dad can see or hear us."

"I know that life and death are two sides of the same coin, that without the other, neither one means anything."

"And you don't know whether the hurricane will hit us?"

"The weather experts say it will probably turn away. That makes me believe it will come."

"You're a cynical person."

"Not at all. I just grew up in Florida and have noticed how many times the weather reports are exactly wrong. They said giant Hurricane Andrew wouldn't hit Miami, but it turned around at the last minute."

We watched the tub fill, found the drain plug wasn't tight, and adjusted it until we couldn't hear the telltale trickle in the pipes.

"Do you remember where you were when Andrew hit?" Orson asked.

"Oh yes. My father had a clothing store, and I went to board it up and put all the expensive stuff in the inside storeroom. While I was dragging suits and coats around, a twister came up and turned the roof to match-sticks. I hid in the men's room. I had a tie in my hand—an expensive one by an Italian designer called Ferragamo—and the wind whipped it into my eye so hard I thought I'd go blind for sure. There's still a patch of skin under my lid that is always cold."

"Any other storms?"

"You're old enough to remember Lloyd and Ivan and Frances and Jeanne. None of those was like Andrew."

"You don't think this one will be big, do you?"

"Heck no. I'm just doing what I need to do to keep your house dry."

"You're not like my dad. He always assumed the worst."

"You probably think that because he liked to be prepared. Pilots think that way."

"If he was so good at thinking ahead, how come he killed himself and left me alone?"

"Maybe he knew you could come stay with me," I said. "At least until the storm is over."

He shook his head. "I want to stick around here."

"No fun being alone in a storm. Not safe, either."

"I'm just not feeling social."

"I'll take you on my bike" I said. "Just put some stuff in a duffel and sling it over your shoulder."

The prospect of a motorcycle ride seemed to change his mind, and he went and packed some clothes.

"What happened to the Triumph," he asked when he met me downstairs.

"It's down for the count. This one's good, too."

"I didn't know BMW even made bikes."

"Since the 1920s," I said. "Some of the best."

When we got home, I took him inside and showed him his room. He put his bag on the bed.

"I didn't mean it about you fucking up Dad's brain," he said, looking at the floor.

"I know."

"I'm sorry I hit you."

"No problem. Want a beer?"

"I'm a minor. You're not supposed to offer me booze."

I went to the fridge and gave him a cold one. He pulled on it like a pro.

"Not your first, is it?" I smiled.

"You're kidding, right?" he belched. He looked around. "You really live this Chinese shit don't you?"

"I started when I was young. It kind of snuck up on me slowly."

He picked an issue off the stack of kung fu magazines Wanda had noticed. "Is the stuff in here real?" he asked, leafing through it idly, unable to really put his mind on anything.

"Some of it is. Mostly it's entertainment."

"So why do you subscribe?"

"I like the pictures. I like looking at some of the weapons. I like learning the Chinese names of things."

"Your teacher didn't teach you Chinese?"

"Just a few words. I'm terrible with languages."

"I can't think of you being terrible at anything."

"I'm horrible at ping pong. My teacher tried to teach me, but I was hopeless."

"But you've gotta have great reflexes."

I spread my hands. "I'm terrible at Scrabble, too."

"What's Scrabble?"

"Never mind. I suck at poker, because my face gives me away, I'm dumb at math, and I can't make a golf club hit the ball even if I have an hour to do it."

Orson started to laugh.

"Anything else?"

"I once crushed a Rubik's cube with an axe because I couldn't figure it out. I had a terrible temper as a kid."

"Is that what got you started training? Your temper?"

"I think my nanny might have taught me anyway, but maybe not."

"So you fought in school?"

"One time I tried to push a kid off a parking garage in Miami."

Orson's eyes grew wide. "Why?"

"He made fun of my green sport jacket. Another time, I kicked my math teacher."

"What!"

"I was in first grade. She said something about my mother, didn't know she was dead."

Orson took another pull on his beer, set it down, and wiped the ring off my wooden coffee table with his hand. "I didn't know your mother died."

"I was four. I don't remember her that well."

"So your nanny was like a second mom?"

"That's right."

"Wow. No wonder you're so good. Any guy that starts kung fu at four...."

I picked up my favorite of the martial arts journals and turned to the weapons ads in the back pages. "I didn't start at four. I started after I kicked the math teacher."

"Your dad got you into it?"

"Hell no. I hid it all from him. He was dead set against me developing any martial skills, was convinced that with my temper I'd just use them to kill someone and end up in jail. My teacher knew better. She knew the arts would do for me what they will do for you: assure the qi flows in the most healthful way, thereby balancing the thoughts and emotions, and also teach the kind of discipline that makes rash action unlikely and violence unwise."

"If you've got yourself all figured out, how come you're not married?"

"I haven't got much figured out, but I'm damn sure I'd be in worse shape without having learned what I know. As to the other, I work a lot, I have certain bad habits, and it has taken me a while to find the right woman."

"What kind of habits? You snore, don't you?"

"I don't even sleep much."

"Could the sizzling girlfriend be the one?"

"What?"

"You know, the *one*, your soul mate."

"How about a soak in the hot tub? Might help you relax."

"We have one at Dad's house. I never go in it."

"Today might be different."

"Like an adult giving me beer."

"Just like that."

I headed upstairs to get my acupuncture kit. Orson seemed to have calmed down greatly, but I knew it was just a matter of an hour or so before shock and grief came flooding back. I figured a few needles might help. When I was halfway up the stairs, the doorbell rang.

It doesn't ring often, and given what was going on, my blood ran sharp. I debated whether to go for my teacher's blade. I didn't want Orson to see me wield it—the less of that the better. Surely a Redfella would not ring the bell or show up in the middle of the day on Monday. Maybe it was Wanda or Roan. Maybe it was Jordan. No, she would wait for me to come to her. She'd figure it was my turn.

I took Orson by the elbow and put him into the downstairs bedroom. "Something's up," I said. "I'm going to close this door. Go into the closet and hide behind the coats until I come get you."

He put down the beer and looked up at me. "Are you kidding or what?"

"Not kidding. We could have some trouble. Just do it."

Seeing the look on my face, he did as I asked.

I made for the door.

42

Bimini Weatherhill rocked back on in-line skates.

"Jeez, Doc," she said. "You gonna hit me or what?"

She wore a bandana tied up over her head. Since I last saw her, a large pimple had erupted on her cheek. She caught me looking at it.

"What are you staring at? Like you're perfect. How about I come in and see if your toilets are all flushed. How about I look around for dirty socks on the floor? There's no Missus Doctor Long Hair, is there?"

"No there is not."

"How did I know?"

Orson came out of the bedroom, beer in hand.

"I thought I told you to stay put."

"She doesn't look too dangerous."

Bimini craned to look over my shoulder. "And this is who, your son?"

"A friend," I said. "He's staying with me for a while."

"Ice cream and beer," she said. "Aren't you the proverbial candy man? So are you going to invite me in?"

I made a sweeping gesture and she blew by me, glided over the marble, and plopped down on the couch.

"My father is just dead," said Orson. "He hung himself at our house."

Bimini blinked. "What is it about you?" she asked me.

Orson sat down beside her. "You're sweating," he said.

"You have manners like he has manners. I don't sweat. I'm a girl. I perspire. You got anything to drink? There's a storm coming and it's 90 degrees and ninety percent humidity out there, not that the two of you would notice, hanging out in here with the shades drawn and the air conditioning on."

I brought her a glass of ice water.

"How come he gets a beer?"

"I think he told you why."

She paused for a minute, looking like she was going to argue, and then took the water out of my hand and began downing it in unladylike gulps. Orson watched her every move, watched the water escape the seal of her lips on the glass and make twin dribbles down her throat. He reached out and dabbed at the rivulets with his finger. She watched him, but kept drinking until the glass was dry. "What's your name?" she asked when she was done.

"Orson."

"I'm Bimini. It took like an hour to get here on skates. And I had to come over that steel deck bridge at the end. I was planning to step up onto the sidewalk but I got going kind of fast on the downside of Atlantic Boulevard while I was looking for the ocean. You can't look down you know, or you lose your balance. Sometimes if you're going fast and you look up, you miss surface things on the road. I almost crashed. I actually reached out and touched a white Mustang. Some drivers are cocks and try to peel out and turn you into a smear on the pavement. This guy was okay. He just waved."

"Probably checking you out in those shorts," said Orson.

"Come on," I said. "She's fourteen."

"Yeah, so? She's almost as old as me."

I reached over and took his beer. He didn't seem to notice. There wasn't much left in the bottle anyway. I told myself it was okay he was boozing and that he had probably done far worse on days when his father hadn't happened to hang himself.

"What can I do for you?" I asked Bimini.

"You said to call you if I thought of anything else. I was going to, but I wanted to see where you live. Pretty cool neighborhood. I don't know how many times I've gone by in my dad's car and never even noticed it over here."

"I thought the same thing," said Orson, shifting closer to her on the couch.

"So what is it that you've remembered?"

"Does Orson know about Raffy?"

"Maybe I don't know about that dude, but I know more about this one than you do," Orson answered, pointing at me. "Like you probably don't know that he's a kung fu master and that he really gives a shit about people."

"I've got to take care of the yard before the storm," I said. "Are you two gonna help?"

"I will if he will," said Bimini.

Outside, the palm fronds that screened me from my neighbor to the west were waving in the light breeze. The sky was titanium gray. Bimini looked at the pool and peeled off her blouse. She wore a red bra underneath.

"Actually, a swim sounds better than helping you with your shit," she said.

Orson removed his t-shirt in a clear sign he intended to join her.

"Come on, you two."

Ignoring me, they went to the pool.

I almost didn't want to follow. I almost wanted to leave them alone. Sanity prevailed and I stayed with them. Orson slid into the water. Bimini sat on the edge and dipped her toes.

"I wish it were cooler," she said.

"So what was it you remembered about Rafik?" I asked again.

"I've been to Bimini," said Orson. "One time, in my dad's airplane. There's not much there. Two islands: North and South. The airport is on the south side; the restaurants and such are on the north in a place called Alice. Sea turtles come out and nest there. We saw them once flying at night on a half moon. Big black shapes—like soldiers invading the beach. Unless you're a fisherman the place is pretty dead."

"Dude," she said. "Don't you think I know all this? Don't you think I've been there? It's my name."

"Doctor Pearl's teacher was an old Chinese lady," Orson said. "She's dead now."

"In the movies those great masters are immortal. What was it, cancer?" Bimini wanted to know.

"Bullets. And she wasn't old. She was young and beautiful."

"Who would shoot some Chinese lady?" said Bimini. "I mean, are there anything but gangsters in this crazy world?"

The sky began to drizzle. I tucked my chaise lounge under my arm and took it inside. I did the same with the umbrella over my little picnic table, and then rolled the table inside too. "Tell me about Rafik now," I commanded when I came out.

"I think it was about me," Bimini sighed. "The evil older woman. As if I could really have an influence on somebody like him."

"You had an influence all right, otherwise he wouldn't have talked about you at the end."

"I've been thinking about that," she said. "And I've decided you made that up. He was fierce; you know that? If he really were awake in the end, he wouldn't have been mushy. I'd like to believe he was thinking about me, but I bet he was too busy fighting. He was full of crazy energy; he had that wild badass heart turned to good. There's such a thin line between the good guys and the bad and he was either going to grow up to be one of the good bad guys, or one of the bad good guys."

"Who is this Rafik, anyway?" asked Orson.

"So that's what you came to tell me?" I said. "That it was about you?"

She gave me a stare that said she thought I was dumb as a stump.

"Don't you get it? They're mob royalty. They've got their clan. They're at the top. I'm a pierced teen from gay Wilton Manors. They probably figured I stole his virginity; they didn't want him to see me anymore, but he came to me every chance he could get. Where there's conflict, there's motive, right?"

"You stole someone's virginity?" Orson asked.

Bimini took some water in her mouth and blew it at him in a fine long spray. Her legs floated up behind her. Orson looked at her with undisguised admiration. Suicide or not, I decided things had gone far enough.

"I'm hip and I'm cool. Now get out of my pool."

"About your teacher," said Bimini. "I bet you find out death is not the end of her. If she's anything like Raffy, there's ever so much more."

43

Keeping one eye on the kids, I made a quick call to my insurance company. On the phone, I explained someone had broken into my place and totaled my motorcycle with a hammer. The woman who took the information said it was an unusual report. She wanted to know if I could identify the culprit. I said no. She asked if I had made a police report. I said no to that, too. I explained that I had been busy doing brain surgery and hadn't had a spare minute. She said they would need one before they could pay on the claim, but that given the circumstances she would try to find an adjuster who wasn't too busy getting ready for the hurricane, and send him over.

Orson fell asleep on the couch. I put a blanket over him. He woke when he felt the material, looked at me, then closed his eyes again and went back to sleep. Bimini watched the exchange in silence.

The squall that had cooled us passed. The hurricane, still out over the Bahamas, did battle with a ridge of high pressure blowing in from the Northwest, having made its way, as these winds do, in a great swan dive from high left to low right on the map. I put Bimini on the back of the old BMW, strapped on a spare helmet, and took her home. She went barefoot on the foot pegs, her skates tied together by the laces and slung around her neck.

The wind chattered as I headed west. At one point a gust nearly took us into the opposing lane. Bimini hit me with her fist.

"Hey," she yelled from inside the helmet I'd given her. "Do that again and I'll make you see stars."

I stopped a block shy of her house because I didn't want to chance a chat with her folks. "Can I see Orson again?" she asked. "We've both lost people. It's nice to sit with him."

I wanted to say that it was up to him, that I wasn't his keeper and that his mother would probably be down soon. "Sure," I said instead. "I can tell he likes you."

She blushed a little, not much, and solemnly stuck out her hand. I shook it. Her grip was strong, and its impression stayed with me as I rode away, stayed with me as I got onto the freeway in the light midday traffic, stayed with me all the way to Hallandale, Aventura and finally Lakeside Memorial Park.

My mother and Wu Tie Mei lie side by side. My mother's stone was obsidian and stately, and emblazoned with a Jewish star. It bears the inscription my father chose.

Helen Pearl
Beloved Wife and Mother—Taken Too Soon

I doffed my helmet and touched my mother's stone. "I'm in love, Mom," I said. "I wish you could meet her, and I wish she could meet you. You were the first woman in my life, and you will always remain first, but Jordan has won my heart. She is graceful and beautiful the way Dad says you were, and willing to look at hard things without flinching, the way I know you did. I also think she has a keen sensitivity to the suffering of others, something you know I endure, and which, from what Dad tells me, I inherited from you."

A new squall moved in. I wasn't ready to leave, so I huddled closer to my mother's bones.

"I don't look at death the same way I did the last time I was here to talk to you. I know it sounds sappy, but I have to believe you will come back as someone close to me, for it seems like souls reincarnate in clusters, and do their work together. I'm watching for you, but I haven't seen you yet.

"Anyway, there is something I have to do, and I'd like to think I have your understanding, approval, and even your help. So if it works the way I hope it does and you are able to watch over me, please do. I know I haven't said it for a while now, but I miss you, Mom. I forgive you for leaving, but I'm really sorry we had so little time together in this life."

As I always did, I waited for a reply, but all I heard was distant weeping. A funeral party was less than a hundred yards away, a dark and indistinct mob of people shuffling to a grieving beat. When I was ready, I moved a few feet to my teacher's stone.

Wu Tie Mei is the only Chinese Jew on campus, probably one of the few Chinese Jews buried in the state. Her marker is white and oval at the top. It bears her name in English, with her last name at the end, in the American standard. Under that was her name in Chinese—the only Asian characters in the park—along with the eight trigrams, or Bagua, of Chinese martial arts fame, something I had to sketch for the stonecutters. I also wrote her inscription.

Tie Mei Wu
A beacon of wisdom and strength to all who knew her.

"So now I'm sure," I said without preamble. "Petrossov, the guy you call Wang, beat his boy to death, probably over his relationship with a girl at school. I know you want me to remember my lives so I don't repeat my lessons, but I don't remember, so all I can do is try to be true to the impulses that rule me now. I am moving closer and closer to a resolution. There's a hurricane coming, but the force pushing me along rose up when the boy died and you showed up; it's not a meteorological force, but something else."

"It may be true that we've had many lives together, but I sure wish you had shared more with me in this one. I wish I knew more about your secret life before you came to America, more about your martial lineage, who taught you the agony points, the death points, the grabs, angles, slice and chokes you taught me."

The rain let off. I licked some of it from my lips. I squeezed my ponytail and felt a trickle run down my bike jacket. The funeral across the way disbanded, leaving the dead in peace.

"I figure you're not here listening, but I've been thinking about why you keep showing up. I've got this idea that you're stuck in some bardo and can't get out until you perform some kind of blessing, some kind of mitzvah, and help me on my path. I'm striving for the memories you want, but so far I can only claim a few insights. I feel you're impatient with me, which you didn't use to be, and that you're judging me harshly. Please, please remember I am just an older version of the same kid you raised: the one who didn't do well in calculus or gross anatomy because that was all about details, and I was more interested in principles. The why of things still interests me more than the how, and I need clearer motivation before I risk violence again, or commit murder for any reason at all."

I'd stored up more to say, but I was suddenly deeply tired. I closed my eyes, and lay down in the wet grass. In my private darkness I saw Rafik's soul take wing; I saw Hugh Cartwright on my table with his face sheared off; I saw Simba George screaming for his arm; I saw Spenser Brownfield's spurting carbuncle and Gloria in her seductive underclothes; I saw Olivia Spode, shorn of her eyebrows and awash in chocolate truffles; I saw Orson and Bimini courting in my pool.

Most of all, I saw beautiful Jordan, queen of my recent days and nights. The tiniest hint of her, just the edge of her eyes, her breath, her voice, her flesh, gave my stomach wings and brought me a smile. In the darkness that had descended upon me, she was the light, and for the very fact of her existence in the world, I was filled with gratitude.

When the others were gone, visions of Wu Tie Mei came to me, and, in answer to my prayers, they were silent, tender gifts: Here she was on a San Francisco cable car, her dangling hand making a hole in the fog; there she was on the raised boardwalk of the Audubon preserve out by Naples, an owl circling around her head. I saw her execute a low kung fu posture, wearing purple silk, her sword raised high. I saw her link her arm through my father's, wearing a smile at once weary and full of satisfaction, a smile that said look I've made it across oceans and beaten the odds and side-slipped politics and history to come to this far shore and be with these, my people.

And there she was on a folding chair, in the audience, glowing as she watched me play Robin Hood in the school play, with my green tights, curly-toe shoes and my little balsa wood bow and a quiver full of plastic arrows. I saw the tears on her cheeks as my father took another woman upstairs to bed. I saw her totally relinquish control as we twisted and plunged on a Busch Gardens roller coaster, her hands folded serenely in her lap. I saw her come off the couch in a rapt crouch as television news showed the fall of the Berlin Wall, and I saw her witness the massacre at Tiananmen Square, her fists clenched in impotent rage.

The rain fell harder, but I would have been happy to stay there forever, my forehead pressed to her tombstone, crying the tears of an abandoned child, but the insistent ring of my cell phone disrupted my peace.

It was my assistant, Kellie on the line.

"Doctor Khalsa has been calling for an hour," she reported. "He says it's urgent."

"I'm not on call."

"He says it's a case only you can handle. Doctor Tremper has opened and is out of his depth."

"I'm on the way," I said.

"He said you should ride fast, Zee. I don't think he was kidding around."

44

I stopped to fill the BMW's tank and pumped hastily, aware that a human life was at stake. Customers around me speculated the impending hurricane might hit us directly. Some called it a whopper. I was sloppy with the filler hose and spilled gas. I rode through the rain as fast as I could. When I crossed the railroad tracks at Dixie Highway, I stood up on the pegs.

The nursing staff saw me coming in and urged me to hurry. I left a trail of clothes in the locker room. I was still pulling on my cap and stumbling with my shoe covers as I entered the O.R. The patient was face down and draped head to foot. The visible flesh was badly bruised. Scott Tremper's face was grim.

"The good news is she's not dead," he said. "The bad news is, if she survives—and it's a big if—she'll play out her days in a chair."

I winced at the loose, loud talk, but I wasn't working with Roan and I wasn't working with Vicky. Monica the nurse was there, but otherwise, this was another man's team. It wasn't my place to start in about what I believed patients could hear under gas.

"Give me the details," I said.

"Twenty-something female, victim of violent crime," Tremper said.

"How violent?"

"Assaulted and left for dead."

"Assaulted how?"

"Tick tock," said Pinnerman, the anesthesiologist, a dour part-timer who probably wanted to get home to watch a ball game. "Let's chat later."

Tremper ignored him. "Minor lacerations to the legs and belly," he said. "No apparent sexual violation, but the spine makes up for it. It's been bruised up and down with some kind of blunt instrument and there's a lumbar fracture that needs fusing. The worst of it is what I found at T9. Take a look at the picture. You really have to hate someone to hurt them like this."

I had washed and washed during my prep but could still smell the gasoline from the filling station on my hands. I went to the light box. The MRI film had been shoved in sideways in haste, but it clearly showed a serious insult to the upper back. The other blows might have been blunt, but this one had been sharp enough to drive the posteriolateral aspect of the vertebral lamina—the bone—right into the cord.

"I'm afraid of the artery," said Tremper. "That's why I asked for your help."

Afraid was the right word. Tremper was a good surgeon. He was Khalsa's lackey so we didn't socialize, but he had a steady hand and was perspicacious enough to know when he was out of his depth. Shards of bone were tickling the artery of Adamkewicz, the major vessel nourishing the spinal cord from below. The vessel wasn't severed, but it was torn and leaking. Teasing the bone away to spare the cord would entail working in and around the tear. If I nicked that artery the way I had nicked little Raffy Petrossov, the gash would open, the blood supply to the cord would fail, and the patient would be paralyzed.

"Did she have feeling below the level of the injury?" I asked, knowing that a neurologist would have pricked her with needles and asked her to wiggle toes, establishing a specific baseline measure of the damage before she was sent up to surgery.

"There's sensation, but it's impaired."

"Motor activity?"

"A hint."

Tremper's answers told me that the woman's spinal nerves were still sending signals to the brain and the brain was sending back a message telling the legs to move. No response would have been a bad sign. The patient had a prayer of walking again if I did my job right, but only a prayer.

"What do we know about her?"

"Not much," said Tremper. "She came in on a wagon. She was in and out of consciousness. Barely coherent, not much help with questions."

Monica wired me up. I put my light on the field, a rectangle of muscle and bone in the middle of blue drapes.

"I took it as far down as I could go. You can see the shards," Tremper said, stepping away.

"Less talk, more surgery," said Pinnerman. "I'm having a hell of a time with her gases."

Tremper had done a serviceable job elevating the splinters of bone from the dura. The field was full of absorbent cotton paddies and Gelfoam, which calmed down the bleeding by giving platelets a matrix against which to aggregate. Still, it was all just a finger in the dyke. The wound needed conclusive repair.

The neuromonitoring technician had the patient wired with a forest of electrodes in her head and more on her hands and feet. "Let's get cracking," he said, as he ran test current across her spine. "She's not stable."

The team rolled the digital microscope into place. They positioned the lens over the surgical site and lit up the monitor so that everyone else could see what I was doing. I leaned over to line up with the eyepieces and went to work. One by one I teased back the last little tiny bits of bone. Little by little, the bleeder came into view.

"Adamkewicz," said Tremper. "I knew it."

I asked Monica for an aneurysm clamp. She looked at me over her mask as she handed it to me. Her glasses showed the tiniest hint of fog on the bottom.

"I smell gasoline," she said. "Did you spill filling up your bike?"

"I was in a rush."

My plan was to stop the bleeding artery by compressing it the same way you compress a garden hose. If I stopped the flow of blood entirely, my patient would never walk again. I needed to reduce the flow to a trickle so that I could work, and then do a fast microsurgical stitch job on the arterial wall.

The psychological pressure was greater than the pressure in the artery, and without my martial training, I'm sure I would have succumbed to it. People who don't practice the martial arts generally don't realize the full extent of the mind/body connection. They don't realize that even dividing the two for the purposes of discussion is an error, that the two are inseparable, and that intention rules the physical body just as much as it rules the head.

When I felt tension at the surgical stakes, I consciously willed it away. I loosened every muscle from the acupuncture crown point at the top of my head, *bai hui*, to *yong quan*, the bubbling well points, one on the bottom of each foot. I contracted points on my chest and sides, too, making a concerted effort to relax. As much of an oxymoron as that seems, it's an apt description, and the consequence of my efforts was the drop in backpressure on the peripheral vasculature, meaning an easier job for my heart, the consequent drop in blood pressure, and as clear a head and positive a frame of mind as I could muster.

"Easy with that clamp," warned Tremper. "You're going to stroke the cord."

Ignoring him, I stretched my gloved fingers with one of Tie Mei's maneuvers, bending them first in toward my wrist and then back the other way to loosen my tendons for the tense work ahead.

I wondered about the patient on my table. Had she ever in her wildest dreams imagined that her life would come down to a sew job, that her future would hang, literally, by a thread? Wheelchair or running shoes, that's what I was about to determine: dancing with a partner or sitting out life on the sidelines; active, passionate romance or lying passively in hope of some tiny sensation. And what about having kids? A young woman in a wheelchair might certainly have a rewarding relationship, but as a dependent herself, motherhood was unlikely.

I retracted the overlying connective tissue and looked at the bleeder. I chose a place on the trunk and snapped on the clamp. The whine of the suction pump grew higher as air entered the mixture. I held the tiny needle using specially designed forceps and guided it into the arterial wall. The clock was ticking. Working along the length of the tear, I fought against odds that said the spine would seize for lack of oxygen, and that the oh-so-delicate network of nerves would die. As always, I used interrupted stitches, tying each one and snipping the ends down close before going onto the next. Tremper started to pace, looked like he wanted to say something, but held his tongue.

I tied off the last stitch. "Bioglue," I said.

Monica handed it over.

The stuff is a wonder. It's made from purified cow serum and a fixative called glutaraldehyde. It looks like bee pollen. I dropped some in around the stitched vessel and gave it a moment to set. I released the clamp. The artery swelled and the tissue went pink. If there were a leak, we all would have seen it on the screen. There wasn't a drop. It held tight.

"Potentials look good," said the technician, referring to the electrical chatter across the spinal cord that was the stuff of messages. "Better, actually."

"Wow," said Monica.

"Bravo," said Pinnerman. "I take back everything I've said about you."

"Nobody denies he's one hell of a surgeon," Tremper clucked. "Do you want to do the fusion or do you want me to take over?".

Spinal surgery is never a cakewalk, but compared to what I had just managed, a fusion was no big challenge.

"I'll finish," I said. "I feel pretty good."

Tremper put up a fresh set of images on the light box. I took a look. It was a straightforward fracture, one wing and a crack in the pedicle, the centerpiece of the vertebral body. Monica moved the drape down to expose the lumbar spine.

The way the spine twists and turns, a crack in a vertebrae can put the cord in peril. Standard technique calls for a screw to be placed in the middle of two adjacent bones and then the movement limited by attaching a rod to both screws. To make sure there is no play, some additional small bits of bone are put into the space between the vertebral bodies as well. That bone is classically harvested from the posterior pelvis.

Tremper put a CD on Pinnerman's player. Sting crooned about fields of gold. I made the incision, moved muscle aside, found a couple of bone fragments, and cleaned them out. Monica was ready with the sterile self-tapping screw kit, and while I inserted them, she made note of exactly how many I had used—that's the kind of penny-pinching that goes on in hospitals these days.

Before I put in the rods that would lock the bones together, I had to get the filler bone from the pelvis. Monica pulled the drape back farther, isolating a small, prepared square on the patient's upper hip.

The woman's lower spine was bare.

There was a tattoo there.

It showed the scales of judgment, rendered in ink.

Everything I knew failed me.

Everything substantial lost mass.

45

Cutting again. Always cutting. Gash, slit, slice, and hack. Cut options, burdens, obligations, and attachments. Cut tumors. Cut to the chase, cut to the bone, cut in front, cut back. Chop, whittle, sever, extirpate, excise, and prune. Cut up, cut down, cut back, and cut away. The sharp edge is havoc: pain, separation, and loss. Cut to wound, cut to win, cut to destroy, cut to kill.

Sculptors cut away and what remains is art. I cut away and what remains is a miracle. I cut to redeem and to deliver. I cut to restore. In darkness I cut, and the world becomes light. In daylight I cut, and life is saved. I cut to erase endless agony. I cut my sweet love's flesh to give her a chance to walk.

Before I cut her again, I touched her flesh with my finger not my scalpel. I disappeared into my memory of her, her fragrance, her softness, her warmth, and her embrace.

"What is this patient's name?" I asked the room.

"Jordan something," Pinnerman answered. "I think the last name is Jones."

I steadied myself against the table as I received confirmation. I let heaven spin.

"Doctor Pearl?" said Monica.

"You don't realize what these touch-and-go procedures take out of you," said Tremper. "The adrenaline comes down and you're toast. Sure you don't want me to finish, Zee? Just a little graft is all."

I sat down on the edge of the surgical table, squeezing a tiny spot for myself by my beloved's feet.

"Pearl," said Tremper. "Are you all right?"

"Jordan Jones is my lover," I whispered. "She is my partner and friend."

There was an immense, stunning, all engulfing silence after my words. I could hear every little instrument beep, I could hear drops of blood fall, I believe I could hear light rays race and molecules bump each other.

The neuromonitoring technician was the first to react. He stood up so fast the metal stool he'd been perched on skittered across the room and slammed into the metal suction canister, the repository for all patient fluids.

Pinnerman was next. "This is not good," he said. "Not good at all."

Monica took my gloved hand in hers and held it. "I'm here for you," she said.

Tremper came around the table and stood studying the field.

"The tattoo?"

I nodded.

"You had no idea before that?"

"I was up against the artery," I said, speaking from orbit, spinning in space, trying to control my breath, trying to hear over the pounding of my heart in my ears. "It was a job."

He touched me on the shoulder. "You did good."

"I want to finish."

"Out of the question."

"Scott," I said. "It's something I have to do."

"Take a walk and come back. We can wait. She can wait."

It was a good suggestion, and I followed it. The harvest amounted to no more than scooping bone with a curette, but it had to be placed between the damaged vertebrae, which brought me close to the cord again, a place I should not be unless I was stone steady. Nothing had been the same since Rafik, not inside my head, and not among my colleagues, in a roost I used to rule.

In the hallway, a couple of attending physicians I didn't recognize gave me a wide berth. The nurses at the station stared. I probably looked like I was drunk. Through the whole excursion I could think only of sweet Jordan, of the courage she was going to need. I was all too familiar with rehabilitation from this kind of injury. I knew the months of agony Jordan would face, the loss of self-confidence, the shattering of her power, her femininity, her world. I saw her struggling to get her shoes on. I saw her shaving legs that might always be useless, imagined her watching them wither away. Slightly ashamed, I remembered the power she had in her thighs, remembered how she had ridden me. I recalled our first meeting, how she had handled molten steel, stoking the fire in the forge. I remembered the ping-pong ball and the fierce concentration on that delicate brow. I wondered who could, who would, have done this to such a beautiful life.

I came up, in the keenest possible agony, with an answer.

Petrossov.

I turned with a cry and kicked at the nearest possible target—an equipment cart. Vials and sharps scattered across the floor. An orderly passing by jumped away in fright. I fought my anger, fought my sadness; I had a real battle with myself right there in plain view. I had been through these battles before, clashes between the way my life was going and the way I wanted it to go. I was an old hand at internal warfare, but even so it took a few minutes for the sane Zee to win. I concentrated on my breath; I contracted the diaphragm on inhale, dropped it to exhale. Starting at the sacrum and then moving up, I filled my back with breath. I let my belly expand as the breath released, dropping, always dropping, increasing my contact with the ground, growing friendlier with gravity.

In time, when I felt stable, I returned to the O.R.

The team looked at me expectantly. I put on my gloves and quickly made a smart, short incision in the hip, over the posterior iliac wing, where the nerves and blood supply were both sparse.

"Khalsa isn't going to like this," Pinnerman said, worriedly. "You knowing her and all."

"Forget knowing her," said Tremper. "Loving her."

"Fuck Khalsa," I said.

"You can afford to say that," Tremper sighed. "The way you are with scalpel and stitch."

Maybe not, but I went to work anyway. I separated the fascial insertion of the gluteal muscles until the outer table of the bone was exposed. I ignored Jordan's curves. My heart would take over again later, but now I needed my hands.

I cut the outer table with a chisel and peeled it away to expose the cancellous bone within. I used a gouge to peel away portions of that inner area like the rind of a lemon.

Tremper stood by my elbow as if he were expecting some egregious error, or, perhaps, for me to collapse. My breath made a furnace of my mask. To help the graft stabilize and take, I roughened the transverse process of the vertebrae in the fusion area using a high-speed drill, then, packed the transplanted bone in under pressure.

"Damn good," said Tremper.

After that, it was all about closing. Methodically, carefully, perfectly, I stitched my lover closed. I kept the loops tight and neat and straight. It was the sew job of my life. By the time I was done, everyone in the room had their eyes fixed on the wound.

I turned to the neuromonitoring technician. I wanted to know what his equipment showed. I wanted to know if her cord was talking to her brain the way it should, and to her legs.

"How about now?" I asked, knowing full well that the fusion and the graft probably wouldn't change anything up at the T9 injury. "Is she going to walk or not?"

The technician looked me straight in the eye. "I don't know," he said. "I wish I did, but I don't."

I bent down and put my lips to Jordan's ear. My nose touched the beautiful hollow at the top of her neck. I remembered whispering to Rafik, the little shell of a boy, his soul already gone. This time there was someone there to hear me.

"You're going to beat this, my love. You're going to dance at our wedding, believe me."

Sobs fought their way up as I walked out of the room, but I beat them down with deadly hands and feet.

46

On the way home, I saw frenzied hordes around gas stations and supermarkets. I saw a fistfight over a bottle of water erupt outside a convenience store. I saw sheets of plywood twist and writhe in the wind like living things trying to be free of the ropes that tied them dangerously to the roofs of cars. I saw a woman on a scooter blown into oncoming traffic by the sail effect of a board she had tucked under one arm. She dodged and sped through to save her skin, and kept going even after the wood knocked a pedestrian to the ground.

Closer to my neighborhood, cop cars prowled the beach road. Mandatory evacuations were expected any time. Petrossov's watcher was gone from the lot next door. My neighbors had closed their shutters. Some had fled to relatives or hotels. Across the street, a guy I knew had staked some palms so they would not blow over in the wind, but left unsupported two expensive Japanese maples, along with a florid, fruiting, South American geiger tree and two tamarinds, exotics that lacked the flexibility to survive the storm.

There was a message on the door from my insurance adjuster. He had come about the Thruxton and was sorry to find me not at home. There was another message on the refrigerator, this one from Orson, telling me he had gone to see Bimini and would probably sleep at the waterfront house. I knew what that probably meant, but I didn't have it in me to track him down right then.

I closed the accordion shutters on my windows and lay down to watch storm reports on TV. Updates came in from hurricane hunter aircraft crews aloft in the eye of the giant white gyre blanketing the Caribbean. There was talk of how global warming was melting the polar ice caps, thereby increasing the frequency and intensity of killer storms and also raising the level of the world's oceans. Globally, high tides would soon inundate low-lying areas. Hundreds of thousands might drown.

Locally, certain Bahamian islands, along with the Florida Keys, were increasingly vulnerable to storm surge. If this particular hurricane came ashore, huge numbers of Floridians could lose their homes because of the way warming exacerbated storm damage.

I had not slept in days and did not expect to sleep then, but Morpheus ignored my fear-cloaked heart and took me to his bosom, where I dreamt about wheelchairs. In that dark land I kept buying lighter and sexier ones for Jordan, wheelchairs that handled like Porsches, wheelchairs that would stop on a dime. I saw myself lift her up and carry her to the bed, her legs a dead weight on my arm all the while. I saw her cry beneath me because of what she could not feel.

In those inchoate dreams, I was certain of my steadfastness despite the fact that our love was new and our commitment unspoken. I had seen the nitty gritty of a paraplegic life, but I would be loyal and true nonetheless. Whether her legs worked or not, Jordan Jones was the woman for me. I had not been looking, but she had come to me with an accepting heart, a deep past, a fascinating beauty, an intricate intelligence, a passion for steel, and a soul to die for. I was not going to let her go.

And so, although I might have come up from slumber stricken with dread, I arose instead with determination and purpose and went to the yard to restore myself. I began with a double broadsword set, a form I found particularly demanding because the slightest wavering of attention could cost me an elbow or an ear, and progressed to a long set with the *guan dao*, that thirty pound halberd so tough on the shoulders. After that, I spent half an hour driving a spear into a dime-sized target on the side of my gazebo, concentrating as fully as possible on both forward and backward movements, and managing to keep all three hundred thrusts inside the perimeter Tie Mei had once set out.

I stretched vigorously after that, dropping deep into Chinese splits— never an easy one for me—and feeling my groin muscles, the abductors of my hip release. I stretched the front and back of each leg after that, hamstrings and quadriceps, and then went on to my shoulders and arms. Only then did I head for a much-need shower.

I doubled over and cried in the middle of frying a couple of eggs, but I recovered, and sprinkled them with paprika and parsley before wolfing them down. I forced myself to eat two slices of whole-wheat toast. I made tea and drank it. I cut a piece of Belgian dark chocolate from a bar and ate it. Tea and chocolate were the elixirs of my life and I knew I needed them for succor and strength, but my mind, consumed by pain, would not allow me to enjoy them.

When I finished eating, I called the nursing station.

Vicky Sanchez was back on the floor. "Jordan's resting comfortably," she said. "She's on an opioid drip."

"Any change in the potentials?" I asked, curious to know if her tenderly treated nerves were conducting electricity.

"I don't think so."

"Is she awake?"

"In and out."

"Did she ask for me?"

"She hasn't asked for anybody. Listen, Zee, I know what happened. I just want you to know how sorry everyone here is, how sorry I am. What a rotten, horrible piece of luck."

"So I gather everybody knows."

"You can't really expect it to remain secret."

"I suppose not. Any word from Khalsa?"

"Not that I've heard. Jordan did ask me about her prognosis."

"What did you say?"

"That I wasn't qualified to answer. That her doctor would talk with her presently."

"Does she know I did the work?"

"I haven't told her. I don't think anyone here wants to be the one to do that. Doctor Tremper was by, but she was asleep. She talked to Doctor Pinnerman. He said he didn't know what to tell her about her prospects; he told her that his job had just been to put her to sleep and make sure she woke up. His bedside manner's not the best, but she actually smiled. Can you imagine? She's lovely, Zee. I hope and pray for her. For you too."

I told Vicky I was lucky to have her around and then I hung up. I got myself ready to go to the hospital. The one thing I had not practiced in my dreams was how to talk to Jordan about her condition, how to urge her to heal without offering false hope or damaging her with pessimism. I decided it would be best to be honest. That's what I would want from her if our situation were reversed.

I called the insurance adjuster and left him a message. I brought in the mail. There were some catalogs, a few bills, and a letter on purple stationary from Anita Broussard. Written in looping and elegant script it thanked me for the job I had done on Denny's brain.

"My father would admire you if he could know you," she wrote. "And I admire you myself."

There was also a package in the stack that bore no stamp. It had my name on the front, along with the words:

WATCH THIS RIGHT NOW

A DVD tumbled out when I shook the box. I put it in my player and sat down to watch. The storm reports were replaced by a clean blue screen, then blackness overlain by wavy lines. An alley appeared. A yellow Subaru was parked off to one side. The camera angle was high, as if on a landing or an old-time fire escape. The back of a head came into view: short hair, breezily cut, a shapely woman with a familiar, graceful gait. While she walked, she buckled her purse and slung it back on her shoulder. Perhaps she had just been shopping, though there was no bag. Perhaps she was on her way back from visiting an ATM.

My heart started to hammer. I grew aware of my tongue.

Jordan made it all the way to the car door before a group of men sprang up from behind a stand of trashcans. Startled, she leapt back, darting first in one direction and then the other, trying to escape. The men closed in, hooting. One, two, three, four, five; all dressed in black t-shirts and trousers, all wearing masks.

I groaned out loud.

Jordan fumbled for her keys, found them, managed to put them into the door. My eyes started watering when they tore her from the car. There was some movement in the camera, amateurish jiggling and bouncing, a quick dip suggesting the lensman had jumped.

She pulled her knife. It was a glorious, fruitless, heart-rending defense she managed, circling and holding them off, slashing out at them, stabbing and waving the blade. They were surprised, I could see by the way they looked at each other, but after less than a minute they coordinated their attack, coming at her all at once.

The men in front grabbed her arm while the thug behind her jumped on her the same way he had jumped on me outside the convenience store. They forced her down onto the hood. One of the five was much smaller than the rest, almost diminutive. He seemed to be the boss, giving instructions by pointing and with low, muffled words I could not understand. Pleading at last, Jordan offered her purse, but they kicked it away. The camera zoomed in on her face, contorted, as they assaulted her with feet and hands, driving her higher and higher up on the hood until the back of her head was up by the windshield wipers, against the glass.

When I saw her eyes, I rolled off the couch and onto the floor. I went fetal as they pulled up her blouse and beat her belly with their elbows and fists. One of them tried to pull off her pants. She kicked at him and started to scream. Up until then, she had only grunted with effort. It was the scream that did it for me. I recognized her voice, but at the same time I did not recognize it. She said no word that I could understand, but I understood the scream all right.

I retched. The eggs, tea and toast came up. The chocolate made a puddle on my hardwood floor.

The video kept running. They worked Jordan's pants down to her knees. The thickset man—somehow I knew he had to be Chazov—set to cutting her raggedly with a key. I had to turn off the film then. I needed blessed silence and I needed water and air.

I crawled to the kitchen on all fours. I reached the sink and put my head under the tap. I soaked my clothes. I flooded the floor. I let the water run and run. Then, shaking, I went back to the television set just the way I had gone back to the operating table, digging deep to do what I needed to do.

I watched them turn her over. The small one took out a hammer. It had a standard head and a long, straight claw. I had seen my grandfather use one once when he was laying mortar for his pond. He'd called it a brick hammer. There was something not quite right about the bastard who wielded it, something liquid and flexible and sickly lithe about the way he moved. I couldn't place it, couldn't figure it, transfixed as I was by the terrible weapon.

The hammer went up and it went down, as pitiless in its repetition as an oil drill in a derrick. I saw the blow that pierced Jordan's spine, knew it by the shriek of pain and also by her strange and hideous opisthotonos: the unnatural arcing spasm of her back that bespoke dire injury. Watching Jordan's face, I knew what she was feeling. This kind of damage is accompanied by Lhermitte's phenomenon, the feeling that an electric shock has traveled to the extremities. The hammer blows were practiced, leisurely, and unspeakable. This monster had done this work before. Finally, Jordan's agony was replaced by numbness. Her face relaxed. She had not yet realized that she could not move.

One of the big men turned Jordan face up again. She flopped as he manipulated her. The little man put the hammer away and in one, smooth movement came up with two guns, one in each hand. Right to Jordan's face he put them: right to my true love's eyes. He dug the barrels deep, and to do this he had to lean forward, and when he did I saw the shape of his chest and realized that he was a she, and that this woman was going to pull the triggers.

In that moment, I realized something. A loose piece of information, one that had been floating around for years, suddenly came to ground.

"No!" I screamed.

A big man stopped the shooter. Muttering a word too muffled to understand, he batted the gun up and out of the way. There was a blast then, and it was impossibly loud even on television. It shattered the Subaru's windshield, but it did not blind and it did not kill.

End of video. Dawn of darkness for me, for Jordan, and for my world.

47

Upstairs, in my walk-in safe, surrounded by burglarproof, bullet-proof, fireproof walls of steel, I stood like a corpse in an upended lead box. Heavy on my soles, I felt the cold of the steel floor through my canvas kung fu slippers. What even my near drowning had failed to do, a terrible revelation—combined with the violation of Jordan Jones—accomplished. Wu Tie Mei said I would find my past by pursuing ever-deeper trances; it didn't happen that way. Transcendence of the present came not through meditation, but from the cocktail that had fueled me through countless lives, juice of hypersensitivity to suffering mixed with tincture of moral outrage.

My memories flooded in like a rhinoceros chasing me down, pinning me to its horn, and then shaking me in the direction of snow-capped emotional peaks. I was caught up in a maelstrom of consciousness, an onrush of images so vivid I could taste them, so deafening they crumpled me, so quiet and delightful and poignant and sad, I worried I would drown myself for the second time in this life by filling my tiny metal coffin with tears.

I relived my Eastern Chou life, standing on the edge of the mountain, getting ready to defend the Kingdom of Qin at the city of Hsienyang, on the edge of the impenetrable Land Between the Passes. I felt the rough belly of the wooden crossbow as I pulled the string up over the stock and engaged the latch. I saw the enemy army swarming in like painted ants in bright armor, and I let the bolt fly and dropped my man. I saw the man who was now Asher, my father, do the same.

I remembered wielding a Three Kingdoms bronze sword, a weapon too fragile and dull for cutting but a serviceable piercing tool, as I fought Ts'ao Ts'ao army as a Yellow Turban rebel, and died on the battlefield on that decisive day in 192 A.D. The bronze crumpled against my enemy's horse, breaking my wrist so that when I ran away from his pursuing lance, the meat of my hand and my fingers jiggled loosely even as I tried desperately, with my other hand, to hold them in place.

I recalled the Shang dynasty courtesan who tried with all her charms to distract me as I worked Mo Tzu's invention—he was a pompous and pedantic man—a resonance box designed to help determine where the enemy was attempting to tunnel under the wall. It was a clever device, made of a pottery jar with a thin piece of leather stretched over the top, a kind of drum in reverse, designed to pick up vibrations from the ground and transmit them to the careful ear. The woman wanted a child by me and was determined to have it right then and there, against the stone, at night, and I had to put my hand over her mouth as we made love so I could listen for the trembling of the skin.

A bomb of gunpowder wrapped in paper flew from a "Sitting Tiger" stone thrower and exploded into the man next to me, who is Orson Cartwright in the life I know best. The soldier's guts burst out and I helped him put them back where they belonged, then used a golden needle to take his pain before helping the next patient remove a spear point from his leg.

A soldier of the Western Han under Li Kuang-li, I carried a halberd against the Hsiung-nu invaders from up north. Most of the elephants were already gone from the Asian steppe, slaughtered and abused by the warring armies of the time, but I had one in my care, a female with a gentle, probing trunk and a loyal temperament. I remembered realizing one day that she was somehow communicating with her congeners at war—ultra-low frequency sound was the answer but I didn't know that back then—but when I tried to tell my general, he laughed at me. The elephant died from a fire arrow attack, and I myself burned to death trying to put her fire out. She sprayed me with water at the end of my time, but it wasn't enough and we went down and out together.

A thousand years later, I fought other marauding barbarians, the Jurchens, as a cavalryman in a Liao dynasty army. My horse and I hated each other, and in an exhibition for my field commander the horse bucked me off and I was wounded. A maid of low station—Roan Cole, but far better-looking—took up the cause of my wounds, and she later became my wife and bore me a daughter with one brown eye and one yellow. When my daughter was twelve, the emperor took her as a concubine and I never saw her again, although from time to time I would get a gift of rice from the court, and my wife would receive cotton for weaving.

I was a member of the personal guard of Li Shih-min, the greatest general of Chinese history and also, if the almond smell didn't deceive me, an early incarnation of my own nanny and teacher. Nephew to the duke of T'ang, my liege was already a military genius at 15, the year I entered his service. I followed him through the campaigns that led to the throne of the Kingdom of Heaven.

Indeed, I was the wife of a ferryman who was Tie Mei as well, and it is true I was skilled with fans, though not nearly so skilled as I was with a fine steel sword, when fighting alongside Jordan, then a lance-man, for the rebel Ming dynasty prince who was to take Nanking and move the ruling seat to Pei Ping, later Beijing, capital of the north.

My memories, truth be told, were not all visual; they played the full range of human senses. I heard babies crying and men dying and women and men grunting in ecstasy, and I heard animals running against hard earth and the sound of water dripping into the corner of a stone prison cell. I heard the tiny tick of newborn birds and the deafening roar of the Yangtze overflowing its banks and carrying villagers downriver, drowning their cries.

Smell is the sense most closely linked to memory, and although my experience transcended any common sense of recollection, I relived the foul stench of city cisterns and the rotting of corpses in the desert. I remembered the intoxicating smell of night-blooming jasmine, osmanthus and wintersweet, the musky odor of my own clothes after battle, and the ripe and heady aroma of a wife waiting months for my return. I remembered animal smells—we've gotten so far from them now, but they used to be everywhere—the rank odor of camels and the steaming scent of buffalo emerging from a soak. I recalled the pungent odor of wolf dung in signal fires, rising uninterrupted in a black column visible for leagues. Best of all, I relived the complex, indescribably comforting odors of home.

My fingertips bore witness to the nearly paper-thin delicacy of azaleas, the smooth hands of children, the density and balance of mahogany and cherry, both splendid as weapon handles or hilts. My hands twitched recalling the heft of weapons I have no name for, spiked ropes and strange maces with bumps and edges like some crazy fruit, spears with shafts so straight they might have been axles. I remembered carrying injured friends on my back, the feel of their blood dripping over my skin. I remember the gossamer threads of an industrious spider touching my eyelids, and the new wonder of doing what is commonplace for me now, touching the surface of a brain laid bare by a war axe. I remembered feeling holes where once I had teeth.

And tastes! I ate crunchy fresh orchids, and drank the tea of the chrysanthemum and lotus. Pork fat dribbled from my lips, smoky and nourishing, and dumplings filled with soup exploded in my mouth with a scalding blast of bamboo and mushroom. I was in castles at times, where I ate oranges and cherries and Persian pomegranates from the Silk Road. Once more I tasted the savory and sweet of soy and duck, and the rough passage of dry gruel, and the hard crack of a winter biscuit soaked in the milk of a yak.

I glimpsed hundreds of other lives as leaves hanging from Chinese branches. Not all the leaves were Asian; in some I was from Europe, Africa, Australia, or the South Sea. I wasn't always a warrior, but the lives in which I did things other than fight were short lives, sad and childless and as unfulfilled as this life would be if I did not follow my teacher's counsel and embrace the true me.

48

"What?" I said into the receiver.

"That's the way you answer the phone now?" My boss inquired.

"Yes. Tell me what you want."

"I'm going to forgive this because I know the stress you're under."

"Does your forgiveness matter?"

"Frankly, no; it doesn't. But I do need to see you at my office."

"Can't we do this by telephone?"

"I'm sorry but there are procedures I have to follow."

I ran an oiled rag over my hammered steel *guan dao*. "I have other priorities right now."

"I can't imagine what those would be."

"Of course you can't."

There was a long pause. "How soon can you be here?" Khalsa asked at last.

"Soon, but there's something I have to do first. Tell the board I refused to see you. Go ahead and say what you have to say, John. And by the way, the Petrossov autopsy bore me out."

"I haven't heard any such thing."

I moved from the *guan dao* to my broadsword, checking it for the tiny pits of rust that were a hazard of living so close to the beach. "You will."

"You have connections to the police now, Zee?"

"As a matter of fact, I do."

"Well even if what you say is true, it's not the point. I made an administrative decision based on hospital policy. You violated it."

"You think the board will back you when they learn the medical examiner's conclusion? You're sucking up to criminals, John. The kid was beaten to death and you're more interested in protocol."

"I'm not more interested in protocol and I don't suck up to anybody.

There are certain realities in a for-profit institution; one of them is we try to avoid unnecessary and expensive legal proceedings. Anyway, I didn't call to debate with you. The fact is when we add what happened yesterday to what was already on the table, disciplinary action is needed."

I put the broadsword down and picked up my favorite hickory staff. I sighted down the length of it, checking for any warping. "What happened yesterday?"

"Come on, Zee. You operated on a loved one."

"I didn't know."

"The name was on the films."

"You know how many people have the name Jones? I was concentrating on the injury, not cruising biographical details."

The staff was fine. I made the same inspection of my spear.

"We like our surgeons to know who their patients are," Khalsa said. "And even after you did know, you proceeded when another competent surgeon was standing right there. That's against policy too."

"You don't like me very much, do you, John?"

"No, I don't. But you are a brilliant surgeon and this is a loss to the hospital."

"I practice at other hospitals."

"Godspeed. When it comes to this hospital, you have no more privileges."

One can't really prepare for those words, not even when you've had plenty of time to do so. Broward Samaritan represented the lion's share of my caseload and I had not recently pursued other referrals; nor would this development assist me in that aim.

I hung up, and immediately tried to talk myself into being relieved. Instead, I found I was devastated. I was out of a job. How was I going to buy food, pay my mortgage, keep up with expenses, repay my school loans? My power base was suddenly eroded. I had talked to Tie Mei of the scalpel and the sword being the yin and yang, the two halves needed to make me whole. Suddenly cut loose from the hospital, I realized that in this world, in this place and at this time, I could not be and do what I needed to be and do without holding on to my physician identity. Never before, not in any of the lives I could remember, had I lived such a clear double life; and now my cover was blown. I went to the kitchen and tried to eat again, but I couldn't keep anything down.

So I got on the old BMW and headed down along the ocean toward Miami Beach. The gusty wind pushed the bike around. Out at sea, the waves were angry. A few cops looked at me from their cars and shook their heads. There was very little traffic; everyone seemed to have hunkered down.

Rachel's condominium building was shuttered up and closed tight. Shaking his head, the doorman let me in. "You gotta be nuts riding that thing in this wind," he said.

Upstairs, Rachel was working on real estate forms. My father had his back to me when I came in, a reading light over his shoulder. When he heard my voice, he tried in vain to stuff something under the pillow. The movement was so guilty I sped around to get a look.

"You're knitting now?" I asked.

"He has a love for fabric," Rachel defended. "He says he's always had it. He doesn't have the store anymore."

"But knitting?"

"It's not knitting," my father snapped. "It's crochet."

"Whatever it is, I need to talk to you alone."

Rachel looked at me, wounded. My tone of voice was new to her and I was sorry for that.

"You can say anything in front of Rachel. She's my wife."

"I can't say this."

"It's all right," Rachel said. "I'll take a walk."

My father glowered at me. Rachel went out the front door with nothing more than her purse.

"So what is so confidential?" he demanded.

"I think you know."

"I certainly do not."

"Jordan was assaulted last night," I said. "Redfellas did it. They put the whole thing on DVD and dropped it off in my mailbox. She'll be lucky if she isn't paralyzed for life."

"Paralyzed," said my father, his mouth opening wide. *"Vey iz mir."*

"The disc told me something I didn't know before. It told me who killed Tie Mei."

My father put his crochet needles down. "Listen to me," he said.

I shook my head. "One of the guys on the disc drew a pair of pistols and was going to shoot her in the eyes. Does that sound familiar? Another one put a stop to it so Jordan would live and suffer. They wanted to punish her and they wanted to punish me, too. That's the kind of people they are. They beat people to a pulp and shoot people in the eyes. You know who they are, don't you, Dad?"

"Please," he said. "You don't understand."

"All this is about you, isn't it? Were you one of them and then you went legit, wanted out? They killed Tie Mei to punish you and now they're at this horrible game all over again?"

Tears slid down my father's cheeks. New wrinkles seemed to appear on his face. It was as if he had been holding them at bay with his newfound happiness but they crept up on him after all, now that I was forcing him to look at the past.

"I was never one of them," he said. "Don't think it and don't say it either."

"You got money from them," I said. "You started the business with a loan."

"You have no right to judge me," he said. "You have no idea what it was to come here from Russia with nothing, to start a life, to try and make a life, to put money aside for you, to send you to school, to be the man of substance your mother wanted me to be."

"This is why Grandpa Lou doesn't talk to you. He knows what you did. That's it, isn't it?"

"He thinks he knows, just like you think you know."

"Petrossov?"

"He was young then. Not the big *macher* he is now. And I paid him back every cent with interest. No bank would help me. I was a nothing. I didn't have your education. I didn't have your opportunities and maybe I didn't have your brains either."

"So you became a crook?"

"Shut your mouth!" he thundered. "You just shut your mouth! I was a businessman. I wanted to make something of myself, and so I took the money and I invested it in the store and the store made a profit and I paid them back but that wasn't enough for them. They wanted a piece, they wanted protection payments, they wanted control, free suits, free this, free that; it never ended. At first I begged. They slapped me around. I pled poverty. They were heartless. I cooked the books; but they kept coming and coming and coming. So one day I bought a shotgun. It's easy to do, buying a shotgun in Florida. It's nothing. You go in, you pay money; you walk out."

"So you shot someone."

My father smiled a sad and awful smile. "I wish I shot the whole fucking pack of those *gonifs*, those *ausvoorfs*. I would have made it self-defense somehow, and if that didn't work and I went to jail that would have been better than the way it turned out."

"Wu Tie Mei protected you," I said, suddenly understanding.

He straightened up. "She was such a woman; even you don't know what a woman she was."

"I know plenty," I said. "I know more than you know."

"Of course you do," he said. "You're my son the doctor. But not about this, thank God. Not about this. She was a tigress. She was a dragon."

"Tell me," I said, slumping down into one of Rachel's dining room chairs. "Tell me everything that happened."

"Four of them came into the store one day."

"One of them was a woman," I said.

"How can you know that?" he asked, looking terrified. "You can't possibly know that."

"Just tell me what happened."

"They came in and I took out the shotgun. They laughed at me; right to my face. I was ready to shoot them. I loaded the shell. It was a big gun and it would have taken out my front window but I was ready to shoot. But they distracted me; they talked, they told lies, they pretended to be afraid, they made razzle-dazzle, and the next minute one was behind me and another was beside me and then their own guns came out."

"Where was Tie Mei?" I asked, needing the answer but not wanting it.

"In the back doing inventory on account of her talent for numbers. She heard them and came out and took one gun away as if she was a tornado in human form. She kicked and punched and whirled and had three of them down on the floor faster than I could even breathe."

"Three," I breathed.

"One stayed out of the fray, hanging by the door: a lookout, I suppose."

"The woman," I said.

"She called out and Tie Mei came up ready with those daggers of hers. She had them with her all the time, you know. Even in bed."

"You know because you slept with her; isn't that right? Why didn't you marry her? That's all she wanted, right? What would it have changed? She was living with us, sleeping with you."

"Please. I know what you think. I wanted to marry her, God how I wanted to, but I couldn't do that to the memory of your mother."

"It was the right thing to do."

"I see that now. Maybe I didn't see it then. Time changes everything and it changes nothing. Someday you'll know what I mean. Tie Mei pushed me down so they couldn't shoot me. She came up to throw the knives and got shot in the eyes for her trouble. Boom, boom; two shots so close they sounded like one. I hear them in my sleep every night of my life."

"That Russian bitch," I said.

"There's nothing you can do," he said. "It's over and done. It was a lifetime ago."

"Ten years," I said. "Ten years is all it's been. You could have gone to the police. You could have gone to the papers. Why didn't you do that? Why didn't you even tell me she died saving you?"

"Better we should leave some things alone," he said.

I went to him. I grabbed him in anger and lifted him off the couch. He was wearing shorts and his legs were thin. His long arms flapped so lightly his bones felt hollow as a bird's. The violence felt familiar to me. It felt good.

My father didn't resist, he just kept looking at me. Finally, I got the message. "It was me," I whispered, letting him down. "I was the reason you didn't fight back."

My father started to cry. "They said they'd kill you. They knew you were just starting out, just doing your internship. They ran before the cops arrived, telling me that if I fingered them they would kill you slower than cooking a roast. That's what they said. They talked about you like you were a piece of meat."

I took him in my arms and smelled his smell, his father smell, that mixture of sweat and cologne and pastrami and age. We held each other for what seemed like forever. We clung together until we heard Rachel's key in the front door.

"Tell me you'll stay away from them," he begged. "Promise you'll let the police do the job. I can't stand the idea of them killing you, too."

"Don't worry," I said. "Everything will be fine."

49

The hurricane stalled just offshore. A dangerous vortex, it whipped the sky and beat the sea, but forecasters were still uncertain of its projected path. Precipitation was light, but when I got to the hospital, I was soaked from the ride. I went to the locker room to put on dry scrubs, only to find my padlock had been cut off, and my name removed from my locker.

John Khalsa was wasting no time.

On my way to the neuro intensive care unit, one of the house staff saw me. I saw something on his face, saw him duck over to the nursing station and pick up the phone. I had just reached Jordan's bed and was about to part the curtains when a burly security guard arrived. Vicky Sanchez hurried along behind him.

"You don't have to do this," she said, tugging on the guard's arm.

"Visiting hours are over," he replied.

"I'm here as an attending," I said.

"You don't have privileges."

"I don't need them to visit a patient."

"I just told you it's after hours."

I took a deep breath, and contracted my torso on the exhale, utilizing a qigong energy technique Tie Mei had taught me. In nature, animals puff up to intimidate a foe. This trick did the opposite. Using abdominal, intercostal and pelvic muscles, I made myself appear smaller, less challenging. It was conflict avoidance, pure and simple.

"May I just spend a little time with my girlfriend here?" I pleaded.

"No way," the guard shook his head.

"He did the surgery. He's the best we have," Vicky implored.

"I got orders from administration."

I put my hand on his shoulder as a way of making an emotional bridge. I did it gently, but he flinched. Deciding then and there that my appeal was useless, I put one stiffened finger onto the back of his elbow and pushed hard on the acupressure point known as *quchi*, or crooked pond. I use this point when I treat nervous patients, as gentle pressure there calms and regulates the body. It has another effect when pressed forcefully. Within seconds, the guard's pallor faded and he clutched his stomach. Vicky watched the whole thing, but my attack was so subtle she missed it completely.

Without a word, the guard tottered off to the bathroom. Ten paces away, he looked over his shoulder as if to say something to me, but the roiling in his bowels overcame him and he quickened his pace toward the bathroom. He would explode from both ends; I knew that much, and I counted on the episode to last long enough for me to have a proper visit.

"What just happened?" asked Vicky.

"I have no idea. Poor guy looked sick."

"Jordan's mother was here. You just missed her."

"Zee?"

The voice was weak, but it was Jordan's. I stepped through the white curtain and over to her bed. I knelt down and laid my head carefully on her breast, avoiding her IV and the cluster of leads.

"I'm here," I said.

I closed my eyes and inhaled the smell of iodine and electrical conducting gel. I was overcome by anxiety and sadness. Psychopaths had done this to her, but I was the bridge that had brought them to her and my feelings of guilt at that were unbearable.

"Why did that man want you to leave?" Jordan asked me.

"It's not important."

"I can't feel my legs."

"I know."

"Zee, what's going on?"

"What do you remember?"

"I'm not really sure what part is nightmare and what part is real."

"Tell me," I said. "We'll sort it out together."

"I went to the bank to get cash for the storm. There was a storm, wasn't there?"

"Not yet."

"You mean it's still coming?"

"It's out in the ocean," I said. "Nobody knows."

"Bad people came to me. Terrible people."

"Not people," I said. "Something else."

"I tried to give them my money, but they didn't want it. I don't know why anyone would want to hurt me. Really, I have no idea. The nurse said I had an operation, Zee."

"The bad people damaged your spine. They did quite a job, but I think we fixed it."

"You fixed it?"

"I helped."

She reached down to stroke my hair. "That must have been terrible for you," she said.

My urge to sob was uncontrollable.

"Don't," she said, hearing me break. "Just tell me I'm going to get my legs back."

"It's complicated," I said.

She used her left arm, the one without the needle in it, to lift my chin so she could see my eyes.

"Don't lie to me, doctor."

I kissed her. She wiped away my tears with her thumb. "I'm not lying," I said. "I'm telling you it's complicated."

"Earlier I could feel my toe, but now I can't."

I felt a leap in my chest. "Say that again."

"Earlier I could feel the weight of the sheet on my big toe. One of the nurses told me to try and wiggle it but all I could do was jerk my leg."

"You jerked your leg?"

"After she went out I did, but I can't do it now."

"That's great news," I said, unable to wipe the grin off my face. "If your spinal cord were permanently damaged, you would not have been able to feel anything, that much I can say. You would not have been able to move anything either."

"But why can't I move now?"

"Here's how it goes," I said, glad to take refuge in technical talk. "First, blood and lymph rush to the site. White cells and the antibiotics in your IV drip work together to fight invaders and red cells bring oxygen to the area. Blood and lymph carry dead tissue and bacteria away from the wound. All this activity has a certain rhythm. It changes according to the demands of the healing process, and it varies according to the time of day. When there is a lot of fluid at the site, the wound swells and can press on nerves, making you lose sensation and the ability to move. As the wound heals and the swelling goes down, you can feel things better. That's why your symptoms are not stable right now."

"I'm not out of the woods yet, am I?"

"I don't know. You may have a long and difficult road ahead."

She took a while to digest this. I watched her face. I listened to the beeping of the monitor.

"We had a great time in Lake Wales," she said at last.

"I've already redecorated my bedroom at home to match the motel."

"Even if I never walk again, nobody can take what we had."

"No," I said. "They can't."

"I've had a little while to think through what happened," she said. "I mean it's really all I've been thinking about."

"Don't," I said. "Better to rest right now."

"But there's a question I have to ask."

I felt my mouth go dry. "Of course," I said.

"Did they hurt me because of you, Zee?"

Unable to face her, I walked toward the door, then the window, then came back to her bed. My mouth worked, but no matter how hard I tried, I couldn't come up with anything to say.

"Did this happen because you stood up to bad people?" she pursued. "Because you wouldn't abandon your principles?"

"We don't have to talk about this now."

"Of course we do. There's nothing more important to talk about. You got in their way, didn't you? You wouldn't back down."

I bowed my head, ashamed of my willfulness, my ego, how little I had thought through the risks my actions might bring to others.

"It was the Russians, right?" she went on. "The mobsters?"

I managed a tiny nod.

"I would have figured this out sooner if they didn't have me all doped up. They hurt me to hurt you, is that it?"

"There's a whole story," I whispered. "It goes back a long time."

"Do you remember what you taught me about the link between intention and cutting?"

"Of course."

"Well, you had no intention to harm me."

"I'm here for you," I said.

"Because you think you owe me."

"That's not why I'm here."

"I'm terrified to be alone like this, but I don't want to be a dead bird around your neck, Zee."

I took her hands in mine. I bent over and kissed her. Her mouth was dry from the medications.

"I mean it," she said. "Guilt and obligation are the enemies of love."

"Let's just take this one day at a time, okay? Please?"

She gave me a small smile and nodded. We sat together for a while. I recognized Vicky's walk as she came close, heard her breathing outside the curtain, saw her shoes, watched her leave again.

"I heard you say you love me at the hammer-in," Jordan said quietly. "You thought I didn't, but even over all the shouting, I could make out the words."

"I'm going to make sure you walk again," I said.

"It's not your fault there's evil in the world, Zee."

"I could have stayed away from you until the Russian thing was over. That's what I should have done. I wasn't thinking like a warrior. I was stupid and selfish and I hate myself for it."

"Hating the energy between us isn't the answer. Hating yourself isn't either."

I squeezed her leg gently.

"I felt that," she whispered.

I squeezed a little lower.

"I felt that too."

"And now?"

"No."

I searched around for a pin. I wanted to do my own neurological exam, but I heard a rustling at the curtain and steeled myself for a security team. I'd make them wait until I was done, that much was for sure. Either that or I'd put them all in their own group hospital room.

It wasn't security. It was Detective Wanda Berkowitz.

"Oh," I said, as she parted the curtain.

"I know you," said Jordan.

"I'm Wanda. We met at the wedding. Xenon's father told me what happened. I'm so sorry."

"Are you here to take a statement?" I asked.

"Actually, I'm here because I'm your sister," said Wanda. "Could I speak with you outside for a moment?"

I went out. She put her hands on my shoulders. "What's going on here, Zee?"

"She was assaulted. I worked with another surgeon to save her life. We don't know if she will walk again. Paraplegia is a possibility."

"You know who did this, don't you?"

"Know who did it? I can't know what you mean. It happened in an alley."

"It's because you wouldn't back off, isn't it? The fucking Mafiya's idea of payback?"

I looked at the floor. There was too much dancing to do, and I felt darkness coming.

"I told you to stay away from them," Wanda said. "I told you to let it be, not to file the complaint, to leave police work to us."

"Are you going to take Jordan's statement or just leave things at giving me a hard time?"

She took her hands off me. Her energy and self-confidence waned and her voice grew softer. Now she was the one who could not look at me.

"They beat their kid and brought him in to die on your table. You wouldn't back down like everyone else around here and just let it lie. You did the right thing, Zee. Now do it again. Tell me what you know. Let me help."

I don't know that I have ever wanted to do anything as badly as I wanted to abandon responsibility, give Wanda the DVD, and duck the job I knew I had to do. The problem was, the perpetrators were disguised, and I was sure the disc had been sanitized. An operation as sophisticated as Petrossov's no doubt knew the ins and outs of forensics. Voice identification might be possible, but justice could not be certain and would in any case bring other painful facts to light. Likely as not, if I worked with Wanda, the tattooed scales of justice on Jordan's sweet back would remain unrequited.

"I wish I knew what you're talking about," I said.

"I'm on your side," she hissed. "I've been on your side all along. But this cutting and killing can't go on. It has to stop right here, or I will have to start asking you very specific questions. Once I start asking those questions, other people will get involved and things will accelerate very, very quickly. I won't be able to help you. You will lose control of your life, Zee. Everything you have and you know, will go away. Do you understand what I'm saying? Please say you do. I can't sit by for this."

"Visit with Jordan," I said. "I know she's glad you're here. I'll just go in now and kiss her goodbye."

As I turned away, Wanda looked infinitely sad.

Inside the room, Jordan beckoned me close. "Is there something else you need to tell me?" she asked.

"Nothing," I said. "Answer Wanda's questions as best you can and then go to sleep. I'll be back to see you in the morning."

"Are you going to need a sword tonight, Zee?"

I flushed; I know I did. I was learning, by the minute, that in this intimate quarter there was no place to hide.

"Rest," I said. "Let nature do its work."

She grabbed my hand with surprising strength. "I finished your sword the night we came home," she said. "It's in a zippered case under my bed."

I marveled at her. I moved her hair off her brow. I kissed her cheeks and her throat and her forehead. I kissed her eyes. "Get all better," I said. "I need you beside me."

"The blade has a name," she said. "I call it Quiet Teacher."

50

I swim below the jellyfish of my past. Bereft of a school, a pelagic wanderer, I am a solitary predator with precious few friends. The long tendrils of the jelly reach down through the depths to sting and stun me. They make it difficult to follow currents and eddies, but at the same time they give me a connection to the world above. With that connection intact, I am but flawed; without it, I am a freak of nature.

I went straight to Jordan's from the hospital. I had no house key, so I broke into her bedroom window by jimmying the latch. If things went well and there was time, I would come back and board the place up before the storm.

The sword case was where she said it would be. I knelt to it and paused with my hands on the black zippered case. I closed my eyes and thought about the long road behind this moment. There was Grandpa Lou's concern for world Jewry, the death of my mother, the arrival of Tie Mei, my father's deal with the Mafiya, and my unlikely training—all incomprehensible without an awareness of the lives that went before. In the context of my reincarnation cycle, the omnipresent hum of violence behind my life made perfect sense.

Tie Mei came to me then, not from the ceiling and not from the window but from some other place entirely, through the very atoms of the wall behind Jordan's bed, floating over the aquarium, waking the electric eel, who rose from the gravel to arc and squirm, thinking to feed. Clad in boots and a coat of fine chain mail, she held two wolf-tooth maces, weapons I had never seen her wield. Smiling, she swung them in a leisurely figure eight.

"Stop gloating," I said.

"I take it I am talking to my old comrade, now?"

"You know damn well who you're talking to."

"Loss," she said. "A casualty of war."

"You played me like a fiddle," I said. "And you didn't care about the price."

"One casualty," Tie Mei said. "She has made your swords before. She was a gimp named Yunling, in the northern forests during the Sung dynasty. Her trick was the water, the minerals in her well. Mixing it into her steel made her blades the strongest."

"She's not going to be a casualty for long," I said. "Not if I have anything to say about it."

Startled, Tie Mei stared at me as if seeing me for the first time. I returned the favor. Having glimpsed the full range of my reincarnation cycle, nothing in life could ever look quite the same to me, least of all my partners in the grand scheme.

"You knew I would avenge you," I went on. "Jordan or no Jordan, you knew I would hunt down the woman who killed you. It has all come down to revenge. That's what all these visits were about, all your exhortations to remember."

"Not just that," she said, letting the maces fall to her side. "You needed to know who you really are. You're changed now. Powerful. Deep."

"I'm changed all right, but I'm not sure I'm better off. Maybe there's a reason people don't remember past lives. Have you thought of that? Maybe there's wisdom to the system."

"Coming to knowledge is always the way. If you don't like knowing more, you need to change your attitude."

"Will I free you from your cycle by avenging your death?"

Tie Mei grew quiet. "Maybe. Maybe you'll free yourself, too."

"Revenge." I said.

Tie Mei sat down next to me on the edge of Jordan's bed. I watched for a dimple in the duvet, but I did not see one. I smelled almonds.

"None of this could have worked if I didn't love you so much," I said. "Violence flowing from love; I find that strange."

For the first time since I'd known her, my teacher cast down her eyes. "Yes," she said. "So do I."

"And guilt," I added. "Something else I didn't want."

She looked at me as if she wanted to say something else but thought better of it. She opened her mouth, and I saw how beautiful her lips were, and I remembered her magnetism and her grace. I suddenly felt badly for blaming her.

"I'm sorry," I said.

She nodded.

"Will I see you again?"

"I don't know."

She leaned over and kissed my cheek. I could not feel her lips, but the aroma of almonds grew strong, and I sensed a tiny tingle on my flesh, the kind you might get if you licked both poles of a radio battery at the same time. Then, as suddenly as she had appeared, she faded, leaving me nothing but a terrible emptiness.

I stayed on the bed, and withdrew the new sword from its leather scabbard. The handle was of dense, tight-grained ebony, and offered a perfect grip. A large black diamond capped off a pommel, shaped like a demon's head. The guard resembled the wings of a bat, a traditional good luck symbol in Chinese martial arts. The wings curved toward the tip to provide a trap for an opponent's blade. The dark Damascus blade looked like raindrops on deep water. A hair from Jordan's head lay on her pillow. I picked it up and dropped it on the edge of the blade. It fell into two pieces.

Sword in hand, I moved through the house, getting to know the blade. I cut imaginary foes and parried imaginary thrusts. The balance, the voice, the flexibility and the weight were beyond what I had hoped for, beyond my wildest dreams. I had never held such a weapon. At length, I wrapped it in a plastic bag to keep it dry, strapped it to the back of the old BMW, and rode home.

My father was waiting in the driveway, inside Rachel's convertible Jaguar. As I pulled up, he stared at the old bike. "How long have you had that?"

"I bought it six months ago. I've been fixing it up little by little. When you told me you were getting married, I sped up the project so I could give it to you for a wedding present."

"Yeah? Then what are you doing riding it around in the rain?"

"It's your old bike," I said.

"I knew that."

"I mean your exact old bike."

"Impossible," he said.

"But true. I found it in Miami. There were photos of you and Tie

Mei in the tool tray. I'll show them to you after the storm has passed.

My father got out of his car and straddled his old machine. He levered it off the kickstand and leaned down close to the fairing. The intimacy of the moment—something only someone who has developed a relationship with a bike can understand—was almost too much for me to watch.

"Rachel's going to love it," he said.

"That's what I was thinking."

He came off the seat and kissed me. "Get in the car for a minute. I've got something for you too."

I slid into the passenger's seat. He handed me a rosewood box. "I should have given these to you years ago," he said.

I knew what lay inside even before the latch gave in to my fingers. My mouth went dry. I started to shake. This time it was my father who had to look away.

I had long imagined them to be bloodstained or pitted, but the daggers were perfect, their handles contoured like bamboo, their blades wicked and flat and perfectly symmetrical and bright.

"I thought the police kept these as evidence," I said.

"The police nothing. I've had them for years. I took them before anyone showed up at the shop."

"You took them?"

"For you. I took them for you. I've kept them oiled, see? There's not a spot of rust on them. They even smell a little bit like almonds."

I gave him a startled look.

"What, you don't think I remember?" he whispered. "You don't think I have a nose?"

"I just...."

"Now, don't say anything that's going to embarrass you later."

"Thank you," I said.

"Just go inside and get your things together and let me drive you someplace safe."

I got out of the car. The rain ran down my face. "I've got it all worked out; you don't need to wait."

He lowered his window and looked at me suspiciously. "It's worked out?"

"I've reserved a hotel. Now go back to Rachel before the roads flood out. I've got things to do to get ready."

"You're sure?" he said. "The storm has turned. It's coming in."

"Don't worry. I told you. Everything's going to be fine."

That's when he got out of the car. He looked tall, and he moved lightly, quickly, with more spring than I'd seen in a long time, maybe ever. I wondered how much of my power and speed I'd inherited from him, how much of my focus. I'd never regarded my father physically that way. I had the sudden feeling there was more about him that I didn't know than I did.

"That's your code for you're going to do something to the Russians," he spat. "You think I don't know about you, with your swords and your sticks."

"I don't have any sticks," I said.

"But you've got swords," he interrupted, slamming the door behind him. "Wanda talked to Rachel. Rachel talked to me. We don't have secrets, Rachel and I. I'm sick of secrets and so is she; we're both too old for them. I'm not sure exactly what's going on, but I know Wanda's worried about you. You're making stress for us with whatever it is you're doing, Zee. I watch the papers. I watch the TV. I got some ideas."

I put up my hands. "Don't," I said. "Don't get ideas."

"You want to ruin what I got with Rachel over some revenge idea, some crazy thing you think you have to set right? You want to do that to your old man? Don't pit one side of this tender new family against the other. Let it go, son. Give us all a chance at happiness for whatever time we got left."

I turned and walked to the front door of the house. He followed me.

"I'm going to set everything right," I said, opening the door.

"Right for you!" he thundered as I stepped inside. "But what about everyone around you?"

I closed the door. Even over the rising wind and rain, I heard him there, sensed him still standing with clenched fists.

"You're throwing away everything! Everything! If you do this, you are not my son! If you go and kill for revenge, you are no kind of doctor; you've learned nothing about compassion. If you do this, I cast you out!"

I felt my tears come up. I stood touching the door handle, my heart and head a jumble. It was the hardest thing I've ever done, keeping that door closed, but I did. I waited for the sound of the car engine starting. It seemed like an age until I heard it.

51

After my father drove away, Orson Cartwright appeared at my back patio door. He was smiling, and held a crumpled Burger King wrapper in one hand, and a soggy copy of Miyamoto Musashi's *Book Of Five Rings* in the other.

"How come no shutters on this door?" he asked.

"Hurricane glass."

"Oh. Hey, what was that all about?"

"My father is worried about me."

"Yeah, but he said he cast you out."

"Bible talk," I said. "From another age."

"Still," said Orson.

"Yes."

"If my father had worried about me, he wouldn't have killed himself."

"Where'd you come from?" I asked him, as the rain suddenly grew strong.

"Don't worry, I'm dry. I've been under the eave. I came back to help you. Hey, it says in the intro to this book that this guy killed the most famous swordsman in Japan with a wooden oar. Do you think it's true?"

"Not an oar, a wooden sword carved from an oar," I said. "Where's Bimini?"

"With her folks," he said, following me into the house. "She invited me to stay over there, but I told her I'd rather be with you."

"We're in an evacuation zone. You shouldn't be here."

"You're here."

"Well, I've got to go out again."

"Come on. The storm will be here in an hour."

"There's a job I have to do. After I leave, call a cab and have him take you to Bimini's place."

Orson dogged me as I went upstairs for my acupuncture kit. "Wow," he said, right at my elbow. "Look at all that weird stuff."

"How long were you waiting for me outside?"

"Couple of hours, maybe. It's really quiet over here. Hardly anybody came by. The cops were around twice. I saw them cruising, and hid in the bushes."

I put together a selection of my largest needles. He asked me what they were for.

"Treating a cancer," I said.

"And what about that other stuff? What's that hook? What's are those vials? What's in that sack?"

"Tools of the trade," I said.

"What trade? Who carries stuff like that around?"

"You're too nosy for your own good."

"Everybody says that. But we're cool, right?"

"Sure," I said. We're cool."

"Even with the age thing?"

"What age thing?"

"You being old and me being young."

"You're not that young and I'm not that old."

"I feel a lot older since dad died, but there's glue between us: you stuck on me and me stuck on you. Am I right?"

"We're friends, Orson. I'm sure we always will be."

He digested that for a moment. "People die from cancer, don't they?"

"It happens," I answered.

Alongside the garage, Orson watched as I stowed everything in the watertight hatch of my racy Greenland kayak.

"You're going paddling?" he said.

"I told you I had a job to do. I have to take the boat to get there. Don't ask any more questions about it, because you're not going to get any more answers."

"You're not going to drown in the storm, are you?"

"No way," I said. "It's a good boat. Now help me carry it to the Intracoastal."

"I thought it would be heavier," he said, lifting the stern.

"It's a special boat. It was a gift."

It took us five minutes to reach the Intracoastal. The water roiled.

Orson held the boat steady between his legs while I climbed in, soaking his shoes.

"You sure about this?" he asked doubtfully.

"I'm sure. Now go call that cab."

The boat was much less stable than the big plastic lug I'd paddled that day off Jake Derringer's yacht, a sports car compared to an SUV. Trying desperately not to tip it over in front of Orson, I dug in and headed south. I hadn't gotten ten feet when he called out to me. I backed up. He waded out into the water and looked me straight in the eye.

"You done this before? Paddled, I mean? You don't look too smooth."

"Just the rain," I said.

"So why not do it on a sunny day? I don't want to lose you, too."

"If I had a son, I'd want him to be like you," I said. "Now go see your girl."

He smiled, and I paddled off. When I was a hundred yards out, I turned around.

Orson was still standing in the water.

52

It took me far longer to reach Idylwild than I expected. The headwind was daunting and the force of the storm at sea disrupted the normal flow of the Intracoastal. The waterway was narrow, but it felt wide; the distance was only a few miles, but it felt galactic. I battled currents and backwash and choppy whitecaps. I learned to keep my paddle low to the boat to save my shoulders from burning, and I learned by trial and error to feather the paddle when it was out of the water so the wind wouldn't use it as a sail. The darkness seemed preternaturally deep, and it masked floating sticks and other debris, so my hull took a pounding.

At one point I saw the flashing blue light of a sheriff's speedboat off in the distance, and I paddled madly down a tributary canal just to escape his notice. I sat bobbing until he passed, his searchlight roving across the water, then waited a few minutes just in case he looped around. There was no way I wanted to explain myself. Being seen out in this night would terminate the plan that had been growing in me for some time now. It was a plan that depended upon the storm. I was out this night because of the weather, not in spite of it.

I paddled south past Commercial Boulevard, Oakland Park, and Sunrise. When I passed under the bridge at Las Olas, I saw the lights of Idylwild glinting off to the west. Petrossov's big yacht was tied tight to the pier; vintage Miss America X was up out of the water on a hoist. He should have moved it to an inland marina, but of course failing to protect his boat was the least egregious of Vlexei Petrossov's trespasses.

I tied up the kayak against the concrete seawall, shouldered my pack, and came up the dock slowly. I noticed the security camera on a post at the end of the walkway. It took a few moments to see that it was moving in a slow constrained arc, first one way, then the other. I waited for it to turn away, then sprinted down the walkway to the gate. There had been a man stationed there when I had last been to the house, but the post was abandoned.

Wu Tie Mei taught me the strategy of dividing the enemy to conquer him. She said it was a 2,500-year-old idea from Sun Tzu, China's most famous general. Now, I had certain memories of the technique, a glimpse of running down a desert dune with a handful of men at my side, the damp smell of the deep forest as I watched a brigade split into two in an attempt to encircle me as I hid in a tree.

Even in the storm, I was certain Petrossov had too many men for me to handle all at once. I had to take them out one at a time. Ideally they wouldn't know what was happening until it was nearly over. There was a path that went from the dock to the driveway and I took it, crouching low along the hedges. When I got to the guardhouse at the front, I found the door shut and the windows steamed up.

I knocked on the glass.

The man named Dmitri came out with a machine pistol at the ready. I shoved a needle straight up into his armpit, targeting *jiquan*, Summit's Spring, the first point on the heart meridian. Done too forcefully, this point stops the heart, but needled more gently it leads to weakness, confusion, and a bewildering sense of being alone in the world. As Dmitri looked desperately around, I took the clip out of the gun and threw it into the bushes, then stepped inside to look at the security monitors.

Some of the images were fuzzy because of the rain, but they told me what I needed to know. I found the next guard walking the perimeter. He was one of the men who had assaulted me, perhaps one of those who had beat Jordan, although I couldn't be sure. If I had come up from the dock a minute later, I would have run right into him. A soggy cigarette dangled from his lips, and he walked an Alsatian on a tight lead. I hadn't seen any sign of a dog in my previous visit, but I had come prepared. The dog started growling. The guard turned around. I ducked behind a hedgerow. The dog strained toward me. I reached back into my pack and took out a small ball of herbs and rolled it down the walkway. The dog sniffed it.

"No!" said the guard, but the Chinese potion was irresistible. Tie Mei had shown me how it worked at the playground when I was a child. It was her one bit of mischief, putting dogs harmlessly and mysteriously to sleep. The dog went down and the guard crouched to feel its chest and when he did I reached out from inside the hedge and jammed a needle into *shuidao*, the watercourse, twenty-eighth point on the stomach meridian, below and to the side of the navel. The resulting explosion in his bowels had him rolling on the ground in pain while I sprinted up the path to the house. A motion-sensor light went on. I threw a rock at it. The tinkle of the glass was muted by the wind.

The cameras had shown two more guards snacking by the kitchen window. I remembered seeing an adjoining breakfast nook during my time in the house. I took a spring-loaded tap out of my back, broke the window there, and shoved a tree branch through it. The men were there in ten seconds.

"Isn't this hurricane glass?" one asked.

"Must be getting really bad out there," answered the other.

I pulled on the branch. I watched the two guys bend over in fascination. One touched the branch as if it were a snake. I wiggled the end. The men bent closer, and I jumped on the branch. As it came up, it caught the first guy under the chin. He had a glass jaw and went right down. The second cupped his hands to the window, caught sight of me and let off a burst of gunfire. Shards of glass rained down. I saw glints in the water behind me, reflections of lights going on upstairs.

The element of surprise gone, I stayed flat on the ground below the window. The guard stuck out his head. It took him a moment to look down, just long enough to reach into my pack and pull out a bottle and open it and throw it on his face.

It was a combination of four different liniments each designed to bring circulation to the site of specific training injuries, the forearm from overuse of a heavy halberd, say, or the knee from low crouches used while employing the spear. All told, there were 34 ingredients, so the sting in the guard's eyes was not merely from the alcohol base but from decaying gecko, scorpion, deer antler, sparrow brain, dragon blood resin, cicadas, flying squirrel feces, toad venom, blister beetle, centipede, earthworm, and some caustic plants.

No sightseeing for him for a while.

I moved around to the front of the house. I took out the glass side panel at the front door and went in so I could watch the stairs. I saw Chazov, the butler, come down with a big pistol in his hand. He wore his service whites and he headed for the kitchen. I threaded my way through all the expensive furniture, making no sound, keeping my eye on the stairs in case someone else came down. He was almost to the kitchen hallway when he suddenly spun around. I dove into an alcove. He fired one shot at me and then another, hitting the antique horse sculpture above me. It tottered on its pedestal as I rolled away. Chazov intercepted its fall, and in that one precious instant I leapt toward him. Crouching and radiating confidence, he turned, horse in one hand, gun in the other. I turned with him, keeping his body between me and the gun, and managed to stay there just long enough to shove a needle into his neck.

He fell and looked up at me from the floor.

"Nobody can move that fast," he said.

"You shouldn't have gone for the horse."

"A museum piece from the Tsar Peter's palace."

"Your last big mistake."

"If you knew how many men...." Befuddled, he started to laugh. Small Intestine 16 is a particularly grotesque point in that it unbalances the emotions before it kills. Tie Mei used to say that the real warrior is full of passion but shows none. I could see he was appalled by his own outburst. "I am dying, yes?" he asked.

"It isn't the first time, and it won't be the last."

He looked at me uncertainly, not following my meaning. "But you are a doctor. Doctor's don't kill people."

"You haven't been reading the newspapers lately."

He started laughing again, fought it, lost, yowled in hysteria, then suddenly grew quiet.

"Tell me I'll be buried in Russia."

"No," I said. "You won't."

"You're not far behind me," he said. "It won't be up to you anyway."

"Yes it will."

"This is revenge for the woman?"

I hit him with a back fist across the face. It was my best shot, very strong, and he hadn't expected it. The flesh on his cheek split, and I was satisfied to see his cheek cave in, signaling a break in the bone.

"Jordan. Her name is Jordan."

He rubbed his face, reached in and pulled out a molar. "A woman nobody will want anymore," he said.

I kicked him in the ribs. "You're wrong about that."

"If I was wrong, you wouldn't be kicking me," he smiled.

I pushed the needle in deeper. He stiffened. The smile left his face.

"I promise I'll be seeing you soon," he croaked.

Then he died. The house was quiet after that, save for the whistling of the wind through the exterior breaches I had created. A rhythmic tapping came from outside the panoramic glass in the living room. A palm tree, bent over in the wind.

South Florida houses are devoid of basements. I knew Vlexei and Natalya were upstairs waiting for me. I felt certain they would not come down. I imagined the firepower they must have in their bedroom.

"Come on down," I called. "It will go worse for you if I have to come up."

When they didn't answer, I went out the front door and threw a grappling hook over the gable. I shimmied up to the ledge, broke a window, waited for gunfire, and rolled in.

I came up in a hallway. I had only an instant to look around before the house was plunged into darkness. Behind me, the eerie green glow of a city generator hit by lightning filled the window. It took a moment for the house generator to click on, but when it did, I saw Galina, in silk pajamas, standing at the end of the hall.

"My parents are bad, aren't they? They do bad things."

"Yes."

"You're bleeding. Did they shoot you?"

I looked down. Blood oozed from a small hole in my side, and I suddenly understood Chazov's promise. I had felt nothing until now, but I was suddenly overcome with fatigue and a sense of doom. I felt for an exit point but did not feel one.

The bullet was still inside me.

"Where are they?" I asked.

"They went downstairs. Don't hurt my papa, okay? He's nice sometimes."

"Go back inside. Hide under the bed and don't come out. Will you do that?"

"You're going to stop the bad things from happening to me?"

"I'm going to do my best."

"I prayed for you to come. I talk to God on my cell phone all the time. Now I know he listens, even though he never says anything."

53

The Petrossovs stood back-to-back in the center of the living room, on a Persian area rug that might have been a khan's. Natalya wore a green silk robe tied at the waist, and while she had her back to me I knew from her posture she was holding her two autopistols. Vlexei was bare-chested and wearing slacks. He had a big, nickel-plated Smith & Wesson revolver in his hand.

They scanned the myriad doorways and windows, the front of the house and the back. The one place they were not looking was the place they had just come from—the stairs. Crouched on the landing, I paused long enough to pop a tiny red pill and to pack my bullet wound with orange powder. Tie Mei told me the reason our troops could never find injured enemy soldiers during the Vietnam War was because of this combination, known as *yu nan bai yao*. The powder stopped bleeding, and the pill staved off shock.

"This is what you get," I heard Vlexei Petrossov tell her in Russian. "This is Rafchik's revenge. My poor darling boy."

"Rafik is in heaven now. He forgives me."

Keeping Quiet Teacher low and to my side, I started down the stairs. Vlexei glanced down the hall.

"Chazov!" he cried.

"What?" his wife hissed.

"Chazov is dead," Vlexei said in wonderment. "How could anyone kill Chazov?"

"I told you those Spetsnaz boys were no good for us," Natalya said, disappearing down the hall to join her husband. "If they were so good up close they would have won Afghanistan. Give them a tank, give them goggles and radios, they're fine. That fancy training isn't worth shit on the street."

Spetsnaz; Russian Special Forces. I was lucky to be alive. I crept down the staircase on my toes, ready to dive over the banister and roll away if I were spotted. I reached the ground floor and peeked around the corner, low and stealthy. I saw Vlexei crouched near his man, while Natalya stood close by, tapping her foot in boredom.

"Look," said Vlexei. "Tsar Peter's horse."

"If he's holding it, he died for it."

"You always hated Chazov," Vlexei said. "But he was a good man."

"You're an idiot for thinking so."

"The doctor is dangerous," Vlexei said, putting the horse back on its stand and looking around.

Natalya spat. "He's the protégé of that Chinese bitch with the sad eyes. She's reaching out from the grave with him. You should have killed him with the boat."

"I ran over him three times! You should have left his girlfriend out of it. You went too far. You always have to push people. You could have charmed him. Why didn't you charm him?"

"He knew!" Natalya yelled.

Crouched by the doorway, I tried to figure how I could take them both out with a sword. Once again, I was going to have to divide to conquer. I rued the superiority of firearms at a distance. Up close, I'd have a chance, but at this yardage it was no go.

"He knew nothing," Vlexei shouted. "Don't you see? You forced him to dig. You forced him to learn."

"I'll kill him, so why worry?"

"Why worry?" Vlexei looked at his wife as if just now realizing she was mad. "Where are the guards? Where is the dog? Chazov is dead and he's out there hunting us, and it's a hurricane outside and you ask why worry?"

"Stop your whining. You're pathetic."

Natalya stepped out of the hallway and looked around. I barely had time to press myself against the wall. Seeing nothing, she turned back to her husband.

"Stop it or what?" I heard him say. "You'll kill me too? That's where all this is going, isn't it. You'll kill me and then you'll make a big show of mourning and then one day soon you'll lose your temper and hammer Galina."

"Shut up and look for the doctor, you idiot."

"Oh, you'll do it all right," Vlexei raged.

"You don't know what you're talking about."

"Sure you do. The woman I married is gone. The monster has taken over. Soon you'll do me, and then you'll do my little girl, and then you'll do our men, then other bosses. When you're finished with us, you'll go out into the world and you'll hammer and hammer until nobody is left."

I couldn't help thinking how sane Vlexei Petrossov sounded right then, how much like a man who had lost the woman he loved and was facing annihilation. I wanted desperately to see his expression, and so I peeked around the corner just as Natalya paused, stared at him as if thinking through what he had just said, raised her two small guns, and before he could utter another syllable, shot her husband through the eyes.

I gasped as he toppled, I know I did, but she seemed not to hear me.

"The crazy doctor did it," she muttered, circling his fresh corpse. "He was a nervous wreck from his botched surgery, his career in tatters, came into our home and killed my poor Vlexei. That's it, officer. That's how it happened."

I watched the trail of red coming out of Vlexei Petrossov's face and felt nothing but grateful I'd not seen my teacher die this way. I thought about all the crimes this terrible pair had committed, all the things Wanda had alluded to but not spoken, a whole history of horror spanning two continents.

Natalya's voice brought me out of my reverie.

"Galina," she cried, the hysterical tone replaced by madness. "Oh, Galina, come see what the doctor did to poor daddy."

Outrage at the notion she would ask her daughter to see her father's bloody corpse on the floor took my better judgment, and I stepped out into the hall. "No," I said. "Not Galina."

It was Natalya's tiny pause of surprise that saved me. By the time her guns were up, I had dropped back into the living room and rolled between the leonine feet of the dining table and a credenza supporting a set of priceless silver.

"Come out, Doctor. Let's talk this over like civilized people."

Knowing she was expecting me to crawl away, I crawled toward her instead, closing in on her fluffy little blood-soaked slippers. I got close enough to smell the stale musk of her, and close enough to hear her breathe like a bellows in the night. The quarters were too close for Quiet Teacher, but they were not too close for my teacher's daggers. I stabbed through her foot with one, and brought the other up into her belly.

Natalya went down screaming, both guns blazing at the table. The solid oak—inches thick and seasoned—did not stop the bullets, but it did deflect them, and they passed by, one by my ear, another by my hip. She slid to the ground weeping in rage and agony, her knee twisted up because her foot would not move. When the guns were empty, I sprang from under the table and cut them from her, taking fingers with them, and bits of bone.

"That was for Tie Mei," I said, coming up onto my feet. "And this, this is for Jordan.

I sliced Natalya's leg using a move called Beat the Grass to Find the Snake from the sublime martial art of Chen style taijiquan. Embracing the principle of the decreasing radius circle I had taught Jordan at the hammer-in, I used a large hip movement in a wide stance and dropped my tailbone so the movement had a small, but important vertical component in addition to the large horizontal one. Thanks to Jordan's wondrous blade, the leg came off at the hip, and in the geyser that followed, Natalya, shrieked and clawed at me. The look in her eyes reminded me of the prisoners at the Broward jail: most alive as death closed in.

I rested for a moment as she bled out.

"I'll see you in hell," she whispered.

"Actually, although I know we've done this before, the way I'm working it, this is the last time for us."

With that, I raised Jordan's mistress of mayhem until the steel glowed from the light of the chandelier. Using a large, two-handed, overhead chop, I took Natalya's head.

I didn't stop there. Somehow, even simple, bloody execution wasn't enough, not for Tie Mei, not for Jordan, not for a boy named Rafik, not for what the pain I'd been through, the upheaval, the loss, the cost of my job, my family, likely my liberty too. I wielded that blade long after Natalya was dead, cutting always through soft flesh only, never through bone. In time there were only wet, red pieces of the monster, and the evil that had motivated it.

When I was finished, when the hate finally began to leave me, I took my daggers back and dug for the bullet again. I found it lodged in my oblique abdominals, and while I couldn't get it out, I took comfort in the fact that it wasn't going to kill me.

I flung the back doors wide and let the storm roar into the house. Paintings juddered and furniture slid in the wind. I turned off the lights, only to find myself standing in the glow of the emergency lights on the tall condominiums across the water. It was strange light—palpable and foreboding—the light of change, the light of deeds done. The moon pressed hard against the thick clouds, making a dull orange glow as I made my way to the dock and lowered Miss America X into the choppy surface of the Intracoastal Waterway.

I dragged Chazov's body out to the boat, and then Vlexei Petrossov's. I gathered what was left of Natalya into the Persian rug, and carried her out to join her men. When all three were in the boat, I went back inside, and found Galina standing at the bottom of the stairs.

The look on her face is one I will take to my grave.

"I told you to stay in your room," I said, panting from exertion and pain.

She just stared at me.

"How long have you been there?"

Still those eyes, still that expression.

"How long have you been standing there? What did you see?"

No answer.

"Tell me."

Not one word—just the stare. We looked at each other for a long and desperate moment. There were so many things I wanted to explain to her. I wanted to tell her how her brother's soul had fled for the sky. I wanted to tell her I had done what I had done in the name of revenge for Rafik and for Tie Mei and for countless other victims. I wanted to tell her I had set her free, but I could not muster it, especially without knowing whether she had seen my keen edge at work.

So, I picked up the telephone and called 911. I said there was a little girl alone in a waterfront house. I said she was all right, but that they should send somebody. I wiped the receiver clean.

"Galina," I said. "God doesn't want you to tell anyone I was here."

"You don't know what God wants," she whispered, her eyes filling with tears.

"I'm sorry," I said, trying not to think about the images that might be in her head. "I know it's not enough, but I did the best I could do."

"I don't know what you are," she said, shaking her head. "But I know you're not God's angel."

"No," I said. "I'm something else."

I left her that way, on the stairs, and went out to her father's speedboat. It took a few precious minutes for me to figure out how to fire up the engines, what with all the primers and chokes, but I got it running, tied my kayak to a stern cleat, and headed away from shore. The wind howled and the waves slapped. A lesser craft would have slid sideways or drenched me in the spray of the storm and tide, but the bow held true to course. Miss America X was some boat.

When I reached the ocean, I loosened a fuel line, set the motor to idle and pulled my kayak close, then leapt over and cast off. I struck one of Tie Mei's special wet/dry matches and gave it a toss. The wind took it. I did it again. The wind took that one too. The third time landed short, but the fourth match did the trick.

A trail of flame came up like an earthbound comet. The roar slapped my face. I held my paddle low, ignored the pain in my side, and let the surf take me in. Even in the Intracoastal, the current was an e-ticket ride and it was going my way.

54

Driven homeward by the forces of nature, I contemplated the flow of the water. Wu Tie Mei always told me to move like water when fighting, to flow easily and gracefully and immediately and without fanfare to the lowest places, behind and under an opponent so as to never meet his force directly, but rather always move to disconnect him from the ground, thereby controlling him. There was more to water, I realized, for in the way it connects every thing it touches, it is a metaphor for the reality we inhabit, the field of energy surrounding and connecting all living things.

I wished I could bring justice to the world without shedding blood. More than that, because I was so irredeemably soiled and so impossibly tired, I wished for a world in which husbands didn't burn their wives with cigarettes, where mothers didn't murder their children with brick hammers, where good people were not shot in the eyes, where a little girl did not have to bear witness, where my lover could rise unaided from her hospital bed and dance. In the same way that a little poison poured into the ocean manages to find the farthest shore, human intentions and human actions pollute or purify the ocean of consciousness. The smallest compassionate act benefits the whole of humanity; the smallest evil harms it. I hoped and prayed and believed that despite the violence of my actions, I had done more to clean the world that night than to dirty it.

At last, I climbed onto shore near my home, and in case there had been any witnesses at all, opened the hatches so my little boat would sink, and set it adrift. I dug in against the gale and the blood loss and the pain, and made my way across the beach road. I was accompanied in my halting march by thousands of itinerant Cuban tree frogs, their intimate places shockingly white as they fled the salty wind in a great and solemn phalanx west.

I found my house still standing, and not one drop of the Atlantic inside. I unlocked the door and entered the stultifying darkness. The power was off, so I lit a set of meditation candles, and their warm light and sweet aroma helped me relax. I lay down on the couch and ate an entire bar of the most special chocolate made from cacao grown in Chuao, Venezuela. I waited for the chocolate buzz—a combination of natural opiates and the ingredient anandamide—then stripped off my clothes, took iodine and forceps from my first aid kit, and prepared to dig the bullet out of my belly.

"What are you doing?" asked Orson Cartwright.

He stood in the doorway to the back bedroom, his shorts riding so low they showed his boxers, his t-shirt announcing "2005—Year of the Cock" in bold black letters.

"I didn't know you were here," I said. "I told you to go to Bimini's place."

"I was waiting for you. You've been shot. That's a bullet hole."

"You watch too much TV."

"I just knew something bad was going to happen. I could feel it."

"You should see the other guy."

Orson paced and circled like a duck lost in a watercourse. He clasped his hands in some kind of prayer, and then unclasped them again. His mouth moved as if his face were coming apart.

"I knew it," he said. "I knew it, I knew it, I knew it. You're going to die. Dad hung himself, you're going to die, and I'm going to be alone."

"You're not going to be alone."

He picked up Quiet Teacher.

"Put that down," I said.

"Why, because I'm going to find blood on it?"

"It's not your sword to draw," I said. "Someday you may have your own, but that one belongs to me."

"So you were in too big a rush to wipe it off. Blood and blood."

I wanted to explain about martial etiquette, something he was going to have to learn eventually. I also felt the urge to discourse on the relationship between a martial artist and his blade, perhaps even drop a little quantum physics in the mix. I wanted to tell him that because swords worked at the molecular and atomic level, they were, after a fashion, nuclear weapons. The energy to share those fine thoughts failed me, though, because I was losing precious bodily fluids out the side of my abdomen, and because I was too exhausted to do much more than breathe. "If you pull that sword, you will be transgressing."

"Like cutting across someone's lawn?"

"Transgressing, not trespassing. Think of it as acting against natural laws."

He laid it down on the coffee table. The house shook with a clap of thunder. "The radio weather report says the storm is turning," he said matter-of-factly. "That's why I stayed here. It only got us with a jab. There was no knock-out blow."

Outside, the wind grabbed hold of the elephant-ear philodendron along my front walkway and snapped it against the window like an angry whip. I put the forceps in Orson's hand.

"Keep the other hand on my stomach; that way you'll be able to feel where the tip is. I need you to follow the bullet's path and stay between the muscle and the flesh, not poke in and not come up too close to the skin. Do you think you can do that?"

"I'm going to vomit," he said.

"No you're not. Now, I'm going to lie back and relax. That will make your job easier. You'll know you've reached the bullet because you'll feel resistance. When you do, I want you to open the forceps slowly and see if you can grab it."

"I'm not kidding," he said. "I'm gonna hurl."

"You'll be fine."

"There's nothing fine here!" he cried. "I'm not a doctor. I need to call an ambulance."

"No calls," I said.

"You're crazy! What if you pass out?"

"I won't, I promise."

"Give yourself a shot, will you do that?"

I closed my eyes. "I took Chinese medicine for the loss of blood. I can't do booze or a painkiller because I don't know how it mixes with the Chinese herbs. You can do me a favor and put on a little music, though."

"What do you want to hear?"

"As you pull it out, I want to hear Neil Young sing 'After The Gold Rush.' The CD is over there next to the stereo."

He went and found it and selected the track. Neil Young crooned.

"Let's get to it," I said.

"The guy sings like a girl," Orson said.

"Still the greatest. Now go."

Orson sobbed once, then his hand grew steady. "This is really going to hurt," he said.

I looked away when the pain came. In my mind's eye, I saw Galina looking at me from the stairs. Orson's work didn't hurt as much as the vision.

"This song is ancient," said Orson.

"Me too," I said. "Now pull it out," I said.

After a long minute, the bullet came out with a sucking sound. "It's flat," Orson said, suddenly fascinated. "Like a hard little mushroom with a cap in the middle. Do you want to see it?"

"I've seen enough for one night," I answered. "Now hand me that needle and thread."

55

Wanda came to see me at home the next evening.

"Petrossov and his wife are missing," she said. "Pieces of his speedboat floated up next to a cruise ship in Fort Lauderdale Harbor."

"Silly to go boating in this bad weather we've been having."

"I heard you had the stomach flu."

"People get sick a lot around hurricanes," I said. "The stress, the overwork and all that."

"Still hurting you pretty bad, is it?"

Wanda was so sharp. I hadn't noticed that I was touching my wound. "You know the flu," I said.

"Petrossov's guards won't talk. I guess their employment prospects wouldn't be too good if word got out something had happened on their watch. My captain thinks that some army got past them. Personally, I don't think it was an army. We found spent rounds in the house, but not that many."

"Would you like some tea?"

She took a bar stool at my kitchen counter while I put the pot on. "There are no organic remains with the boat," she said. "The divers have a theory about the rough weather causing a fuel leak but I'm not buying it."

"You're not?"

"Petrossov's little girl is in the custody of the state. She was in the house for whatever happened that night, but she's shut tight as a clam. Won't say a single word. The docs say it's post-traumatic stress."

"This is *Ti Kuan Yin*, otherwise known as Iron Goddess," I said, taking the jar of leaf out and shaking some into the pot. "Very fine tea, very subtle. Good with chocolate."

"You want to show me your belly, Zee?"

"I've got some terrific stuff just in from Belgium, from a special

296

contact I keep there."

"Please lift your shirt."

"I met Galina when I stopped by the house to offer my condolences. She's charming. If nobody comes forward to take care of her, I suggest Vicky Sanchez. She's a neurosurgery nurse at Broward Samaritan: the best of the best. She lost a little girl the same age to leukemia."

"I'll see what we can do with Child Protective Investigative Services. Now would you pull up your shirt for me, Zee?"

I turned the gas up a little higher to speed up the boil. "Actually, you caught me on the way to visit Jordan."

"With the flu? Aren't you afraid she'll catch it?"

"I'm past the contagious phase."

"Show me the wound, Zee."

I moved away, put the tea jar back in the cupboard. I was afraid she might make a grab for me to look at my belly. "Some bad folks passed away," I said. "The world is lighter and cleaner than it was. I'd say that's a boon to the police department and the community in general."

"I might agree," she said. "But there are things I have to know. It's my job. I have to make my decision from a fully informed place. Now, I can bring you with me to the station and we can take a look at your wound there."

"No wound, just a flu."

Wanda sighed. "There's a lot we can do to build a case, Zee, and I'm not just talking about whatever happened to the Petrossovs. There are witnesses we can go back and talk to if we take you into custody. We can tell them you're in custody, ask them to ID you, reassure them you won't be exacting revenge."

"This teapot is made from purple Yixing clay," I said. "The Chinese say it acts like a filter and removes bad tastes from the water. They say it's the best possible material for brewing."

The kettle began to sing. I took it off the heat. Wanda chafed at the distraction, rubbing her forearms as if she cold. "Maybe we should go down to the station now and we can have tea some other time," she said.

"You say you want to make a decision from a fully informed place. Maybe I can give you some information you might not have. Do you remember Simba George, the guy with the bar that burned down?"

"He bled out through his arm."

"He used dried pinto beans in a mayo jar as a timer to set off a pipe bomb."

"I'm sure the arson investigators have the bomb figured out by now."

I made a show of counting the infusion time: 20 seconds, and not a second more. "He really had no idea when it would go off," I said after I took the leaves out.

"We found his suitcases. We know he was getting ready to leave town."

"He was happy to rid the world of a couple of generations of drunks," I said.

"And you know this because you're psychically connected with his ghost, right? That being one of your special powers?"

"Someone I know died in that fire. Hell of a guy, I can tell you that."

"This isn't working for me, Zee. In fact it's getting worse."

"I want our family to hang together."

Wanda sighed. "I hate that you're my family, Zee. I hate what this is going to do to my mother."

"Drink your tea."

"You know I have to take you in."

"All right," I said. "But I want you to make an informed decision."

"What's that supposed to mean?"

"I'm going upstairs," I said. "I'll be right back."

"You'd better be."

I brought the DVD down and put it in the player for her. "Go ahead and watch this. I'll be in the back yard."

"It's not too nice outside," she said. "Maybe you could stay where I can see you."

"Just watch the disc, okay?"

I went out through the French doors. The pool was littered with leaves, but I looked longingly at the hot tub anyway. It would be a while longer before my wound was closed enough to soak. If Chazov had shot me in the hand or in the foot I could have wrapped myself and gone in. Ruptured in the middle, I would have to wait.

I circumnavigated the yard, taking a post-storm survey in the twilight. There were branches on the ground, a piece of my neighbor's roof on the swale, two broken birds of paradise, a wind-stripped African daisy, broken bamboo, and a pencil cactus leaking sap. Other than that, things weren't bad at all.

After about five minutes, Wanda appeared at the French doors. I went inside and sat with her. The TV screen was dark, and her eyes were swollen and rimmed in red.

"Show me your sword," she said.

"You can't take it."

"Show me the sword, Zee."

I brought out Quiet Teacher.

"Jordan made it," I said. "It's what she does."

"At the wedding, she told me she was a receptionist."

"Is that right? Well maybe I had something to do with that. She's a bladesmith, Wanda: a mistress of steel. She forges metal, hammers it out, folds it, treats it, shapes it, and sharpens it. She infuses each piece with her spirit. She's a true artist."

I pulled Quiet Teacher from its scabbard. It made a soft whistle. Wanda gazed at the figure of the Damascus, at the filigree work and at the devilish bat wings.

"However did Jordan learn to make something like this?"

"Her father taught her. Metalwork is her family tradition. It's like you being a cop."

She touched the tip and it came away a red bloom. She put her finger to her lips.

"You clean this between uses, yes? I mean there's nothing...."

"I clean it."

"To sterilize it and then protect against rust."

"You're a natural," I said, putting Quiet Teacher away.

She didn't smile back. "The disc I just watched...."

"Was hand-delivered to my mailbox."

"I'm going to take it. It's not good for you to keep it. As your sister, I can tell you that."

"It's the last thing I would ever want to keep. Thank you."

"You have nothing to thank me for. I don't condone anything you did. Not one single thing, do you hear me? And I can't guarantee you won't go to jail. I have to take myself off the case. This isn't going to go clean and easy for you."

"I've never had clean and easy," I said.

"I don't feel sorry for you."

"I'm not asking you to."

"I'm confiscating the sword."

"No."

"Don't push your luck, brother. The sword goes with me."

I moved then. The look on Wanda's face told me she hadn't been expecting anything like the speed with which I took the sword. Reflexively, she reached for her gun, then stopped, hand on the holster.

"If someone finds it with you, your career is over," I said, sliding it back into its scabbard.

"If someone finds it with you, your life is over."

"Let's think about the issue for a few days," I said.

"In those few days, the sword stays locked away. It doesn't see the light of day. It doesn't even see a candle."

"I've still got the flu," I said. "And anyway, I never learned to use a sword."

She shook her head, still angry and shaken from the way I had disarmed her.

"I wish you and Martin would come see me up here when the moon is full and the night is clear," I said. "We could sit outside and use the tub and watch the bamboo and smell the jasmine."

"If Jordan can join us, it's a deal."

"Oh, she'll be here," I said. "Believe it."

Wanda stood. She took a couple of steps toward the door. It looked like her legs were tied to my furniture. "I had a talk with my mother," she said. "I thought she could talk to your father, that he would have some influence on you."

"He mentioned it," I said.

"It's a big problem for them, right at the start. Your dad's in denial."

"He just says he is," I said.

"They slept in separate rooms for the last couple of nights."

"Great."

"I hate you for this, Zee."

"I get that."

"If I were you, I wouldn't be making any travel plans. If you have to drive anywhere but the grocery store, I want to know about it."

"I never plan," I said. "Change is life. Everything is impermanent. You have to go with the flow."

56

John Khalsa met me in the lobby. "I heard you were on the way in," he said. "I wanted to see you."

"I've been an arrogant ass, and I owe you an apology," I said.

"Stop," he said. "Sucking up doesn't suit you."

"Forget what suits me. I should have worked with you not against you to get that autopsy done, and I should have been more professional when I realized I was working on my girlfriend."

Khalsa stared at me distrustfully, as if waiting for me to add something that would turn my apology upside down.

"Your dismissal is a committee decision," he said, when I had nothing more. "I don't have the power to reverse it."

"I understand. I made my bed and I'll lie in it. I just wanted you to know I'm sorry."

I walked toward the elevator. Khalsa went with me. "Did you do something to the security guard who tried to keep you out that night?"

"Do something?" I asked innocently. "I just asked nicely to see my girl."

"You've got more trouble than you know," he said as I pushed the button to call the car. "The DEA has been to see us. They think you write too many pain scripts."

"Better to be rid of me," I said. "I'm an all-around pain in the ass."

"There's one agent who seems to have it in for you."

"The Texan?"

"That's him."

"Testosterone," I said, stepping into the car.

Khalsa got in with me. "You'd recognize it," he said.

"What?"

"Testosterone."

I shrugged. "I just take care of my patients, that's all. When I see suffering, I do what it takes to end it. Law enforcement likes things in neat little boxes. It's a control thing. If I were on the street with them every day I'm sure I would come around to their way of thinking. If Agent El Paso were in the office with me day after day, I'm sure he'd come around to mine."

"Maybe not," said Khalsa. "Look. I still don't like you. I still think you're a hothead and a loner. You'll never be a team player."

"Guilty as charged. I know. I'm an ass. If begging would help, I'd beg for my job back. I'm not shit without my blade."

"There are other hospitals," he said. "And maybe things could change here, though I wouldn't count on it."

"I'm taking time off anyway," I said. "I've got a private patient to look after."

He managed a wry smile. "Jordan's test results are encouraging. I'm beginning to believe you saved her cord."

"Me too."

"Rehab is going to be something, though. I still don't know that she'll walk."

"Of course she will," I said.

"Right," he said. "Of course she will."

The elevator door opened on Khalsa's floor. There was a commotion in the hall, so I stepped out with him to see what was going on.

"Dr. Khalsa, I'm glad you're here," said the floor nurse. "We're having trouble with a patient. He's here to have his sutures checked and he's brought his dog. We've told him animals are not allowed in the hospital, but he keeps saying he's an attorney and he knows the law and the Chihuahua saved his life and she stays with him."

"What's this guy look like?" I interrupted.

The nurse was startled for a moment, but answered. "He's a big bald guy, looks like a Hell's Angel ..."

I didn't wait for her to finish.

"Where is he?"

She pointed at a treatment room, and I hurried down the hall, ignoring Khalsa's call. I threw open the examining room door. The room took on a crepuscular shimmer, and I was sure I was hallucinating once more.

"Hey Doc, you look like you've seen a ghost," said Big Steve.

Luna barked a greeting.

I found I couldn't speak.

"Doc, you okay?"

I still couldn't find my voice so instead I went over and touched him experimentally on the shoulder. He was flesh and blood and hard as concrete.

"I heard you were blown to smithereens," I said.

"Almost. The blast got my bike. Killed a kid, too."

"But you were in the bar...."

"Luna took me outside. She's good that way. She lets me know when she has to go. I got a nasty gash on the leg, took thirty five stitches."

I couldn't help myself. I hugged him. He looked bemused. "You got a traffic ticket needs fixing? I hope it's nothing more than that."

"Nothing at all," I said.

As we spoke, I saw Steve as he looked in the brilliant sunshine of the battlefield outside the Mongol summer capitol Shangdu, as we fought together for the Emperor Hongwu, Steve with his giant battle axe, me with a pair of willow-leaf broadswords.

I told him briefly about Jordan and that we would all be together again soon. He didn't say anything about the "again" part, even though he hadn't met Jordan yet. I think he knew what I meant.

I got on the elevator again and went up two more floors. When the doors opened, Jordan was waiting, accompanied by quite a crowd of hospital staff.

"You're a goddamn midnight sun," I said, leaning over her wheelchair to kiss her.

"Amazing what a little makeup will do."

"It isn't makeup I'm looking at."

"Eye of the beholder," she said.

"Then how come all the orderlies are green with envy?"

"That's not envy, Zee, that's their hospital uniform."

We got into the elevator. I pushed the button. Together we watched the lights blink down. I stroked her hair. She took my hand, my sword hand, and down we went, our hearts in our throats, hoping we were ready for whatever the next days would bring.

Just before the doors opened on the new day, I could swear I smelled almonds.

Please sign the guest book at www.thecuttingseason.com to be kept informed of the next installment of Dr. Xenon Pearl.

About the Author

Arthur Rosenfeld is a martial arts teacher, writer, speaker, and coach. His martial arts training spans more than twenty-seven years, and includes instruction in Tang Soo Do, Kenpo, Kung Fu, and Tai Chi Ch'uan. Rosenfeld is a critically-acclaimed, best-selling author of six novels (Avon Books, Bantam, Doubleday Dell, Forge Books), two non-fiction books (Simon and Schuster, Basic Books), several screenplays, and  numerous magazine articles (*Vogue, Vanity Fair, Parade,* and others). He consults for the pharmaceutical industry as a recognized expert on aspects of chronic pain. Arthur Rosenfeld resides in South Florida.